"A betrayed beauty and a devastated artist find hope and healing in *The Painted Rose,* the lyrical and richly emotional debut by talented newcomer Donna Birdsell."

—Mary Jo Putney,
New York Times bestselling
author of *Dancing on the Wind*

"In *The Painted Rose,* a passion for art and flowers weaves a web of healing between past pain and present love. A delightful debut romance."

—Jo Beverley,
New York Times bestselling
author of *Winter Fire*

"Donna Birdsell's terrific debut novel, *The Painted Rose,* is a deeply moving story that truly celebrates the healing power of love. With an emotional story that is both dark and tender as well as intelligent, and with sympathetic characters, this is a must-read for lovers of romance."

—Jacqueline Navin,
author of *The Heiress of Hyde Park*

The Painted Rose

DONNA BIRDSELL

BERKLEY SENSATION, NEW YORK

THE BERKLEY PUBLISHING GROUP
Published by the Penguin Group
Penguin Group (USA) Inc.
375 Hudson Street, New York, New York 10014, USA

Penguin Group (Canada), 10 Alcorn Avenue, Toronto, Ontario M4V 3B2, Canada
(a division of Pearson Penguin Canada Inc.)
Penguin Books Ltd., 80 Strand, London WC2R 0RL, England
Penguin Group Ireland, 25 St. Stephen's Green, Dublin 2, Ireland (a division of Penguin Books Ltd.)
Penguin Group (Australia), 250 Camberwell Road, Camberwell, Victoria 3124, Australia
(a division of Pearson Australia Group Pty. Ltd.)
Penguin Books India Pvt. Ltd., 11 Community Centre, Panchsheel Park, New Delhi—110 017, India
Penguin Group (NZ), Cnr. Airborne and Rosedale Roads, Albany, Auckland 1310, New Zealand
(a division of Pearson New Zealand Ltd.)
Penguin Books (South Africa) (Pty.) Ltd., 24 Sturdee Avenue, Rosebank, Johannesburg 2196, South
Africa

Penguin Books Ltd., Registered Offices: 80 Strand, London WC2R 0RL, England

This is a work of fiction. Names, characters, places, and incidents either are the product of the author's imagination or are used fictitiously, and any resemblance to actual persons, living or dead, business establishments, events, or locales is entirely coincidental.

THE PAINTED ROSE

A Berkley Sensation Book / published by arrangement with the author

PRINTING HISTORY
Berkley Sensation / September 2004

Copyright © 2004 by Donna Birdsell.
Cover art by Danny O'Leary.
Cover design by Lesley Worrell.
Interior text design by Kristin del Rosario.

ISBN: 0-425-19804-9

BERKLEY® SENSATION
Berkley Sensation Books are published by The Berkley Publishing Group,
a division of Penguin Group (USA) Inc.,
375 Hudson Street, New York, New York 10014.
BERKLEY SENSATION and the "B" design
are trademarks belonging to Penguin Group (USA) Inc.

PRINTED IN THE UNITED STATES OF AMERICA

10 9 8 7 6 5 4 3 2 1

For my husband,
with all my heart.

Chapter 1

ENGLAND
JUNE 1777

Afternoon sun touched the quiet English countryside like the hand of Midas, turning to gold each blossom and leaf, each weatherworn stone lining the lane. It was a color impossible to reproduce on canvas, the same way a moment in time could not be relived nor a fleeting joy be recaptured in the heart.

Lucien Delacourte pondered these things for only a moment before more pressing thoughts consumed him.

Would the tutoring position that had been offered him still be available? He had not sent word to his potential employer, the Earl of Darby, or even to his mentor, Henri, that he would accept it. Lucien had needed the freedom to change his mind on the way to England. When he left France, he decided that if the post had already been filled, he would simply continue on to London, where he might find some kind of work.

A dire lack of funds, however, had now made that option inconceivable.

The meager pay he drew working on a transport ship

from Paris to Weymouth had paid for food and transportation only as far as Southampton. He had been forced to travel by foot from there. Should Lord Darby turn him away, it would mean a long, hungry walk to London.

He passed a farm ringed by a crumbling stone wall. The stench of a hog pen drifted on the breeze. Two bony horses wandered over to the wall and eyed him with a mixture of suspicion and hope. When he offered them nothing, the horses lost interest and ambled back into the field.

Lucien shifted his satchel to the other shoulder and hunched against the sunshine, not raising his head again until he drew closer to the village. Soon the sounds of civilization reached him. The metal clanging of a smithy's hammer, the rumble of an oxcart, a child's happy shriek. His chest constricted.

Tessa, my Tessa. God rest her soul.

He willed himself forward.

At the smell of cooking meat, Lucien's stomach contracted painfully. His last meal had been days ago.

When he crested a hill, the village lay below him. Carts bounced through rutted streets, parting an ocean of townsfolk. Bright flashes of color, the kerchiefs of milkmaids, bobbed among the brown work clothes of farmers. He soon reached the point where the country lane became a proper road. A wooden placard mounted on a pole announced the village of Whitford in crude lettering.

So this was it.

Lucien stepped onto a hard-packed street. The presence of others rubbed his senses raw as he emerged from the solitary world of a foot traveler. He braced himself before moving into the crowd.

"They're burnt."

The voice seemed to come from nowhere. For a moment, Lucien thought it had followed him from Paris. The hair on his arms bristled.

"They're burnt," the voice repeated. Lucien's heart pounded against his chest as he looked for the source of the whisper. An old woman, leather-skinned and dressed in rags, leaned against a squat stone building. She scurried across the cobblestones, snatching at his sleeve as he passed.

She opened a dirty cloth, revealing two black loaves of bread. Lucien stared at them as the past caught him once again—even here, in the middle of godforsaken England. He choked on the bile inching up his throat.

The old woman held the loaves up to Lucien's face. But instead of bread, he saw the bodies once again . . . one small, one larger, intertwined on a stretcher . . .

"Stop!" He broke the old woman's grasp and backed away, but the heel of his boot caught on a loose stone. As he fell backward onto the street, his satchel burst open and the contents clattered out onto the cobblestones.

The old woman cursed him before she hobbled off with her bread, leaving Lucien alone with his macabre vision.

Suddenly a hand descended from above. It was a farmer's hand, rough and square, dirt entrenched in the lines of the palm. Lucien clasped the man's wrist and allowed himself to be pulled up from the ground.

"Pay no heed to old Eliza," the giant of a man said. "She's a pure nuisance with that wretched bread."

Lucien brushed the dirt from his breeches. "Thank you."

"You must be recently arrived in Whitford," the farmer said. "I'm Oliver Stagg. What name have you?"

"Delacourte. Lucien Delacourte."

Stagg's smile was pleasant enough, though nearly toothless. He looked down at Lucien's things strewn on the street. "What are these?" He picked up three corked tins.

"Pigments."

Stagg shook one of the tins near his ear. "Pigments?"

"Paints. I am an artist." Even as he said the words, Lucien

wondered if he still had the right to use the title. He pushed a roll of canvas back into the bag. Stagg retrieved a few brushes and pencils from the street and handed them to Lucien, who stuffed them into the pack and secured the ties before hoisting it to his shoulder.

"Thank you again." Lucien nodded and turned to go, but felt Stagg's heavy hand on his shoulder.

"Not meanin' any offense, but you look gave out. Could you stand a draught?"

Lucien debated his answer. He finally said, "I could, but to be truthful, I am lacking coin at the moment."

"Not to worry." The farmer jingled the coins in his purse. " 'Twas a good day for Stagg. Care to join me at the tavern?" The farmer's eyes held a glint of curiosity.

Lucien hesitated. He wasn't in the mood for questions, but his hands still shook and his belly rumbled with hunger. Perhaps a draught of ale would help to fill the void.

"Lead the way," he said.

As he followed Stagg into the heart of Whitford, Lucien averted his gaze from the children.

It was a market day, and the square thrummed with activity. Stagg skirted the path of a drover herding sheep to a makeshift pen, and turned left onto a narrower street. The farmer seemed to accept the noise and redolence of the marketplace without a second thought, hopping over piles of dung, ignoring the wails of the vendors. Lucien, however, was still reacquainting himself to these cruder aspects of civilization.

"Here." The man gestured to a narrow green door. Above it hung a sign festooned with the images of a hog and a dove.

Lucien entered first, standing still while his eyes adjusted to the lack of light. Men scattered at the tables and lined up at the bar glared at him with suspicion until Stagg came in behind him and clapped a hand on his shoulder. They turned back to their cups.

"Ale?" Stagg asked. Lucien nodded, his throat too dry to speak. He slid onto a stool. Stagg signaled the tavern keep with an upraised hand.

Out of the corner of his eye, Lucien studied the other patrons of the Hog and Dove. There were a few merchants, but most of the men appeared to be farmers or craftsmen of some sort, probably in the village for market. The friendly banter between them grew louder as they forgot about Lucien.

"Me wife's cousin's daughter is workin' on the hill," said one. "She's come out from the city."

All chatter ceased.

"Go on, Belk," someone urged. "What does she 'ave to say about it?"

"Not much," Belk answered. "She's only been up there a fortnight." He sucked his teeth.

"What do the others tell 'er?" someone else asked. "The ones who been up there longer?"

"Not a thing," Belk repeated. "Most of 'em come from London like her, and their mouths may as well be sewn up. She's been told to mind 'er own puddin' where the lord and ladies are concerned, and if she don't, she'll be out without a penny."

Stagg jumped into the conversation. "What does she say about the house?"

Belk stared wistfully into his empty mug. A half-dozen men scrambled to pay for the next draught. Belk waited until his cup was filled, then took a long pull before answering Stagg's question.

"The house," Belk said with some drama, "is grand."

"Indeed?" Stagg studied Belk with exaggerated surprise before swatting him with his hat. "We can tell *that* from th' middle o' town. But what is it *like*?"

Belk squinted at Stagg.

Lucien cleared his throat. "I believe Mr. Stagg is asking

about the feel of the place." The others nodded and murmured.

"Right. The feel of it," Stagg agreed.

"Oh!" Belk nodded solemnly. "Very sad, indeed. Like
it all happened jus' yesterday, says the wife's cousin's
daughter."

There was much murmuring and throat clearing all
around.

"Damnable pity." Stagg downed the rest of his ale in
one gulp.

A question drifted forward from the back of the room.
"Has she seen the Phantom?"

Stagg slammed his mug on the bar. The crowd grew
quiet. "I'll not hear such talk about that poor soul."

A moment of silence was observed before the room
once again buzzed with conversation. Lucien had a difficult time following it all. Whispers of a phantom. Heads
shaking in disbelief. Nodding. Spitting. Endless questions
it seemed no one could answer.

In the midst of the talk, the tavern keep set two wooden
bowls and a loaf of brown bread between Lucien and Stagg.

"Eat up," Stagg said, pushing a bowl toward him.

Lucien tasted the fare. Lukewarm mutton stew. To him,
however, it may well have been manna. He shoveled bits of
meat and vegetables into his mouth, sopping up the gravy
with chunks of the bread and washing it down with huge
gulps of ale. When he'd finished, another bowl appeared
before him.

As he ate, the talk continued around him. He caught
only snatches of conversation, so when his appetite finally
was sated, he said, "Forgive my ignorance, Stagg, but what
is the house we are discussing?"

"The one atop the hill," the farmer said. "What is known
as Elmstone."

Lucien swallowed deliberately. "Elmstone House? The
home of the Earl of Darby?"

Stagg raised a brow. "The very same. What of it?"

" 'Tis my destination."

Stagg's ruddy complexion gave way to white, and the tavern fell silent. Lucien's gaze swept the room.

The men stared into their mugs.

Chapter 2

A short time later, Lucien stepped back out on the square.
He had learned not one more thing about Elmstone House,
Lord Darby, or the mysterious "phantom." Conversation
turned to weather, harvests, and similar mundane subjects
after Lucien revealed his destination. When he told them
he would be instructing Lord Darby's sister, Stagg gave
him an unfathomable look that seemed equal parts admira-
tion and sympathy.

What was it about Elmstone that caused a room full of
grown men to gossip like fishwives? Lucien shrugged his
pack onto his shoulder and gazed up at the estate looming
above the village. He would find out soon enough.

He set off, forgoing the road for a route cutting straight
over the countryside. The land was pretty, but rose on such a
slope that halfway up it Lucien's legs grew weak from the
exertion. He had stopped to rest on an outcropping of stones
when he noticed a faint ribbon of smoke curling against the
sky. His eyes followed it to the source—a cottage so artfully

nestled against the hill it was almost invisible through the trees.

A thin man garbed in servant's livery—curious clothing for a caretaker, Lucien thought—appeared from around back. He disappeared into a copse of trees and moments later appeared again, this time upon a fine caramel-colored mount. Staying close to the tree line, horse and rider headed up the hill toward the manor. Lucien watched with envy as the man disappeared from view, then he stretched his aching legs and once more took to the path.

At last he reached the hilltop, where the overgrown path met with a cobbled drive. Lucien followed it straight to the gate of the manor. He realized he could discern more about the place from the middle of Whitford than from where he now stood, for the house was concealed behind ivy-covered ramparts and tall hedges. A rope dangled through a hole in the stone wall next to the iron gate. When he pulled it, the crisp clang of a bell rang out from a box atop the wall.

Lucien patted the dust from his breeches as he awaited a response. Since it would not have been wise to tramp through the English countryside dressed as a French courtier, he had driven himself deeper into debt with the purchase of the clothing he now wore. Unfortunately, his fine English jacket and breeches had already grown shabby with the sweat and grime of travel.

Several minutes passed before a liveried servant appeared at the gate and peered through the iron bars.

"Help you, sir?"

"Yes. Kindly inform Lord Darby that Lucien Delacourte is here to serve him."

The servant cast him a wary look. "There has been no mention of your arrival, sir."

Lucien feigned a look of surprise, then lied, "I am afraid I do not understand. I am here to serve as tutor to Lord

Darby's sister. Monsieur Henri Valmetant undoubtedly notified his lordship several months ago."

The servant seemed unsure of what action he should
take, so Lucien pressed on.

"I am certain Lord Darby would wish to see me."

The servant shrugged. "Remain here, please."

Lucien scrutinized the gate as he waited. It was quite
beautiful, wrought with delicate roses on the edges and tall,
leafy elm trees at the center. The gate looked relatively
new—forged within the last decade, at least—and although
it was lovely, there was no mistaking its true purpose. The
sharp pikes along the top would deter any intruder who
valued his ballocks.

Lucien dropped his pack and peered through the bars.
Two figures descended a narrow brick walk toward the gate.
The first was the servant to whom he had spoken, the second
a tall man in leather breeches and a rough brown shirt. A
huntsman, perhaps? Or the stable master?

When the two approached, however, Lucien realized his
mistake. Although dressed in the garb of a common man,
one could not disregard the air of aristocracy the second
man possessed. The man in brown was not the stable master, but the Earl of Darby himself.

The scowl Lord Darby wore did not give Lucien hope.
He forced his own face into a suitably pleasant expression.

"Lucien Delacourte? I am afraid I have had no notice
from Monsieur Valmetant about your arrival," the man said
through the gate.

Lucien repeated his show of surprise. "But I sent word
to Henri two months ago. He did not inform you of my ac-
ceptance?"

The earl shook his head. "When I failed to receive a reply
from Valmetant, I assumed he could find no suitable tutor."

"Perhaps I should have sent a missive directly to you.
Please accept my deepest apologies for the confusion." Lucien bowed, holding his breath.

Lord Darby seemed to consider the situation for a moment before motioning to the servant to unlock the gate.

Lucien grabbed up his pack and stepped onto the grounds of the estate. "I hope my arrival has not caused undue anxiety."

"That remains to be seen. Come. Let us discuss this inside."

They walked along a path that wound beside the tall gray manse. As the servant hurried ahead, Lucien said, "Your home is spectacular. When was it built?"

Lord Darby swept an arm toward the house. "My family has resided at Elmstone for three hundred years. My great-great-great grandfather was given the land by King Henry the Seventh for his valiant service in the Battle of Bosworth Field."

The residence seemed not so much ancient as gracefully aged. Much of the architecture was medieval, but recent touches such as ornate cornices and architraves lent an air of elegance to the functional square form. Altogether a home to be appreciated, at least from the outside.

Lucien turned his attention from the home to the man, and took stock of James Essington, Earl of Darby. He was a striking figure, lean and dark with intense brown eyes and a stern mouth. His manner was aloof, yet surprisingly unassuming. They walked side by side, which seemed not to disturb Lord Darby in the least. Such a thing would never have occurred at Versailles, where a nobleman did his utmost to stay ahead of his lessers, and his equals for that matter, at all times.

"I look forward to meeting your sister," Lucien said.

Lord Darby slowed. "There are a few things we should discuss. Had I known you were coming, I would have explained our somewhat unusual situation in a missive beforehand. Since I did not know you would be arriving, I suppose we shall have to discuss it now."

"Does your sister still wish to learn to paint?"

"Yes, very much so."

"Have you hired another tutor?"

"No."

"Then there is nothing to worry over," Lucien said, with a confidence he certainly did not feel. Nothing to worry over?

Nothing, except he was not altogether sure he could still paint. And he had just lied to his new employer within minutes of their acquaintance. And he had never taught another person anything about art in his life. For Lucien, a sense of disaster loomed in the shadows of Elmstone.

His words seemed to appease Lord Darby, however, who quickened his pace once again. Soon they arrived before a tall, arched doorway. The same servant who unlocked the gates now stood before the open door.

"Find Miss Witherspoon," Lord Darby told the servant. "Send her to the hall."

"Yes, m'lord."

Lord Darby lingered on the portico for a moment, again seeming to deliberate over his decision. Lucien searched for the words to convince the other man, and perhaps himself, that he belonged there.

"Sir, I am one of King Louis's favored artists. I have studied my craft since I was nine years of age. I have practiced it, perfected it, lived and breathed it. I have cursed it and embraced it. But above all, I have always loved it. It would be an honor to teach it. I hope you will allow me to do that."

Lord Darby's eyes held a peculiar look. "How lucky you are to have such strength of conviction. To know what you want from this life and to take it. It must be liberating."

"On the contrary, my lord. It can be quite stifling when you know of nothing else."

Lucien followed Lord Darby into the vast hallway of the manor, where they were intercepted by a dour-looking man who appeared to be suffering in his formal attire. By his slightly hunched bearing, Lucien recognized him at once as the man he had seen leaving the hidden cottage.

"Delacourte, this is my valet. Arthur, Mr. Delacourte has come to teach my sister to paint. When Miss Witherspoon arrives, tell her to prepare a room for him. He will be staying on indefinitely."

So, he would stay. Lucien drew his first real breath since he'd left Paris.

Arthur nodded to Lord Darby. "Of course. However, there is a matter which requires your immediate attention, your lordship."

Lord Darby frowned. "The south field again?"

"Yes, sir. I have taken the liberty of having your horse saddled. The mount is waiting at the stables."

"I shall be on my way momentarily." He turned to Lucien. "Where is your baggage? Did you leave it in town?"

"No, no. Unfortunately my trunk was misplaced at the docks. I am afraid I have but the clothes on my back."

Lord Darby shook his head. "Incompetence is indeed the scourge of the traveler. We shall have my tailor come up tomorrow. In the meantime, please take comfort in my home. Should you wish for anything, do not hesitate to summon Arthur."

The valet appeared less than pleased with Lord Darby's offer. If possible, the man looked even stiffer than when they had entered the great hall. He gave Lucien an acid look and shuffled off, presumably in search of Miss Witherspoon.

"I am afraid I must attend to this matter immediately," Lord Darby said.

"I would not want to interfere with your business. I shall find a corner in which to rest until your return."

"Nonsense. Feel free to explore Elmstone as you wish. I am certain Miss Witherspoon will be with you in short measure." Lord Darby disappeared through an archway on the side of the hall.

Left to his own devices, Lucien stood in the center of the shining tile floor, listening to the quiet. The hall was clean and cool. Black and white. Not at all revealing of the person he had just met.

He waited for Miss Witherspoon, but when she failed to appear, he grew restless. He considered Stagg's question to Belk in the tavern. What was the manor like? What was the feel of the place? Thus far, he could not fathom it. He determined that exploration was the key to forming a clear answer, if only for himself.

Lucien deposited his satchel in a corner, chose a direction, and began to walk, deciding for the moment not to think about what lay ahead for him in this strange place.

Though Lucien had spent plenty of time in the homes of both friends and strangers, he found he was never quite at ease living amongst another man's things. The furniture, the carpeting, and especially the artwork were so profoundly personal in each home, he felt as if he were dwelling inside another's mind. Each home had a different emotion.

As he wandered through the manor, Lucien found it difficult to pinpoint Elmstone's emotion. Was it sadness, as the men in the tavern had professed? No, not quite. Melancholy, perhaps, with a whisper of secrets to be uncovered.

Lucien absorbed the silence.

There had been a time when he could not abide silence. He could not be alone. He had found comfort in crowds, had prospered amidst the multitudes. Solitude was something he had never expected to want or need.

Until the fire. Everything had changed after the fire.

Lucien followed a corridor to a richly appointed library, where he scanned the titles of the books, took note of some excellent statuettes on the mantelpiece, and breathed the thick scent of leather. He was examining the fine detail in the chair rail when he noticed a set of doors leading outside to a small courtyard.

When he opened them, fragrant air flooded the library. The yard was surrounded by a wall covered with climbing white roses. At the base of the wall, pale pink and deep red blossoms tangled with the white, reminding Lucien of sunset on the canals of Venice.

On the right side of the courtyard, a stone walkway lined with heather led to a tea table. Lucien followed the path and sat in one of the chairs. His gaze meandered over each bloom that surrounded him. If he counted, he was sure to find hundreds of varieties of flowers. The garden reminded him of one at Versailles, albeit on a much smaller scale. A feast for the soul as well as the eyes.

He yearned to set his easel in the middle of this magical place, to mix the paints and lose himself in the colors—the very thought of it made him weak. But he knew the moment he picked up a brush, he would fail miserably, as he had the last thousand times.

Something within him fought against the yearning to paint, against his nature. It would be wrong to sate his own desires when Katrina and Tessa could not. To feel *life* when they could not.

Lucien clasped his hair in his fists and pulled hard, harder, until the need to create something beautiful ebbed away. Then he retraced his steps back to the great hallway, where the cool black and white would not tempt him.

He had been foolish to come. He would fail here, just as he had in Versailles. Just as he had in Paris. Perhaps he should just return to France and let one of his less civilized creditors slit his throat. At least it would end the nightmares.

The pack containing Lucien's things was not beside the stairs where he had left it. He set off toward the rear of the house, hoping to find someone who could direct him to his belongings.

A woman in a gray frock whisked through the corridor directly ahead of him and disappeared around a corner. He hurried to catch her, hoping she might be the elusive Miss Witherspoon.

The woman's step was light and quick, like that of a girl, but the sway of her hips left no question of her maturity. Lucien lost sight of her on several occasions, so quickly did she walk. When she *was* in view, she stayed just far enough ahead that he was reluctant to call out for fear of startling her, so he simply followed. She had to stop eventually.

The woman passed through a drawing room and another set of doors, finally emerging into a garden even lovelier than the one he had visited earlier. This yard was larger and more refined. Blood roses formed a fragrant arbor over part of the garden. A wide grass path led to the center, where half a dozen marble nymphs danced in a pond lush with water lilies and floating greenery.

The woman in gray knelt in a corner of the garden and snipped roses from one of the bushes. Lucien approached, but she appeared not to hear. He paused, for some reason unwilling to alert her to his presence so soon. He watched for a few moments as she worked.

Her movements deft and practiced, she chose only the most perfect blooms, laying them next to her in a neat pile as she cut them. Her arms were long and slender, and moved like the reeds in the pond. The gray dress was plain but fashionable and of high quality, unusual for a servant. Hair of smooth, dark sable was pinned up beneath a gray hat.

Lucien cleared his throat loudly and the woman turned in surprise.

Now it was Lucien who was startled.

Layers of gossamer lace hung from the brim of her hat, concealing her face. The sun's light cast through the lace from behind, revealing only the silhouette of her head and neck. She made a small noise and rose quickly to her feet.

Lucien believed she would have backed away had the bushes not been blocking her retreat.

"Miss Witherspoon?"

Her laugh was nervous, yet oddly enchanting. "No. Miss Witherspoon is attending to something at the moment. I am Sarah Essington. And you are?"

"Pardon me, my lady. I am Lucien Delacourte, recently arrived to serve as an art tutor."

"Lucien . . . Lucien Delacourte? Tutor? I am afraid I do not understand."

Lucien bowed. "Do pardon me. I have just arrived, and your brother was called away before he could make the introductions. Are you the lady who wishes to learn to paint, or is there another sister?"

"No. It is I you shall be teaching. But I understood Monsieur Valmetant could not provide a tutor. At any rate, I never would have expected . . . well, you've certainly come far." She gathered up the flowers, her hands trembling slightly, and placed them in a basket.

Lucien took a few steps back. "You are distressed, I see. I am very sorry to have startled you."

"Please, think nothing of it. We do not have many visitors here, so new faces tend to unsettle me. And James did not tell me to expect you . . ."

"It would seem Valmetant's word of my arrival failed to reach your brother." Lucien repeated the lie he had told the earl, which somehow seemed even more distasteful this time. "Lord Darby has been kind enough to welcome me despite the confusion. He's asked your Miss Witherspoon to prepare a room."

As he spoke, Lucien attempted to peer through the lace. Despite its delicate weave, he could make out only vague details of Sarah Essington's face. Perhaps the veils served to shield her from insects or the sun?

"In any event, now that you are here, I shall make good

use of you." She handed him the basket of roses she had collected. "Hold these, please. I have just a few more to cut."

Lucien stood behind her as she knelt, noting the subtle bend and sway in her back as her hands avoided thorns and moved skillfully through the bushes. The daylight illuminated the bare white of her forearms almost to the sheen of the marble nymphs in the pond. He mixed the hues of her skin in the palette of his mind before he could stop himself.

"A few more," she said over her shoulder. The force of her breath caused the veils to ripple away from her neck. It was long and pale and graceful, like that of a swan.

"The garden is lovely," he said, trying to direct his gaze elsewhere.

"Thank you. I planted most of the bushes and flowers myself. The gardeners helped, of course. There's so much to do. But I attempt to do as much as I can on my own." She handed him the last of the flowers, then brushed dirt from the front of her skirt.

"You are responsible for the gardens?"

"Yes. You might call them my obsession. Fortunately, my brother indulges my whims."

"Is my presence due to a whim, as well?" His words surprised him. Even more surprising was his desire for a favorable response. It mattered little if her interest in painting was a whim. He would collect his compensation either way.

Lady Sarah did not seem bothered in the least by the question.

"I wouldn't say my interest in painting is a whim. More a fervent desire. Come with me." She strolled beneath the fragrant canopy of roses, checking the condition of leaves and buds as she went. They entered the house into a dark, echo-filled dining hall, where Lady Sarah deposited the flowers in a large blue vase. She arranged them quickly, and set the vase in the center of a massive table. She still had not turned back the veils.

"Please, forgive me for delaying your comfort. You

must be quite weary from your travels. Are you in a terrible hurry to find Miss Witherspoon?" Her voice was calm now, smooth and musical. The female version of her brother's.

"No hurry," Lucien replied. Any thoughts of leaving this place had receded to the back of his mind. Foremost now was the desire to see Sarah Essington's face.

"Good. Then I shall show you round the rest of the gardens before we attempt to find your quarters."

Lady Sarah escorted Lucien through six gardens, including a fragrant kitchen garden boasting dozens of varieties of vegetables and herbs. She identified many of the plants and their common—and uncommon—uses.

Each of the estate's gardens was unique in color scheme and design, from sweeping, natural landscapes to formal alcoves with mazes, walkways, and giant stone urns. There was a small, glass-enclosed room as well, an orangery where Lady Sarah experimented with local flora, exotic plants and flowers, and fruit-bearing trees.

As they walked, she kept the veils in place, and Lucien came to suspect it wasn't for the sake of insects. It would seem Lord Darby's sister bore some sort of affliction. Some deformity of birth, perhaps? He felt a curious twinge of disappointment, though her malady should not have mattered to him, either, unless it affected her ability to learn.

There appeared to be no chance of that. Her subtle wit and fluid conversation proved there was no defect of the mind. She could speak easily on most any subject, from the operas of Haydn to the poetry of Edmund Spenser. Never had Lucien conversed so effortlessly with a woman, not even his beloved Katrina.

Lady Sarah's reaction to him, however, was curious. Though she seemed pleased that he had arrived, she seemed equally apprehensive of his presence. She was congenial, but careful to keep a good distance from him as they walked.

Lucien's initial distress at the beauty of Lady Sarah's gardens was gradually offset by his interest in the woman herself, and he was surprised to find himself wishing there were more than six gardens on the grounds of the estate.

"I assume your botanical interests keep you rather busy," Lucien commented as they completed the rounds and arrived back in the dining hall. "Why do you wish to take time away from them to paint? It is an art which takes much study and practice to master."

Lady Sarah removed her gloves and motioned for him to follow her. He recognized the corridor they traveled as the one which led to the hall.

"It's true I am quite involved with my gardens," she said. "Throughout the spring and summer, I cut the best of the blossoms and hang them to dry, press them in books, or seal them in wax. I catalogue them and collect the seeds for the next year's planting. I have even sketched most of them. But I have discovered that sketching just cannot do them justice."

"Sketching and painting yield quite different results, it is true. But why do you feel such a necessity to use oils?"

"It's simple, really. You see, I am compiling a comprehensive volume which I hope will be of interest to the Royal Botanical Society. King George also has a keen interest in botany, and I would like to present him with several depictions of his favorite varieties along with the book."

"Painting for the king? Quite ambitious."

She laughed. "From the tone of your voice, I suspect you meant to use a word other than 'ambitious.'"

"Not at all."

She laughed again. "It's quite all right to say it. It is madness!" She turned to him abruptly and put a finger to the veils, as if to shush him. "Perhaps it *is* madness. But

I've heard"—and here her voice lowered to a whisper—
"I've heard that King George is a bit mad himself!"

Now Lucien laughed as well, carried away by a sense of
collusion, of an intimacy created by the hush of the hall
and the warmth of her breath on his cheek.

They mounted a winding staircase as Lady Sarah spoke
aloud once more. "I daresay I shall never aspire to such
success as you've garnered with your king, but I hope my
liege will at least appreciate my efforts."

His king?

"What do you know of *my* king?"

"Ah! Here we are. I believe this will be your room," she
said.

She pushed the door fully open, revealing finely appointed quarters laid out with dark wood furnishings, rich
paneling, and gold and green carpets. The bed was done up
in rich green damask, the curtains tied back with gold tas-
seled ropes. On a bench at the foot of the bed lay Lucien's
leather bag.

"Miss Witherspoon has a fondness for this room. Do
you find your quarters acceptable?"

Acceptable? He compared the room to the last filthy
hovel in Paris that he had called home, and almost laughed
aloud. "Most acceptable, thank you."

He stroked the rich coverlet with his fingertips.

Lady Sarah seemed to be suddenly seized with discomfort, and backed toward the door. "Very well, then. Shall
we expect you to supper?"

"Yes. And thank you for an enchanting excursion."

"Yes. Well." Her voice held a note of—what? Surprise?
Gratitude? "Cook serves promptly at eight."

She closed the door behind her, leaving Lucien to his
own devices.

He disrobed and poured water into a fine porcelain basin,
washing the grime of travel from his hands and face and

neck. He shook the dust from his clothes as best he could and lay down on the bed, all the while thinking of Lady Sarah and her veils.

Was she the reason Elmstone was the subject of such morose conversation at the Hog and Dove? Could she be the "phantom" of whom Belk and Stagg and the rest spoke? A flicker of anger sparked in his gut. For them to speak in such a manner about a woman they did not know was reprehensible. Lady Sarah was no more a phantom than he was a vagabond. She seemed to be a perfectly charming, albeit somewhat enigmatic, woman.

Lucien tried to imagine Lady Sarah's face, but found he could not. For once in his life, his imagination refused to fill the empty canvas of his mind.

A cabinet clock in the hall struck the eight o'clock hour as Lucien descended the stairs in the rotunda. He tried to recall the way to the dining hall. To the left? No, to the right, he was certain.

He hurried through the winding corridors of the manor, acutely aware he was late for his first meal at Elmstone. At last he heard the muted chinking of cutlery on china.

Dinner had begun without him.

The room was nearly dark. Heavy curtains hung closed over the doors to the garden, the singular source of light from the outside. A tall candelabrum in the center of the table, next to Lady Sarah's floral arrangement, provided the only illumination. Through the shadows, Lucien saw Lord Darby's sister. She still wore her veils.

He stood in the open doorway until she called him in.

"Forgive my tardiness," he said, directing his apology to Lady Sarah, since Lord Darby seemed to be absent.

"Of course. I hope you are recovering from what must have been an exhausting day."

A waspish female voice emerged from the gloom. "If he

endured a tour of your gardens, he must surely be exhausted."

Lucien searched for the source of the voice, spying a murky silhouette at the foot of the long dining table. A dark-eyed beauty with sharp features leaned forward into the glow of the candles as Lucien's eyes adjusted to the dim light. The woman's expression reminded him of a French courtesan who had just spied a tower of sweets.

"As Sarah has neglected to make the introductions, I shall take it upon myself," she said. "I am Julia Essington, Countess of Darby."

Lucien rounded the table to greet her, and she held up a slender hand. He clasped it lightly and bowed low over her fingertips. "Lucien Delacourte, here to serve as tutor to Lady Sarah."

"As always, I seem to be the last one informed of the arrival of new guests." She smiled thinly.

"That is altogether by design." This voice, which came from the opposite end of the table, was feminine as well, though decidedly older. "Should you be the first soul our guests encounter, Julia, the vast majority would be scared away immediately."

A tiny bird of a woman with a spray of turquoise feathers in her graying hair moved into the light. An old-fashioned neck ruff added to the parrot-like image she conveyed.

Lady Darby withdrew her hand from Lucien's and directed a withering look toward the bird. "Now, Mother. You really ought to behave."

"I'm *not* your mother," said the older woman. "And I will behave any way I wish."

Lady Sarah said, "Mr. Delacourte, this is *my* mother, the Dowager Countess of Darby."

He bowed over her hand as he had Lady Darby's. The dowager waved him off. "You may address me as Dowager. At my advanced age, I could very well expire before one is able to complete my title."

Lucien took a seat across from Lady Sarah, realizing that they were the only four present at the long table.

"Is Lord Darby unable to attend tonight?" Lucien asked. The chinking and scraping stopped.

"My husband rarely attends meals these days," Lady Darby answered. Her frigid tone made Lucien think better of asking why.

The chinking and scraping resumed. Supper passed with painfully little conversation. Lady Darby was sullen throughout, though she did spend a great deal of time watching Lucien eat, as though he were an exotic animal she had never before seen. It reminded him of the time a rhinoceros was presented to King Louis. For one solid week, all of Versailles spent their days and nights observing the beast's habits.

If Lucien were to be honest, though, he was hardly one to criticize. He spent a good deal of *his* time observing Lady Sarah, who ate not one bite of the delicious fare.

Lady Sarah and the dowager murmured a few comments to one another during the repast, and Lady Sarah made a small effort to promote a conversation with Lucien, but all parties seemed vastly relieved when the meal was over.

"As there are no other gentlemen about, perhaps you would like to join us in the drawing room?" Lady Sarah helped her mother from the chair as she spoke to Lucien.

"Thank you for the kind offer, but I believe I shall retire. It has been an eventful day."

"Of course. Good night." Lady Sarah escorted the dowager from the room, while Lady Darby lingered in the doorway.

"Should you be in need of some company," the countess said as she slipped her hands into a long pair of gloves, "please do not hesitate to seek me out. As I said before, my husband is rarely about these days and I would find it rather stimulating to have someone new to talk to."

She gave him a pointed look before she, too, disappeared, leaving Lucien alone in the shadows to contemplate this strange trio of women, as well as the route back to his quarters.

Chapter 3

"For Heaven's sake, come away from there," Sarah's mother said. "Your gardens will be there in the morning."

Sarah turned her back to the moonlight streaming in through the windows of the small sitting room in her chambers. In warmer weather, she left the windows open to the fragrance of the gardens below, wanting to enjoy every possible moment with her flowers.

On rare occasions she dared to walk the gardens at night, without her veils. But it stirred such a longing to be free of them, she didn't do it often. Perhaps she would tonight.

"You act like a mother doting on her children," said Merri.

"What?"

"The gardens. The flowers. You act like a mother doting on her children."

"How ridiculous," Sarah said, without conviction. There was much truth in her mother's observation.

In a way, the flowers were her progeny. She raised them from seeds, nurtured them, fussed over them, fed and cared for them as if they were an extension of herself. For so long she had wanted to learn to paint, to recreate her "children" in the cold of winter, to fill her home with the beauty of the gardens when they were bare.

"Soon," she said aloud. "Soon, I'll be able to paint them."

Merri sighed. "Well, I *am* happy you've found something else to interest you. Something that will keep you out of the dirt for a spell."

"How do you suppose James came to hire Lucien Delacourte, of all people?"

"I'm sure it's no coincidence. The way your brother has doted on you since the accident, I'm surprised he didn't try to resurrect Michelangelo the first time you mentioned an interest in learning to paint."

"I would rather have Monsieur Delacourte."

Sarah had known of her tutor long before he arrived at Elmstone. Before the accident, she had traveled several times to Paris, where Delacourte's signature was coveted by a small but discriminating group of collectors. One of them was Sarah's father. He purchased a rendering of a French garden in spring, which now graced a wall in their drawing room.

Sarah had devoted hours to staring at it. During the long days of her recovery, she lost herself in that work of art. The colors transported her. The delicate depictions of rosebuds inspired her to try and recreate such beauty on the grounds of Elmstone Manor.

"James must have gone to great lengths to hire Mr. Delacourte," she said.

"He knows how much you admire him, my dear."

"I do admire him, but . . . Frankly, I don't enjoy having a stranger in the house. I wish we would have had some sort of warning. I would have prepared."

"Prepared? Whatever for?"

Sarah shrugged. "For the curiosity. For the questions he's bound to ask about my veils."

Her mother looked surprised. "I should have thought he'd asked them already."

"No, but he will. Curiosity triumphs over proper manners every time."

"In this instance, I certainly hope it will. You need someone to question you. For more than seven years you've hidden yourself away, behind these walls and behind those veils. It's time you rejoined the world."

"I have no desire to rejoin the world, thank you. Perfect strangers staring and pointing, asking rude questions. I do not wish to share my life that way."

"My dear, when was the last time you spoke to anyone who isn't a relative or a servant?"

Sarah tugged at her veils. "A while, I suppose."

"Two years. It was two years ago, my dear, when Sir Richard Cannon stayed with us. Whatever happened? I thought you and he had struck up a friendship of sorts."

Sarah wandered over to the window again. "Not really."

The truth was, she had indeed struck up a friendship with Sir Richard, but it was cut short when her brother discovered some perceived unsavory detail about his character. James forced him to leave in the dead of night. Though Sarah had no romantic designs on the gentleman, her brother's overprotective nature left her angry, and more than a little hurt. It was proof she could never regain his respect. Not after what had happened on the night of the accident.

"I would like to see you married before I die," Merri said, suddenly.

Sarah smiled. Her mother's voice actually conveyed hope.

"Perhaps you should retire now, Mother. You're beginning to sound delirious. Where is Miss Witherspoon?"

"The Devil's teeth. It will take me longer to find her than it will to walk to my rooms alone," Merri said, struggling to her feet.

"Shall I help you?"

"It's only three doors away. I don't think I'll expire with the effort."

"Good. Then I'll look for you tomorrow at breakfast," Sarah said as her mother hobbled from the room, her cane thudding on the carpet in the hallway. She listened as the door to Merri's quarters opened and closed, then locked her room from the inside and put the key in a wooden box on her dressing table. It was the only key in existence. She kept her door locked at all times, lest someone enter and find her unveiled.

She removed her veils and hat, along with her hairpins, before returning to the window. She leaned out and stared up at the moon.

A familiar yearning seeped into her bones.

The fact that Lucien Delacourte was handsome hadn't escaped her notice. The accident hadn't marred her vision, nor destroyed the normal urges a woman might feel toward a man as attractive as he. It simply had taught her not to act on them. Fate had punished her dearly for quenching that thirst once.

Now, even if she wanted to, she could not engage the interest of a man like Lucien Delacourte.

It was a pity she had not met him in Paris, when she was young and had no trouble attracting handsome gentlemen. Back then, she'd indulged in amorous pursuits with the confidence only a very young and naïve girl could possess. Never had she imagined it would all end so abruptly.

Life had been so different then. *She* had been so different then. She had admirers and parties and adventures.

And she had Duncan.

Sarah swept her straight, unbound hair over her shoulders. Starting at the bridge of her nose, her forefinger traced the long scar that ran above her right eyebrow, across her forehead, and down her right cheek to the shallow cleft in her chin. The shape of half a heart.

The rough skin beneath her fingertip tingled at her touch,

still sensitive after nearly eight years. Once an angry red slash, the scar had turned silvery white over time, as if it were now only a ghost of the nightmare she had lived.

In a way, it was.

Once she ceased leaving Elmstone, the pain lessened. There were no more questions or whispers or sympathetic stares. She no longer cried when she looked in the mirror. It was a *fait accompli*. Her life had changed.

Without the time-consuming trappings of vanity, Sarah had accomplished much more than she ever imagined. She had the time now to read books she never dreamed she would read; to learn things she never thought possible. Work in her garden gave her purpose. She tried to forget Duncan and her terrible weakness for him, and had come to realize there was more to life than being admired for her beauty.

But Lucien Delacourte had awakened that long-forgotten wish to be admired. What was it about him that stirred such wistful thoughts?

True, he was an arresting study of manhood, with golden coloring and iris blue eyes that commanded one's attention. But she had seen plenty of dashing men in her time, and looks did not sway her as they once might have. She suspected her interest in him lay in his talent, in the way his work had moved her so long ago.

Her restless hands searched a desk near the window. She withdrew a packet of papers from a drawer and unfolded them, studying them in the moonlight. The sketches she had drawn were passable; some might even be considered good. But adding color to the images was a daunting thought. She was lucky to have such a fine tutor.

She donned her veils and rang for her maid a full hour earlier than usual. She wanted to be at her best tomorrow for her first lesson with Lucien Delacourte.

* * *

Lucien had spent too many days sleeping on dirty floors or bug-ridden ticking not to appreciate having a soft, clean place to lay his head. He fell into a deep sleep shortly after he stretched out on the bed. Though his body was content, his mind could not be still. As soon as sleep came, so too did the dream.

Versailles again. Another night spent at court, sketching, laughing, drinking. Lucien was in favor with the king, and nothing could be more exhilarating.

He had begged Katrina to accompany him, but she did not want to leave Tessa.

"Ah, my love, do not make me go alone," he said, as Katrina poured him another glass of wine.

She laughed as she stroked his cheek. "Are you so afraid of Madame Du Clair that you need an escort?"

Lucien grabbed his wife about the waist and dragged her onto his lap, nuzzling her neck. "As a matter of fact, I am. I swear, the last time I caught her looking in my direction, she was licking her lips."

Katrina gave him a playful push and wiggled from his grasp. "No doubt she'd just devoured a tray of marzipan."

Lucien raised a brow. "You jest, but do I detect a note of jealousy in your words?"

"No. Just a note of regret that Tessa and I will have to make do without you for another evening."

He finished his wine and Katrina took the empty glass, kissing him gently on the forehead.

"It won't be much longer before my sketches are complete," he said. "Then I'll be home for a good long while."

Katrina's eyes sparkled. "Ah, yes. Working. We still won't see much of you, but at least you'll be in the other room rather than lost among the noblemen at court. If we press our ears to the door, we might even hear you take a breath."

Lucien knew she teased him. Nevertheless, she spoke the

truth. When he wasn't at court, he did spend most of his time painting. But aside from a few good-natured complaints, Katrina rarely took him to task for constantly working. She seemed to understand his nature so fully, to accept his ambitions as necessary to his existence.

He felt a sudden, powerful need to have her by his side that night, to serve as his small bit of sanity in the sea of lace and perfume and illusions.

He kissed her neck softly. "Let me send for a nurse to stay with Tessa. You can accompany me to court, and we will eat and drink and dance under the stars until you can bear my company no longer."

She tangled her fingers in his hair and pressed her full lips to his. "What makes you believe I can bear you this moment?"

"Katrina—"

"My sweet husband, the king and queen of France have no place in their court for the daughter of German peasants."

He pulled her tight against him. "But you are my wife. You belong with me."

Her smile was indulgent. "Go, Lucien. Make your sketches and hurry home . . ."

He'd tried to hurry home. But there was always one more sketch to be made, one more joke to hear, one more glass of wine to drink. It was morning when he finally stumbled home.

The sight that greeted him turned his blood to ice.

Black smoke hung in the sky, turning day to night. Below it raged the fires of hell. Dozens of villagers gathered on the square outside the burning villa.

His home.

Katrina's closest friend knelt on the ground, weeping.

"What happened?" He shook her. Her face was blank. "Where are Katrina and Tessa?"

"We had breakfast together. We laughed."

"Where are they?"

"Terrible," she moaned. "It was terrible. Tessa, she was playing with your brushes." The woman sobbed uncontrollably.

Lucien felt dizzy. He slapped the woman's face. "Tell me!"

"She . . . she knocked over the cup. The turpentine soaked her skirts. When she passed by the fire . . ."

Tessa!

He tried to push through the people, but they held him back. It was too late. The villa collapsed, sending a shower of orange sparks toward the crowd . . .

Lucien half woke, though his eyes refused to focus in the silver-gray light. He tried to will himself back to Katrina and Tessa. Back to that horrible night. If only he could go back, he could change things. He could stay with them, carry them from the burning villa. Or at least die with them.

His mind refused to take him home.

He rose from the bed and pulled open the heavy curtains, looking out upon the vast countryside. His arms were bare, slick with a sheen of sweat that reflected the moonlight.

His gaze caught the shadow of a figure moving through the garden directly below his window. Servants meeting for a tryst, perhaps—Or something else?

A chill passed over him despite the warmth of the night. This place harbored so many secrets, perhaps it harbored ghosts as well.

The figure disappeared beneath the trellis, and Lucien turned his attention back to the garden itself.

Even by the faint light of night it was spectacular. White and pale pink blossoms captured the moonbeams on their petals, appearing to float in the breeze, their dark green stems invisible in the shadows. The nymphs frolicked in the pond, alive with the magic of the moon.

Lucien's thoughts strayed unexpectedly to Sarah Essington, wondering again at the veils. He sensed that to ask

her about them would break the tentative trust they had
built that afternoon, and he did not wish to do that.

Their lessons would progress much more smoothly if
they were comfortable with each other. They were off to a
fair beginning. Lady Sarah was easy to listen to, refreshing
after years of forced court banter.

During their brief time together, Lucien had studied the
woman in the way he'd perfected years ago. Outwardly, he
gave only a casual glance as he captured each small detail,
each mannerism and movement that defined a person. The
skill had served him well, until now. He found he could not
use it with Lady Sarah. He could not see her eyes or her
mouth—a person's most expressive and revealing features.

Lucien breathed in the seductive smell of the roses,
and concentrated. He envisioned Sarah's long, graceful
arms; her slender fingers encircling the stem of a rose;
the slight sway of her hips as he followed her through the
passageways; the thrum of anticipation in her voice as she
spoke of learning to paint . . .

Suddenly, Lucien felt a hunger he had not experienced
in an eternity: the desire to be interested, to be excited by
something. Whether this desire arose from the gardens or
the pending lessons, he could not be certain.

But of course, it did not matter.

He would not allow himself the luxury of emotions. To
feel anything would serve only to prove he was alive, betraying his beloved Katrina and Tessa each time he drew a
breath.

Chapter 4

The sun warmed Sarah's back as she weeded a section of the east garden. The flowers were awash in the creamy yellow light of morning, dew balancing in the hollows of petals and leaves. She longed to remove her veils.

Although the thin gauze impeded her vision only slightly, taking the sharp edges away and perhaps muting the colors by a shade, she wished to see with naked eyes by sunlight rather than moonlight. But for fear of someone happening upon her, she kept the veils in place—always.

She burrowed her fingers deep into the earth, feeling a pulse there. The life of the plants and flowers, or her own? Both, she decided. They were one and the same. She needed them as much as they needed her.

Sarah heard footsteps behind her. She turned, half expecting, half longing for them to be the footsteps of the artist. Instead, her brother approached.

"What brings you out here so early?" She tossed a handful of weeds into a wooden bucket and accepted James's hand.

"Breakfast," he said.

He escorted her to the stone terrace, where a silver tray piled high with scones, figs, honey, cream, and biscuits graced the center of a table. A smaller table beside it bore an ornate tea service etched with vines.

James pulled Sarah's chair out and handed her a damp linen for her hands. "I've not had a chance to warn you. A guest arrived yesterday—"

"Delacourte."

James looked only mildly surprised. "You've met him, then?"

"Indeed. I showed him round the gardens after I found him wandering the grounds in search of Miss Witherspoon. Where *does* she get away to?"

"No doubt she hides in the pantry in order to escape Mother's unreasonable demands."

Sarah smiled at the image of the proper Miss Witherspoon cowering behind a barrel of potatoes. "Mmm. Mother *can* be a fright at times."

"At times? We shall have to raise poor Miss Witherspoon's salary again if we hope to keep her here."

Sarah knew James was only half joking. "It would be well worth the cost," she said. "Now, tell me. How is it that Lucien Delacourte has come to be my tutor?"

James shrugged. "Can you imagine my surprise when I discovered him standing at the gate? Since I assumed Monsieur Valmetant could not convince him to fill the position, I had been seeking other alternatives."

"Michelangelo, per chance?"

"Michelangelo?" James looked perplexed.

Sarah laughed. "Never mind. I'm thrilled he's here. But have you noticed he seems a bit odd? Distracted?"

"In what way?"

"Oh, I cannot say for certain. It's as if a chilly breeze follows him about. He doesn't smile."

"One never knows what drives the artistic temperament."

Her brother diverted his attention to the breakfast tray, and Sarah knew she had lost him for the moment. He ate in silence until he'd tried at least one of everything on the table. Sarah watched with amusement, remembering him as a boy of twelve, two years her senior and nearly twice her size, who once ate so much pigeon pie he had to be carried up to his rooms.

Whatever happened to that boy? James's appetite was one of the few things that remained of the brother she'd teased and played and fought with. He had changed almost as much as she had.

When James had taken the edge off his appetite, Sarah said, "I'm looking forward to beginning my lessons. Perhaps when I'm finished, I will be able to render the lot of you in oils."

"I hope you can," James said. "You know, we have no decent portrait of Father. Nothing to help our children remember him . . ."

Sarah bowed her head.

"Sarah, I am sorry. I didn't mean—"

"Please, James. I know I will never have children. I have come to terms with my fate."

He frowned. "It doesn't have to be that way. I could find a decent match for you."

"I would be far too old by the time you found someone you approve of."

"What do you mean?"

Sarah sighed. "You're much too protective, James. Do you remember what happened with Sir Richard?"

Her brother's face turned red. "The man was despicable. He—"

"Never mind. It doesn't matter."

"Yes, it does. I cannot allow anyone to hurt you the way Duncan Lavery did. But I do want you to be happy."

"I *am* happy, in my own way. I'm not alone. I have my

family and the gardens. I'm so much more fortunate than many."

James shook his head.

"Perhaps Mr. Delacourte would paint you," Sarah suggested, attempting to change the subject. "Do you think he could truly capture the Earl of Darby's most prominent feature?"

James dribbled honey on a scone. "What? My nose?"

"No!" Sarah laughed. It was only in these few moments, before the cares of the day had worn away at him, that James resembled the laughing young man he had been. "Your keen intelligence is your most prominent feature. However, your nose follows close behind."

"Watch what you say, sister dear. Our features are more similar than you might care to admit."

"Ah, James. Fortune has blessed me, for I have my veils. You, however, are doomed to confront the world with your naked face each morning."

"And never has the world been so favored."

"Who, pray tell, is favored?" Julia glided through the open doors and out onto the terrace. She wore a petulant look, as well as a gown more suited for a night at the opera than a quiet breakfast in the garden. Her powdered hair was looped and braided in an elaborate fashion.

She patted her coif. "Do you like it?"

James stood to greet his wife. The smile he wore earlier had dimmed considerably. "A bit overdone for breakfast, isn't it?"

Sarah noted the tension that had gathered in his jaw. A pebble of guilt rattled in her chest. If not for her own failed engagement, James would not be bound to a woman he didn't love and couldn't respect. But political alliances demanded a marriage—any marriage—between their two families. Her ill fate had touched them all, her brother most especially.

"Figs and scones again," Julia complained, ignoring

James completely. "If I'm forced to eat another fig, I may begin to sprout them."

"Not to worry, Julia," Sarah said sweetly. "Fig trees prefer to grow in warm places."

Julia sent a scathing look her way. "I'm simply pointing out that we have them *every single day.*"

"They're my mother's favorites," James reminded her. "You know how Cook dotes on Mother."

"Which reminds me, didn't we discuss taking on a different cook?"

"We did, and I said absolutely not. Mrs. Hopstead has been with us for nearly twenty years and I see no good reason to let her go . . ."

Only half listening to James and Julia's bickering, Sarah lifted a cup of tea beneath her veils and sipped the tepid liquid. It had taken a long time to lose her self-consciousness enough to eat and drink in the presence of others. Before then she had taken many meals alone in her rooms. Eventually she perfected a way to bring things to her lips beneath the veils without exposing her face, but she rarely practiced this feat in the presence of anyone besides her mother, James, and Julia. Thus, when Lucien Delacourte appeared on the terrace, she put her cup aside.

"Fine morning," the artist said, bowing to those present. An unruly blond curl slid over his forehead. The jacket he wore stretched tight across his shoulders as he bent, and Sarah measured the width of them with her eyes until she noticed Julia watching her. A sly smile played on her sister-in-law's lips, as if Julia had somehow guessed what she was looking at.

Sarah nervously adjusted the fine lace kerchief adorning her neck. Why had she chosen to don such a frivolous thing this morning? Heavens, but it caused her to itch.

James motioned Mr. Delacourte to the table. "I understand my sister bullied you into a lengthy expedition yesterday."

"Bully? Never. It was a pleasure, I assure you." Mr. Delacourte smiled. It was the first smile Sarah had seen him affect. Broad and dazzling, it evinced not one shred of true happiness. Still, it managed to curl Sarah's toes all the same.

"A pleasure, eh?" said James, wryly. "No doubt you'd find a leeching enjoyable then."

"Now, James," Julia scolded in a honeyed voice. "Just because *you* prefer a muddy wheat field to the beauty of a garden doesn't mean you should scorn someone with more discriminating taste."

All trace of humor left James's face. "My dear, have you met Lucien Delacourte? He has come to teach Sarah to paint."

"We became acquainted last eve, at supper. You might have introduced us all to him there, had you bothered to make an appearance." Julia directed her comment to James, but her eyes remained trained on the artist. "Delacourte. Delacourte. The name sounds familiar." Julia's brow puckered in concentration. "I could not seem to get it out of my mind all the night. Where have I heard it?"

"London, most probably," Mr. Delacourte said. "My father was English. He was raised in London, and we lived there for a time when I was a boy."

"I suppose that would explain your excellent English," said Sarah, reaching for a teacup. Julia, however, was quicker.

"How ever did you end up in France?" Julia poured a cup of tea and set it before Mr. Delacourte, flashing Sarah another maddening smirk.

"My mother was French. When I showed a proclivity to painting, we took up residence in Paris so I could study there under Valmetant. I have lived in France most of my life."

"Oh! Now I remember. I've heard of a Mathilde Delacourte," said Julia. "Are you any relation?"

"We are first cousins, though we have not seen one another in many years."

Julia tapped her chin. "She has a brother, too. He married up— He married well, didn't he?"

"The daughter of a baron, I believe."

"Perhaps if you're going to be with us for a while, we can arrange for you and your cousins to become reacquainted," Julia said. "In any event, it will give us a good excuse to get out of this God-awful village and visit London."

Mr. Delacourte shifted in his chair. "Are you from London originally, Lady Darby?"

"Heavens, no. I was reared in Pickney, not half a day's ride from here. Much smaller than Whitford, if you can imagine, and teeming with Catholics. Impossible to find even a mediocre hat there. But then James rescued me and brought me here, where it's quite easy to find a mediocre hat." Julia stabbed at a fig on the tray.

James's features clouded, but Julia seemed not to notice. Or perhaps not to care.

"You are fond of hats?" Mr. Delacourte asked her, obviously trying to ease the sudden tension at the table.

"Not particularly, no. What is the hat situation in Paris these days, monsieur?"

"Almost nonexistent, I am afraid. Hair is more the fashion. Rather tall hair."

Julia patted her coif.

"Enough about hair and hats and the like," said James. "Tell us, Delacourte, when will Sarah's lessons commence?"

Her new tutor seemed relieved at the change of subject. "We could begin this afternoon, if Lady Sarah so desires."

"I do," Sarah replied. "I'm quite anxious to start." An understatement, to be sure. She had been awake half the night thinking about it.

"Is there a place we can work without interruption?"

"Perhaps the gardens?" she suggested. "It's such a lovely day."

"Might I join you?" Julia said, before Mr. Delacourte could answer. "I am fair to bursting with curiosity about how an artist works. Perhaps I could serve as a model."

"I am afraid there is much for Lady Sarah to learn before we even begin to paint. It will be many weeks before we need any sort of model."

"I see. Well, maybe I could join in the lessons. I am certain Sarah wouldn't mind if—"

"Julia," Sarah's mother snapped from the doorway. "Anne has been looking for you all morning. She's waiting for you in the kitchen."

The men rose from their seats as Merri approached. Her expression was one of supreme annoyance.

Julia stood as well. "Mother. I trust you had a good night?"

"I haven't had a good night in years," the dowager replied. "Anne is in the kitchen." She took a seat next to Sarah, bestowing a frosty look upon her daughter-in-law.

Julia, her mouth pinched into a tight line, left without another word.

"Mother," said James, a genuine smile returning to his lips, "you look lovelier than the tulips this morning."

"I should certainly hope so, as tulips are dead this time of year."

"Oh?" James looked to Sarah, who nodded. He cleared his throat. "Well. I suppose you *would* look lovelier then, wouldn't you?"

Merri waved a hand impatiently. "Your power to charm me escaped when you outgrew your nursery togs, my boy. Now, put a few figs on my plate and you may just win me over again."

Merri plucked a teacup and saucer from the tray and pushed them toward Sarah, who was in the process of

smoothing a wrinkle from her mother's sleeve. "Stop fussing with my clothing and give me some tea."

"Glad to see you in such a pleasant mood today." Sarah
poured from the elegant service.

"Have you forgotten the way to my rooms?" Merri said.
"It's been a week, at least, since I've seen you there. You
used to visit me every morning."

"You exaggerate, Mother. I was there the day before
yesterday. We sorted your needles and threads, remember?" Sarah leaned over and kissed her mother's cheek.

"That damnable lace," Merri complained. "Can't I have
a kiss from my daughter instead of the Phantom of Whitford?"

Mr. Delacourte seemed shocked by Merri's words. But
the barb had little effect on Sarah, who had borne her
mother's frustration with the veils a thousand times. "What
has happened to make you so disagreeable this morning?
Did Miss Witherspoon forget to rub your feet?"

"Be careful, Mother," said James. "Mr. Delacourte will
begin to think you're a nasty piece of work."

"Why should I care what he thinks?"

Sarah sighed. "You are incorrigible. Father would be
shocked at the woman you have become."

"My dear, were your father still alive, I would not *be* the
woman I have become. 'Twas the loss of a good man that
sparked my temper."

An image of her father appeared in Sarah's mind. He
was so kind, so gentle. She missed him.

She spooned some honey into her mother's tea.
"Enough?"

"It will do. Now, Mr. Delacourte, how long will you be
staying with us?" The dowager focused her attention on
Lucien. Before he could answer, she said, "Well! My
daughter was right. You *are* a far sight more handsome in
the daylight than in that dungeon in which we dine. Lady

44 DONNA BIRDSELL

Darby's ill attempt at elegance makes everyone look terribly ghoulish."

Mr. Delacourte seemed amused, not the least bit embarrassed by her mother's words, though Sarah certainly was. This was one of the rare times she was happy to have the veils, for the unnatural warmth of her cheeks would certainly be visible without them.

Merri pressed on, oblivious to her daughter's discomfort. "Did you know we have one of your works? My husband purchased it for Sarah, I believe, on a sojourn to Paris some years ago."

Mr. Delacourte straightened. "Indeed?"

"Our Sarah has been a collector of paintings for many years. It was a love she shared with her father. She's spent a great deal of time examining your painting, in particular."

Sarah pinched Merri's knee beneath the table. Her mother was impossible!

"Perhaps you would care to revisit your painting after breakfast, Mr. Delacourte?" Sarah said.

"Most definitely. I am curious to see which of my works caught your interest."

"Interest? Obsession is more the word. I cannot count how many hours she's spent in front of it," said James. "It's the reason I sought you for the tutoring position."

Again, Sarah was glad for the veils. She considered spilling her tea into her mother's lap to create a diversion. Before she could lift her cup, though, Mr. Delacourte turned to her.

"Might I ask what you find so appealing about this particular painting?"

Her mother was saved, for the moment.

Sarah set her teacup back in its saucer. Why should she feel embarrassed to be an admirer of this man's exquisite ability? This was an opportunity she had longed for many times while sitting before his painting. How often had she wanted to tell him what that garden scene had meant to her, had done for her? But she knew he could never fully understand how his painting had saved her life.

"Your work inspired me during a time in my life when I was greatly in need of inspiration."

"A most excellent compliment," Mr. Delacourte said softly.

For a moment it seemed as if they were the only two at the table.

"Well!" said James, breaking the spell. "I'm afraid I must take my leave. There is much business to attend to. Mother, tell Cook not to expect me for supper."

"Does she ever, these days?" Merri gave James a disapproving glare. He looked away, brushing an imaginary crumb from his jacket.

Sarah stole a glance at her tutor, who seemed too absorbed in his own thoughts to notice their little drama.

He seemed so utterly out of place here, like an exotic orchid in a field of wildflowers. What could possibly have lured him to Elmstone when he held such an enviable post at Versailles?

Lucien was reluctant to teach in the gardens, as Lady Sarah suggested. The colors bit into his consciousness with such sweet savagery that he did not know if he could concentrate there. Instead, he chose a sunny alcove off the drawing room in which to set up his easel.

Lady Sarah sat on the edge of the window seat, watching. He imagined her eyes beneath the veils—alert, intelligent, shining with curiosity and enthusiasm.

For this first session she had worn a sensible gown of dark blue silk that left her arms bare to the elbows. The soft down of hair on her forearms caught the sunlight filtering through the window. Her wrists were narrow and unadorned, as were her hands, in which she held a packet of folded papers.

"Are you ready to begin?"

"I am," she replied. Her voice was hushed, as if she were speaking in church.

"Will your veils impede your vision in any way?"

Her back straightened. "They tend to dim my vision a bit. However, I thought we could proceed with our lessons here and I'll complete them, if necessary, upstairs in my rooms. Will that pose a problem?"

"Not at all."

As Lucien requested, a servant had fetched two stools, which he set before the empty easel. He gestured to one, and Sarah took a seat. She sat behind his left elbow, out of the path of the sunlight.

"What have you there?" he asked, pointing to the papers she held.

She hesitated only briefly, then handed him the packet. "Sketches. I thought they might give you some idea of my abilities, or lack thereof."

He unfolded the papers and smoothed them on his leg. The drawings were done in charcoal, neat and unsmudged. The first depicted several small, star-shaped flowers. The lines were precise and smooth.

"Very good. What is this one?"

"*Campanula persicifolia.* Paper flower."

"And what are the colors?"

"Blue or white petals. Deep green stems and leaves."

He studied the drawing for a moment, then picked up a small tack from a nearby table and fixed it to the frame of the easel. He looked at the second page. A tall stalk with a cone-shaped cluster of blossoms. "And this?"

"*Stachys byzantina.* Lambs' lugs. Medium green stalks with lilac spires."

Together they looked at four more, Sarah giving the names and colors. With each description her voice projected more confidence. The last, a rose in bloom, was rendered with impressive detail.

"This is one of my own varieties," she said, with unmistakable pride. "I've not yet named it."

Lucien tacked the rose to the easel's frame beneath the other charcoal drawings. "These sketches are quite good. Have you had lessons?"

"When I was a girl, as part of my studies. Though I didn't take the time to work on it until after the . . . until the last several years."

After the what? he wondered. He said, "Your lines are quite natural. Often times it is difficult for novices to depict the intricate shapes and curves found in flowers. They're different from the shapes of the human form, and can be more difficult to capture accurately."

She laughed. "For me, plants and flowers are much more familiar than the human form, because I've spent so many hours in the gardens observing their movements and growth. I know them quite intimately."

"It is apparent in your drawings. I believe the greatest works are those for which the artist has a great love, an intimate understanding of the subject's soul. I see it here."

"Thank you."

"Do not thank me so quickly. While these drawings are more than adequate, painting is a very different means of expression. To make your work exceptional, not only must you be proficient with your lines, you also must add something of yourself. We have much work to do before you will be able to properly portray these wonders on canvas." With that, Lucien withdrew an apple from his pocket and held it up into the sunbeams crisscrossing the room. "What do you see?" he asked.

"An apple."

"What else?"

She hesitated. "The stem, the skin . . ."

"Before you are able to paint this apple, you must truly examine it. Look deeply. Find, if you can, its soul."

Sarah sat quietly for several minutes, studying the apple

as Lucien studied her. She was so still, so focused. He envied her that. He had been unable to find such stillness for far too long. Was that the reason he could no longer paint?

He watched the veils flutter subtly with her breathing. It was the only movement he could detect.

"What do you see?" he asked again.

"An apple blossom that aspired to be more."

"And?"

"A gift of sustenance from Nature."

"And?"

"Something that will remain perfect only for a short period of time before it softens and rots and eventually disappears back into the earth."

"Very good. You need such insights to capture the essence of the apple while it is still here, within your reach. You are not just painting a subject, but capturing a moment in time forever. Unless, of course, you dislike it, in which case you may simply paint over it."

Her voice lowered again to the church whisper. "I've lived many moments I wish I could simply paint over."

The melancholy in her voice struck his heart.

"As have I," he said. "As have I."

Chapter 5

Julia slouched in a chair in the corner of the drawing room. Other evenings she would be dreaming up an excuse to leave. But not tonight. Tonight, suffering the company of her husband's family was almost worth the effort.

Dinner had been an altogether miserable affair, as usual. In a rare mealtime appearance, James had prattled on about the fields again, as if he were a common farmer rather than a member of the peerage. All the talk of seeds and weather and planting schedules—she would never fathom his devotion to the dirt on which this musty old manor stood.

Speaking of musty, that old nag Merri had been casting cold looks about all night, no doubt devising some new way to make a nuisance of herself. And Sarah . . . Well, what could be said about her dear, damaged sister-in-law? The veils were beyond tedious. Julia fought a daily urge to rip them from her face.

The only bright spot had been the presence of the artist. Mr. Delacourte spoke of Paris and Rome and Vienna—all the places Julia would rather be than weary old Whitford. Those were the places where she belonged.

Her lips curled into a lazy smile as she stole a glance at Mr. Delacourte's—Lucien's—profile. He sat on the settee, dutifully listening to Sarah's pitiful attempts at conversation. Something political. War, or some such. Things women should never speak of. How could he actually manage to appear interested?

Julia's attention wandered from Lucien's deep-set blue eyes to his angular chin and down to the blond hair curling over the collar of his coat. Her gaze traced the breadth of his shoulders, the width of his hips, his long, lean legs.

Julia chewed on her lower lip. She knew of something sure to pique his interest more than Sarah's tired conversation. Lucien would soon discover that life at Elmstone was akin to living in a graveyard, complete with a phantom, a ghost, and a vicious old ghoul. Unless he made an effort to keep his blood pumping, he would find himself half-dead as well.

Over the years, Julia had done rather well at keeping her blood pumping, but it was slowing fast. Aside from the occasional tryst with Robert, one of the groomsmen at Elmstone, the last bit of true excitement she had was when an old schoolmate of James's had paid a visit.

James had invited Sir Richard Cannon hoping he would take a fancy to Sarah. The two did seem to enjoy each other's company, but Julia couldn't bear to see his attentions wasted on someone so boring. It wasn't long before Sir Richard fancied *her* instead. Quite well, as a matter of fact.

She curled a lock of hair around her finger, trying to catch Lucien's attention. Instead it was her mother-in-law who took notice.

"Have you something to add to this conversation, Julia?" The ghoul's very voice turned Julia's blood to ice.

Julia projected a wide-eyed stare. "I'm afraid I could never aspire to the eloquence of our dear Sarah."

"Quite true." Merri shot her a look of supreme disgust and turned to Sarah. "How was your first lesson, my dear?"

"It went very well, I believe. What do you think, Mr. Delacourte?"

"I agree. Dowager, your daughter has a natural artistic instinct. I look forward to working with her."

The old ghoul looked positively smug. "No doubt she inherited her abilities from me. I was quite the artist in my day, you know."

"Is that so?" Lucien said.

"Yes, I spent a great deal of time in Munich, working under a student of Mengs."

"What made you abandon your efforts, madame?"

"Alas, I married my dear husband. All thoughts of the artistic bent were soon displaced by the duties of a wife and mother."

"At least *you* will not have those worries, Sarah," Julia said brightly. "You shall no doubt be free to pursue your artistic endeavors for as long as you wish."

The room fell silent.

"Julia." James's voice was low, but there could be no mistaking the warning it held.

"What?" She feigned innocence. It was criminal the way James always took up for Sarah, when he knew better than anyone there was no hope for his sister. Even without the scars, Sarah was well past the age of marriage. She was also an unmitigated bore. "Isn't it kinder to help Sarah face the truth? To prepare her for a life of . . . well, of gardening and painting, rather than encouraging false hopes?"

"I harbor no false hopes, Julia. You can be certain of that," Sarah said quietly.

Julia suddenly could not bear another moment in the drawing room, despite Lucien's tantalizing presence. "I fear I've grown very tired."

She rose and gave her mother-in-law a perfunctory kiss on the cheek, affording Lucien an enticing view of her cleavage as she did so. Then she turned to her sister-in-law. "I'm truly sorry if I have offended you, Sarah. Please believe my comments were only meant to encourage your talent."

"The day your words discourage me is the day I molder in my grave."

"Honestly, Sarah. Must everything be so morbid?" Julia sauntered over to James. "I shall be up in my rooms," she murmured.

His face was unreadable. "Have a restful night."

No chance of that, Julia thought, as she climbed the stairs. Her dreams, she knew, would be filled with visions of a certain Frenchman.

Damn James. He wouldn't help to ease her restlessness tonight. In fact, it had been months since he'd performed his husbandly duties.

No matter. Robert was always available.

And if she so desired, she could simply bide her time and wait for Lucien. That he would come calling some night soon, she had no doubt.

They all did.

James tried not to reveal the relief he felt as his wife left the drawing room. While Julia could be callous, her words were, most likely, the truth. Sarah would never be married because she wouldn't allow him to name a match for her.

In truth, he could force her to marry whomever he chose. But he would not. Not when he was the cause of all her unhappiness to begin with.

James hadn't slept a full night in years. In the darkness he relived the events of that evening over and over again. The accident—and the fact that she'd left the ball alone—was his fault.

It was his fault Sarah was scarred. He should have

escorted her home himself. It was his fault she hid herself away behind the gates of Elmstone.

God knows, he tried to make it up to her. Whatever she wished, he strived to make it so. But the little things he did for her could never bring back the innocence and beauty, the vibrant life that had been hers before the tragedy.

James tried to shake his despair. He smiled at his mother, who seemed to enjoy Delacourte's company. However, as usual, he could not read his sister's thoughts. Those damnable veils hid her feelings so well they could be a stone wall.

Was she happy Delacourte was here? He knew she'd wanted to learn to paint for a long time, but he also knew her discomfort with strangers. For her to accept someone new into the private world she had created proved the extent of her determination in this matter.

Only when Sarah was truly happy could he forgive himself the role he played in her fate. He smiled at her and she nodded.

"I believe I shall also bid you all a fine evening," Sarah said, rising. "Mother, shall we go?"

"Miss Witherspoon is devilishly slow. Where is she?" Merri complained.

"No doubt dusting your thimble collection or sewing bows on your nightcap," said Sarah.

Merri wagged a bony finger. "She's hiding in the kitchen, gossiping with Cook. She's forever gossiping with Cook."

"Wherever she is, I hope she's had a chance to sit down for a moment," James muttered.

Merri stooped as if to kiss him on the cheek, but pulled his ear instead. "A son shouldn't take such a tone with his mother."

"Come, now." Sarah laughed. "I'll escort you."

"Fine. James, please exhume Miss Witherspoon from

the kitchen and send her to my rooms. I have a few things I'd like her to do before I retire for the night."

James rubbed his ear. "Whatever you wish, Mother."

Merri smiled. "Much, much better. Now, Sarah," she said as her daughter led her from the room, "we must work on *you*. Do you think a good pinch could get you to remove those veils?"

Their patter grew softer as they made their way toward the stairs.

"Exceptional women," said Delacourte.

"Indeed," said James. "They do add life to this place. I cannot imagine Elmstone without either one of them."

"Lady Sarah's gardens are quite extraordinary."

"The finest private gardens I've ever seen. Although I imagine you've seen some spectacular gardens at Versailles."

"Naturally. Though they lacked the loving hand your sister has given these."

"It's a pity the gardens are the only beneficiaries of her loving touch. I've long thought she would make an excellent mother. Have you any children, Delacourte?"

The artist's glass slipped from his fingers and bounced at his feet. Brandy splashed onto his stockings and shoes and soaked into the thick wool carpet beneath his feet.

"I am so sorry!" he said, retrieving the glass from the floor. "Let me fetch a napkin or something—"

"Never mind. I shall ring for the maid. She'll take care of it."

James crossed to the bell pull as Delacourte stood above the spill, nervously raking at his hair.

"Perhaps you should go and take care of your shoes."

Delacourte seemed relieved at the suggestion. "I will. Again, I am sorry."

"Think nothing of it, really."

The artist bid him good eve, and hastened from the

drawing room. James wondered at his odd behavior. It was just as his sister had said. The man seemed a bit off.

When the family had all retired for the evening, Lucien re-turned to the drawing room. He stood before his painting, which hung on the far wall.

He remembered it well. It was one of the first in a study of the gardens of Versailles, capturing a small corner in a courtyard. He painted it just after his marriage to Katrina, before Tessa was born, when he believed they would have their whole lives together.

After Katrina and Tessa's deaths, after two years of loneliness, he never thought he could feel connected to another soul again. But something was happening to him here. He felt a desire to be part of life again. He wanted to know where Lord Darby disappeared to, and what made the dowager's tongue so sharp.

He wanted to know why Lady Sarah hid behind her veils.

Lucien wandered into the alcove where his easel stood. Lady Sarah's drawings still hung on the board, and he grazed them with his fingertips, tracing the slight tracks left by the pressure of charcoal on paper. He imagined her, veils flung aside, tense with concentration, laboring over every detail.

He tried to envision her face. Did she and her brother share the same features? The same dark eyes and thoughtful brow? The same aristocratic nose? Were her lips pale pink like magnolia blossoms, or the deep red of rose petals?

Lucien sat before the easel, recalling their lesson that afternoon. He told Sarah to look deeply at her subject, and to find its soul. Was he still capable of such a feat? He doubted it. How could he possibly find the soul of a subject when he could not even find his own?

How could he teach someone a skill he himself had lost more than two years ago? Madness.

But it was too late now to leave. For one thing, he had no money. Where would he go? How would he get there? He had to remain at least long enough to collect his pay.

Besides, to desert Lady Sarah might cause her to abandon her dream to paint, and he did not wish to be responsible for that. He had to keep trying, for Lady Sarah's sake and for his own.

As he rose from the stool, he saw her in the doorway.

Tessa.

She was fairylike. White-blond curls tumbling over slim shoulders, wide eyes with thick lashes staring up at him in the half-dark. She possessed both the shyness and curiosity of a six-year-old, at one moment looking as if she might flee, the next gazing with longing at his easel.

He shook his head. "It cannot be. You are gone. I watched . . . I saw it with my own eyes."

But no, there she stood.

"I am sorry, so sorry," he whispered. "I never should have left you that night."

He wanted to tell her to come in. Come close. God, how he wanted to touch her hair. But she was not real, merely a vision. A ghost come to haunt him.

He pressed his palms against his eyes. He felt disjointed. Numb.

When he opened his eyes, Tessa was gone.

For a moment Sarah lay abed, caught between her dreams and the sunlight creeping into the room. She dreamed of Duncan. His deep green eyes searched hers as he held her close to him in the garden.

"Will you be my bride?" he whispered.

"Yes," she replied, over and over again.

And then he kissed her, his lips warm and promising.

How many years she had watched him playing in the fields of Cambert Hall when her family would visit his, yearning for that moment.

He hardly noticed her at first, but when they grew older, his indifference turned to interest. Soon, they had shared their first dance. Then their first walk alone in the gardens. Then their first sweet kiss . . .

The nasty caw of a crow outside her windows woke her fully, and Sarah remembered. Duncan did not love her anymore, if he ever truly had.

She rolled over on her side and closed her eyes. The dream burned away like fog in the sun, and Sarah sighed. She was one day farther away from that life. One day closer, she hoped, to being happy with this one. She had been content for quite a while now. But to be truly happy . . .

And then she remembered her lessons.

A surge of excitement propelled her from the bed. It was, indeed, a new day. There was much to learn from Mr. Delacourte. Or rather Lucien, as he had asked her to address him. And she was just Sarah now to him, as well. They discovered during their third lesson that polite formality seemed only to serve as a barrier to the communication necessary for their purpose. Once they shed their manners, the lessons had taken a much different tone.

She rang for her lady's maid, and began her toilette. She washed her face and brushed the tangles from her hair, then pulled it back into a knot at the base of her neck. Like most other days, she didn't linger at the mirror.

A knock at the door prompted her to don the veiled hat that lay on a chair.

"One moment, please, Becca." Sarah straightened the hat and pinned it in place, then lowered the veils. She removed the key from its wooden box and unlocked the door.

"Good morning, miss." Rebecca looked as if she were still half asleep.

"You really should get to bed a bit earlier," Sarah said with a motherly cluck.

"Yes, miss." The girl trudged into the room and went directly to the dressing table, where she removed a tin box from one drawer and a fresh linen shift from another.

"Shall we get you out of your nightclothes, Lady Sarah?"

Becca's hands moved deftly over the buttons on Sarah's back. She opened the tin of lavender talc and dusted Sarah's shoulders and arms, then handed her the shift.

"When will William return?" Sarah asked as she slipped into the shift. William was Rebecca's new husband, a tinker who traveled through the towns from Whitford to London and back. They had met outside the London residence, where Rebecca had worked for a time before coming to Whitford to serve Sarah.

Rebecca grinned. "It'll be another month or so. And none too soon. I miss him terribly." The two had been married but half a year. William had been traveling most of that time.

Rebecca adjusted the straps of the shift on Sarah's shoulders and helped her into a soft silk underskirt. Sarah patted the young woman's arm. "Give me a few days' warning, and you shall have a week free."

"Oh, thank you, my lady! 'Twould mean the world to me."

The maid hurried to the wardrobe and removed one of several gray gowns, which she dropped into a puddle on the floor. Sarah stepped into the circle formed by the soft fabric and Rebecca pulled the gown up to her shoulders. The sleeves hugged Sarah's arms tightly to the elbows, where a short ruffle of lace peeked out from beneath the gray. The modest neckline, too, was trimmed with lace. The hem was plain, a concession made by the draper purely out of practicality. Sarah's constant walks through the gardens soiled any type of trim beyond recognition.

Rebecca fastened the gown and tugged it here, gathered it there, smoothed it over Sarah's hips.

"You have the shape of an angel, miss, and if you don't mind my saying it, you should wear a bit of color. You might attract something more than bees. Like a certain French painter, perhaps?"

Beneath the veils Sarah's face grew hot. She would never get used to Becca's bluntness. And what good was the shape of an angel when you wore the face of a demon? "Gray suits me just fine, thank you."

"Hmmph." The maid gathered up the toilette items and deposited them in the drawer. She fussed over Sarah's gown once more, then gave a quick curtsy. "Will that be all, miss?"

"Yes. Thank you, Becca."

The maid hurried from the room, no doubt headed for the kitchen for a bite of breakfast before her day of laundering and mending began.

Sarah pinned her veils to the bodice of her dress with a simple brooch. On a whim, she dabbed a few drops of perfume on her wrists—something she hadn't done in months—before heading off to the gardens.

Chapter 6 ❧

Lucien missed breakfast altogether and took the noon meal in his room. He arrived downstairs to find only Lady Darby and Sarah present in the library. Sarah was reading a book as Lady Darby worked on a bit of tatting.

"Where is everyone this afternoon?" he asked.

"My husband ran off at an ungodly hour to mingle with the other farmers," Lady Darby answered. "Mother is back in her rooms with Miss Witherspoon, applying some smelly poultice to her knees."

Lucien sank into a chair and rubbed his eyes. He had been at Elmstone a fortnight. In that time he had been visited by the ghost of his dead daughter on three occasions. Each time he had been sitting at the easel in the alcove of the drawing room, trying to work up the nerve to pick up a brush, or even a pencil or a piece of charcoal, for he knew it would not be long before his lessons with Sarah progressed to the point where it would be necessary.

Each time Tessa appeared she would come no closer

than the doorway, where she would stand in silence . . . curious, fearful. Accusing?

He had seen her in Paris a number of times, but never with such stunning clarity. He would almost swear she lived again.

Oh, Tessa, ma petite. *Why didn't you listen to me? Why couldn't you leave my things alone?*

Lucien tried to focus on the present. "Lady Sarah, have you practiced your technique for today's lesson?"

"I have, though I'm finding the deflection of light from an angle to be a bit troublesome. The shadows seem unnatural."

The anticipation in her voice made him smile. He recalled his own enthusiasm when he first began his lessons with Valmetant, and that remembrance alone made this venture worthwhile. If he could not paint, at least he could pass his knowledge on to someone who, if not quite as technically talented, was at least every bit enamored of the process as he.

"The sunlight through the fog should prove an interesting twist this afternoon," he said.

She regarded him with a look of concern. "You seem tired today, Lucien."

At Sarah's use of his familiar name, Lady Darby's head snapped up. She made no effort to hide her interest in their conversation.

"I had a restless night," he said.

"Would you care to forgo our lesson for the day? I could work on my shadows until tomorrow."

The offer was tempting. If he could just lie down for a few hours, perhaps he could rid himself of the dull ache in his head and the burning eyes. But he knew how much Sarah looked forward to these lessons.

"No," he said. "We have too much to do."

"If you will both excuse me," said Lady Darby suddenly. "I have a busy morning." She gave Lucien a secretive little smile as she hurried past.

"I've not seen Julia move so quickly since the draper received a new shipment of Turkish silk," Sarah said. "Where could she be off to in such a rush?"

When Sarah and Lucien arrived in the drawing room alcove, Julia was already seated next to the easel. She had changed from the beribboned mauve gown to a less beribboned green one. "What shall we be learning today, monsieur? Or shall I address you as Lucien, as Sarah does?"

Sarah seethed with frustration beneath the veils, but her tone remained civil. "I thought we discussed this when Mr. Delacourte first arrived, Julia."

"Did we? I couldn't help but notice how enamored you've become with your little sessions, and I thought perhaps I should discover why." Julia cast a flirtatious look at Lucien, who seemed more amused than disturbed.

Sarah took two deep breaths. "I'm afraid I must ask you to leave. These lessons are not open to the entire household. We have much to accomplish, and you will surely be bored."

"Why, Sarah, I'm hardly the entire household. You'll scarcely notice me. Unless there is some other reason you want me to leave?"

Sarah wanted to slap Julia's patronizing smile from her face. "The only reason I want you to leave is that these lessons involve Mr. Delacourte and me alone."

"Ahh. *Alone.* And therein lies the problem."

Sarah's face warmed. "What problem would that be?"

"Yes, what problem?" said Lucien.

Julia raised her brow. "Oh, dear. How could I possibly have questioned your virtue? Still, if *I* entertained such a thought, surely others might, as well."

"Just what are you implying, Julia?" said Sarah.

The other woman shrugged. "A man and a woman spending quite a bit of time alone together . . . well, the servants might begin to gossip. What better reason for me to stay? We cannot have your reputation sullied, dear sister."

Lucien's look of amusement dissolved into annoyance. "Lady Darby, you cannot mean to suggest—"

Sarah stilled him with an upraised hand.

"By your own words, Julia, who would have me? What man would possibly want to sully the reputation of the Phantom of Whitford?" She fought to control her anger. "I am asking for privacy. For a bit of peace so that I might learn to paint. It's what James wants for me."

Julia smoothed her skirts over her lap, obviously refusing to budge from the stool. "James isn't here at the moment. As lady of this house I'm in charge in his absences, which are quite frequent of late. My husband's coin pays the tutor's wage, and I wish to stay for this lesson."

Before Sarah could do anything she might regret—but would certainly enjoy—Lucien stepped between them.

"Very well, Lady Darby. Stay," he said. "It makes no matter to us." He turned to Sarah. "Do you have the drawings you have been working on?"

Sarah fought against her anger, realizing that Lucien's reaction was the only sensible one. They had to quell Julia's bizarre notions immediately.

"Certainly. I have the drawings right here." With trembling hands, she handed him the papers and sat on the stool beside him.

Lucien tacked her sketches on the frame of the easel as he had for each lesson, taking great pains to ignore Julia's rustling and coughing on his other side. He studied the work for several minutes, nodding.

"The form and content are both good, but you're fighting the light," he said. "Your expectations outwit your eyes. You expect the light to fall in a straight line, but in truth, light bends. It deflects. It reflects. It illuminates from many angles."

He moved his stool closer to Sarah's and pointed to one of the drawings. "This chestnut, for example. You perceive the shell to be smooth. It is what your hands tell you when you touch it. But the touch of light feels more. It feels the ridges and pocks not discernable with human fingertips. You must draw what you see, not what you feel."

"I've always considered touch to be the most useful of the senses," said Julia. Lucien ignored her, which gave Sarah an inexplicable feeling of satisfaction.

"I want you to try a different approach," Lucien said to Sarah. "Capture the shadows rather than the light."

This time the subject would be a fig pilfered from the breakfast tray. Lucien placed the fruit on the windowsill, where the fog-filtered sun played over the mottled green skin.

"Where are my paper and pencil?" asked Julia.

"I thought you didn't care for figs," said Sarah.

Lucien coughed into his hand. He passed Julia a drawing board and pencil.

Sarah tacked a fresh piece of paper on the board in her lap. She would create a rough sketch here in the drawing room and then retire to her quarters to work on the details without veils obscuring her vision.

"Will you be drawing today?" Julia asked Lucien.

"No, I will not."

Sarah wasn't surprised. In the weeks they worked together, Lucien had never actually drawn anything. He showed her sketches, of course. They were exciting—precise and detailed. Beautiful. But to her knowledge, none of them had been done on the premises of Elmstone.

Just as Lucien had never asked why she wore the veils, it never occurred to her to ask why Lucien never sketched with her.

Julia, however, had no reservations.

"How is it possible to teach a lesson without doing the exercise yourself?"

Lucien bowed under Julia's stare, but then his discomfort seemed to change to anger.

"I have already completed these lessons many times over, Lady Darby. However, *you* have not. Are you ready for me to review your work?"

Julia smiled. "No thank you, *Lucien*. I believe my curiosity has been assuaged. I shall leave the both of you to your studies."

Upstairs in her chambers, Julia stared out over Sarah's wretched gardens. She couldn't escape them, damn it. Every time she looked out the window, she was reminded of Sarah's little hobby.

Now it would seem her sister-in-law had found another distraction. But what exactly was it? Painting, or the artist?

To Julia, who at one time or another had used every device known to women to attract men, Sarah's pitiable attempts to gain Lucien's attention seemed almost childish. The shy laugh. The accidental brush of a hand. The feigned interest in his every word.

Really, what could one expect from a woman who had hidden herself away for so many years? Naturally she would be lacking in the art of seduction.

Poor, pathetic Sarah.

Julia drummed her fingers on the window seat. She had to admit, her own efforts to seduce the artist were failing. She would have thought a man of Lucien's experience could recognize flirtation quite easily. However, he wasn't responding properly to her subtle overtures. Perhaps it was time to be a bit more obvious.

She pulled the satin-tasseled bell rope near her bed and waited impatiently for her girl to arrive.

Agnes, shoulders hunched and head bowed, plowed through the door like a mule pulling a cart of stones. "Yes, mum?"

"Do try to stand up straight, Agnes." How many times had she spoken to James about finding a more appropriate servant for her? Why did Sarah always get the good ones?

"Yes, mum." The mule craned its neck.

Julia sighed. "Never mind. I want a bath. And I want to wear something marvelous to supper this eve. I must look absolutely captivating."

Lady Darby's thigh pressed tight against his beneath the table.

Lucien tried without success to remove it, knowing it would not be long before her foot would be entwined with his.

There was a time he would have been flattered by Lady Darby's outrageous flirtations. She reminded him of the courtesans at Versailles—dangerously attractive and much too available. Experienced, exotic, ever-present. The pleasures they offered were difficult for a man to resist.

It would be easy to take pleasure with Lady Darby, if only to assuage the fits of lust suffered by a man two years without a woman. But he did not want her, no matter how easy it would be to take her. He would not cuckold his employer, though he suspected Lord Darby would not care if he did.

Even without his lack of interest in Lady Darby, there was a more compelling reason.

Sarah.

Should he dally with Lady Darby, Sarah would most certainly find it out. Lady Darby did not seem the sort to be discreet. And Sarah would disapprove, he was sure.

He would do nothing to hurt or disappoint her.

He cherished the warmth that had grown between them. Not only did their friendship aid in their lessons, it gave Lucien a sense of purpose—a reason to rise each morning. He looked forward to learning more about Sarah every day.

There was much to discover about her, even beyond the continuing mystery of why she wore the veils. Any dalliance with Lady Darby would most certainly send that to ruin.

So, for the fourth time that evening he moved his leg away from Lady Darby's. He turned to the dowager. The older woman was blinding, even in the dim light of the dining room, in a red gown rigged out with lemon yellow rosettes.

"Did you have a restful day, Dowager?"

Merri made a face. "I have absolutely no need for restful days. I shall rest long enough when I'm dead. I had quite an active day, thank you."

"Really? What did you do?" Sarah said.

"For one, Miss Witherspoon escorted me through the white garden, where I noticed a pack of caterpillars making off with the leaves of the cheiranthus. I must say, I was both shocked and pleased."

"Pleased?"

"Yes, pleased. It means, my dear, that you've actually neglected an inch of the gardens. Which means you've found something else to hold your interest. Which makes me very happy indeed." Merri's smile bordered on the triumphant.

Sarah leaned back a bit in her chair. "Now I'm the one who is shocked and pleased," she said.

"Why is that?" Merri asked.

"Because you've actually said you're happy."

Merri attempted to retrieve her ever-present scowl, but it was lost in her momentary joviality. She erupted into laughter, the skin around her eyes crinkling like aged paper.

Just then Lord Darby entered the dining room. His look of surprise drew another whoop from Merri, and resonant laughter from beneath Sarah's veils.

"What an occasion. Laughter at the dinner table, of all things," he said. "Mother, have you been taking whiskey in your tea again?"

Lady Darby, sullen beside Lucien, spoke. "How nice of you to join us, dear husband. Mother has just commented on the sudden change in Sarah's interests. I find it quite curious myself. Tell us, Sarah, what is it that has captured your fancy more than your roses?"

"Yes, tell us, Sarah," said Lord Darby, though his voice held none of the mocking lilt his wife's had. He took his seat at the head of the table and gave his sister an expectant look.

Sarah shook her head. "Oh, stop this nonsense, everyone. My lessons have taken a great deal of my time, but don't work yourselves into spasms. The gardens won't fall to ruin. I'll make sure of that."

Lord Darby unfolded his napkin. "Tell us what you're learning."

Lucien watched them as they spoke to one another, noting the familial similarities. The dowager and Sarah had many of the same mannerisms. They both cocked their heads to the left when listening, and their shoulders rolled when they laughed. Lord Darby and Sarah shared the same penchant to use their hands to illustrate bits of conversation. All three had a habit of fiddling with the silver.

These resemblances fascinated Lucien, who had spent no more than a few hours with his parents during any given month of his life. In their bid for higher social status, his parents had traveled extensively, attended many fetes, and generally relinquished his upbringing to Monsieur Valmetant. So if he had inherited any of their mannerisms, he did not know. Nor would he ever know, as they were both long dead.

Although he had been with them only a few weeks, he already preferred this family over his own, despite their impairments.

He especially liked the dowager. Her love for her children shone through her temper, as did her sadness for Sarah's predicament, whatever that may be. He imagined how he would sketch this wry old bird—softening the edges, brightening the eyes. He envisioned her as a younger woman, stubborn, strong, and beautiful.

This idea to sketch the dowager was so subtle, Lucien almost did not realize what had occurred. He'd thought of working—of creating—and no sense of panic loomed!

A feeling of anticipation curled through his stomach, tempered with only a hint of fear.

Beneath the table Lady Darby brushed her hand against his knee. He did not hide his annoyance as he pushed it away. He wanted nothing, nothing at all, to interfere with this moment of hope.

That night Lucien sat in the drawing room alcove alone again, but this time was different from the others. He was drawing. He was creating, and it felt wondrous.

Beneath his fingers, charcoal scratched against paper as the dowager emerged from the page. Intelligent eyes. Strong jaw. Cleft chin. Wide mouth. At first the strokes were unsteady and tenuous, but as he worked, they grew strong. He felt his confidence returning with each line.

When he finished, he heard a soft gasp behind him. His breathing stopped and he turned, expecting to see Tessa in the doorway. But tonight it was Sarah who stood watching.

"That was Mother ten years ago," she said. "Before Father passed on. How? How did you know?"

Lucien shrugged. "Monsieur Valmetant once told me I have the gift of an inner eye."

Sarah stood behind him to study the sketch of her mother more closely. The scent of her surprised him. He would have expected roses or gardenias, but instead she smelled of grass and sunshine.

"Astounding," Sarah said. "You have actually succeeded in making my mother look pleasant."

Lucien laughed. "Even a lioness has soft fur."

"But one must never forget her bite." Sarah reached over Lucien's shoulder to stroke the apple of her mother's cheek. A smudge of charcoal darkened the pad of her fingertip. Without thinking, Lucien took her hand and brushed the black dust from her finger. Her skin was warm and smooth, like a rose petal in the sun. He held her hand to his cheek and closed his eyes. It was only when Sarah pulled away that he realized what he had done.

He cleared his throat. "You may have it when I am finished."

"Have what?" Her voice wavered slightly.

"The drawing, of course."

He shaded the flesh of the dowager's neck and redefined the lines of her nose before removing the sketch from the board.

Just then he heard a rustle at the door. His heart lurched. Without turning, he knew Tessa had come.

Chapter 7

Sarah reached for the drawing just as it slipped from Lucien's trembling fingers. His face was ashen. Even his lips had lost their color.

"Lucien, what is the matter?" She feared he was having some sort of attack.

His body folded at the waist. She grasped his elbow just as he pitched forward on the stool. The momentum sent them both to the floor, as the stool clattered to the ground beside them.

"Lucien! Lucien, speak to me!"

He didn't answer. His breathing was shallow and uneven. From her position on the floor Sarah spied a shadow at the door, but she could not see clearly through the veils. "Who's there?" she demanded.

A little girl slipped into the circle of lamplight.

"Anne! Thank heavens. Go fetch your father at once. If you cannot find him, get Arthur or Miss Witherspoon. Anyone. Go!"

Sarah heard the retreat of Anne's little boots. She struggled to her knees. Lucien lay beside her on his stomach, one arm wedged beneath his chest. She pulled his shoulder, trying to roll him onto his back, but failed to move him. He was too solid. She stroked his arm, trying to rouse him. She touched his cheek, and he groaned. The sound gave her hope.

Just then James ran in, and together they were able to get Lucien onto his back.

"No, no," he murmured again and again.

James opened the buttons of Lucien's jacket and loosened his collar while Sarah fanned him with the sketch of Merri. Finally, Lucien opened his eyes.

"Are you in pain?" James asked. Lucien shook his head. He tried to sit up, but Sarah held him to the floor with a firm but gentle touch.

"Lie still," she said. "Take a deep breath. And another."

When his color returned, she allowed him to rise.

"What happened?" asked James.

Lucien's voice did not rise above a whisper. "Tessa."

James righted the stool and helped Lucien stand. "Who is Tessa?"

"My daughter."

Daughter?

"Tessa," Lucien said. "In the doorway. I saw her there."

James put a hand on Lucien's shoulder, urging him to sit on the stool. "As far as I know, we have admitted no visitors."

Lucien laughed, but the sound was far from jovial. "You do not understand. My daughter, she is . . . she is dead."

Sarah's arms broke out in gooseflesh. The sorrow was drawn on Lucien's features as clearly as Merri's smile on the likeness that now lay on the floor. So many things had suddenly become clear.

Sarah looked at her brother. He nodded and quietly left the room.

She took Lucien's hand in hers and rubbed his knuckles against her palm. He leaned into her as if he could think of nothing else to do, and she cradled his head against her side. Something long dormant moved within her as she comforted him.

She raked Lucien's thick blond hair away from his forehead with her fingers. When he wrapped his arms around her waist, she didn't dare to breathe. It felt as if she had never touched another soul this way.

With the creak of the drawing room door, Lucien suddenly pulled away.

"I think we may have solved this ghostly mystery," James said, entering. Anne was by his side.

He took the girl to Lucien and she stood before him, her sweet face peering up into his.

"Tessa?"

Sarah could hear Lucien's anguish in the name.

"Not Tessa," said James. "Anne. My daughter. Lady Darby is a firm believer that children should be seen and not heard, so Anne usually keeps to the opposite end of the house, under the supervision of her governess."

The air was thick and still. A candle on the windowsill sputtered, breaking the silence.

Lucien turned away from Anne and covered his face with his hands. He wept soundlessly.

"Let us leave Mr. Delacourte alone for a while, shall we?" Sarah asked, taking her niece's hand.

Anne nodded. James followed them as they slipped quietly from the drawing room. Out in the hallway, Anne began to cry.

"Mother told me to stay away. She'll be so angry if she finds out I disobeyed her." She sobbed loudly.

"There, there," said Sarah, stroking her hair. "We won't tell, will we, James?"

His eyes were dark, but he shook his head. "Your secret is safe with me."

Anne sniffed. "What about Miss Elsey?"

"We won't tell her, either," said James. "But you must do as you are told from now on."

"I only wanted to watch him," Anne said. "I didn't mean to upset him so. Aunt Sarah, what did I do?"

"Nothing, my sweet. Nothing."

James patted Anne's shoulder awkwardly. "I believe he misses his own little girl."

"What happened to her?" Anne asked through her sniffles.

James looked to Sarah as he answered. "Perhaps one day he will tell you."

Sarah was in the white garden examining the damage done by the caterpillars when Lucien appeared. A stubble of beard shadowed his chin, but the dark circles beneath his eyes, which had been present since he arrived at Elmstone, were gone.

"Did you sleep well?" she asked.

"Better than I have in years." Lucien sat on the ground beside her, stretching his legs out on the grass.

Sarah picked a few brown leaves from a rosebush. She had decided not to mention the previous night's events, for fear of embarrassing him, but Lucien broached the subject himself.

"I must apologize for missing our lesson this morning, as well as for my outburst last evening."

"No need to apologize. I have quite enough to practice with regard to our lessons. As for your outburst, it was hardly that. Clearly you had a moment of great emotion, and a person should never feel guilty for such a thing." She stood and picked up the cloth on which she knelt, and then placed it in front of the next bush.

As she moved from plant to plant, Lucien moved with

her, watching. She could feel his gaze focused on her movements, and despite a cool breeze, she began to feel warm.

Without warning, Lucien reached for her hand. A ripple of excitement danced through her belly.

"I thank you for what you did for me last night," he said. The deep baritone of his voice raked over her suddenly sensitive nerves. "It has been a long time since someone has been so kind to me."

Gently she withdrew her hand from his, unable to withstand her reaction to his touch. "I have no wish to pry into your affairs, Lucien. I don't want you to think you must explain."

"But I do. I want to explain. Now, if you will let me."

For one brief moment Sarah was torn between the desire to know about his daughter and the fear of discovering he had a wife somewhere in France. But it shouldn't matter. The fact that he was married should mean nothing to her.

Only, it did.

She had grown to care for Lucien in this short time. Could it be she wanted more than his friendship?

No! He was her teacher. Her tutor, and nothing more. She must remember that. But to pull away from him now, when he seemed to need her so, would hurt him. She couldn't do that. She would listen to his secrets, and hope that he wouldn't expect her to reveal her own.

Lucien awaited her answer.

"Continue." Sarah resumed her work. She watched him as he spoke. The pain he carried in his heart showed on his face, and it matched her own so fully she feared she could not bear to see it. She turned away.

Lucien lay back on the grass, speaking to her, to the sky, to the garden around him.

"Your niece is the same age as my daughter Tessa was when she died, along with her mother. Tessa was as sweet a little girl as God ever delivered upon this earth. Since her death I have been plagued with images of her—she seems to follow me wherever I go."

Sarah was quiet. What could she say? She, too, had memories that wouldn't leave her be.

Lucien continued. "I left Paris partly to escape these visions, but when I arrived here, they seemed to grow worse. Always Tessa. Always in the doorway, just as she was in Versailles, when she was alive. My curious girl who wanted only to learn to paint. But I was too consumed with my own work to teach her. I sent her away time and again, always promising one day I would teach her.

"When I believed I saw her here, I thought . . . I thought she had come to punish me because I am teaching someone else. The guilt nearly drove me insane. Over and over she came to the drawing room, never saying a word. I suppose I went there to see her, too. To punish myself," he said. "I did not know about Anne."

Sarah turned in time to see the anguish on Lucien's face. His eyes were closed, as if he could block out the memories of his wife and child with such a meager act of resistance.

She wanted to touch him, but found she could not. Instead, she told him about her niece.

"Anne is, I'm sure, very similar to your Tessa. Most little girls have the same wishes, the same dreams. Anne cannot decide whether she wants to be a gypsy or the queen of England."

Lucien's smile spurred her on.

"Anne is quiet, but she loves to be around people. Unfortunately, Julia won't allow that. She encourages the servants to keep Anne away from the adults, hidden up in the schoolroom with the governess or out in the kitchen with the cook. She believes children have no place in proper society until their social skills are firmly established. That's why you've never seen her, except at night when her governess is most likely asleep. I should have told you about her, but honestly, her cloistering is a bone of contention in the household."

"What about your brother? Does he agree with Lady Darby?"

Sarah shook her head. "Poor James. He has no notion what little girls need. I think he's a bit bewildered by the fairer sex. As you can see, we outnumber him here. And as a result he spends quite a bit of time away from the house."

Sarah moved the cloth to the next bush.

"Mother and I try to liberate Anne as often as possible, but Julia is her mother. Ultimately, Julia's word must be abided when it comes to Anne's upbringing. Mother and I agreed to that for James' sake."

"I am sorry to say I was much the same as your brother." Lucien sat up. He raked a dry leaf out of the grass with his fingers and toyed with it. "I did not spend much time with our daughter. My wife bore the burden of raising Tessa."

His wife. Sarah tamped down a spark of curious jealousy at those words. "Did you agree with her methods?"

"I wish I could say, one way or another. But the truth is, I was seldom home. I did not truly know my daughter. I loved her, but I did not truly know her. I did not know my wife either, for that matter. Now it is too late."

Sarah waited for Lucien to say more, but he fell into a lengthy silence. She sensed that the conversation, at least as it pertained to his wife and child, was finished.

Lucien followed as she completed her rounds in the garden. She shook the cloth out and removed her gloves. "Would you care for a bite to eat?" She looked up at the sky. "It's just about noon. I believe Cook has roasted a duck, but if you would rather have breakfast, I'm certain we could arrange it."

They walked side by side. Lucien took the cloth from

her arm and carried it as they wound their way through the
garden paths toward the house.

"The noon meal will be fine," he said. "But I should return to my quarters first. Make myself presentable."

She laughed. "You do look a bit rumpled. I'll see you in
the dining room, then. Afterwards, we can visit Anne in the
schoolroom. I know she would like to see you."

Lucien slowed his pace. "I . . ."

"Lucien, I won't force you. But perhaps you need to
face these fears, this guilt you hold about your daughter. I
know it would be good for Anne, too. She feels responsible
for what happened last evening, and to see you smile would
put her at ease."

He nodded. "In that case, I will go."

The schoolroom reminded Lucien of his own early child-
hood prison, complete with a severe-looking governess and
stacks of musty books. Anne sat in a little chair far from
the only window, intent on her lessons. In the daylight, the
differences between Anne and Tessa were more apparent.
Where Tessa's hair had been nearly white, Anne's was
closer to spun gold. Her face was not as round as Tessa's,
and her nose was thinner. But they both had the same eager
demeanor.

Anne gave Lucien a tentative smile when he and Sarah
entered, and he returned it with one of his own.

A sharp pain speared his stomach. He remembered how
Tessa sparkled whenever he paid her the slightest bit of attention. Why had it been so hard for him to do?

He and Sarah entered the schoolroom and sat quietly in
the corner while the governess finished her lesson, though
it was clear Anne's concentration had been broken by their
arrival.

"That will be all, Miss Elsey. I believe Anne has had
enough for today."

The governess snapped her book shut. "Lady Darby will not approve of this," she said on her way out.

Anne giggled behind her hand. Lucien and Sarah joined in, and soon the three of them were laughing aloud.

"Thank you, Aunt Sarah. My head is so stuffed with history I couldn't have learned one more thing today."

"Not one more thing? Are you certain?" Lucien said. "Your Aunt Sarah and I were hoping you would join us for our lesson today, which might require you to learn just a bit more."

Anne's eyes grew wide. "You'll let me watch?"

"No," he said. "We expect you to work with us."

Her smile was the only answer he needed. Images of Tessa drifted through his mind like bright clouds on azure. The pain in his stomach flared like a hot coal.

Anne jumped from her seat, almost tripping over her skirts. "When? Where? What will we do?"

"Be calm," Sarah chided. "First, you must change clothes. We cannot have you messing your pretty gown with charcoal. Then you may meet us down in the drawing room. Have you eaten?"

"No, but I'm not hungry."

"Your mother is going to be angry enough at me already, without Cook telling her you took no luncheon." Sarah herded Anne to the door. "Go dress, and I'll bring something to the drawing room for you to eat."

"Hurrah!" Anne raced from the schoolroom, her boots making a terrible racket on the bare floors.

Sarah turned to Lucien. "Thank you."

The way the light fell on her, Lucien imagined he could see the curve of her smile through the veils.

The pain plaguing his stomach lessened to a dull ache.

While Lucien instructed Sarah and Anne on the principles of contrast, Julia fumed in her rooms.

Miss Elsey had informed her of the schoolroom raid, and she was not pleased. In fact, she considered it an unpardonable offense on the part of her sister-in-law.

"I can forgive the artist," she said, more to herself than to Agnes, who was helping her into a fresh gown for tea. "Men cannot be expected to understand such things. But Sarah is another matter altogether."

"Mmmf-mmm," replied Agnes, her mouth full of pins.

"I'm afraid I really must insist Anne keep away from Sarah altogether." It was clear Anne favored her aunt's company over that of her own mother—a situation Julia would not abide. Julia had tried repeatedly to keep the two apart.

"I cannot have Anne believing Sarah's ridiculous notion that women don't need men to be happy. It just isn't normal. Oh, Agnes. The bodice should be much tighter than that."

"Mmmf-mmm."

"As I was saying, the only reason Sarah believes such nonsense is because she has no choice. But I will not have my daughter accepting such foolishness as truth. As far as I'm concerned, women were put on this earth *solely* to be admired by men. It's the only way for a woman to get what she wants in this world."

"Yes, mum." Agnes had removed the pins from her mouth and was tying the sash at Julia's waist.

"For Heaven's sake, men hold the land, the wealth, and the law in their hands."

"'Tis true, mum."

"But a woman who is admired by these men, *she* holds the power. The sooner Anne understands that, the better off she'll be."

Which was precisely why Julia had kept her locked away, learning how to be a lady before she came in contact with the world. Besides, keeping Anne away from the visitors served Julia's own purposes as well.

Men acted much differently toward a woman who had

borne a child. The title of mother suggested an air of frumpiness not at all conducive to the art of seduction. In short, motherhood had a tendency to cut into her pleasures.

Now that Lucien had met Anne, it would be all the more difficult to bed him. And bedding him had become an obsession. Never, ever had she failed to snare a man she wanted. It was a matter of pride.

Only, she was having a devil of a time getting Lucien to even notice her, and she knew why. He spent too much time with Sarah, who was obviously making him believe that his appointment as tutor required him to devote every moment to her whims.

What Julia needed was a distraction. Something to take Sarah's mind off her lessons, and Lucien.

What Julia needed—or rather, *who*—was Duncan.

Chapter 8

The pounding at the door was a perfect match to the pounding in Duncan Lavery's skull, so he did not realize at first they were not one and the same. Until the shouting began.

"Lavery! Open the door, Lavery."

"Shut your bloody pie hole!" He discovered too late that shouting caused a deep, slicing pain behind the eyes when one had gone so deep into one's cups the night before.

He stumbled out of bed, tripped over the sheet tangled around his legs, and landed flat on his face on the cold stone floor.

Damnation. Where in bloody hell were the carpets?

Then he remembered. They'd been taken the day before, along with the majority of his things. Bloody bastards.

"Lavery, open the damned door. I know you're in there. I can smell you from here."

Ballocks. Celeste's brother again. Couldn't her family leave him in peace? They had taken everything but a few bottles of liquor and the lumpy featherbed on which he slept. What else could they possibly want?

Bugger all. If Evan insisted on seeing him immediately, then see him he would. Duncan opened the door without a stitch to cover him.

Evan snorted with amusement. "No wonder my sister left you. It appears you had little to offer her."

"What do you want at this hour of the morning?" Duncan scratched himself and turned back to the room, rooting through the dirty clothes strewn about on the floor.

"It's well after noon, Lavery. Can't you tell time, either?"

"Go away." He pulled on a pair of rumpled peacock blue breeches and began the search for a suitable shirt.

"It will be my pleasure to leave you to your stink. I'm here only to deliver something."

"That's a switch, considering yesterday you took everything."

Evan proffered a letter. "It's addressed to you. Somehow it got into Celeste's things."

"Perhaps because yesterday they were *my* things."

Duncan discovered a decanter in the corner that still contained a few fingers of brandy. He uncorked it and took a healthy swig.

Evan gave him a disgusted look. "After everything you've done to Celeste, you're fortunate we left you with anything at all. Including your life."

"Oh, yes. So fortunate." Duncan snatched the letter from Evan's fingers and studied the seal.

Cousin Julia.

He dismissed Evan with an imperial wave. "Thank you. You may go now."

"Stay far from my sister, Lavery, or you shall rue the day."

"Try and stop me, Evan. Celeste is my wife."

"A Gretna Green wedding with a witness who can't be named? 'Tis no more that a joke."

"It wasn't such a joke for the past six months."

"Not until you made it so, with your drinking and carousing," Evan said bitterly.

Duncan burped. "I've appealed to the courts, and I'll soon have England's law behind me."

"England's law? Maybe. But never my family's law. We'll kill you, Lavery. I swear it." Evan spit on the floor. "As I said before, keep away from my sister."

When his brother-in-law had gone, Duncan took the brandy decanter into bed with him and opened the letter, expecting Julia's usual discourse on her boring country life. Well, she would get no pity from him this day. At least she lived in relative comfort, possessing such things as furniture and carpets. And food.

Hugging the decanter to his side, he read:

Dearest Duncan,

I cannot explain what a misery my life has become. Every day spent in this dreadful, drafty monstrosity James calls home, stranded so far from London I scarcely remember how civilized people live.

Join the club, thought Duncan. He took another pull from the decanter.

Recent events, however, have presented an opportunity for some relief. A very interesting gentleman, an artist, has come to stay at Elmstone for a while. My hope is to know him more intimately, but certain obstacles stand in my way.

Duncan laughed aloud. Dear Julia had the tactical skills of a general on the battleground of carnal dalliances. Duncan bore witness to dozens of campaigns leveled at unsuspecting men, from nobles to groomsmen. This artist didn't have a prayer against Julia's arsenal.

One of these obstacles is a woman to whom you were betrothed for a time. Yes, Duncan, it's true! Our poor Sarah seems to have taken a fancy to the man, if you can imagine. They spend a ridiculous amount of time together under the guise of tutor and student. I'm afraid, dear cousin, that Sarah's devotion to your memory is finally beginning to wane.

Duncan took another swallow of brandy. It burned in his throat.

So Sarah was beginning to forget him. It shouldn't have bothered him, but for some reason it did. Her wealth was merely the half of it. The rest was a matter of pride.

Sarah was a woman who had loved him beyond reason. Who had given herself freely to him before their wedding, and who, with the blind faith reserved only for those truly in love, was sure he would marry her afterward.

He might have, too, if not for that bloody awful accident.

Sarah had been so lovely then, and so deliciously naive. When they attended a ball together, every man in the room cast him envious stares. And the women! The women considered it a challenge to take him away from one so beautiful. The deadly sin of jealousy aided him more than once in bedding some of the most eager-to-please ladies in London.

Duncan had no qualms about his behavior. Marrying Sarah wasn't his idea to begin with. His father pressed him into the engagement, as it was a good political match for both families. The Essingtons had power and money; the Laverys had land—lots of it.

At first Duncan resisted the match, but soon he realized the merit of the situation. Before they were betrothed, he'd had no luck getting Sarah into his bed. Once he tied himself to her, his luck changed. He decided that, should she become tiresome, he would do something so despicable she would sever the engagement herself.

His only regret was that he'd bedded her only once before her coach went over and ruined her pretty face.

Bloody shame, it was.

That was long ago, however, when he was young enough and handsome enough to have whatever tail he fancied. The going was a bit rougher now. Years of drink had taken their toll, and there were precious few ladies of breeding who fell willingly into his arms these days. It mattered not. There were plenty of those without breeding who would.

He took another drink and continued reading.

> *If Sarah's defection doesn't sufficiently prick your pride enough to pay us a visit, I have yet another reason.*
>
> *Word has reached me your lovely bride, Celeste, will no longer abide your appetite for chambermaids. I have it on good authority that her father has removed her from your house, citing an invalid marriage.*
>
> *I imagine he's taken her dowry, as well. Or at least what was left of it.*
>
> *I daresay poverty is not a condition that suits you, Duncan. Your expensive tastes can hardly be supported by the meager stipend your father gives you—so what will you do?*

What would he do?

Celeste had been a stroke of luck. A rich spinster, almost easy on the eyes, who wanted children before she grew too old to birth them. Though they never had any success there, Duncan was willing and able to keep trying. But when Celeste's demands for him to live a temperate and respectable life increased, so too did his appetite for other women.

Bringing him to his current predicament. What *would* he do now that Celeste and her money were gone?

I propose this, Cousin Julia wrote.

Come to Whitford. Distract Sarah and resurrect the feelings she once had for you. Give me some time to work on the artist without interference.

If you do it, I will make it worth your while. Enough money for a new wardrobe and a year in London. That should be ample time for you to find a rich old woman willing to take care of your needs.

I will await your reply. Do be quick.

Your loving cousin,
Julia

Duncan took another long pull on the decanter and mulled over Julia's proposition.

He had no doubt he could distract Sarah. For God's sake, she'd taken up with a painter of all things. Duncan was certain he could win her back. He might be frayed about the edges these days, but the Lavery charm was still intact.

Why, he might even do Sarah a favor and take her to bed, for old times' sake.

He finished off the brandy, remembering the way Sarah's body fit neatly against his. His thoughts grew fuzzy as he planned his grand entrance to Elmstone . . .

"*Absolutely not. Duncan Lavery is not welcome in this house, ever.*"

"But James," Julia tried on her most reasonable voice, "Duncan is my cousin. My family."

"He is vermin, and I will not have him here." James's

adamant posturing at the foot of her bed left her grasping for another tack.

She tried wheedling. "But I need my family. You know how lonely I am, with you always out in the fields like a common farmer. Sarah and your mother hardly speak to me."

"I'm sure you have given them good reason."

She tried petulance. "If Duncan cannot come here, then take me to London to meet him. I'm so bored here, I hardly know what to do with myself all day."

"Perhaps you could spend some time with your daughter."

She tried seduction. "Please, James. I really need to see my cousin." She crawled down to the foot of the bed and kneeled before him, rubbing her hands over his chest.

He pushed her away. "No. Duncan Lavery broke Sarah's heart. He is not to cross this threshold, and that is my final word."

Julia smiled. She had overlooked the most obvious way to persuade him. His precious sister's heart.

"He broke her heart, it's true. Which is precisely the reason he *should* come," she said. "Sarah is still in love with him, James. Can't you see it? And he's in love with her, too. He wrote to me, bemoaning his youthful decision to leave her. He said he had made a terrible mistake by not marrying her."

"And what of his current wife?" James gave her a sardonic look. "Will he bring Celeste with him?"

For once Julia was glad her husband spent all his time in the fields, where he could not possibly have heard of Duncan's indiscretions.

"He and Celeste have parted ways," she said. "Apparently, their marriage wasn't quite legal. Besides, Celeste could not abide Duncan's devotion to Sarah."

"Forgive me if I don't believe you, Julia, but your motives are not always pure."

"I resent your malicious remark, but I will excuse it because I'm feeling charitable today. Of course I have my own motives, but I'm thinking of Sarah, as well."

James paced before the windows, staring out as if something beckoned. "You're hardly an authority on my sister's likes and dislikes."

"James, I swear it! Sarah is still in love with Duncan. Why else would she moon so whenever someone mentions his name? Of course, how would you notice such a thing when you're never here." She paused to let her words sink in. "Wouldn't it be wonderful if they reconciled after all these years?"

James didn't answer.

"It would make Sarah very, very happy." Beneath her sincere expression, Julia silently celebrated. She knew she had found the magic words.

"Very well," he said. "But if Sarah shows the slightest desire to throw Duncan out on his ear, so help me, Julia, he will go."

She smiled openly now. "As you wish, my lord."

Chapter 9

The days had grown cooler but the sun was still bright in the drawing room, where Lucien and Sarah held their daily tutoring sessions. Occasionally Anne would join them after her lessons; however, on this day they were alone.

Lucien had been sketching madly since the night he met Anne. Portraits, landscapes, anything that captured his fancy. Still, when he picked up a brush to paint, an inexplicable panic gripped him. His hands shook. His heart raced. His stomach rolled until he had to leave the easel and return to his rooms, defeated again by the fear of failure and the memories of the fire.

But now Sarah had progressed to the point where she could no longer learn without doing. It was time for her to paint.

Time for him to confess that he could not.

He looked at Sarah beside him as she studied the shading on a drawing he had done.

Sometimes when they were seated in a certain way, when the sun shone just right through the window, he could

make out her profile through the veils. In his mind he tried
to fill in the shadows and guess at the colors of her eyes,
her lips, her cheeks.

God, how he wanted to see her. He had not realized how
badly until just this moment. Sarah had done so much to
heal his heart, and he did not even know what she looked
like.

No, that wasn't true. He knew she was beautiful. No
matter what she looked like beneath the veils, she was
beautiful. He had come to respect her tenacious will, her
wit, her enthusiasm. And the way she had drawn him into
her family and made him care again—especially with Anne.
He owed her so much.

He owed her the truth, even if it meant he would have to
leave Elmstone.

"What will we do today?" Sarah asked.

"Today we prepare for tomorrow."

"And what will we do tomorrow?"

He forced the words from his mouth. "Tomorrow, you
paint."

"Ah."

He could hear the smile in her voice. She had been waiting for this moment. "But why not today?"

"As I said, today we must prepare for tomorrow." Lucien had assembled a frame the night before, which he'd
hidden behind one of the curtains. He retrieved it and
placed it on the easel.

"First we must ready our canvas. Come down from your
stool so I can show you how to stretch it."

They worked together, Sarah holding the canvas in
place while Lucien tacked it to the frame with a small hammer. He had not been so close to her since the night in the
drawing room when he first met Anne.

He watched her fingers as she worked. She wore a small,
square garnet on her left hand, but the other was bare.
Her fingers were long and tapered, lightly browned from

working in the gardens. The scent of the fresh honeysuckle she wore in the band of her hat infused the air about them.

Several times their hands met over the canvas, but Sarah did not pull away. She seemed to have become as comfortable with his touch as he had with hers.

When they had finished tacking, Lucien gently hammered small wooden wedges into the corners of the frame until the canvas was taut and smooth. Then he examined it from every angle, checking for flaws and wrinkles.

"Readying the canvas is an important task," he explained, when they were seated before the easel. On the table beside him lay a leather pouch filled with white powder, a cask of glue, and a large bowl. He poured some powder and glue into the bowl, mixing it until it was smooth.

"What is that?" Sarah asked.

"Gypsum. When mixed with hide glue, it is called gesso. We will apply it to the canvas as a primer. It seals the surface of the canvas and provides a neutral base for our paints." Lucien handed Sarah a large brush. "Coat the entire surface. Make certain not to forget the corners."

Sarah followed his instructions, carefully applying the mixture to the canvas. When the entire square was covered with white, Lucien cleaned the brush and bowl. Then he lined up half a dozen small tins on the table.

"What are those?"

"Our pigments. Tomorrow we shall create a simple palette and begin to experiment with color. Are you ready?"

Anticipation radiated like heat from her skin. "I fear I cannot wait," she said.

If only I could, he thought.

That night, like most others, Lucien paid a midnight visit to the drawing room. Though he now knew it was Anne and not Tessa who had visited him there, he still felt close to his daughter in the quiet of the night.

This night, however, he would not be alone.

The dowager sat motionless before the fireplace, an open book lying across her lap. She did not stir as he approached. He stood beside her and cleared his throat. Still she did not move. He peered into her face. Her eyes flew open.

Lucien started.

"I'm still breathing," she said.

"I am glad. Would you mind some company, or would you care to be alone?" he asked.

"Company, please. Sit down."

Lucien pulled a chair closer to hers and sat.

"The nights are growing cool again," she said. "Summer is almost over."

"Yes. Are you warm enough?"

She smiled sadly. "My body is warm. But my soul, Monsieur Delacourte, is another matter entirely."

"How is that?"

"The end of summer gives me a chill I cannot shake until spring comes round again." She closed her book and balanced it on the arm of the chair. "My husband died in autumn, and the cool of September always reminds me of his passing, I suppose."

Lucien stared into the flames. "My wife and daughter died in the spring."

The dowager stretched a hand out to him, and he took it. She gave it a squeeze and they sat in silence for a long moment.

"What do you think of my daughter?" She asked suddenly.

Lucien's heart beat faster. He let go of her hand. "Sarah is an excellent pupil. Very adept."

The dowager issued a low chuckle. "I meant, what do you think of her as a person? As a woman, to be precise." She squinted at him in the firelight.

"I admire her greatly. I have never known anyone like her."

The old woman nodded. "When Sarah was a child, everyone adored her. The townsfolk in Whitford would watch for her to come down the hill each day with a basket of treats for the children. She would tie her skirts up to her knees so she could run faster. Quite unladylike." She smiled.

"Sarah is special," she continued. "I have always known that about her. But I don't think she knows it about herself. I fear she'll wither here, even as her gardens bloom. She'll waste all the love, all the goodness God blessed her with because she's too afraid to leave this place. Will you help her, Lucien?"

What could he possibly do to help Sarah? She had not even confided in him why she wore the veils. For a moment he considered asking the dowager, but then he realized he wanted to hear it from Sarah's lips alone. He wanted Sarah to trust him enough to tell him why she hid herself away.

"I do not know if I can," he said.

He feared his time at Elmstone was limited. His services would surely be terminated when Sarah and Lord Darby discovered his inability to paint.

"But will you try?"

Lucien nodded.

"Good." The dowager swiped a tear from her cheek. "Will you help me to my rooms?"

A gust of wind swept through the kitchen garden, rustling the tufts of herbs around Sarah, who hunched over a patch of ruined sage. She would have to speak to James about the wall. It was the lowest one at the manor, and obviously something had jumped it to munch on the herbs and vegetables.

She collected the few pungent leaves that remained for Cook, who would prepare a shank of lamb for supper. As she leaned forward to cut some thyme, the ground vibrated beneath her palms.

The wind abated and she heard a sound that matched the vibration. A low rumble, as if a storm waited just outside the garden gate.

She straightened, catching muffled shouts in the distance. The rumble grew louder and she could feel it now in her knees. Suddenly the sun disappeared. Sarah looked up, and screamed.

The black belly of a horse hung directly over her head, so close she could reach up and touch it.

She scrambled back against the wall. Stones dug into her back but she hardly noticed. She trained her attention on the riderless beast landing before her. It turned to face her, snorting and slavering, its head swinging in a mad arc.

The horse's front legs, the only white on a field of black, jerked out a bizarre dance. The animal lurched toward her, rising up on its haunches and pawing the air mere inches from her face.

Her limbs refused to move.

The wind kicked up, swirling leaves around the horse's hind legs. The beast shrieked as its hoof landed a glancing blow to Sarah's shoulder. The force of it nearly blinded her with pain.

She gripped her shoulder, watching in horror as the beast trampled the small garden, shredding tender herbs with razor hooves. Twice it would have trampled her as well, had she not been pressed as tight against the wall as she could manage.

Pain threatened to steal her consciousness. As her world grew dim, three groomsmen burst through the garden gate in pursuit of the mad beast.

They chased it from one end of the garden to the other, finally cornering the wailing horse near the kitchen door. Two of the men trapped the horse between them while the other threw a rope around its neck. If it were able, the horse would have breathed fire.

Covered in foamy sweat and writhing against the rope,

the horse made one last attempt to buck its captors before it whinnied its defeat. Men and beast looked exhausted. Two of the groomsmen led the horse through the gate.

"Awful sorry, Lady Sarah," said the third. He twisted the hem of his shirt nervously in his hands. "I can't imagine how that horse got out of the stables. Are you hurt bad?"

Sarah breathed deep through her teeth. "I will be fine, Robert," she said. "Go help your friends."

"Yes, Lady Sarah." He followed the other two through the gate and closed it behind him.

Fighting the pain, Sarah struggled to her feet and stumbled through the ruins of the garden to the kitchen door.

"Rest assured, I will get to the bottom of this," said James. "I cannot understand how that horse got into the garden." He clenched his jaw so tightly his teeth hurt. Just like the night her carriage ran off the road, a groomsman had to come to Sarah's rescue. Yet again he, her own brother, had failed her.

"It was an accident," said Sarah. Her arm was propped up on a pile of pillows in the library.

The physician had just gone, after poking and prodding the bruised shoulder for what seemed like an hour. Finally, the man prescribed a poultice of comfrey and rosemary, and plenty of rest.

A knock on the library door yielded one of the groomsmen.

"Robert. Come in," said James.

The young man removed his hat as he stepped over the threshold.

"I demand to know what happened this morning," said James. "For God's sake, man, Lady Sarah could have been killed."

"I can't say, m'lord," said Robert, twisting his hat in his hands. "The horse got away from us."

"That horse was to be sold weeks ago. He was impossible to break. Someone will pay for this grievous error."

Robert grew pale. "Yes, m'lord."

"Please, James." Sarah sounded exhausted. "It was no one's fault. You said yourself the horse was wild. Can we not just forget this happened?"

Robert looked up from his cap for just a moment, a strange look in his eye. Then, just as quickly, he lowered his head again.

"Please let me handle this, Sarah. The servants must learn their positions depend on their performance."

"I understand, m'lord," said Robert. " 'Twill never happen again."

James could feel Sarah's pleading look through the veils. It was always that way with her. She couldn't abide causing ill will. If he did release Robert from their service, Sarah would be miserable knowing she was the cause of it.

And Robert *had* come to her aid in the garden, as much as James hated to think about it. He supposed he owed the man something for that.

James sighed. "I'll decrease your pay for six months' time—a fair lesson, don't you think? And I expect that horse to be gone by the morrow. I don't care what you do with it, just get it away from Elmstone or I'll put the beast out of its misery myself."

"Yes, m'lord." The groom hunched into a slight bow. "Will that be all, m'lord?"

"Yes. You may go."

Robert hurried for the door.

"Wait," said James. "One more thing. Saddle my horse. I shall be ready for him in a quarter of an hour."

"Yes, m'lord."

Robert made his escape.

"Do you promise to rest for the remainder of the week?" he asked his sister.

Sarah groaned. "I suppose. But I was going to paint this afternoon."

"No painting. You heard the physician. You are to keep your arm completely still."

"I know, I know. Will you have someone notify Lu— Mr. Delacourte before he prepares for our lesson?"

"Of course." He bent to kiss the top of Sarah's hat. "I will see you later."

"Where are you off to?" she said.

But her brother had already disappeared.

Chapter 10

"*Drink this.*" *James held a cup to Leah's lips, but she re-*fused it. He touched her forehead again. It still burned hot with fever.

He had spent the entire morning at the cottage, beside the narrow bed at the window. He held Leah's hand and read to her—excerpts from a book of poetry—but he doubted she was even aware of his presence most of the time.

It was well past noon when he spied the rented carriage grinding up the side of the hill toward Elmstone. He gave Leah's hand a squeeze. "I must go. I'll be back tomorrow."

He signaled to the nurse sitting at the foot of the bed, working a bit of tatting. She rose and took his place.

"Make sure she takes some water," he said.

The nurse nodded.

In four strides James traversed the cottage's rough-hewn floor and emerged into a neat dirt yard. His horse was teth-ered within a small ring of trees so as not to be visible from the road. He untied it and mounted quickly. As he started up the hill, he saw the carriage arrive at the gate.

Damn. He had no idea this would happen so quickly. He had forgotten to warn Sarah.

Sarah was fair to bursting with excitement as she and Lucien settled in for the day's lesson. She rubbed her shoulder. In the past week, most of the swelling had gone, leaving only an ugly black circle to remind her of the horse's hoof. She was ready to paint.

She took a deep breath to calm herself as Lucien removed a long pouch from his bag. He untied the leather string and unrolled the pouch on the table. Inside were many narrow pockets, each holding a well-used paintbrush.

Her fingertips hummed with anticipation.

She glanced over at Lucien, who didn't seem to share her acute anticipation. She touched his hand lightly. Did it tremble?

"You seem almost as nervous as I," she joked. "If I didn't know any better, I would think this was your first time painting, as well."

He stared at the brushes in his fist. "I must confess something. I have not been completely truthful with you."

She removed her hand from his. "Lucien, if I am not ready . . ."

"No. You are ready. It is I who may not be. You see, I—" A loud rap at the drawing room door interrupted him.

She and Lucien stood mere inches from one another, frozen in the intimate posture of revelation.

Another rap.

"Please enter," Sarah said loudly, all the while watching Lucien's face. She heard the door open, but no accompanying footsteps. Reluctantly, Sarah tore her gaze from Lucien to see who had interrupted their lesson.

Duncan.

Sarah's gasp caught in her throat at the sight of him. Time fell away, transporting her back to the days of their courtship when he would stand in that spot on the rug, that same smile on his lips, waiting to escort her to a ball, or out to the garden, where he was sure to steal a kiss . . .

She tried to fill her lungs, but the air seemed to crackle with every breath.

"Duncan," she whispered.

His smile turned her knees to aspic.

"Sarah, my Sarah. How I have missed you."

She was aware of Lucien's presence beside her, and reached for his shoulder to steady herself. When he took her elbow, her knees gave out. Lucien supported her weight, but Duncan hurried to her side and wrested her from Lucien's grasp.

Duncan led Sarah to the settee and she flopped, most ungracefully, onto the cushioned seat. Through the buzzing in her ears she heard Duncan attempt to dismiss Lucien.

Ignoring Duncan completely, Lucien came over to the settee and touched her shoulder. "Would you care for some water?"

She nodded, afraid to speak lest she scream, or sob, or otherwise give herself away.

"Excellent idea, my man," Duncan said. "You may fetch it whilst Sarah and I have a proper reunion."

"A proper reunion?" she said, when she finally caught her breath. "And me without a pistol."

Had Duncan forgotten how he'd left her when she was hurt and suffering? How she'd waited in vain to hear from him in the awful weeks and months after the accident? How he'd taken her foolish heart and smashed it to a million pieces?

"Go on, man. Fetch the water," Duncan commanded again.

Lucien stood stubbornly beside her. "I will leave only if Lady Sarah so wishes."

She did not. But she refused to let Duncan witness any further insecurity.

She nodded to Lucien. "It's fine. Duncan is an old acquaintance. You may go."

"As you wish."

Lucien gave Duncan a look of warning before he strode from the drawing room, pushing the doors wide open on his way out.

"Mr. Delacourte is not a servant, Duncan."

"Really? Are tutors now considered members of the family?"

Sarah's cheeks grew hot. "Mr. Delacourte is in the employ of our family, but he is not here to serve you. You will not order him about."

Duncan laughed. "Of course not. I merely asked him to fetch you some water. Or perhaps you would care for something stronger?" He moved to the sideboard and gestured to a decanter of brandy.

"No."

He shrugged. "If you don't mind, I believe I shall take a draught for myself. It was a long journey from Cambert Hall. You remember Cambert Hall?"

"Of course. The accident did nothing to my memory."

Duncan's shoulders hunched ever so slightly at the mention of the accident. Sarah felt an ugly twinge of satisfaction.

He poured a glass of brandy, downing it in one gulp, and then poured another before he returned to the settee. He took a seat beside her, his leg almost touching hers. He was much too close for comfort, but she refused to move away.

"You seem surprised I'm here," he said, staring intently at her.

"Not at all!" She forced herself to look into his eyes, though she knew he could not see hers. "It's only been eight years since I've last seen your face. Or should I say, since you have seen mine? It was then you told me our marriage was off, and I've not heard a word from you since. Why ever should I wonder about your presence here?"

Duncan's smile didn't falter. He moved his head about, attempting to peer at her through the veils. Sarah sat perfectly still. What did it matter if he managed to catch a glimpse of her scars? He'd done far more damage to her heart than the broken wheel of that coach had done to her face.

"I cannot blame you for being upset," he said.

"Upset?" She laughed.

"What I did to you was horrible, Sarah. Unforgivable. But I'm here to beg your forgiveness just the same."

She desperately wanted the brandy Duncan offered earlier, but she realized she would have to stand in order to get it. At the moment, she still didn't trust her knees to hold her.

Duncan slid closer to her on the settee. He reached for her hand, but she snatched it away and buried it in the folds of her skirt.

"You want my forgiveness, Duncan?"

"Desperately."

"Fine. You are forgiven. Now please, leave this house."

Duncan's mouth formed the angular pout she had come to know so well when they were betrothed. "I cannot leave, Sarah. I've missed you terribly. I realize now what a blunder I have made."

He spoke, but she barely heard him. Instead, she looked at him, truly looked at him, for the first time since he had entered the room.

His eyes were still the clear green they'd always been, framed with smoky black lashes beneath dark slashes of his brow. But his hair had thinned out a bit on top, she noticed, and the buttons on his coat stretched tight across his middle.

Compared to Lucien, Duncan seemed soft and weak. But her feelings about Duncan were so tangled . . .

"Didn't you hear me, Sarah? I said I've missed you."

For one slip of a moment, she wanted to believe him. She wanted so much to slide into his embrace and forget the horrors and hurt of the past eight years.

Before she could reply, a breeze swept through an open window and the scent of roses infused the air, reminding Sarah of all she had gained since Duncan had left her.

"Go back to Cambert Hall, Duncan. Go back to your wife."

Duncan stood. "I cannot, Sarah. My marriage is a sham. When I confessed to Celeste that I could never love her as I love you, she left. She's returned to the bosom of her family, and I have come here for you."

Sarah was speechless.

Here was the man she once had loved above all else. The man she had dreamed of and pined for and cried over. The man she had mourned as dead, buried in her mind and resurrected over and over in her dreams. Now this man stood before her, professing his love. Insisting he had always loved her.

But instead of joy, she felt only anger.

"How dare you?" she said. "How dare you come here, to my only sanctuary, to disrupt my life again? How dare you tell me after all this time that you love me? Well, I don't love *you*, Duncan. I want you to go. Leave me in peace."

Duncan's features hardened momentarily before reddening—in what? Anger? Humiliation?

"It doesn't matter if you believe me today, Sarah. I'll be here for a while. I've come for a long visit with my dear cousin, and in that time, I intend to win your heart again."

Duncan marched from the drawing room, pulling the doors closed behind him.

Never, even in her darkest days, had Sarah felt so alone as in the still of the drawing room that afternoon.

* * *

"I'll put him out on his ear, if that's what you wish." James stood before the fireplace in the drawing room, a glass of port in hand.

Sarah sighed. "No, don't bother. He no longer affects me." James didn't seem to notice her discomfort. He was much too absorbed in his own mood at the moment.

If James sent Duncan away now, her feelings for him, whatever they may be, would never abate. This was her chance, perhaps the last chance, to get him out of her mind for good.

James swirled the liquid in his glass. "Julia somehow convinced me you still cared for him, and I wanted to believe it. But I guess she would have said anything to get me to allow Duncan to visit. I'm sorry, Sarah."

"No need to apologize, really. Julia has every right, I suppose, to have visits from her family. I harbor the man no ill will. But I must admit it was a bit shocking to see him again. In any event he's here now, so we shall all have to make the best of it."

James wandered over to the window. "Quite."

"Is there a problem? You seem distracted."

"The fields, again, I'm afraid. Seems there's been some sort of scourge there. Bugs or something."

"Hmm. Troublesome fields, this year."

"Indeed."

"Would you like my help? You could bring me a few clippings. After all, I do have some experience ridding plants of insects."

James swallowed the rest of his port before answering. "Thank you, but that won't be necessary. I believe we have it under control now."

"James, is there something you would like to discuss? You're hardly ever here anymore. When you are, you seem so distracted, and—"

"James!" Merri directed a venomous expression at her son as Miss Witherspoon escorted her into the room and to her favorite chair. "What in the Devil's name is that black-guard doing in this house?"

"Good evening to you, too, Mother." James wandered over and gave her a kiss on the cheek. "I assume the black-guard you refer to is Duncan Lavery?"

"Is there another blackguard in residence?"

James sat down across from Sarah. "Duncan has come to visit Julia, who assures me that if Sarah has any problem at all with the arrangement, she will send Duncan straight away to the Hog and Dove for the duration of his stay. However, Sarah has convinced me she has no qualms about Duncan's staying here."

Merri scowled. "Bully for Sarah! But what about the rest of us? What if *we* cannot abide his presence?"

"Calm yourself, Mother," Sarah said. "Surely we can extend a bit of hospitality to family."

"Family? Pah! That man is no family of mine. Nor, for that matter, is that cold-hearted shrew you married, James."

"Take care, Mother. You are speaking of my wife." But if his words were harsh, James's tone lacked conviction.

"How could she invite the Devil's henchman into our home? Why, I have half a mind to kick his posterior to the door myself. I'm not too old to do it!"

"Good evening, Dowager." Duncan strolled into the room as if he were crossing London Bridge. "I see you're as spirited as ever."

"If you value your tongue, Duncan Lavery, you'll take care not to wag it at *me*." She turned to Sarah. "Shall we proceed to the dining room and leave these men to converse on their own?" It was clear her mother expected James to give Duncan a dressing-down.

"I would rather wait here until supper," Sarah replied, ignoring her mother's tart look.

Duncan brushed past Sarah, his trousers touching her skirts, on his way to the sideboard to pour a drink. He downed it quickly, pouring another before taking a seat facing the women.

"Where is Julia?" James asked Duncan.

Duncan shrugged. "I haven't seen her for several hours. I imagine she's preparing for dinner." He turned his attention to Sarah. "Good eve, Lady Sarah. I trust you have recovered from the shock of my arrival."

"Quite easily, thank you."

Duncan drained his glass and gave her a serious look. "The last thing I want is for you to feel uneasy in my company."

"That you have been able to abide your *own* company after what you did to my daughter astounds me, Lavery. Although it does prove what I've always suspected."

Duncan turned to Merri, a wry smile on his lips. "What is that, Dowager?"

"That you are completely devoid of a soul."

Duncan laughed a great, loud laugh, his chair shaking with the exertion. "Ah, how I've missed your rapier wit. But I do hope you shall discover—as I hope all of you shall discover—that I'm a changed man."

Duncan directed his comment to Sarah. She turned away.

Where was Lucien? she wondered.

Lucien had just finished dressing when there came a soft knock at the door. He expected it was Anne, sneaking away while Miss Elsey was napping to bring him a new drawing to exclaim over.

He opened the door to find not Anne, however, but Lady Darby. A shy smile played on her lips.

Lucien held his amusement in check. Lady Darby wearing a shy smile was akin to a cobra wearing shoes.

He bowed. "Lady Darby. To what do I owe the pleasure of this visit?"

She sidled into the room and closed the door behind

her. "I realize it's entirely inappropriate for me to be here. What would people say? However, I wished to speak with you alone."

"I see."

"I know you and Sarah have grown rather close. I'm concerned for her welfare."

"Oh?"

She moved closer, placing her hand on his forearm. "I'm feeling a bit apprehensive over inviting my cousin to visit."

"Why is that?" Lucien pulled tactfully away from her touch and moved to the mirror on the pretense of adjusting his jabot.

Lady Darby came up behind him, meeting his gaze in the mirror. "I'm afraid Duncan's presence will be difficult for Sarah, given their history together."

"Their history? I do not understand."

"Oh! I assumed Sarah told you. The two were once betrothed. It ended badly, I'm sorry to say." She reached around him to smooth the front of his waistcoat.

Lucien's jaw tightened. This bit of information would certainly explain Sarah's reaction in the drawing room this afternoon.

"Lady Darby, why ever would you invite the man here if you knew it would upset Lady Sarah?"

Julia moved closer, brushing her breasts against his back. "I had hoped it would help Sarah to see him. You see, she still cares for him. And my cousin has confessed an error in judgment by leaving Sarah. He hopes to win her back."

Lucien's stomach tightened at the thought. "Why would you discuss this matter with me?"

"I know Sarah has come to trust your opinion, Lucien. I hoped you would speak to her regarding this matter. Convince her to give my cousin another chance. My husband is very much in favor of the match."

A sinking feeling gripped him with Lady Darby's words.

He had no call to feel so deeply for a pupil, but he also had no call to interfere in her life.

"I am afraid I cannot help you," he said, breaking from the circle of her arms and brushing past her to make his escape. "Lady Sarah has not confided in me; therefore, I do not believe I should involve myself in this matter. The affairs of her heart are none of my concern."

Lady Darby followed him to the door. "I must say I'm relieved to hear those words."

"Why?"

"I'm ashamed to admit I suspected something between the two of you. I'm happy I was mistaken. After all, Sarah's heart could only be broken once again. There surely could be no future for the two of you, being of such different backgrounds."

"Indeed."

"Besides, you're quite the handsome, well-traveled gentleman. You should have more than a woman who covers her face and refuses to leave her home." Lady Darby reached up, stroking his cheek with her fingertips. "You need someone a bit more . . . adventurous."

Lucien opened the door. "Shall we adjourn to dinner, Lady Darby?"

Lady Darby's smile brightened. "As you wish."

Chapter 11

When Lucien arrived in the drawing room with Lady
Darby clinging to his arm, there was a decided pall over
the occupants.

Lord Darby seemed to be in another world. The dowager
wore a bitter look, and Sarah sat stiffly on the sofa while a
bleary-eyed Duncan Lavery ogled her from a nearby chair.

"Are we late for a funeral?" Lady Darby said.

"If the dowager had her way, it would be mine," said Lavery. "Where have you been keeping yourself, Cousin Julia?"

"I'm afraid I got a bit, ah, distracted." She looked at
Lord Darby, but he was still miles away.

Lavery shuffled to the sideboard with an unsteady gait.
"Anyone care for a brandy?"

No one answered him.

"Brandy, Delacourte?"

"No." Lucien glanced at Sarah. She seemed to be looking directly at him, her posture hopeful. "May I sit beside
you, Lady Sarah?"

"Certainly."

Had he detected a note of relief in her voice?

Lucien sat, taking care not to touch Sarah's gown, or make any seemingly improper gestures to her person. He had to remember that they were student and teacher. Any sign of friendship or affection would be completely inappropriate.

With a possessive look, Lavery rounded the end of the sofa to stand beside Sarah. She turned her back to him, focusing her attention on Lucien.

"You must be terribly hungry, Mr. Delacourte. I realized as I dressed for supper that we completely forgot the afternoon meal. I suppose my excitement over our lesson is to blame."

"What did you learn today from our dear Lucien?" The dowager sent a sugary smile Lucien's way, and he bit back a laugh. A sugary smile on her was the equivalent of Lady Darby's shy one.

"Mr. Delacourte pronounced me ready for actual paints," Sarah said. "We were just about to begin with them when we were unexpectedly interrupted."

"Good heavens," said Lady Darby. "You mean to say you haven't yet painted? Whatever have the two of you been doing all this time?"

"Yes, what *have* you been doing?" Lavery interjected.

"Preparing," said Sarah.

"Preparing?" said Lady Darby. "How difficult can it be to brush some paint on a canvas?"

"Just as a priest must prepare for his vows," said Lucien, "so must an artist prepare for her paints."

Lavery gave him a blank stare.

"What Lucien—What Mr. Delacourte means is that putting paint to canvas is a commitment one does not take lightly," Sarah said.

Lady Darby snapped open her fan. "Yes, well. While

all of this talk of priests and preparations is quite fascinating, I'm famished. Shall we proceed to the dining room?"

"Hear, hear." Lavery raised his glass as if to toast, and polished off the contents in one swallow.

Lady Darby hurried over and snatched the glass from his hand, depositing it on the marble sideboard with an audible clunk. "Walk with me, dear cousin."

The group filed *en masse* toward the dining room with Lady Darby in the lead, exerting a viselike grip on Lavery's elbow. Lucien suspected she was holding him up.

When they were seated, Lucien found himself opposite Lavery, giving him a chance to take stock of the man.

What had Sarah seen in him?

Lavery might be considered handsome in an artless sort of way. His skin was of an alabaster hue, making his deep green eyes all the more striking. Dark hair and narrow, symmetrical features lent a cold, chiseled air.

He stood just an inch or two taller than Lucien, but the regal set of Lavery's shoulders made him appear much larger than he was. Had this self-possessed demeanor played a role in Sarah's infatuation? Confidence could be quite an aphrodisiac.

Sarah sat to the left of Lavery, trapped in the shadow of her former beau. She seemed nervous, fidgeting with her unused silver, twisting her napkin between her fingers. Did she still harbor feelings for Lavery? Perhaps Lady Darby had been telling the truth. There was no accounting for the female heart.

Lady Darby took full advantage of her position beside Lucien, once again rubbing her thigh against his beneath the table. And again, he moved his leg away.

"Begging your pardon, Lady Darby."

She smiled coquettishly, but her efforts went unrewarded. Lord Darby hardly seemed to notice his wife, or the rest of the people around him, as he made quick work of the food put before him.

The dowager cast daggers the way of Duncan Lavery, who swallowed his third glass of wine before the meat had even been served. "Have you had quite enough?"

Lavery looked at her, clearly startled that she would address him at all. "Enough what?"

"Enough brandy. Enough wine. You scarcely touched your food. Are your meals strictly of the liquid sort these days, Duncan?"

Lavery had the decency to color a bit—mottled pink stained his alabaster cheeks. "Sorry. I s'pose I'm still a bit worn from the journey."

"Hmmf." The old woman poked at the roasted quail on her plate.

Beneath the table, Lucien felt Lady Darby kick her cousin's ankle. Lavery gave her a sheepish look before struggling to stand.

"If you will all excuse me, I'm rather exhausted. I'm afraid I am poor company tonight," he said.

"As if you're ever good company," said the dowager. "By all means, go. If we're fortunate, you'll keep on going, straight out the door."

"You're a despicable woman." Lady Darby threw her napkin on her plate and followed Lavery out.

"Mother, you are terrible," said Sarah, stirring in her chair. For a moment Lucien thought she would rise and follow the others, but then she settled back in her seat.

Lord Darby continued to eat, seemingly unfazed by the drama unfolding around him.

The dowager shrugged, and took another bite of her quail.

"What has possessed you?" Julia paced the length of her cousin's quarters as he lay facedown on the bed, rumpled

and sleepy. "I had no idea how bad things had become. You're a stinking drunkard."

Duncan giggled into his pillow.

Julia came to an abrupt stop. "You find this amusing, do you? Well, this is no farce, cousin. If you insist on acting the sot, you'll have no hope of winning back Sarah's affections. Even *I* find you disgusting."

"Oh, stuff it up your arse, Julia. I had a few sips of wine with my meal. What's the harm?"

"A few sips? You had a decanter of brandy before supper began, and several glasses of wine with your soup. Had I not dragged you from the table, no doubt you would have had a few dozen more."

Duncan licked his lips. "I'm feeling dry. Can you bring something up for me, or shall I ring the chambermaid?"

"You would do well to stay away from liquor. And from chambermaids." Julia stamped her foot in frustration. "Go to bed, Duncan, and consider your future for a while. If Sarah refuses you, you won't get a penny from me. In a few months' time, instead of drinking fine brandy from crystal glasses, you shall be drinking cheap ale from a wooden mug. That thought alone should enable you to crawl from the depths of your cups for a fortnight or two. At least until you pry Sarah from the artist's side."

Duncan rolled onto his back and belched. "Mmm. The artist. I hate to be the one to deliver bad tidings, dear cousin, but Delacourte hardly seems to notice you."

"How can he possibly notice me when Sarah commandeers every moment of his attention? My husband pays Lucien well to occupy her. I'm sure he doesn't want to jeopardize his commission by ignoring his charge. That is why you must distract Sarah. Give Lucien time to appreciate my charms."

Julia knelt beside the bed. "Please, Duncan. It's why I asked you here. This will be the perfect solution for the both of us. Besides," she said, pushing to her feet, "I understand, from a reliable source, that very shortly Cambert Hall will no longer belong to you."

"What?" Duncan struggled to sit up.

Julia nodded. "It would seem your father is quite displeased with your separation from Celeste. He lost a very influential ally in Celeste's father."

Duncan deflated into the featherbed.

"Take heart, cousin," Julia said. "You have a genuine timid old spinster right under your nose. All that's left is for you to seduce her once again."

Sarah was vastly relieved to be back in her rooms. The way Duncan had hung on her every word, taken every opportunity to touch her in some way, truly disturbed her.

Since his arrival, Duncan's relentless attentions stirred a cauldron of memories and long-forgotten feelings. Sarah found herself caught somewhere between hatred and love, between attraction and pity, for a man who had fallen apart.

The changes she had noticed when she first saw Duncan in the drawing room had to be related to his drinking. He had once possessed an edge, a keen sense of observation, and a biting wit. Alcohol had changed him, had turned him soft and blurry, like a man standing in fog.

On the other hand, his new vulnerability gave him a sort of doleful allure—the kind possessed by stray mongrels and orphans. Sarah felt an inexplicable urge to protect him. Protect him!

He was the source of her greatest shame. If she hadn't been weak, she would be his wife right now. She would have several lovely children, and a wonderful social life. Her face would be unmarked . . .

She pulled her shawl close around her shoulders and pushed thoughts of Duncan from her mind. If all that were true, there would be much she would have missed as well.

She focused her thoughts on her gardens.

The weather grew colder by the day. Soon the blooms would fall from the flowers and the browns of autumn would ransack the countryside. She typically disliked this season, but this year it didn't seem so maudlin. This year she had her lessons.

This year, she had the company of Lucien.

She wondered what Lucien thought of Duncan, and what, if anything, he had learned of their courtship.

Why hadn't she ever told Lucien about Duncan? Why hadn't she told him so many things? Lucien had opened his heart to her about Tessa. He had shared so much, and she so little. She was a terrible friend.

Suddenly, it became very important that Lucien know everything.

The corridor was drafty and dark. Everyone apparently had retired to their quarters and the candles had been extinguished.

Sarah carried a single taper in a silver holder. The flame sputtered and spit, causing her to slow her pace. She didn't relish being alone in the dark, even in her own home. It reminded her too much of the night of the accident, when she'd been trapped beneath the carriage for what seemed like hours.

She stayed close to the wall as she counted the doors. Lucien's was the fourth on the left, she remembered from the day he had arrived. The green apartment.

She rapped lightly on the door. There was no answer, so she rapped again, this time a bit harder. She heard shuffling from deep within the room before the door creaked open.

Lucien stood before her clad only in breeches, and those half buttoned as if he had pulled them on in haste.

"Sarah? What are you doing here?" He stuck his head

out into the hallway and looked about. It occurred to Sarah that he might be expecting someone else. Or did he have someone else with him already?

One of the staff, perhaps? She'd overheard the maids discussing Lucien's attributes on more than one occasion. She felt a momentary flare of jealousy before he stepped aside and motioned her into the room.

"You should not have come here." His voice was almost a whisper.

Sarah supposed it was the height of impropriety for her to be alone in a man's room so late at night, but she simply didn't care. Living her life behind the walls of the estate allowed her not to give two shakes about what was proper anymore.

"I'm sorry to wake you," she said, "but I needed to speak with you."

"What is it?" He took her candle and used it to light one on the dresser. He retrieved his shirt from the bedpost and pulled it on without bothering to button it. Sarah followed the path of golden hair that ran from Lucien's chest to his stomach, and disappeared below the waistband of his breeches.

Her mouth went dry. She tore her eyes away from his bare skin and focused on his face.

"There is something I must tell you." Her veils moved with her breath, and in turn, so did the candle. She set it upon a small, round table against the wall and gestured for Lucien to sit on the chest at the foot of his bed.

She sat beside him and examined her hands so she wouldn't be tempted by the trail of curls. The red garnet she wore glinted in the candlelight. "I couldn't sleep. I feel . . . I want you to know I care a great deal for you. As of late, I've begun to think of you as a friend."

"And I, you."

"Good. Because I'm in need of a friend just now, and I had hoped you would be willing to serve in that capacity."

He reached out as if to take her hand, but seemed to think better of it. He tucked his hands beneath his legs. "Of course. What is it?"

"You've confided in me, you've trusted me, and that has touched me more than you can possibly know. In turn, I've not been as trusting of you. I've not been a worthy friend because I've not placed my confidence in you."

"Sarah, it is not necessary—"

"It is necessary for me. It's been an eternity since I've had a friend. I seem to have forgotten how to behave with one. So I would like to confide in you."

Lucien was silent. She turned toward him, and he nodded.

"You may have sensed my discomfort with Duncan Lavery."

"I did."

"The reason his presence vexes me so is because we were once betrothed."

"Lady Darby divulged as much."

Sarah was surprised. When had he spoken to Julia alone? She stole a glance at Lucien. His head was bowed.

"Well, I don't know how much you have heard. But I want you to hear the entire story from me, directly."

He nodded.

Sarah stared at the candle flickering on the table. She took a deep breath. "Eight years ago I suffered a terrible accident. A week before Duncan and I were to be married, I was returning at night to Elmstone from a ball we attended together. Something spooked the horses, and my carriage overturned. The vehicle broke in half when it rolled into a gulley. A spoke from one of the wheels slashed my face. I was fortunate not to have been rendered blind or deaf. But I wasn't fortunate enough to hold Duncan's interest.

"When he saw my face after the accident, he put an immediate end to all plans for our union."

"Bastard."

She emitted a small, bitter laugh. "Ours was an arranged match, so few people were surprised when Duncan called it off. But I was. I loved Duncan, and I thought he cared for me. I was devastated."

Lucien did take her hand now, curling his fingers around hers and warming her palm against his.

The tears began to flow beneath the veils, but her voice remained steady.

"At first I believed Duncan would return to me after the scandal died down, when he'd had time to think. When he'd had time to consider how his actions had hurt me. But he didn't. I waited for weeks. Months. But he never returned. In the meantime, I recovered from my injuries in seclusion, but there were so many questions, so many rumors about my face, about Duncan.

"By the time I was well, I refused to leave Elmstone. I allowed that if my own beloved couldn't stand to be near me, mere acquaintances and strangers would certainly be offended by my presence.

"Perhaps I was rash. But I decided I could lead a perfectly good life behind these walls, and I have."

Lucien squeezed her hand. "You say it has been good, and maybe it has. But has it been everything it could have been?"

"It has been different than it would have been. More than that, I cannot say."

"What of your friends? What did they do to help you?"

She swallowed against the lump growing in her throat. "When I was younger, I visited Whitford daily, counting nearly every resident of the village a friend. But after the accident, when I decided to stay within the gates of Elmstone, not one of them bothered to visit. That these so-called friends could forget me so easily was the second-worst lesson I learned after the accident."

"It must have been terrible for you. But surely there was someone?"

She shook her head. "Lucien, you've given me such happiness as of late. Knowing I'll be able to finish my botanical catalogue, and knowing I'll have a way to spend the cold winter days until I can once again tend my roses, has given me great peace."

Lucien rubbed his thumb over hers, sending a shiver of heat through her. "Don't you wish for more than peace and contentment, Sarah? Don't you deserve more?"

A small sob escaped her throat. "I cannot! This is my lot, my punishment."

Her scars were her punishment. But had she really learned her lesson? When Duncan had walked into the drawing room, she'd felt a moment of hope, the possibility of redemption.

"I must confess," she said quietly, "that when I saw Duncan again, the feelings I once had for him resurfaced. When he told me he was here to beg my forgiveness, part of me rejoiced."

Lucien released her hand abruptly and moved to the fireplace. The low light of embers cast a glow over his face.

"Do you want him?"

She swallowed hard. "No! But I've always been weak where Duncan is concerned. He told me he intends to win me over. I cannot let him back into my life, Lucien. I cannot!"

"I will help you, then. I will protect you from him, and from yourself, if that is what you wish." He sat beside her again, and she grasped his arm.

"You would do that for me?"

"Only if that is what you truly wish."

"It is."

"Then we shall become inseparable, you and I. I will provide a constant barrier between you and Lavery. He cannot court your affections if he cannot get close enough to do it. Eventually he will give up and go away."

Sarah sighed with relief. "Thank you, Lucien. Your friendship has become my saving grace."

Lucien raised her hand to his lips and brushed it with a tender kiss. "It will be an honor to serve you, Lady Sarah Essington."

Chapter 12

Sleep evaded her.

Sarah was so relieved by Lucien's offer to help her, she could think of nothing else. To have a friend—a true friend—after all this time alone was a blessing. Trusting another person had been more than difficult; it was almost inconceivable. Until Lucien.

Though she rarely admitted it, her isolated existence was painful. The loneliness hurt, but the real problem lay with her memories. Living as she did, she had to fight against bitterness every day. She especially fought against her memories of Duncan.

She had trusted him so completely. She had offered up her heart and he had sacrificed it for his own vanity, making it clear he could not bear to be seen with a damaged woman.

If she had not given herself to him just hours before the accident, his abandonment would have been easier to bear.

Memories of their single night together flared in her mind after years of repression.

Duncan had held a masque in honor of their forthcoming marriage at his home, Cambert Hall, several hours' ride from Elmstone. Sarah was to stay the night, along with many of the other guests.

It began as a most romantic evening. Duncan treated her as if she were the only woman in the world. He fetched her punch, commandeered every dance, and never left her side.

Near the end of the night, Duncan whisked her away from the crowd. He insisted he couldn't wait for her until their vows were spoken. He expounded on the purity of their love, their common destiny, and convinced her that their forthcoming commitment would erase all wrong in the eyes of God and the Church. So she went willingly up the servants' stairs to his quarters while hundreds of guests danced and mingled in the ballroom below.

In his quarters, Duncan surrounded the bed with candles. Their light cast an ethereal glow over the white coverlet. He removed her gown with such tenderness, such devotion and reverence in his eyes, all trepidation fled.

Sarah remembered every moment so clearly. Duncan's soft kisses and whispers. His broad hands on her back, her breasts, caressing her in places she previously would have blushed to even think of. The sharp pain, and Duncan's comforting words when her barrier was breached. When it was over, he kissed her forehead and helped her to dress. Though she knew it should have been a magical moment, Sarah felt ashamed. She wanted nothing more than to return to her home.

Duncan, however, wanted to return to the ball.

Sarah was mortified when he refused to accompany her on the long ride to Elmstone, sending his valet in his stead. The servant, eager to deliver her so he could spend the rest of the night at the Hog and Dove, pressed the driver ever faster over the dark country roads.

The next thing Sarah remembered, she was trapped

beneath the splintered remains of the carriage, staring up at a full moon which turned red as blood streamed into her eyes . . .

Sarah pushed the awful images to the back of her mind, locking them in the dark room reserved only for unthinkable horrors. She thought she had long passed the time for such morbid reminiscing. However, the ugly recollections did serve a purpose.

They reminded her never, ever to trust Duncan Lavery.

Lucien once again admired the deft movements of Sarah's arms and shoulders as she pruned a low-growing rosebush.

"I knew I would find you here," he said.

She turned. He could feel the warmth of her smile through the veils, and through the chilly breeze.

"Lucien!" She collected a few of the branches she had cut and placed them in a basket.

Lucien helped her to her feet. He took the basket and walked with her beside a stone wall, his shoulders brushing the errant leaves of late-blooming climbers.

"I fear these darlings will not last much longer. A frost is coming," Sarah said.

"I have felt a chill in the air as of late, too."

"Are you sure it's not coming from Mother?"

Lucien laughed. "Her disposition has not improved since Lavery's arrival."

"For once I'm grateful for her ferocious demeanor. Perhaps it will serve to shorten Duncan's stay. She made him miserable at breakfast, though he did seem a bit peaked to begin with. I cannot imagine he felt very well after the amount of drink he imbibed at supper."

They strolled toward the house under an archway formed of yew trees, which blocked out most of the sunlight. The path was mossy and damp, the air crisp. Sarah gathered the short cape she wore tight around her shoulders.

"Has he always been that way?" Lucien asked.

"A drinker, you mean?" Sarah shrugged. "Perhaps he had the potential. I really cannot say, since my every thought of him then was colored with affection. When you care so deeply for a person, you tend to overlook their faults."

"He seems to have plenty."

"I suppose. But there was good in him, as well. He was quite endearing in a spoiled, mischievous sort of way. He was polite and refined, always knew the proper thing to say, and could charm the stockings off any woman from five years to fifty."

"A useful talent, indeed." Suddenly Lucien did not care to hear another word about Duncan Lavery. "Tell me, what is that bush over there?"

"Rhododendron. It blooms in the early spring. The flowers are pink and white. Quite beautiful, really."

"And that one?"

"Where has this sudden interest in bushes come from?"

Lucien shrugged. "From my complete and utter disinterest in Lavery, of course."

Sarah laughed. "I must commend your honesty. And while we're on to other subjects, am I ever going to paint?"

They climbed the stone steps to the terrace. When they arrived at the top, Lucien handed Sarah the basket. "I wondered when you would come around to that. I shall meet you in the drawing room in half an hour."

The early autumn sun infused the room with a deep yellow cast, mellowing the vibrant colors of the furniture and adding imagined warmth to the air.

Sarah was already settled on the stool before the easel when Lucien arrived. He closed the door slowly behind him, and seemed to take an eternity to cross the room.

"Am I such a terrible student that you're dreading this class?"

"Of course not." He rubbed the back of his neck. "Where is my stool?"

"Over in the corner. You seem disturbed."

He fetched the seat and pulled it beside hers, ignoring her observation. "Shall we begin?"

He fumbled with one of the pigment tins lined up on the table. The lid popped off, spewing a dark yellow powder into the air. The fine dust floated in the beams of sunlight, finally settling on the easel, the floor, and Lucien's sleeve.

"Sorry." He shook some of the remaining powder into a bowl. "This is your pigment."

He uncorked a tall bottle and held it beneath her nose. She flinched against the strong odor.

"This is a mixture of linseed oil and resin of turpentine, which we shall use as a binder. When we mix the binder and the pigment, it makes paint. The more binder we use, the thinner the paint. The thinner the paint, the more quickly it will dry. It is best to use thinner paint on the first layers."

He added a few drops of the oil to the bowl, and extracted a flat-edged palette knife from the pouch of brushes. Using the knife, he worked the pigment and oil together until the mixture was the consistency of thin syrup.

Then he rooted through his leather satchel and withdrew a teardrop-shaped palette made of dark wood. He scraped the paint from the bowl onto the palette.

Sarah watched, mesmerized, as he repeated the process with three more powders, making the palette come alive with puddles of color. Dark red. Vivid blue. Midnight black. When he finished, he handed the palette to her, hooking her thumb through the hole in the middle.

The wood was heavier than she had imagined it would be, catching her off guard. Her wrist lurched beneath the weight. She quickly righted it.

"The paint will not slide off," he teased.

She stared at the bright colors against the dark grain of the wood. "What shall I do?"

"Well, now you must practice holding the palette for a few days."

He must have sensed her disappointment, for he began to laugh. "I am only joking. What I would like for you to do is to study the colors. Take note how they look in the light. Mix them at your will. Become familiar with the constitution."

Sarah hesitated, but when Lucien made no move to help her, she took up a fan-shaped brush and lightly touched it to the spot of blue paint.

"Take a bit more," he said.

She did as he instructed.

"Now brush it into the middle of the palette, near your thumb. Excellent. Now take a bit of the yellow—just a small bit, mind you—and work it into the blue. Fold the colors into one another."

A bright green emerged on the palette beneath the brush. "Exactly the green of Scots briar leaves," she said with satisfaction.

"A fine color." Lucien smiled. Sarah smiled back, but then she realized he could not see her. Suddenly, she resented the isolation her veils inflicted much more than she appreciated what they hid.

"I want you to know I'm smiling, Lucien."

"I know. Try some more."

For nearly an hour she created endless hues on the palette using just the four colors Lucien had mixed for her. The purplish reds of roses, the yellow-orange of a lily. The range of greens from rosebushes to yew trees—the colors of her gardens blossomed beneath her brush.

While attempting to recreate a spectacular shade of violet she could see only in the spring, Duncan wandered into the drawing room.

"Pardon me," he said. "I hope I'm not interrupting." He took a seat anyway, balancing a glass of brandy on his knee. The sky blue jacket he wore looked slept in, while his embroidered waistcoat bore a stain of questionable origin.

Despite her wariness, Sarah's heart went out to him. Something truly terrible must have happened to change him from such a vibrant, charming man into this sad fellow drinking brandy in the morning. Nevertheless, he'd intruded upon their lesson.

"Excuse us, Duncan. We're working and do not wish to be disturbed."

Duncan imparted a lopsided grin. "I promise to be on my best behavior. Mum as a doorknocker."

Sarah saw Lucien's jaw tense. Would he confront Duncan? There was really no point to it. Their lesson was just about finished.

She reached out and squeezed Lucien's arm.

"Never mind," she whispered. "He looks about to fall asleep, anyway."

"He should not be here," Lucien said, loudly.

"Perhaps not. But the sun has disappeared behind some clouds. The room is getting dark, so I imagine our lesson will end shortly."

Lucien's expression was a curious mix of annoyance and relief. "Shall we clean up for today?"

"Fine."

Sarah put her brush in a cup of turpentine to soak.

"No!" Lucien growled. "You never leave your brushes in the turpentine."

Sarah flinched at the harsh tone. "I'm sorry, Lucien. I only meant to soak them for a minute before I cleaned them."

He squeezed his eyes shut and rubbed his temples. "Please forgive me. I just . . . I want you to be careful."

"Of course."

As they finished cleaning up, a bleary-eyed Duncan monitored their every word and move.

When they made to leave, Duncan struggled to his feet. "Stay, Sarah? I had hoped we could spend a few moments talking."

"We have nothing to talk about." She wiped clean the last brush and placed it, bristles up, in an empty cup to dry.

"Please, Sarah."

Something in Duncan's voice struck her as desperate. She looked at him closely. He didn't seem well. Perhaps he was ill. Pity welled reluctantly within her.

"Very well. Just for a moment."

"I will stay with you," said Lucien, returning from the doorway to stand beside her.

"That won't be necessary," she said.

"Lady Sarah—" Lucien's eyes gave warning.

"It will be fine, Lucien. I shall be but a moment here. If you like, you may wait for me in the library and I'll be along directly."

Lucien's fingers curled, but his face remained passive. He looked at her for a long minute, his eyes unreadable, before stalking from the drawing room.

Duncan flopped back into his seat. "For a moment I thought I might have to call him out."

"For heaven's sake, Duncan, don't be an ass."

He looked hurt. "Clearly I must protect you from that man. He's a lecherous sort, no doubt about it."

Sarah ignored Duncan's ridiculous ramblings. "What did you wish to speak to me about?"

"Come here." His voice was thick and slow.

"No."

"Let me see your face."

Sarah was momentarily taken aback. Then she began to laugh, soft and humorless.

"You've already seen my face, remember? One time was all you needed to decide you no longer loved me."

"Not true!" Duncan lurched to his feet again. "I never stopped loving you. Never!"

Sarah started for the door. Duncan reached out, more quickly than she imagined he could have in his condition, and caught her elbow.

"You must understand I had a reputation to uphold. I am not a titled man, Sarah. Other than my holdings, all I had was my reputation."

She slapped his hand away. "And you made me believe all I had was my beauty. But while it appears you've lost that which you treasure the most—your precious reputation—I've gained something much more enduring than beauty. My self-respect."

Sarah ran from the drawing room as quickly as her trembling legs could manage. It took every last ounce of strength for her to make it up the stairs to her chambers.

She locked the door behind her and tore the hat and veils from her head, scattering pins everywhere.

So that was why he left her? His precious reputation? The handsome, charming Duncan Lavery couldn't take a damaged wife—not when he could easily have a perfect one.

Sarah threw herself on the bed and cried as she should have the night Duncan broke off their engagement. She had been numb then; the tears would not come. But she wasn't numb anymore.

It hurt. Dear God, it still hurt. But it was going to get better, because now she had Lucien's help.

Lucien!

She hurriedly donned her veils and ran from the room, hoping against hope that he was still waiting for her in the library.

Chapter 13
❧

Sarah never came. He waited, but she never came.

Lucien finally walked out of the manor, through the gates, and over the fields alone, Sarah's disregard weighing heavily in his steps.

She had seemed so sincere when she told him she wanted nothing to do with Lavery. So grateful when she accepted his assistance to keep her away from the drunken sot.

It had pricked Lucien's heart to hear about Sarah's accident and Lavery's subsequent betrayal. How a man could tear apart the dreams and hopes of such a lovely young woman, Lucien would never understand. The man was a rodent.

But even more baffling was why Sarah still acknowledged the wretched cur's existence.

Without forethought, Lucien's feet carried him down the rough-hewn path toward Whitford. Was this the same route the young Sarah trod each day on her way to the town? Images of a carefree girl running among the tall grass and wildflowers plagued him. He suddenly wished he'd known Sarah then.

Just as suddenly, he wished he knew her now.

All he had assumed of Sarah—that she was strong, confident, and intelligent—had been dismantled by her reaction to Lavery. Why would she subject herself to Lavery's company so willingly after the way he had hurt her? He would only cause her misery again.

He wondered what they were doing at that moment. Perhaps rekindling their forgotten affections? His mouth went dry.

Lucien imagined so many distasteful scenarios involving Sarah and Lavery that by the time he reached Whitford, he would happily have given his right leg for a mug of ale and a shot of whiskey.

He hurried through the streets, nearly crushing a hapless chicken beneath his heel in search of the Hog and Dove. Once he got his bearings, he stood before the door of the tavern in less time than it took to walk from one end of Elmstone to the other.

When he entered the establishment, again he was greeted with hostile silence until one of the patrons stepped forward.

"You the bloke went up to Elmstone? The painter?"

Lucien nodded.

A buzz spread through the common room until Oliver Stagg, the burly, good-natured farmer Lucien met when he first arrived in Whitford, plowed through the crowd. His nose and cheeks were bright red, and he listed to one side like a great, unbalanced galleon.

"Another good day at the market, Mr. Stagg?" Lucien said.

The farmer laughed and gestured toward the bar. "Sit down, Delacourte."

Lucien took the proffered stool. The roar of the patrons had dulled to a low buzz. Lucien felt several dozen pairs of eyes on his back, but he did not acknowledge them. He wanted a drink, and would not be cowed from his purpose.

The barkeep sauntered over to where Lucien and Stagg sat.

"Ale?"

"Yes." Lucien reached into his coat pocket for his purse.

Stagg grabbed his wrist. "My coin is good for it. As you said, 'twas a good day at the market."

"I get the notion most days at the market are good for you."

Stagg laughed again, the red in his cheeks deepening to scarlet. The barkeep plunked two mugs down in front of them. Lucien made to take a sip, but again Stagg stayed his hand.

"Well, then?"

Lucien's attention turned from his mug to the farmer's broad face. "Well, what?"

Stagg raised a brow. "Ah. Is that how it will be? And after my coin filled your mug?"

"I did not ask for it. It was you who offered."

"Aye. But you took it quick enough."

There were shouts of "Aye! Aye!" all around, matched with accusatory glares and angry murmurs.

Lucien slid his mug toward Stagg. "I cannot tell you anything."

More angry murmurs.

Lucien stood. "Please hear me. Lady Sarah is my pupil. I cannot betray her confidence, or the confidence of her family."

The tavern erupted. A skinny merchant in green breeches and a brown waistcoat stood and pounded on a table. "She's more ours than yours, man. We've known her since she was a child. We've not seen her for eight years, nor heard a dozen words about her in all that time. 'Tis our right, as her friends!"

Lucien attempted to speak over a round of cheers. A barmaid huddled in a corner, wiping the perspiration from her brow with the back of her hand.

He looked about the inn's common room. All eyes were focused upon him. The air was thick with expectance.

What would they do if he just walked out? They were angry, but he did not think they would stop him.

Lucien remembered what the dowager had told him. How Sarah had always been friendly with the people of Whitford, coming down from Elmstone to visit each day. How she had cared for them, and they for her.

And he remembered, also, what Sarah had told him. Not one of them had ever come to see her.

"Why should I tell you anything? You could have asked Sarah yourselves, eight years ago, if any of you had bothered to walk up that hill. If any of you had bothered to inquire after her."

The tavern erupted anew.

"Quiet, mates. Quiet!" Stagg held up his arms to silence the crowd. To Lucien, he said, "Who told you such?"

"Lady Sarah herself. She said not one of you bothered to pay her a visit after the accident. Not one."

" 'Tis a lie."

"You mean to say you did see her?"

Stagg spit on the floorboards. "No. But we tried enough. We was turned away at the gate every time, on Lord Darby's orders. We was told she din't want to see anybody."

Lucien looked about the tavern. The concern he read in the eyes of these men and women made him believe their interest in Sarah was more than mere curiosity.

But if he relented, if he answered their questions, would he be betraying Sarah? She valued her privacy, yes. But did she value it above friendship? Above the concern of so many old friends?

"You cannot know how we've missed her, worried for her," Stagg said, his voice ragged. "Tell us about her."

Lucien exhaled through his teeth. "What is it you wish to know?"

A wave of excitement crested forth from the crowd. The man who paid for his ale was, out of common courtesy he presumed, the first to present his question.

"Is she terribly sad?" Stagg asked, his red face stone serious.

Lucien considered his answer carefully. "No. I would not say she is sad. I think Lady Sarah has an unbreakable spirit. But she does seem lonely."

The crowd encouraged Lucien to take a mouthful of ale.

"Is she well?" This from a portly gent off to Lucien's left.

"Yes. At least, she seems perfectly healthy to me."

"Are the gardens as lovely as we hear?" The question came from the back of the room. Female. One of the barmaids, he assumed.

"In fact, they are magnificent. Lady Sarah has a rare talent for creating beauty."

Another mouthful of ale.

Lucien answered question after question, drank mug after mug of ale, until the curiosity of the people of Whitford seemed almost sated, and he was most definitely drunk.

However, one last question remained.

"What does she look like beneath the veils?"

Lucien could not tell from whom the question had finally come. It did not matter. It was the question they had all wanted to ask. The question that hovered in the smoke above the room, and at the bottom of every mug of ale.

Lucien's head spun. His mouth went dry, despite the enormous amount of drink he had just consumed.

"I cannot say. I have never seen her without them."

All was silent.

Lucien's stool scraped noisily on the wooden floor. He pushed open the door of the Hog and Dove and walked out into the cold night, leaving the good people of Whitford to make what they would of his answers.

He trod the uneven countryside under the autumn moon, attempting to walk off the effects of drink as well as the guilt brewing within him. Perhaps he should not have revealed so much about Sarah at the Hog and Dove. She would feel betrayed when she found out.

Well, too bad. He felt betrayed as well. Sarah all but drove him to the Hog and Dove when she sent him to the library so she could be alone with Lavery.

The man sickened him. He'd once had the love of a wonderful woman, but even such a rare gift could not deter him from his life of decadence. Lavery would never be able to see beyond Sarah's veils. He would never understand that beauty was fleeting, the least important element in the search for a woman's truest heart.

Sarah knew Lavery would never change. So why? Why would she give him even a moment more of her time?

Perhaps she deserved what she got. And perhaps Lucien had read too much into his friendship with the lady. He assumed Sarah valued his opinion. That she cared for him.

This was clearly not the case if today's incident in the drawing room was any indication.

Lucien slipped on a stone in the pathway and landed on his back, staring up at the moon. The white orb swung through his line of vision as if hanging on the end of a hypnotist's chain. Back and forth. Back and forth.

He closed his eyes, but the swinging grew worse.

He rolled up onto his knees. The ale in his belly threatened to spill out onto the moonlit path. Taking several deep breaths, Lucien lurched to his feet.

Dear God, please let me get back to my quarters.

Julia froze. Were those footsteps she heard?

She tiptoed to the door and opened it a crack, peering into the hall.

No one about.

She closed the door quietly, and continued her search of Lucien's room. Thus far her efforts had yielded nothing interesting, but she was determined to find something that would give her an advantage when it came time to seduce this man properly. Some sort of insight into his deepest thoughts and desires.

She picked up the wine-colored jacket hanging over the back of the desk chair, recalling how snugly it stretched over Lucien's broad shoulders. She brought the coat to her nose and inhaled his scent. Her heartbeat quickened.

He would be one of her finest conquests.

She opened one of the desk drawers and removed a handful of drawings. The first few were flowers, imbued with excellent detail. However, deeper into the pile she discovered some simpler drawings. She squinted at the signature in the corner. Not Lucien's, nor even Sarah's. It was that of her own daughter, Anne.

When had the child made these? Anne must have sneaked away from her governess to spend time with Lucien. And after Julia had warned her, in no uncertain terms, to stay clear of their handsome houseguest.

No doubt Sarah had something to do with this rebellion. For some reason, Sarah believed Julia did not afford Anne enough attention. In Julia's opinion, children were little more than a nuisance until they were old enough to come out into society. Until then there were nannies, governesses, tutors, convents, lengthy travels, and above all, very large houses.

Julia stuffed the papers back into the desk drawer, vowing to keep a close watch on Miss Elsey and her daughter. She discovered little else in the desk besides pencils, charcoal, and fresh sketching paper, so she moved on.

Atop the dresser was a gilt frame. She opened it to discover two miniatures, one of a light-haired woman and one of a girl about Anne's age, with blond curls and blue eyes the same shade as Lucien's.

She opened the bottom drawer of Lucien's dresser and

sifted through a neat pile of soft linen shirts. Beneath them, toward the back of the drawer, her fingers brushed something flat. Paper. She slid her hand beneath the pile, careful not to disturb the garments, and fished it out.

"Well, well. What have we here?" she murmured.

It appeared to be a correspondence, delivered to Lucien at a Paris address. A letter from a lover, perhaps? The blunt edges and dirt-smudged seal suggested it had been read often.

Julia eagerly unfolded the sheaf of paper and examined the signature. Much to her disappointment, the missive was not from a woman but from a Monsieur Henri Valmetant. She read it nonetheless, in the unlikely case it held hints of decadent proclivities. It did not, but she pocketed the letter anyway.

It was not quite what she had been hoping for, but it would do. Yes, it would do very nicely.

She made her way to the door and opened it a crack, finding herself eye to eye with . . .

An eye.

"Oh!"

"Lady Darby, I presume?" Lucien said, pushing the door open slowly.

Chapter 14

Duncan walked past the door to Sarah's chambers a dozen times that morning, not because he hoped to see her but merely because he wished to be near her.

Truly, he did not know what insanity had invaded his mind. Sarah suddenly possessed a powerful attraction, like that of a rat to a flea.

He had watched her the night before at supper, as he had every moment since his arrival. He was searching her veils, her home, her life for some sign of the Sarah he'd once known. The Sarah he could convince of anything; who accepted his word as gospel; who could not take a breath without him. To Duncan's great surprise, he could not find her.

Gone was the lovely but insecure girl who once longed to be his bride—the girl who had seemed to care for little but gowns and gifts and parties. In her place was a woman who was complex and curious, compassionate and forgiving. A woman whose present refinement was far more intriguing than her past beauty.

Duncan had expected to find a broken woman, desperate enough for love and affection that she would even accept the man who had once dashed her dreams. Instead, he'd found just the opposite. Sarah did not want him back.

No, it was even worse. *She* pitied *him.* He could hear it in her voice.

How dare she?

Why should little Lady Sarah, the Phantom of Whitford, be so content behind her veils, while he was so utterly miserable? Bloody hell.

Duncan wandered past Sarah's door again, as if the proximity to his sudden nemesis would give him some sort of clue how to foil her. Instead, his notions of conquest and revenge melted inexplicably into fantasies with a much more, well . . . *tender* feel.

Julia smiled. There was nothing quite like waking to a man's touch.

She stretched her arms over her head to encourage the hand that was stroking her back to move to the front. She wiggled her bottom until she was nestled against something stiff and unyielding.

The magic hand stroked her backside, her legs, her thighs. She moved her hips, pressing her pelvis against his palm.

"Mmm, Lucien."

The heavenly stroking stopped. "What did you say?"

Julia's eyes popped open. She bit her bottom lip. "What?"

Robert, the groomsman, took her by the shoulders and rolled her onto her back. He looked into her face. "What did you just say?"

"Nothing."

"Yes, you did. You said a name."

She pulled away and rolled over. "I said, 'Let me sleep,' you fool. The sun hasn't yet risen."

Silence.

She held her breath.

At last Robert rose from her bed. "I had hoped to pleasure you once more, m'lady, before my duties in the stables take me away from you."

Julia sighed. Robert was a decent enough lover, but recently he'd become far too serious. She'd grown bored of his protestations of undying love.

Still, it never hurt to start one's day off right.

She looked at the young servant standing at the foot of the bed, breeches in hand, an eager, intense look on his face.

"Well, if you insist . . ." She opened her arms.

Lucien groaned. His head ached and he was cold, so cold. He opened his eyes.

What was he doing on the floor with his shirt half off and his breeches unbuttoned?

Lady Darby.

He sat bolt upright. Why did Lady Darby keep popping into his thoughts? He had the vague feeling he'd run into her the night before, but could not seem to remember where.

Something else plagued him as well. A sense of guilt. But why?

And then he remembered.

He'd gone to the Hog and Dove, drank barrels of ale, and quite indiscriminately trumpeted Sarah's life to the tavern. He had given such little thought to her sense of privacy he may as well have climbed on a pulpit in the middle of town and announced to all of Whitford her secrets.

He was no better than Lavery, was he?

Sarah was sure to feel an overwhelming sense of betrayal if she found out. Or rather, *when* she found out. He had every intention of confessing his misdeeds.

The gray light of morning fought its way through the window, illuminating his room just enough so that he did not need to light a candle. He quickly righted his clothing, washed his face, and went in search of some bread and tea to ease the queasiness in his stomach.

As he passed the library, he spied Lord Darby slouched in an armchair near the fireplace, rearranging the pieces on a marble chess set as if playing a game against himself.

"Are you winning?" Lucien asked from just inside the door. He noticed Lord Darby's boots were wet.

The man looked up, his gaze unfocused. "What?"

"I asked if you were winning."

"Oh. Actually, no." Lord Darby gestured to the chair across the table.

Lucien sat and glanced at his employer. There were dark circles beneath his eyes, and his skin looked sallow. "Are you feeling ill, sir?"

"*I* am in perfect health."

Lucien felt a stab of worry. "Is it Sarah, then? Or your mother?"

Lord Darby sighed. "No. They're both well. Everyone is fine. Pay no attention to my dismal mood."

Bright orange embers began to darken in the bed of the fireplace. The skeleton of a log shifted on the grate, and scraped against the back of the fireplace wall.

"Shall I add more wood?" Lucien asked.

"Only for yourself, if you wish. I was just about to leave." But Lord Darby remained in his seat, as if held mesmerized by the dying fire. Lucien knew all too well the power of fire to hold one hypnotized, motionless. Unable to react . . .

He turned away from the flames and studied the chessboard. One of the queens was missing.

"If I may be so bold, your lordship, you seem disturbed. Is something amiss?"

Lord Darby turned his chair and stretched his boots toward the warmth. "Indeed, there is something amiss when a man feels compelled to hide in the library to escape his wife. There is something amiss when his life has been one painful mistake on the heels of another." He might have been on the verge of weeping, but he straightened his back and slapped his knees. "Ah, well, Delacourte. We all must live with the guilt we have created for ourselves."

"Perhaps. But Lady Sarah taught me that there are ways to free ourselves from that guilt. Or at least use it to become a better person."

Lord Darby stood. "My sister is wise beyond her years. If only she could learn to embrace that wisdom for her own benefit. Good day, Delacourte."

Robert had finally gone, out Julia's window and down the ropes Sarah had attached to the wall of the house for her climbing vines. He'd left at sunrise—a risk they would be certain not to take again. He could have been seen by any number of curious eyes.

Julia seriously considered lying abed all day. What was the point of rising? There was absolutely nothing to do in this dreadful old pile of stones. At least, not yet.

Not until she was able to catch dear Lucien.

She'd come so close the night before. She'd almost had him undressed when he passed out on the floor. If only he hadn't been so drunk.

Then again, if he hadn't been so drunk, he might have taken issue with her nosing about his room while he was out.

It was just as well. She wanted him completely sober for their first encounter. The longer she waited, the sweeter it would be.

Julia shut her eyes, imagining what it would be like to feel Lucien's long, lean body stretched out beside hers. To see him panting over her, wild and unpredictable, like James had never been.

"Soon, Lucien," she whispered. "I promise."

Chapter 15

As soon as *Sarah opened her eyes, Lucien was in her* thoughts. She had looked for him all evening after her disastrous discussion with Duncan.

It amazed her how much she had come to rely on Lucien as a person she could trust with her thoughts and secrets.

She stretched and rolled over into a narrow patch of sunlight falling across the pillows. The fire had died overnight, and the room held a definite chill. She snuggled into the covers up to her chin, unwilling to brave the cold to ring for Rebecca just yet.

If not for her lesson this morning, she would be tempted to stay abed until dinner, at least. But just the thought of painting—painting!—propelled her from the warm cocoon of bedcovers and across the icy floor to the bell pull.

She quickly brushed and plaited her hair, and tied it in a roll at her neck. She then affixed a small blue cap to her head and with a row of small pins attached two matching silk veils, checking the mirror to be sure they obscured her image but not her vision. When she heard the knock, Sarah withdrew her key from the box and hurried to the door.

Rebecca entered bearing a tray of hot tea. Behind her came Thora, the young girl whose duty it was to clean the hearths and start the fires in the women's quarters. The girl carried a bucket blackened with soot, and kept her eyes glued to the floor as she scurried to the fireplace.

"Good morning, Lady Sarah." Rebecca placed the tea tray on a small table etched with flowers and poured a cupful of the steaming amber liquid.

Sarah sighed with delight. Was there anything better than hot tea on a cold morning? "Thank you, Becca. Good morning to you. And to you as well, Thora."

"Yes, mum," the girl mumbled, staying bent to her task.

Sarah thought it odd, as Thora always had a friendly word as she went about her work. Sarah turned to Rebecca, who whispered, "When she leaves . . ."

Sarah drank two full cups of tea before she felt warm enough to continue her toilette. The fire now blazed, and Thora collected her bucket and shovel. She gave a quick bob before bustling out the door without another word.

"Heavens! What has gotten into her?"

Rebecca shook her head. "More tea?"

"Not unless I want to float away on it. Now, tell me, Becca. Why is Thora so quiet this morning?"

Rebecca went to the wardrobe and pulled open the doors. "Thora sneaked out of the house last night."

"Oh?"

"She went to Whitford. To the Hog and Dove, y'know, because she fancies the innkeeper. Only God knows why. The man is twice her age, and he's got a mole on his chin the size of a—"

"Yes, yes. A mole. But what of Thora? Is the man giving her some sort of trouble? Doesn't he care for her?" Sarah slipped out of her dressing coat as she spoke.

Rebecca pulled a deep blue wool gown from the closet and smoothed it out on the bed. She put her hands on her hips. "Oh, he gave her trouble enough, but not the sort you think. He told her something that upset her. Something about Elmstone."

A small, cold seed of dread settled in Sarah's stomach. James paid the staff very well to assure that no news from the manor should reach the village. When he found out that details of their lives had been revealed, someone was certain to be let go.

Sarah sat on the bed beside the gown, clad only in a shift and stockings. "What exactly did the innkeeper tell Thora?"

Rebecca plopped down on the bed beside Sarah and sighed.

"Becca?"

"'Tis not true, lady. I just know it. 'Tis not true."

"What is not true?"

"That Mr. Delacourte has been spreading tales of Elmstone. Yet Thora's innkeeper swears it be true."

Sarah shook her head. "How could it possibly be true? I don't think Lucien has ventured past the walls of Elmstone since he has arrived."

Rebecca shrugged. "The innkeeper claims Mr. Delacourte was there yesterday afternoon. Says he answered a bushel of questions put to him by the rabble. Questions about you."

Sarah's tongue lay in her mouth like a piece of dry toast. The seed of dread grew, uncurling in her stomach like a nasty vine. Suddenly cold again, she wrapped her arms about her waist as Rebecca went to fetch an underskirt.

Could it be? Was Lucien at the Hog and Dove when he didn't show up for tea, nor for supper? She tried to picture him at the tavern, drinking ale and telling tales of the most private sort. She couldn't.

Rebecca helped her into her undergarments, and then

her gown. She fetched a needle and thread from the drawer of Sarah's dresser and loosely stitched a narrow bit of lace to the neckline of Sarah's bodice and on her sleeves. As usual, the hem of her skirt was free of decoration.

"If you ask me," said Rebecca as she worked, "Mr. Delacourte seems too much a gentleman to do such a thing."

Sarah forced herself to take several deep breaths until the creeping vine of dread withered and disappeared. She tucked her veils into her bodice, noting with some satisfaction that her hands did not tremble a bit.

"I don't believe a word of it," Rebecca said.

"Nor do I."

Lucien was her friend. Her confidant. Her tutor. There was simply no possibility he would betray her like that.

Was there?

"We missed your company at supper last evening." Sarah watched as Lucien prepared for their lesson, setting dabs of paints on the well-worn palette.

When he didn't reply, she said, "I missed you this morning as well, in the gardens. I suppose I've come to rely on your help."

Nothing.

"The hostas are turning brown. I picked some leaves to dry, but the cold took the last of the flowers in the night."

He had yet to look at her directly. Sarah took a deep breath, and tamped down the fear that once again threatened to unnerve her. Damn Thora and her mole-ridden innkeeper.

"Lucien, are you angry about something?"

He shook some cobalt powder into a bowl. "No."

"Then what is it? You've been scarce since our lesson yesterday, and I feel as if you are keeping something from me."

Lucien set the bowl carefully aside. "I suppose I wonder

why you stayed alone in the drawing room with Lavery yesterday. Why, after accepting my offer of protection, you purposefully put yourself in the position you said you wished to avoid."

So his silence was due to anger, not guilt, after all. Sarah sighed with relief.

Lucien was absolutely justified in his annoyance with her. Why *had* she stayed with Duncan after she had sworn to avoid him?

"I honestly don't know," she said. "Perhaps I needed an apology, or an explanation. Something that would allow me to put my ill feelings to rest. Unfortunately, Duncan is incapable of true regret. I realize now I feel little else but pity for him."

"Pity? Whatever for? For callously leaving you when you most needed him? For failing to right his wrongs until eight years later, after you have locked yourself away from the world because of him?"

Sarah's tightly strung nerves were plucked by his words. "You presume too much. I didn't choose to live a sequestered life because of Duncan alone. There were other people, other circumstances that drove me to do it."

She left her stool and walked to the window.

"Besides," she said, "Duncan wasn't the only person who forgot about me. Everyone did. Even the many so-called friends I had in Whitford forgot me. There was no point to leaving Elmstone when there wasn't a soul who cared if I did."

Lucien shook his head. "Not true, Sarah! The people of Whitford *do* care about you. They have spent many hours thinking of you and praying for you, and waiting for your return."

His words sent a shock through her. "What," she asked slowly, "would possess you to make up such lies?"

"I . . ." Lucien's voice dropped, "I was in Whitford yesterday, at the Hog and Dove. I spoke to them."

It took a moment for Sarah to fully realize what Lucien had said. What he had admitted.

It was true. Everything Thora had said was true.

Sarah shook her head. "You spoke to whom? What exactly did you say?"

"I told them the truth."

"The truth?" She could hear her voice rising, taking on a note of hysteria, but she was powerless to control it. "What *truth* did you tell them?"

Lucien spread his fingers out carefully on his knees and sat up straight. His jaw tensed, but his gaze did not waver.

Dear God, she thought. *Let this be a dream.*

"What truth, Lucien?"

"Everything. I told them everything they wanted to know."

"Ah." Sarah crossed her arms over her stomach, as if the action would hold her together. She feared her breakfast would soon escape her. "I was so foolish. Foolish enough to believe we were friends. You . . . you betrayed me."

"No!"

"Yes, you did." Sarah fought to breathe. The air beneath the veils was thick and hot. "You know how deeply I value my privacy, yet you used your position as my tutor and my friend to spread gossip."

"Not gossip. The *truth.*" Lucien raked his fingers through his hair, causing the curls to fan out wildly at his temples. He looked half mad. "Those people harbor nothing but concern for you. They miss you, Sarah."

A sob escaped her throat, and with it, the tears came too. "I'm sorry, but I simply cannot believe that. If they truly cared, they would have come to see me. But they forgot."

Lucien reached for her hand, but she pulled away.

"They did not forget," he said. "Many of them paid a visit in the beginning, but they . . . they could not get through the gates."

"What do you mean, they could not get through the gates?"

"They were turned away. Perhaps you were not well enough yet. I do not know. But they tried."

"No!"

"It is true. They believed you would come to them when you were able, but you never did. They feel as betrayed as you."

Sarah sobbed aloud, and again Lucien tried to take her hand. She slapped him away. How could he have been so callous? The vine of dread that once coiled in her stomach now gripped at her heart. Her veils caught her falling tears.

Lucien let her cry for a while. Then he stood and held out a hand. "Come with me."

"Where?"

"To Whitford."

Sarah's misery turned to panic. "I cannot!"

"Try. If you truly cannot do it, we will turn back."

"No. There is nothing there for me. I have no need to leave Elmstone. I—"

"Damn it, Sarah." Lucien stood before her, his arms outstretched, pleading. "You have no need to leave this place, ever? I do not believe that for a minute. I have witnessed your loneliness. I have seen how you sit at the windows, as if you wish you could break through them and run down the hill. Well, there is nothing at all to stop you." His voice dropped to a whisper. "Come with me."

He held out his hand, silently daring her to take it.

Emotions warred within her. In one blink, she imagined the villagers staring and pointing, whispering behind their hands about the Phantom of Whitford. Or worse yet, running from her in revulsion.

In the next blink, she envisioned walking through town, greeting old friends, hearing the sounds of people in the marketplace. How much had things changed since she last was there? Had her memory of the place remained true?

She took Lucien's hand.

Chapter 16

Before Sarah realized what was happening, she was through the drawing room door, across the great hall, and out onto the drive. The autumn phlox growing around the drive blurred to white as she and Lucien ran, giving the illusion of running through clouds. Cold air stung her bare forearms and chilled her cheeks beneath the veils, but she knew if she turned back for her wrap, she would never come this far again.

She seemed to float above the ground, Lucien pulling her along like a kite through the gates, out into the countryside and down the hill. She looked over her shoulder at Elmstone. She had not seen it from beyond the gates in eight years. It looked cold and distant, like a fairytale castle.

Sarah was vaguely aware of Lucien speaking to her and she answered him, although she had no real idea what she was saying. The rhythm of her heart pounded madly in her ears. As they descended the hill, her feet required no instruction. It was as if they remembered each overturned stone and gully on the path.

In no time they had reached the bottom of the hill and stopped at the edge of Whitford. The sights and sounds and smells reached out to shake her from her dream state. Like grass in the moments before a storm, she trembled.

Lucien took her gently by the shoulders and turned her to face him. "Do you wish to turn back?"

Sarah took a deep breath. "No."

He kept hold of her hand and tucked it beneath his arm. "Shall we walk to the square?"

She nodded.

Thus far, not a soul had taken notice of her. She and Lucien stood off to the side of a small, but busy, thoroughfare. People hurried about, carrying baskets and pushing carts—proof that life had indeed continued without her. She and Lucien drifted into the current of people, letting it carry them to the marketplace.

Sarah recognized no one. She could hardly comprehend what everyone was doing, so lost was she in her emotions and memories. It was too much. She pulled Lucien's arm to stop him from leading her into the square. Before they could turn back, however, Sarah's worst fear was realized.

She was noticed.

A maid struggling with a basket of wheat came to a dead stop in the middle of the street, causing several people behind her to bump into a pile. They followed the maid's startled gaze directly to Sarah.

An invisible rope of tension lassoed, one by one, each person in the square, drawing them to a standstill. Soon there were dozens of pairs of eyes trained upon her.

Sarah felt like the only fox at a hunt, backed against the rocks with the dogs creeping ever closer. She tried to drag Lucien back toward the hill. He would not budge.

"Please," she whispered.

He shook his head. "It is too late."

Sarah's legs wobbled, but Lucien held her upright until

she had no other choice but to stand straight and still while the whole of the village ogled her.

Just when she believed the humiliation would cause her to expire on the spot, she recognized one of the spectators. It was Mrs. Putney, the baker's wife!

And Mr. Dunkling the cobbler.

And there, beside the hog pen . . . could that be Lacey Seton? She was just a child the last time Sarah had seen her.

And there! Old Jackie, toting his cart of sorry-looking apples, which others bought out of pity, for he had no one on this earth to call family. It was rumored he never smiled, and yet he was smiling at her.

In fact, they all were smiling—every one of them. Some of them were crying, as well. They looked upon her not with fear or morbid curiosity, but with genuine interest and concern.

At long last, someone dared approach. Mrs. Addy, the rector's wife, wormed through the gaping mass. Sarah used to help the woman with her garden, and many a day would sit beneath the shade of a tree sipping tea and discussing the persnickety nature of roses.

"Lady Sarah?" Mrs. Addy's question was soft, hopeful.

"Yes."

The woman rushed forward, heedless of Sarah's startled twitch. Lucien let go of Sarah's hand, relinquishing her to Mrs. Addy's arms.

In turn, several others stepped forward, some nodding or bowing, some enclosing her in familiar embraces. The villagers swept Sarah through the square on a tide of affection. It seemed as if everyone wanted to touch her.

Not one soul attempted to peer beneath her veils, nor did they voice the questions she so feared. They merely seemed happy to have her amongst them once again.

Sarah sensed Lucien's presence beside her throughout.

She appreciated it, though she knew his protection was not necessary.

In some ways, it was as if she never had been gone. Once again she was a girl, chatting with everyone she met, catching up with old friends.

She and Lucien trod every inch of the town as Sarah soaked up all the changes, redrawing the map of Whitford in her mind. She listened to problems, dispensed sympathy, and measured out advice, and each small interaction filled her with an indescribable joy.

"Thank you," she said to Lucien, again and again, sometimes aloud and sometimes by her touch.

He just smiled and gathered her close to his side as he escorted her through the streets. He seemed to understand that some invisible chain had finally been broken.

"But I don't want to go home," Sarah said. *"It seems like a* prison to me now, after this taste of freedom."

"Elmstone cannot hold you anymore," he said. "You are free now, to come and go as you wish."

"I know. But I need just a few moments longer."

Lucien allowed her to say her goodbyes as he commandeered a wagon and its driver, anticipating Sarah's exhaustion. She had already spent hours reacquainting herself with Whitford, from the shops and streets to the people— so many people—who wanted to see her, touch her, speak to her. But it was time to go now. It was nearly dark and much too cold for the gown she wore.

"Come now, climb in," he said, handing her up into the back of the wagon. "We've got to get you home."

"Oh, Lucien, thank you. Thank you for taking such good care of me."

Sarah drifted off against his side as they bumped up the hill to Elmstone.

Lucien smiled, looking back over the day with a sense of immense satisfaction.

At first Sarah had been skittish, like a colt new to the saddle. But when she realized the respect of the villagers was genuine, she welcomed their attentions with grace and sincerity.

Lucien had a sense of what she was experiencing. The lancing of such emotional wounds allowed the bitterness to drain out. Sarah had taken the first step to healing, just as he had done when he met Anne. She was allowing herself to feel again. To care.

Sarah had taught him how, and he had returned the favor.

A sudden incline in the road caused Sarah to slide toward the open back of the wagon. Lucien held her gently, shifting her weight until she nestled in the V of his legs, her back pressed against his chest as she slept. When he wrapped his arms around her to keep her from falling, he could feel the gentle rhythm of her breathing and the damp chill of the night on her bare forearms.

Lucien removed his coat and tossed it over Sarah's shoulders, disturbing the veils tucked into her bodice. He realized how easy it would be for him to lift them, to see what she deemed too horrible for anyone's sight but her own. The temptation was so great he actually raised a hand to do it.

Then he stopped. He could not betray her trust again. Sarah had forgiven him his "gossiping" with the villagers, but he knew she would never forgive him that. He leaned back against a wooden slat.

"Gettin' sore back there?" the driver shouted over his shoulder.

"No, we are fine," Lucien answered.

"Good. Won't be long now." The driver went back to his whistling.

With the wagon's bumping, the hem of Sarah's gown

rode up on her leg, exposing a well-turned calf clad in sheer white stockings. The sight of it was infinitely more provocative than Lady Darby's calculated flirtations. Lucien groaned softly, and Sarah stirred in his arms.

With some effort, he pushed all thoughts of her hem—and what lay above it—from his mind.

Sarah was his pupil. He should not have allowed his involvement in her affairs to run as deep as it had already, but that could not be undone. He could, however, keep it from going any further.

He must. For leaving her would be difficult enough once he was discovered to be a fraud. A painting instructor unable to paint . . . There could be no doubt Lord Darby would send him on his way the moment his deception was revealed.

He pushed that thought from his mind, choosing instead to focus on the happiness of this day.

The wheels of the wagon chattered on the stone drive, causing Sarah to stir.

"It is time you were awake." Lucien nudged her from the crook of his embrace. "We are almost to the gate."

Sarah stretched, showing no outward surprise to be seated between his legs, as if it were the most natural thing in the world. "I imagine we've been missed by now. They're probably waiting for us at the gate."

"Perhaps we should lessen the shock by sitting a bit farther apart. For propriety's sake, of course."

Sarah laughed and moved away from him. She stretched her legs out in front of her in the wagon, picking the hay from her skirt. Her movements, though always graceful, seemed lighter and freer than they ever had before.

The wagon rumbled to a halt at the gate. The driver leaped from his seat and tugged the bell rope. Arthur appeared within moments.

"What do you want?" he asked the driver, in a most unpleasant tone.

Lucien jumped down from the wagon and stepped into the manservant's view. "Good evening."

"Mr. Delacourte. What a peculiar mode of travel you have chosen. You *do* know we have carriages at your disposal. Or perhaps you feel more at ease in a hay wagon?"

"Good eve, Arthur." Sarah rounded the wagon.

The servant froze in mid-smirk. His jaw began to work, but no sound issued forth.

"Close your mouth, Arthur. It's only me."

"Yes, Lady Sarah." Arthur stood behind the gate, no doubt trying to behave as if admitting Lady Sarah into Elmstone was a daily occurrence. He failed miserably.

"Open the gate, Arthur." Sarah's amusement was tempered with a hint of annoyance. "In the future, I trust you shall be more cordial to visitors."

"Of course, Lady Sarah. Begging your pardon."

Ashen-faced, Arthur fumbled with the key, stepping aside when the iron gate swung open.

Lady Sarah clasped the wagon-driver's hands in hers. "Thank you, Peter." The gratitude in her voice was not just for the ride to Elmstone, Lucien knew, but words to be taken back to all the villagers for their warm welcome.

"Will we be seeing you again, Lady Sarah?" Peter asked.

"Most assuredly." Sarah hooked Lucien's elbow and they strolled through the gate. "I cannot wait to tell Mother where we've been."

Arthur hurried past them to open the great doors of the house. The servant disappeared immediately, no doubt in search of Lord Darby.

They discovered Merri in the drawing room, chastising the beleaguered Miss Witherspoon for misplacing her favorite book.

Sarah interrupted the diatribe. "Miss Witherspoon, would you be so kind as to have tea brought round?"

With a grateful look, Miss Witherspoon hurried off.

"How could you dismiss that thoughtless girl while I was dressing her down?"

"Actually, I allowed Miss Witherspoon to escape for your own good. You know you shouldn't become over-wrought. It's bad for your stomach."

Merri plopped into a chair. "Why concern yourself with my well-being? Heavens, I hardly catch a glimpse of you anymore. I looked everywhere for you this afternoon. Where the devil did you get to?"

"Whitford," Lord Darby said as he entered the drawing room, a look of reproach on his face.

"What!" said Merri.

"She went to Whitford," Lord Darby repeated. "Sarah, did anyone accost you? Did they harass you in any way?"

"Harass me? Of course not, James. Besides, Lucien was with me every step of the way."

The dowager thumped a hand to her breast. "Whitford! I do not believe it!"

"My word," Sarah said with a giddy laugh, "You would think King George just marched over the threshold, the way you are behaving, Mother."

"King George who? This is a thousand times more exciting." The dowager swiped at her eyes with the back of her hand.

"Are those actual tears?" Sarah said. "Will miracles never cease?"

"Apparently not." The dowager took Sarah's hands in hers. "You did it, by God. You did it." Her voice was thick with emotion.

Reluctant to bear witness to this private family moment, Lucien took his leave. His heart felt lighter than it had in ages, until he was skewered by Lord Darby's eyes.

Sarah tied a colorful silk kerchief over her shoulders, smoothing the fabric into place.

As was their custom on Sundays, the residents of Elmstone planned to meet after chapel in the drawing room for
a few hours of whist or cribbage. Sarah was not particularly good at either, but she enjoyed the time with her family, and of course Lucien.

She unlocked her door with the beribboned key to exit
her quarters. While locking it from the outside, a shadow
loomed over the keyhole. She looked up, surprised to see
Duncan behind her, his lips twisted into a crooked smile.

Sarah's heart knocked against her ribcage.

"Duncan, you scared me near to death. What are you
doing lurking up here in the hallway?"

The whites of his eyes gleamed, even in the dim, win-
dowless hall. "I must speak with you."

"It will have to keep," she said. "Mother and James are
waiting in the drawing room."

Duncan's smile changed to a sneer. "And Delacourte as
well?"

"No doubt. Julia will likely make an appearance, too.
We're playing whist. Will you join us?"

Duncan leaned over, placing his hand on the wall beside
her shoulder. His breath reeked of brandy and tobacco.
Sarah could see the dark stubble of whiskers on his jaw.

"I don't care to play games with your lover."

Sarah's heart renewed its pounding. "My lover?"

"Delacourte," he spat.

"You are ridiculous." She slipped beneath his arm and
started down the hall. Duncan lumbered close enough behind to step on the hem of her skirt if he so chose. Sarah
kept a moderate pace, sensing that if she let her discomfort
be known, he would attack.

"Everyone knows Delacourte is your lover."

"Please, Duncan. I have no time for your cockeyed ramblings."

He laughed, but it sounded more like the snarl of a wolf
on the trail of something small and weak.

She refused to be Duncan's prey.

Near the top of the stairs in the rotunda she whirled to face him. Duncan lost his balance and would have careened into her if she hadn't stepped to the side. Instead, he stumbled against the rail.

"Don't provoke me, Duncan. I won't tolerate it. Lucien is my tutor and my friend. He is not my lover, but if he were, it would be none of your concern."

"It certainly would be, since you're going to be mine."

Sarah blinked. "Is it the drink that has made you so thickheaded? Or were you the same when we were betrothed, but I was too enamored of you to notice it?"

"Ah! You admit you loved me."

"I did love you, I don't deny it. But there is little danger of that now, I assure you."

Duncan slumped against the rail, rubbing his jaw as if she had punched him. "Why, Sarah? Why won't you give me another chance?"

The ice surrounding Sarah's heart thawed just enough to allow her to be honest with him. "I care for you, Duncan, but you're losing yourself to the drink. I hardly recognize you anymore. I fear you'll meet an early grave if you don't change your ways."

A hoarse, rhythmic, sucking sound emanated from Duncan's throat, and Sarah realized he was sobbing.

"I need you, Sarah," he whispered. "Please help me."

"I cannot. You must help yourself."

Duncan leaned heavily against her, his tears soaking her shoulder. Sarah propped him up as well as she could until his sobbing ceased. She was sorry for his pain, but it was of his own making. The drinking, the lies, the women—it had all caught up with him.

But who was she to judge him? Everyone had a cross to bear. So when he reached for her, when he wrapped her in his arms, she didn't pull away.

She didn't have the heart to rub salt in his wounds.

* * *

"Where is Sarah?" Lucien paced the length of the drawing room, still in a state of near euphoria from their adventure in Whitford the previous afternoon. It had spurred him to take a risk of his own.

Unable to sleep the night before, he had crept down to the drawing room to make another go at the canvas, hoping Sarah's breakthrough would somehow give him the strength to paint again.

It did not, but even his failure at the easel could not erase the happiness he felt over Sarah's triumph.

He knew the dowager felt the same, but he could not understand Lord Darby's obvious disapproval. For a man who purportedly wanted Sarah to be happy, her joy over leaving Elmstone did not sit well with him. He had yet to show up for their celebration.

"Will you please go and see what's keeping my daughter?" The dowager called to him from the card table in the corner. She wore a secretive little smile, which was almost obscured by the flounces of lace piled one on top of the other from her shoulders to her neck. Her head looked like a dried apple lying atop a snowdrift.

"Where is Lord Darby?" he asked.

She shrugged, the mountain of lace rising to bury the point of her chin. "One never knows. He promised to be here, so I suppose he'll be along shortly."

"Then perhaps I should go find Sarah."

"Please do, before you wear a hole in our best carpet."

For dignity's sake, Lucien kept himself from running out of the drawing room. He was a grown man, after all, not an excitable child. But he felt like a child, bursting with the prospect of new things to come.

He pushed the worry out of his mind about his inability to paint. Now that Sarah had broken the barriers of Elmstone, the world was theirs to explore. He imagined taking long walks with her through the countryside, or spending hours at the market. He even harbored the hope that one day they would travel to Paris and Rome and Vienna together, to study the works of the Great Masters.

Lost in his daydreams, Lucien ambled into the hall just as the clock chimed. He put a hand on the banister and was about to climb the stairs of the rotunda when he saw them.

Sarah and Duncan, locked in an embrace.

Kissing.

Lucien turned on his heel and left without a word.

Chapter 17

Sarah finally found Lucien in the nursery with Anne. They had their heads together, laughing over a drawing Anne had scratched out with a piece of charcoal.

Lucien spotted Sarah first. He gave her a dark look before turning his attention back to Anne's drawing.

Why would he act so, after the experience they had shared just yesterday?

Sarah debated leaving Lucien and Anne to their game, but thought better of it. Anne was her niece and Elmstone was her home. She had every right to be there.

"What are the two of you conspiring over?"

Anne's head snapped up. Her startled expression quickly turned to a smile when she saw who was at the door. "Aunt Sarah, hurry! We've drawn the most wicked picture of Miss Elsey. Isn't it wonderful? Look. She's covered with warts."

Sarah bit the inside of her cheek to keep from laughing. "Dearest, you really mustn't do such things. Miss Elsey would be heartbroken if she knew you depicted her so callously."

Anne resumed her work. "Good. I hate her."

"Anne!"

Anne shrugged. "Well, I dislike her very much. She never lets me outside this awful room. All day I must work on my needlepoint, or read boring verses, or watch her sleep. She snores!"

Sarah stroked her niece's hair. "We must always try to forgive people their transgressions. It's the mark of civil beings."

"I suppose," Anne said. "But forgiving Miss Elsey isn't as much fun as drawing wicked pictures of her."

Sarah stifled another laugh and looked at Lucien. He, too, seemed to be struggling to keep from laughing. For a moment everything seemed right again—until he rose and went to the window, turning his back to the both of them.

"Could a fresh tart lure you away from your masterpiece?" Sarah asked her niece. "Cook just put them out to cool. I'm certain she would turn the other way long enough for you to steal one."

"Will you wait for me to return, Lucien?" Anne asked.

"Only if you promise to steal a tart for me, as well."

"Of course." Anne flashed them an impish smile before bounding from the nursery.

Sarah perched on the edge of a miniature chair, picking up the drawing of Miss Elsey.

"I rather like the large growth on her nose," she said.

Lucien was silent.

"The hair growing from her chin is quite accurate."

"The detail is impeccable," Lucien said. "Perhaps I have taken on the wrong student."

Sarah placed Anne's drawing back on the little table and folded her hands in her lap. "Do you regret coming to Elmstone House?" she asked, though she really did not care to hear the answer.

Lucien sighed. "No. I do not regret coming here. It has been a rewarding position in many ways."

"But you're not happy with me right now."

Lucien still stood at the window, looking out over the gardens. "Were you sincere when you told Anne we must forgive everyone their transgressions?"

"Yes. I believe it's the only way we can be happy with ourselves. Why?"

"There is something I must tell you. I have been such a coward. I . . ."

Sarah rose and moved to his side. She was so close she could smell the morning frost that had melted and dried on his boots. "What is it?"

Lucien seemed to search for her beneath the veils. Light shone through the window and across the planes of his face, the violet rays of sunset deepening the hue of his eyes.

"Lucien?"

The guilt in his eyes disappeared, replaced by something fierce. Something that could be dangerous. The sun's fiery light tangled in Lucien's hair, setting his golden curls ablaze. Sarah's breathing quickened with a mixture of fear and anticipation.

He hooked an arm about her waist, dragging her tight against him.

"Oh." Her veils fluttered softly with the syllable.

She closed her eyes. The moist warmth of Lucien's breath penetrated the thin gauze of her veils, caressing her cheek. His lips were a hairsbreadth from hers. This mere promise of a kiss was so much more sensuous than the unwelcome assault Duncan had launched earlier, on the stairs.

She wondered briefly if Lucien could see through the veils, but when she opened her eyes, the room was bathed in shadows. The sun had disappeared behind a distant hill leaving nothing but a misty glow, as if the countryside had absorbed the light and now cast it back in faint imitation of the sun's brilliance.

Lucien stood completely still, as if afraid to break a spell. There was an unasked question in his hesitation. Sarah answered it with a tilt of her head.

She felt only gentle pressure at first, before the heat of Lucien's lips flooded through the silken wall dividing them. The caress of his tongue against her lower lip sent a jolt of desire surging through her that pooled between her thighs, in her abdomen, in her tightening nipples. The tip of Sarah's tongue touched Lucien's through the veils.

His fingers traced her backbone, coming to rest at the base of her neck. His forearm pressed against her back, driving her breasts tight against his chest. Could he feel her heart beating? Surely it would plunge through her chest at any moment.

She twisted her fingers into his hair, tightening her grip as a shock of heat thundered through her veins. She whimpered against his mouth, igniting a firestorm. The veils were drawn taught, forming an impenetrable barrier between them that was at once frustrating and erotic.

Lucien took her bottom lip in his teeth, and she prayed the thin fabric would give way against the passion of the kiss.

"Sarah, please. The veils. I—"

"Aunt Sarah!"

The sound of Anne's footsteps wrenched them from the embrace.

Sarah's veils hid her embarrassment, but Lucien wasn't so fortunate.

"Whatever is the matter with you?" Anne asked him. "Your cheeks are red." Luckily, she did not wait for an answer before chattering on. "Look! I remembered the both of you. Cook turned her head for a moment, and I managed to spirit away two of them. Berry and mincemeat." She reached carefully into the bib of her pinafore and withdrew two flattened pastries.

Lucien cleared his throat. "Thank you, Anne. We will enjoy them immensely knowing you pinched them from the kitchen with your very own hands."

"Shall we?" Sarah's voice was shaky. She motioned to the table and they squeezed into the miniature seats. Sarah split her tart with Anne.

The three of them sat in silence as they enjoyed the treats. By the time they finished, the room was all but dark.

"I hope this will not spoil our appetite for supper," Sarah said, mostly to show a good example for Anne.

"Aunt Sarah," her niece moaned. "You always tell me life should be adventurous."

Sarah laughed. "I suppose eating tarts before supper could be considered adventurous. What do you think, Lucien?"

"Absolutely. But not nearly as adventurous as what your aunt did yesterday."

"What did she do? Did she play a nasty trick on Mother?" Anne looked hopeful.

"No, I am afraid not. But she did go to Whitford."

Anne gasped. "Aunt Sarah! You left Elmstone?"

"I did."

The events of the previous day rushed over her again, like ocean waves against a cliff—wild, frightening, and exhilarating. She had left Elmstone!

The urge to kiss Lucien again, right then and there, nearly overwhelmed her. Sarah took a deep breath.

Anne gave her an excited hug. "May I go with you next time?"

"We shall see," Sarah said, as she swept the crumbs from the table. "Now I think Lucien and I ought to go. I'm sure Miss Elsey will be back any minute, and we don't want to be caught doing anything remotely adventuresome."

"Like kissing?" Anne laughed as she ran from the nursery, her picture of Miss Elsey in hand.

It wasn't until much later that Sarah thought to wonder what confession Lucien had been about to make.

Even Julia's haughty demeanor couldn't sour Sarah's mood that night. The last two days had been incredible, and Sarah was having a difficult time deciding what was the most thrilling—her journey to the village or Lucien's kiss.

"Good evening, dear Julia. I trust you had a pleasant day?" Sarah addressed her congenially as Julia took her customary seat to the right of James at the card table.

"James, I believe your sister has struck her head on something. Call for the physician at once."

Sarah laughed. "Must a bit of pleasantness that passes between us be put down to a head injury? How sad!"

"What the devil has gotten into you? And what's all this about?" Julia indicated a table covered with trays of sweetmeats, fruit, marzipan, and an open bottle of champagne.

"We intend to have a celebration," James said, without enthusiasm. "We received a remarkable bit of news."

Julia raised one eyebrow. "Let me guess. The wheat fields survived the frost."

"The crops are doing well, as a matter of fact. However, there's much more exciting news." James raised a glass of champagne and tipped it toward Sarah. Duncan's gaze followed the arc of the glass. "My sister went down to Whitford."

Merri's eyes gleamed as James poured her a glass of champagne. "Close your mouth, Julia, before that sharp tongue of yours slips out and causes damage to your lips."

Duncan's gaze moved from the champagne glass to Sarah. He gave her a tentative smile. Lucien's lips tightened.

"Please. Let's not make more of this than is warranted," Sarah said.

"In my opinion," Merri said, "what is warranted is a

grand celebration, not this miniature affair. How about a feast of some sort? Or a ball? Or perhaps a—"

"Good heavens," Sarah groaned.

Merri sighed. "Fine. I suppose I must settle for these meager salutations. Lucien, would you care to do the honors?"

"May I, Lord Darby?"

"If you feel so compelled."

Lucien raised his glass. They all followed suit, including Julia, who still seemed stunned by the news, and Duncan, who seemed inordinately pleased.

As Sarah turned to face Lucien, the memory of the kiss they had shared in the nursery played in her mind, pushing the words of his salute to the outer reaches of her consciousness. She heard vaguely his testament to her courage, her fortitude, and her spirit, all the while imagining the feel of his lips against hers, the heat of his breath, the way he held her. She knew Lucien had just been swept up in the heightened emotions of the moment. That their kiss was an experience that would not, nor could not, be repeated. But it had been wonderful just the same.

Lucien apparently concluded his speech, for Merri shouted, "Hear, hear," and they all raised their glasses again. Sarah drew her glass beneath the veils and took a sip of the champagne. It tingled sweetly on her tongue. She couldn't remember champagne ever tasting quite so good, and she savored it until she realized Duncan was staring at her.

"What is it, Duncan?"

He actually blushed. "Nothing. I just . . . Well, I'm glad for you."

Glad?

"Thank you," Sarah said. She noticed he had not touched his glass of champagne.

What could he be up to now?

Chapter 18

"*Your abilities as a thespian have certainly improved in re-*cent days." Julia bit into a pear, then dabbed the corners of her mouth with a fine linen napkin. She and Duncan were the only two taking tea in the salon.

Sarah and Lucien were embroiled in another "lesson," and wouldn't allow anyone else in the drawing room. Only God knew where James had gone, and Merri was, mercifully, taking her tea upstairs in her rooms.

"Whatever do you mean?" Duncan buttered a scone and bit into it with relish. For once he actually was drinking tea, instead of brandy or rum or whatever other spirit moved him at the moment.

"Come to think of it, I haven't seen you take anything more potent than a cup of chocolate in days."

"You noticed! Do you suppose Sarah has, as well?"

"Has what?"

"Noticed that I haven't taken spirits."

"Ah!" Julia grinned. "I understand. You've been tippling in seclusion, so as to convince Sarah you've changed."

Duncan looked injured. "I've done no such thing. I haven't had a drop."

"It's an excellent strategy, I must admit. After all, you shall have many days and months to drink whenever, and whatever, you wish—after you've properly seduced Sarah. Lord knows you may have to remain pickled just to tolerate the Phantom's presence."

"By the Phantom, I assume you are referring to Sarah?"

"Who else?"

Duncan frowned. "I wish you wouldn't speak of her in such a manner."

Julia rolled her eyes. "Really, Duncan. Leave off with the charade. It's just the two of us here." .

"There is no charade, cousin. I have a great deal of respect for Lady Sarah. I don't appreciate you maligning her name."

Julia placed her teacup in the saucer with exaggerated care. "Dare I believe my ears? *Respect?* Is there no one who can escape the little mouse's spell? My God, Duncan, come to. The woman is a hermit!"

"Not anymore. She went to Whitford."

"Huzzah," Julia said flatly. "Why, she may as well have taken a ship to America for the way everyone exclaims over it."

Duncan shrugged. "I happen to believe Lady Sarah has a great deal of courage."

"You have lost your mind."

Duncan chewed his scone and considered her. He swallowed deliberately and said, "When Sarah and I were betrothed, I overlooked a great deal about her character. Perhaps I wasn't ready to see it then. But I've grown to admire her greatly this past fortnight."

"Surely you jest."

"I only pray she'll agree, for a second time, to become my wife." Duncan finished off his tea, dabbed his lips with a napkin, and stood. "Good afternoon, cousin."

Julia watched him exit the drawing room, his back straight, a spring in his typically morose gait.

Was Duncan actually in love with Sarah?

It simply couldn't be possible. Duncan craved excess. He reveled in social dalliances and illicit affairs. He lived for conflict. True, a few weeks at Elmstone could turn almost anyone into a bore, but she never would have believed it could happen to Duncan.

He wasn't the only one headed for Bedlam. The entire house had gone mad. The entire village, for that matter.

Julia had paid a rare visit to the apothecary yesterday in search of some red pomatum, and every word on people's lips seemed to be about Sarah.

Oh, how wonderful Lady Sarah is. How sweet. How courageous and kind and generous. Julia pasted a smile on her face and gritted her teeth as villager after dirty, odiferous villager accosted her, asking her to deliver some message to Lady Sarah, or to wish her well, or some other such drivel.

Julia wanted to retch.

She vowed never to go to Whitford again without a decent disguise, or at least a servant who would discourage any conversation between a countess and a peasant. Why, it was indecent the way they had treated her, with no regard for rank or title.

Julia picked a currant from a scone. This was all Sarah's doing. Members of the peerage just did not mix with commoners the way she did. She'd set a bad precedent, and the rest of them were paying for it dearly.

She threw the scone back onto the silver tray. If something, anything interesting didn't occur soon, she was going to be as fat as one of the ever-present cows cluttering the vistas of Elmstone's every window.

* * *

It was almost as if a magic faerie had heard Julia's wish.

That very afternoon James had returned home to announce that he was needed in London. Something about a wheat levy.

"When will we leave?" Julia asked, unable to contain her excitement. "I have so much to do! Oh, James, this is so exciting. Will we attend the theater? Or the opera? It isn't quite the Season, but no matter. I'm certain there will be some sort of entertainment. I shall need a new ball gown, and a riding habit. We must write to the draper immediately. I—"

"*You* will be staying right here in Whitford," James interrupted. "I will be going to London alone."

Her frenzied pacing came to an abrupt halt. "Beg your pardon?"

"I said you will not be joining me. I have important business to attend to. This isn't a pleasure jaunt. I'll be returning as soon as possible. It's harvest time, and I'm needed here." He removed his gloves in an infuriatingly slow manner.

"Poppycock. I'm going, James. If I must ride on the box with the driver, I am going. I refuse to be imprisoned in this stone monstrosity one moment longer. Winter will soon be here, and then we shall be trapped for months in this godforsaken bog, but I *will* have a new winter wardrobe in which to die of boredom."

James sighed. "Julia, be reasonable—"

"No, James. I will not be reasonable. In fact, I will be the most *un*reasonable female you have ever known. If you don't take me to London, I'll go myself. And I'll tell anyone who will listen how my husband keeps me prisoner in his home because his sister is—"

"Stop!" James raked his fingers through his hair. "Very well, come if you must. But I warn you, it will be a short trip."

Julia unleashed her most radiant smile. "Oh, James, this will be wonderful! Trust me. We shall have all sorts of fun. We shall attend every dance, every dinner we can possibly manage. It will be grand."

And she would visit a certain shop which sold naughty unmentionables and featured an unusual selection of scents and perfumes. Lucien would be unable to resist her.

Julia hummed to herself, planning her shopping excursions to Cheapside and afternoons at Vauxhall, when James doused the fires of her ebullience.

"Julia, my dear," he said, "don't forget to instruct Miss Elsey to pack a trunk for herself and Anne."

As it turned out, Anne wouldn't be the only annoyance to accompany them to London. Merri decided it was imperative she visit a friend in London. Duncan, too, insisted on making the trip for reasons he refused to divulge.

Julia never would have objected to Duncan's presence had he not been acting so virtuous as of late. He'd always proven to be excellent company in the past, but Julia could not abide his incessant and annoying smile. A week in London spent in the company of a grinning idiot, an ill-humored old woman, a husband with dirt beneath his fingernails, and a six-year-old child. What fun.

Julia was in the nastiest of moods when the procession of four carriages, one used solely to carry their baggage and one filled with servants, rumbled away from Elmstone in the direction of London, just as the sun rose over the horizon.

Duncan rode in the same coach as she, sitting across from her and gazing out the window at the sunrise.

"Lovely morning, isn't it? I don't think I have ever truly appreciated the sunrise."

"Perhaps because it always arrived along with a headache." She gave an irritated pull on the lap blanket they shared.

Duncan turned his attention to her at last. "You're a ray of sunshine today. What has you so peevish?"

"Peevish? Heavens be, Duncan. Why in the name of the Devil did you insist on accompanying us on this journey? You should have remained at Elmstone to keep an eye on Sarah and Delacourte. You should be using this opportunity to secure a courtship with her, without the old dowager foiling your every effort."

Duncan smiled in his new, insipid manner. "The dowager has been quite civil as of late. I believe she's coming round. And I happen to have an excellent reason for making this journey to London. I'm withdrawing from the courts my suit against Celeste and her family. I'll agree the marriage was illegal. I'll be free."

Julia rolled her eyes. "And what will you use for money in London? Or have you forgotten that a lack of funds is the sole reason you came to Elmstone in the first place?"

"Truthfully, cousin, I had hoped to appeal to your generous nature . . ."

"Absolutely out of the question."

"Come now, Julia. I shall repay you the moment Sarah and I are married. It's simply a matter of time, I assure you."

Julia yanked at the lap rug again. "What makes you so certain you'll win her hand after all?"

Duncan leaned his head against the back of the seat and smiled. "I can hear it in her voice. She's begun to care for me again, Julia. Or perhaps she has never stopped caring for me. And the truth is, I care for her, too. I would never have thought it possible, but I do."

Julia curled up against the side of the coach and closed her eyes. "I am so happy for you. Wake me when we arrive in London."

* * *

"What are you thinking about?"

James searched the woods for a glimpse of the tiny cottage's roof as the carriage rumbled down the hill. "Pardon?"

Merri squinted at him. "What are you thinking about at this moment? You seem lost, and I fear I cannot reach you where you are."

James cuddled a sleeping Anne closer to him and pulled a blanket up to her neck. He cherished these moments, when she was warm and sleepy and smelled of cinnamon and talc. She was so much the opposite of her mother, so innocent and trusting. He wished he knew how to be close to her when she was awake, but he didn't. He simply didn't know how to talk to little girls.

James spoke to his mother in hushed tones. "I was thinking about the harvest. How much work we will have—"

"Bullfeathers," Merri whispered. "You are no farmer, my son. You're a caring lord to your tenants, but I've never known you to have such an abiding interest in every small detail of the land as you have these past months. Nor do I believe you would travel the whole way to London to debate a wheat levy. You may have the others convinced, but I know you too well. There's something else afoot."

"Your limber imagination is getting the best of you again, I'm afraid. I desired a respite in London."

"Hmmpf. You illustrate my point beautifully. You cannot abide London. Why are we making this journey, James?" His mother's eyes seemed to burn a hole in his conscience.

He focused his gaze on the top of Anne's head. She'd removed her hat as soon as they climbed into the carriage. The part in her hair, which was not quite the shade of brown as his, was perfectly straight, revealing the delicate white of her scalp. Anne could never stand to wear hats. James suspected it was because Julia wanted her to.

He didn't have to look up to know his mother still stared at him. James ached to share his burden.

He sighed. "It's true. I have other motives for this journey.

I have an appointment to see a physician in London."

Merri leaned forward, her gaze anxious. "Are you ill? What's the matter?"

James reached for her hand and gave it a small pat. "That's what I hope to discover. Please, mention this to no one, especially Julia."

Merri sat back in her seat. "If it would be possible to avoid all conversation with her for the rest of my days, you can be assured I would."

Chapter 19

The house was blessedly silent.

With her family and many of the servants gone to London, Sarah luxuriated in bed an extra hour before summoning Rebecca. The maid was in a pleasant temper, whistling a happy ditty as she arranged a tray of dried fruits, fresh bread, honey, and tea on a table beside the window.

"What has you so happy this morning?" Sarah asked.

"William's coming. His apprentice ran ahead and left word. He'll be here in two days."

"Oh, Becca! I'm so happy for you. Of course, you shall have a few days off. As long as he's in town."

"But who'll serve you? There are precious few servants left behind."

"Not to worry. I'll make do somehow. You just enjoy some time with your husband."

"Oh, I cannot wait to see him. I expect my clothing and I will part company for a few days, at least."

"Becca!" Sarah's cheeks burned.

The maid laughed. She went to the chifforobe and

retrieved a gown. "I hope I get with child," she said. "I've always wanted a child."

"Me, too," Sarah said quietly.

Rebecca stood with her hands on her hips, staring. She took the gray gown she'd retrieved back to the cabinet and chose another—a heavy silk of moss green. The neckline dipped a bit lower than Sarah's other gowns, and it was one of the few gowns she owned with decoration on the hem. It wasn't the sort of thing Sarah normally would don when working in the dirt.

"I'm going to dig in the garden this morning. I cannot wear that gown."

"So, don't dig."

"But—"

"Trust me, Lady Sarah."

Sarah shrugged. "I suppose I can collect a few specimens today."

Rebecca's tune was contagious. Sarah hummed it softly as she ate beside the window. The garden had lost much of its color with the recent bite of a frost. Somehow, though, the onset of winter wasn't nearly as dispiriting as it used to be. The promise of painting—and Lucien's company as well—made the browns and grays of the season seem almost enchanting this year.

She must do something special for Lucien, she decided. Something to show her appreciation for all he'd done. She pondered this as she finished her breakfast.

Outside, the air was damp and frigid. Basket in hand, Sarah followed a pebbled path from the front doors to the formal garden, collecting a few specimens along the way. She wrapped them carefully in paper to be dissected and catalogued later.

The wind pushed the veils against her face. The soft silk rubbed against her cheeks and lips, bringing to mind Lucien's kiss.

The thought of it warmed her to her toes.

The mere fact that a man like Lucien could forget her disfigurement, if only for a moment, instilled her with hope. Though Sarah knew Lucien could never fall in love with her, at least he'd been able to touch her. At least he could care for her as a friend. And if Lucien could do so, perhaps she'd underestimated others as well. Perhaps she didn't have to be relegated to a life of confinement.

Perhaps it was time to have a bit of faith.

She stood facing the wind, her veils embracing her cheeks, pondering her newfound hope.

Lucien was up before dawn, the rumble of carriage wheels rescuing him from a restless sleep. He had dreamt of Katrina again, but this dream had been far different from the others.

In this dream, the hands of onlookers could not stay him from the burning villa. He braved the scorching flames, moving through the heavy black smoke and searing heat, calling his wife's name. He found her curled up in their bed and knelt beside her. He tried to gather her in his arms, but she pushed him away.

"Your love is not strong enough to carry me," she whispered.

Try as he might, he was unable to lift her. The fire crept closer, encircling the bed and finally climbing the bedcovers. Before he could witness Katrina consumed by the flames, Lucien awoke.

He rose, not bothering to light a candle. The room was frigid. He washed and dressed in the dark, and sat on the window seat to watch the sun rise.

Katrina and Tessa had lost hundreds of sunrises and sunsets. Thousands of laughs. Hundreds of thousands of small moments that build upon each other to create a lifetime.

And all the while he had lived those moments, building

his own lifetime without them, despite his best efforts to the contrary. He had come to Elmstone to escape life, but had found it instead. He had allowed himself to forget his wife and daughter on too many occasions, when it was his duty to keep them alive within his heart. It was the only life possible for them.

Katrina's words haunted him. His love had not been strong enough to carry her. He had betrayed Katrina's memory with a kiss.

He could not allow it to happen again.

"Concentrate, Sarah," Lucien chided. *"Use the brush as an* extension of yourself. Each stroke colors the canvas, yes. But it also adds texture, and light, and depth."

The afternoon lesson, their first since her foray to Whitford, bore a pleasant tension for Sarah that had not been present at previous lessons.

She was acutely aware of Lucien's every move, breath, subtle gesture. As he had taught her to do, she took note of the way the sunlight played off his features: the way the shadows added a dramatic hollow to his cheeks and made his brow appear even stronger; the reddish tints playing through his thick curls; the changeable blue of his eyes. Though she'd studied him before, this time it seemed as if her eyes were brand new.

She held the brush out to him. "Show me."

He pushed her hand away. "No. You will learn more by doing it yourself."

A slender fern stood in a vase beside the easel. Sarah had been trying to recreate it for days, but hadn't been able to capture the essence of the wispy frond.

She mixed a different shade of green on the palette and used a longer, lighter stroke. Still her rendering was lacking.

"Show me," she said again. This time she refused to be denied. She pressed the brush into Lucien's hand.

He held it away from him as if it were an asp. His face tightened and his eyes grew dark. He made a move to return the brush to her hands, but he gripped it so tightly his knuckles were white.

Sarah removed the wooden palette from her thumb and hooked it over his. From the pure-color paints daubed along the edge, Lucien rapidly mixed a rich scale of greens and browns below the ones Sarah had created. He studied the canvas for only a moment before approaching it. The tip of the brush was a hair's breadth from the surface when his hand began to shake.

Lucien's arm dropped to his side. He bowed his head. Sarah assumed he was thinking, but when he looked up, there was such a flare of determination in his eyes she knew there was something more to his hesitation.

Again Lucien reached toward the canvas, only to have his hand tremble like that of an old man. His jaw clenched. Deep lines of exertion appeared on his forehead as he seemed to force his hand toward the canvas.

A growl of anguish tore from his lips as he threw the brush across the room. He kicked the easel onto its side and swept his arm across the table, sending tins of pigment, brushes, and the fern in the vase clattering to the floor.

"Damn me. Damn me," he swore, over and over again.

"Lucien—"

"No! I cannot. Damn me." His fingers clenched his hair. He was a man unhinged, pacing, his harsh breaths sounding like sobs.

"Lucien, stop. Please."

He crouched in a corner, his hands still gripping the hair at his temples.

Sarah approached him slowly, as one might approach an injured animal, and laid a hand on his shoulder. He flinched. She stroked his hair with a gentle caress until her hand met with his. Their fingers entwined and Lucien pulled her down beside him and buried his head against her shoulder.

"I am so sorry," he whispered. "Please forgive me."

"Forgive you?"

He did not speak.

"Lucien, tell me, what is there to forgive?"

His breathing was ragged. "I have done you a great disservice, dear lady. I have pretended to be someone I am not, and I am afraid it is you who will suffer most for it."

A shiver ran through her. "I don't understand. Tell me." She shook his head from her shoulder and stood. "Tell me!"

Had he murdered someone? Had he lied about his wife and child? She waited, trying desperately to control her errant thoughts.

"I cannot paint."

Lucien's admission hung in the air, which reeked of spilt linseed oil and turpentine. He slid from the crouching position onto the floor in the corner and stretched his legs out before him. Leaning back against the wall, he closed his eyes, as if waiting for the world to come down upon his head.

"I . . . Are you not Lucien Delacourte? Is that what you're confessing? If you've lied about your identity—"

"No. I am, indeed, Lucien Delacourte. But I am not the celebrated artist to the king and queen of France."

"I don't understand. You *are* the Lucien Delacourte who painted that piece on the wall?" She pointed to the French garden.

He nodded.

"You're the Lucien Delacourte who studied under Henri Valmetant? The one whom my brother contacted to serve as my tutor?"

"Yes."

"You're the Lucien Delacourte commissioned by King Louis to serve in his court?"

He bowed his head. "Not anymore."

Finally, she understood. It wasn't a case of mistaken identity at all. He'd lost his post with King Louis. He no longer believed in the magic of his own work.

For a man like Lucien, whose whole life had been dedicated to his art, the loss of it could only be devastating. She must help him bring it back.

"Stand up," she said. She took him by the elbow and pulled until he rose to his feet. "You're going to paint for me."

She steered him to the mess in the middle of the floor. Together they righted the easel and picked up the tins and brushes, returning them to their proper order on the table. The last thing Sarah picked up was the palette. It had fallen paint-side up, so the liquid pools of color still dotted the palette's surface. She hooked it over Lucien's thumb and squeezed his hand.

"Paint," she said.

He took a deep breath and dipped a brush in one of the circles of paint. He approached the easel like a man walking into a fierce wind. Some invisible force seemed to be pushing him back.

Sarah laid her hand on his shoulder. "It will be beautiful," she whispered.

Without warning, the brush and palette clattered to the floor. Lucien grabbed her arm and pulled her close. His fingertips caressed her cheek through the veils.

"Sarah . . ."

He found her lips with the pad of his thumb. She kissed it and he groaned, sweeping her tight against his chest. Sarah felt fragile in his arms, as delicate as the fern that now lay at their feet. She was suddenly weightless, free of the endless days and nights spent aching for a moment such as this.

She cut the moorings of those unanswered desires, leaving them to drift into the past as Lucien kissed her. The act was far less innocent, far more urgent, than the time in the nursery.

He caught her bottom lip in his teeth and the veils between them gave way, tearing across the length of Sarah's mouth. As her lips parted in surprise, Lucien slid the tip of his tongue gently between them. She pulled away, startled by the raw heat, but Lucien wouldn't permit her to escape. His fingers caressed her spine before winding through the hair at the base of her neck, freeing it from the hairpins that held it beneath her hat. He reached up to stroke her cheek and she could smell the linseed oil on his hands. It was sweeter than the scent of a rose.

Sarah felt as if she were melting, but Lucien held her aloft as their lips searched again for the breach in the veils. She ached to breathe, but could not. She wanted to stand, but could not.

Lucien stroked her back, his touch as soft as the brush of a flower suddenly buffeted by a breeze. The beat of her heart pulsed between them, in her chest, her belly, her thighs. Or was it his pulse? She could not discern.

Then as quickly as it had begun, the tempest quieted.

Lucien was so still, she should have known what was to come.

"Sarah, my Sarah," he whispered. "I need to see you."

Chapter 20

Lucien's words ran over Sarah's consciousness like ice-cold water, cooling the ardor that had built within her. She drew away and pushed his hand from her cheek.

The loose-limbed euphoria that had gripped her during the kiss still lingered. She staggered over to the settee and leaned a hip against the fat velvet arm to steady herself.

Lucien's breathing was labored. "Sarah, please. I am sorry. I did not mean to frighten you."

Her spine stiffened at his words. "Frighten me? Hardly. Betray me is more the word. I thought you understood. I trusted you."

"And now you do not? Why, because I want to see your face?"

"Yes."

He stretched his arms out, palms turned up to the ceiling. "Is it so wrong, Sarah? I care for you deeply. I think you know that. I desire you. God help me, I know it is wrong, but I desire you. I want to caress your cheek, kiss your neck, feel your skin—"

"Stop!" She turned away from him, unable to listen to any more. "Please leave. I cannot . . ." Her voice gave out.

She heard him sigh behind her.

"As you wish, my lady. I did not mean to offend you."

When she turned around, the drawing room was empty. As empty as her heart, and twice as cold. Sarah wrapped her arms about her waist, willing herself not to cry.

She stared out the window. She touched her lips through the hole in her veils. They were cold now, very different from just minutes ago when Lucien had warmed them with his.

Why did he have to ruin everything? One look at her face and she would never see him again. He would run, just as Duncan had. But she knew he'd go much farther and faster. A man accustomed to beauty such as Lucien had seen—nay, had painted—could never abide such imperfection.

Had she imagined they could be together without his ever seeing her face? She supposed that's what she had hoped for. She realized now how foolish she'd been to think he would never ask her to reveal it. He'd certainly left quick enough when she refused.

It would seem that, either way, she was bound to lose him.

Lucien made it halfway to his chambers on the steam of righteous indignation before regret slowed his feet.

How could he have been so lacking in sense? He knew all too well the depth of Sarah's determination to hide her scars. She had not allowed even her mother to see her face. Why should he expect her to grace *him* with that privilege?

Because he had believed her trust for him went beyond that of friendship. Because he had *wished* it.

God help him, he could no longer deny what he felt for her.

Katrina was gone. Tessa was gone. No matter what he

did or how often he remembered them, he could not raise them from the grave. But he was alive, damn it. To spend the rest of his life as if he were dead would be a sin against God and their memories. It was time to stop grieving. He would never stop loving them, but he could no longer deny his feelings for Sarah.

He had to be honest with Sarah in every way. He would confess both his lies and his feelings. But what did he have to offer her? He was naught but a destitute liar who had once, long ago, been a fine painter. Even if he were still a court artist, their match would not have been deemed acceptable. He had nothing to tender a highborn lady.

Lucien arrived at his quarters with a heavy heart. He stoked the fire, removed his boots, and stretched out on the bed, pulling the counterpane over his legs.

He stared into the flames.

He desperately wanted to seek Sarah out, to tell her how he felt. But he refused to be the cause of more scandal in Sarah's life. She was only beginning to emerge from seclusion. If he made his affections known, it would only serve to drag her into another tangle of gossip and speculation. No, he would not be the cause of such pain.

He lay there he knew not how long, numb in his heart and mind. Then, as the last log grew black in the grate, he heard a commotion in the hall. Running. Unintelligible shouting, and then a banging on his door.

"Fire!"

Lucien opened the door to a frantic servant in shirt-sleeves.

"Arthur, what—"

"Come quickly, please! There's smoke coming from under the door of Lady Sarah's room and we cannot open it. She has the only key."

"Sarah!" As if in a nightmare, Lucien stumbled along the darkened hallway, following the billow of Arthur's white nightshirt.

The servant pounded on Sarah's door. When there was no answer, Lucien pushed him aside.

"Open the door. Sarah, unlock the door!"

He heard a soft rustle behind the gilded wood, and for a moment believed it to be the rustle of Sarah's skirts. But then he realized he'd heard that sound before.

Flames.

Lucien laid a palm against the door. It was hot to the touch. He looked to Arthur. The man's eyes were wide with fear.

"We must break it down," he said.

Arthur stood rooted to the spot. Lucien backed away from the door and charged it, ramming it with his shoulder. Pain shot down the length of his arm. The servant stared at him in horror.

"Help me," Lucien snarled, and backed up again. This time Arthur followed his lead. Together they butted their shoulders against the door. The full weight of both men cracked the frame. They threw their weight against it again. Finally, it gave way.

Flames surged from the room as if a great, fire-breathing dragon dwelled within. Two topiaries, one on each side of Sarah's door, were consumed with flames. Lucien covered his face with his forearm and plunged through the wall of fire. The room was thick with smoke. Lucien's eyes burned. He gagged, and stumbled back to the hallway for air. Arthur had disappeared.

Lucien dropped to his belly, snaking beneath the arch of flames and over the hot stone floor toward Sarah's bed-chamber. He reached the room quickly, but could not see through the smoke. The thick wool carpets smoldered.

Nightmare and reality collided. He may not have been able to rescue Katrina in his dream, but he would not fail Sarah.

Silk wall hangings blazed. To his left stood a washstand holding a basin and pitcher. He crawled to it and reached up for the pitcher. He doused his shirt with the remaining water, tore a strip of the linen from the bottom, and tied it over his nose and mouth.

He attempted to stand, but could see nothing through the black haze save the red-orange of flames. Crawling on all fours through the burning maze of carpets, he continued on until his shoulder met with a bedpost. Rising to a crouch, he swept an arm over the bed until his hit Sarah's ankle.

"Sarah!"

A weak cough answered his cry.

He gripped her leg and dragged her across the bed until she slid down into his arms, bringing a tangle of bedclothes with her. Her hair, loose from its usual bindings, obscured her face. Lucien freed her from the sheets. He removed his sodden shirt and pulled it over Sarah's head to protect her from the acrid smoke.

He shook her, but she lay limp in his arms. His heart thumped erratically against his ribs. He could not lose her. Not like this. Dear God, not like this.

With Sarah cradled in his arms, he stood, momentarily losing his sense of direction. Stifling smoke filled his lungs. He spotted a doorway and plowed toward it, only to discover it was the way to Sarah's closet.

He cut left. Groping along the wall he came again to the washstand, now on fire, a burning landmark to his destination. The door to the hallway lay directly ahead. Closing his eyes and gathering Sarah close, he charged.

Cool air shocked Lucien's senses. Nausea overwhelmed him. He gulped air. His lungs wheezed fitfully with every breath, but he hardly noticed it. Sarah had not yet moved in his arms.

He staggered a few paces down the hall, as far away from the burning room as he was able to walk, and laid Sarah on the burgundy runner.

"Please, God, let her be alive."

Lucien reached for the damp shirt still swathed about Sarah's head when he heard a shout.

Arthur rounded the corner with three other servants trailing behind. The upstairs maid hopped nervously behind Lord Darby's manservant. The cook, clad only in her chemise, waddled next around the bend, her face red, her eyes bulging like those of a codfish. One of the stable hands, in dirty, half-buttoned breeches, brought up the rear of the motley parade. They each carried buckets in both hands, and the scene was so familiar to Lucien he almost gave in to his nausea.

He knelt over Sarah, freeing only her mouth and nose from his shirt, leaving the rest in place to conceal her face. She would not wish to be exposed to her servants, nor to him.

"Extinguish the flames at the door," he commanded. "We must keep the fire from spreading."

Arthur stood before Sarah's room, hesitant.

"Hurry, man, lest we all go up in flames."

Lucien strode to the group huddled behind Arthur and snatched a bucket from the maid's grip. He ducked beneath the flames licking through the doorway and dumped the water onto one of the topiaries.

"Give me another."

Arthur reached for the maid's empty bucket and handed Lucien one of his. Again Lucien doused the burning topiary.

After emptying three more buckets, the flaming topiaries had been extinguished.

"Is there no one else about?" Lucien asked Arthur.

"These were all I could find. Many servants went with Lord Darby to London, and Lady Sarah gave the others a free evening."

"Then the five of us will have to be enough."

"You mean for me to enter that room? I cannot!" said Arthur.

"You will. We will work together to put out the flames."

"But how are we to do it?" Arthur's voice had taken on a note of hysteria.

Lucien grabbed him by the shoulders. "Listen to me. We will work our way into the room from the door. Do not try to move past the flames." Lucien pointed at the stable hand. "You."

"Robert."

"Robert, come with us."

"What should we do?" asked the cook.

"You women will take the empty buckets and fill them," Lucien said. "Do not stop until Arthur tells you the fire is completely extinguished."

Lucien tore one of the sleeves from Arthur's shirt, ignoring the man's horrified expression. He soaked it in one of the buckets. "Tie this over your nose and mouth. Stay as low to the floor as you are able. First, we will soak the carpets well so they do not catch fire again."

Lucien and the servants worked feverishly, in silence, until Lucien was certain the fire was under control. In the hall, he removed the piece of linen that covered his mouth and drank with his hands from a full bucket of water.

"You will have to finish here," he said to Arthur.

"You're leaving?" asked the servant, a note of panic in his voice.

"I must attend to Lady Sarah. Now go, finish putting out the fire." Lucien nudged the manservant toward the door.

Lucien watched Arthur and Robert duck into the doorway before he turned his attention back to Sarah. The maid and the cook eyed her as they waited for the men to emerge. Lucien glared at them, and they turned their gazes back to their buckets.

He knelt beside Sarah. The gentle rise and fall of her chest told him she still breathed, but her eyes were closed. He tried to rouse her, but to no avail.

Ignoring the aching in his every muscle, Lucien again

gathered Sarah in his arms and headed for the stairs. He would take her down to his quarters, far enough away from the fire to assure her safety.

He gave no more thought to the fire. The walls and floors of the manor were constructed of stone. The flames would not spread as long as Arthur and the others kept them from reaching the runners and tapestries in the hallway. The manor would survive.

Lucien prayed Sarah would, too.

As he entered his quarters, the sun made its first appearance on the horizon. Sarah, huddled against his chest, had not issued a sound nor stirred even the slightest as he carried her there.

He laid her gently on his bed, tucking a pillow beneath her head. It appeared she had suffered no burns, but her skin, where bare, was mottled with dark smudges from the smoke and ash. He took her hand. It was bone cold.

He knew he should light a fire, but could not bring himself to do it. The thought of creating that destructive element with his own hands made him shudder. Instead, he lay down beside Sarah, pressing his body against hers to warm her.

His damp shirt still concealed most of her face. He could not leave her this way. He must uncover her and allow her to breathe easily.

With an unsteady hand, he reached for the shirt and slowly unmasked her.

Chapter 21

Had he dreamed of such beauty, he would not have believed it possible.

Sarah's skin was as pale as the moonlight that had flooded her gardens the first night he spent at Elmstone. The delicate arch of her brow crowned almond-shaped eyes. They were fringed with dark lashes that fanned over the shoal of her cheekbones like the soft sable of a paintbrush. Her nose, a smaller version of Lord Darby's, turned up just slightly at the tip. But her lips were what entranced him. They were full and lush, the color of blood roses and petal smooth. He had caught but a glimpse of them through the tear in her veils when they had kissed.

The scar she hid so diligently—a thin, silver crescent moon that rode the planes and hollows of one side of her face from brow to chin—did little to mar her lovely countenance. With great care, Lucien traced it with his fingertips, as if to smooth it as he would a line of paint that had come too thick off the side of a brush.

His hand moved from her face to her hair, spread like a

fine silk mantle over the pillow. He tangled his fingers in it and brought a handful to his face, breathing deeply. Beneath the heavy smell of smoke he detected the heady scent of earth and wind that had aroused his senses too many times to count. The scent that aroused him even now . . .

Lucien rolled off the bed, cursing the lascivious thoughts that would only hinder her care. He retrieved a basin of water and a square of linen from his washstand and carried them to the bed. Taking Sarah's hand again in his, he bathed her skin with the linen, wiping the smudges of ash from her forearm, fingers, and wrist. Her hand was delicate, but slightly roughened by her work in the gardens. He stroked the lines of her palm. What strength these hands possessed. What tenderness, too. Her touch had served to soothe him on more than one occasion.

He repeated his ministrations on the other hand, and then her feet and ankles, studying them as closely as he did her hands. But he did not dare extend his aid to her calves, which lay bare to him as well. Instead, he found a blanket and covered her with it, not trusting himself to warm her any longer.

As he returned the basin to the stand, there came a knock at the door. It swung open before Lucien could reach it.

"The fire is out," said Arthur, in a tone which suggested it was no thanks to Lucien. The manservant's once-pristine shirt was now a muddy gray. His black breeches were wet and torn. The maid stood behind him with a tray. "How does Lady Sarah fare?"

"Not well," Lucien answered, moving into the doorway to block the servants' view of the bed. "She has not yet opened her eyes."

"Elizabeth brought some tea and an herbal poultice, should the lady have any burns. May we?" Arthur gestured into the room.

"I will take it, thank you. If I need anything else, I will be sure to ring."

Arthur's face clouded. "This is not proper, Delacourte. The lady should be moved. She should be cared for by women."

"I will see to her care. But I will be sure to let you know if there is any way you can be of service."

Arthur's face grew as gray as his shirt. He made no move to relinquish the space in the doorframe.

Sudden suspicion stirred in Lucien's mind.

"By the way, Arthur, how did you discover the fire?"

"Why, I smelled it, of course."

"From your quarters downstairs, on the other side of the house?"

The maid followed this exchange with interest.

Arthur glared at her, and she shrank back. "I—I happened to be passing Lady Sarah's rooms, and—"

"In the middle of the night?"

The servant's face turned from gray to red. "Not that it is any of your concern, but I was retrieving a personal item from Lord Darby's quarters."

"You are quite right," said Lucien. "It is none of my concern. I am sure Lady Sarah will appreciate the tea."

Lucien took the tray and closed the door.

He set the service on a small table and poured a cup of tea. The herbal poultice caused the room to smell like a stable, so he wrapped it in a towel and put it out in the hallway, then locked the door behind him. When he returned to the bedside, Sarah was stirring.

Perhaps the poultice held some merit after all. No doubt the stench of the thing woke her.

He sat on the edge of the bed and took her hand, rubbing her knuckles with his thumb. "Come out, Sarah. Come to me," he chanted quietly. "Open your eyes."

Her breathing was less labored, but still she lingered in a sleep-like state. He brushed a stray lock of hair away from her eyes, catching the strands and wrapping them around his finger. A soft moan escaped her lips.

"Come back to me, Sarah."

The sun was fully risen now, and Sarah's eyelids opened slowly against the morning.

Lucien's throat constricted. At long last he looked into Sarah's eyes. They were of a warm, chocolate brown, shot through with shafts of gold that rivaled the color of the sunrise. They engaged him wholly.

"Lucien." Sarah's smile was tentative, confused.

"How do you feel?"

Her brow wrinkled in puzzlement. "Feel?"

"There was a fire in your quarters."

"A fire? I . . ." Her hands flew to her face. "My veils!"

He caught her wrists, encircling them gently. "I have already seen it."

She struggled from his grasp and covered her face with her hands. "Turn away."

"Sarah—"

"Turn away!"

He turned his back to her, but remained beside her on the bed. His hip rested against her leg, and he felt her draw away.

"What of my quarters?" she asked, her voice shaking.

"I cannot say for certain, but I imagine they are almost completely destroyed."

She issued a muffled sob, and he turned toward her.

"Stop! Please do not look at me. I must decide . . . that is, I must figure out what to do. All my . . . everything in my quarters was destroyed?"

"Most likely. The fire was still burning when I brought you here. Arthur and a handful of servants put it out."

"Dear God, did they see . . .?"

"Your face? No. I had covered you with my shirt, so you would not breathe the smoke. I removed it only here, in the privacy of my room."

Sarah was silent for a long while.

Lucien wondered what she was feeling. Was she uncomfortable here, alone with him? Or was she mourning the loss of her personal belongings?

"Sarah, please let me turn. I have seen everything already, and I just want to talk to you."

The bed shook softly. He turned to look at her. She had covered her face with her hands. Tears streamed through her fingers and down her wrists. He took her in his arms and she leaned hesitantly against his chest. Her hair cascaded over his bare skin, raising gooseflesh.

"I want you to leave," she said, her voice muffled.

"Fine. I shall go ask Cook to prepare some broth for you. Is there something else you would like?"

"You misunderstand," she said. "I would like you to pack your things and go."

His mouth grew suddenly dry. "Leave Elmstone?"

"Yes." It was but a whisper, though to him that single word rang louder than a church bell.

He grasped her shoulders and moved her out to arm's length. "I will not leave Elmstone. I will not leave *you*."

"Of course you will. I'm making it easy for you. Now you'll have no need to make excuses."

"Uncover your face."

"No."

"Damn it, Sarah, uncover your face."

Quickly, as if to spite him, she withdrew her hands from her cheeks. She glared at him, heat blazing in her eyes. Lucien felt as if, for the second time in mere hours, he had walked into an inferno. But this time he was prepared to burn. This time, he welcomed it.

He tangled his fingers in her hair and dragged her mouth up against his, tasting the salt of her tears on her lips. He had caught her by surprise, and she allowed the assault for a moment before she tried to pull away.

He tightened his grip and she relented, melting against

his chest. As the kiss deepened, all signs of Sarah's hesitance fled. She answered his onslaught with one of her own, raking his chest as if searching for his soul. She need not have looked further than his eyes, for they would have shown her anything she wanted to see. At this moment, she owned him completely.

A choice beckoned.

The flowers outside the window were dying, retreating to the soil for protection from the cold. Sarah could do the same—hide herself away, protect herself from the cold fear of rejection. Or she could choose to open herself.

The warmth of Lucien's hands, his mouth, his words thawed the frost that had formed, layer by layer, over her heart. Whether it was the fire, or their friendship, or perhaps even pity, what Lucien offered her was a chance to escape—if only for a few moments—the confines of her veils. When it was over, things would go back to the way they were. She would don her veils and he would pretend he had never seen her without them. To do otherwise would only invite scandal, and she could not abide any more of that. But she wanted to be with Lucien more than anything she had ever wanted before.

Without breaking their embrace, Lucien swung his legs onto the bed and stretched out against the length of her. A shock rippled over her body as the hot brand of his bare skin pressed against hers. The silken hair of his chest brushed against her arm; the rough wool of his breeches slid over her naked calf. Evidence of Lucien's ardor pressed hard against her hip. She moaned, the sound catching in her throat.

He freed his hands from her hair to stroke the sensitive skin of her neck, pausing to feel the beat of her pulse at her throat. She was utterly exposed to him, so completely vulnerable to his touch, his lips. His sight. She broke the kiss to turn her scars against the pillows. Lucien touched the tip of his tongue to her earlobe, causing her toes to curl.

He drew away and combed her hair back from her temple with his fingers. Cupping her chin, he turned her to face him, exposing the ugliness she'd fought so hard to conceal.

"You cannot hide anymore, Sarah," he said. Lying over her, he placed a kiss at the start of the white, serpentine line above her brow. "I know you."

He kissed the curve of it at her temple. "I know you are kind. More kind than any woman I have ever known."

He kissed the ridge of it over her cheekbone. "I know you are courageous and determined."

He kissed the jagged stretch of it on her cheek. "I know you are compassionate to a fault."

He reached the merciful end of the scar, kissing the cleft of her chin. "I know you cannot help but love, in spite of the pain it has wrought."

She dared not breathe, for fear of waking from this dream.

He looked into her eyes. "Love *me,* Sarah, and I vow I will do everything I can to undo that pain. Love me."

Her cry was captured by his kiss. She arched against him, her nightgown pulling taut over her chest. He captured a breast in his hand and rubbed his thumb over the sensitive peak. She cried out.

"God forgive me, but I need you." Lucien moved his mouth to her breast. The rough stubble on his chin penetrated the thin fabric of her nightgown. The friction chafed her skin, igniting her desire. With a trembling hand, he untied the ribbon that gathered the garment at her neck. He pushed the thin fabric over her shoulders and it fell away, baring her breasts.

Lucien's mouth descended to her nipple, sparking a fire at her very center. She wound her fingers into his hair, pulling him closer as he laved the tight crest with his tongue. Awash in sensation, she was unable to muster a shred of modesty or denial. She slid down his body, her lips finding his in a searing kiss. As if acting of their own accord, her fingers searched for the buttons of his breeches, meeting Lucien's hardness with unabashed desire.

With sudden urgency, Lucien stripped the nightgown down to her waist, exposing her to the navel. He ran a string of frantic kisses across her breasts, her ribs, her belly, before tugging the gown over her hips and down her legs.

The chill of sudden nakedness was soon replaced by the warmth of Lucien's body as he moved to cover her. He smelled of smoke and desire, of lust and healing.

He raised his head, his eyes again searching hers—this time for assurance, for permission. Sarah answered him with a kiss.

She longed to forget the pain. She longed to love and be loved. She wanted to be free.

She opened herself to him and he entered her, moving through her like wind through the branches of a willow. Moving and stirring and bending her soul until the force of their lovemaking carried her over the treetops and out into a world she had thought was lost to her forever.

Chapter 22

Sarah lay still as a stone, unwilling to break the intimate cocoon Lucien's body formed around hers.

If she could only emerge from it as a butterfly would—transformed and beautiful, a delicate creature able to float at will on a breeze.

Where would she fly? Anywhere. Everywhere! All the places she had missed during her years of confinement. Impossible, she knew. But the freedom of their lovemaking alone would sustain her for the rest of her years. It had to, for she knew such a respite from her solitary world would never occur again.

Instead of sorrow, however, she felt only joy. Lucien's breath on her neck calmed the uneven rhythm of her heart. The steady weight of his limbs served to anchor her in the dream. They had come together so often during the day that her body ached with sweet exhaustion.

She lay warmed by his body until the inevitable occurred. He moved, breaking the spell, fracturing the safety of the cocoon.

Before Lucien was completely conscious, Sarah rose and moved into the shadows in which she had dwelled for an eternity, her insecurity returning by degrees.

He sat up and tossed back the bedclothes, the bare skin of his shoulders and chest aglow in the setting sun.

"Sarah, where are you?" Lucien squinted in her direction.

"At the washstand."

Even in the waning light she could see his smile. "Do you need my assistance?"

Her reply was interrupted by an insistent pounding at the door.

Lucien put a finger to his lips, urging silence. He hastened from the bed and struggled into his breeches, then donned the shirt he had used to cover her face during the fire. He combed his hair with his fingers as he strode toward the door. As he passed the washstand, he took Sarah by the shoulders and steered her toward the bed.

"Lie down, and cover up," he whispered. Then he cleared his throat and pulled open the door.

"What is it?" he demanded.

Beyond the door Sarah heard Rebecca's voice, startled but not cowed.

"I come to see my lady, sir. Elizabeth fetched me from Whitford after the fire. I know Lady Sarah is here."

Sarah frantically searched for her nightgown, which was buried beneath the coverlet.

"It is not a good time. Come back in an hour." Lucien attempted to close the door, but Rebecca would not allow it.

"I must see her now."

"Let her in." Sarah pulled the covers up to her nose and covered her cheek and forehead with her hair. The room was nearly dark, but she would not chance Rebecca seeing her face.

The maid entered with more caution than she had shown at the door. She moved slowly into the room.

Sarah stopped her when she reached the foot of the bed. "Come no closer, Becca. What do you want?"

The maid drew herself up to her full height. "I come to see for myself that you're unharmed. Elizabeth told me of the fire. I was worried."

"Thank you. But as you can see, I'm unharmed. Lucien has taken excellent care of me, though I do appreciate your concern."

"You're well? Truly?"

"Outside of a severe headache from the smoke, I'm fine."

"I see." Rebecca remained by the foot of the bed, fussing with the coverlet. "Shall I return to Elmstone to care for you?"

"Go. Be with your husband. He's only here for a short time. I'll manage."

"Indeed, it would appear you've managed fine up until now."

"Before you leave," Sarah said, "please arrange to have someone prepare new quarters for me as soon as possible."

"Of course, my lady, if you're certain that's what you want." Sarah sensed a note of amusement in the maid's voice. *A pox on her!*

"It is."

"Very well, then. Are you sure I cannot be of service?"

"I appreciate your concern. But it will undoubtedly be a few days before I'll require your services. In the meantime, you should be with William."

Rebecca bobbed her head. "Very well, Lady Sarah. I will return in four days. If you should need me before then . . ."

"I'll have Elizabeth fetch you. Thank you, Becca."

The maid all but skipped from the room, and Sarah knew she would press for details the moment she returned.

"I should have anticipated such interference. I am sorry," Lucien said.

She sighed. "There's no avoiding Becca, I'm afraid."

Lucien lit several candles in a stand. The glow illuminated the corner in which he stood. He seemed uncertain as to what action to take. "How do you feel?"

"Cold. Will you light a fire?" She didn't think she could bear his touch at the moment. Her need for him was overwhelming, but she had to think.

Did Arthur or Elizabeth suspect anything? She knew she could trust Rebecca with any secret, but Arthur was loyal to her brother. If James discovered this tryst, Lucien would suffer. Sarah doubted her brother would look upon this union kindly. It would mean Lucien's dismissal, for certain.

She had known this morning, even as she accepted Lucien into her arms, that it could be the only time. But the reality of it left her aching. Would it be possible to stand beside him at their lessons each day, sit across from him at every meal, enjoy his company at the card table without desiring more?

As she watched him build the fire, her mind mapped the taut muscles of his back, the mole at the base of his neck, each curl of hair from his chest to his navel. She had memorized the landscape of his body, from the curve of his earlobe to the dimple of his ankle.

She loved and had been loved in return. For only one day, true, but it would have to be enough. The only thought more awful than never lying in his arms again was to never see his face again. Especially now that she had seen it so clearly, without her veils.

When he had finished making the fire, Lucien stripped off his shirt and crawled onto the bed, lying down next to her and taking her hand.

"It won't be long before they have my room prepared," she said.

"I could tell Arthur you are not well enough to be moved."

"No. I must go."

"I will visit you later."

She felt the sting of tears in her eyes. "Lucien, we cannot. If James discovers this . . . We cannot raise suspicions amongst the servants, especially Arthur."

He played with her fingers, stroking them, kissing them, curling them in his fist. "I want to hold you one more time."

Her tears fell to the pillows. She pulled her hand gently from his. "We cannot take that risk."

He bent over her and kissed her softly on the tip of her nose. His voice was a rough whisper. "I will go see about your new rooms."

In a fresh shirt and breeches, his body still humming from its proximity to Sarah's, his skin still bearing smudges of soot, Lucien strode through the halls of Elmstone seeking Arthur. And seeking order for his chaotic thoughts.

He cursed his lack of restraint. He had taken advantage of a woman he had grown to care for and respect when she was at her most vulnerable. God help him, he had wanted her, wanted to make love to her, his position at Elmstone be damned. He had forgotten about Katrina and Tessa, about Paris and his debts.

About his lies.

All that had mattered was Sarah. He had finally seen her. He had finally touched her and loved her, and now, he must let her go. He only prayed their actions were not revealed to Lord Darby, for Sarah would, he knew, feel deeply ashamed.

After the first time they made love, Sarah had told him about her night with Lavery—how discomposed she had felt afterward, and how he had abused her affections. She believed her scars were punishment for that night.

Lucien never wanted her to feel that way about making

love with him. But the highborn lady and the lowly artist, together forever? It could never be.

He made his way to the hall and saw Elizabeth entering the drawing room, a duster in her hand.

"How does Lady Sarah fare?" The maid twisted the duster in her fingers.

"Much better, I am happy to report. She asked me to inquire about her new rooms," he said. "Are they ready?"

"Yes, sir. In the east wing, on the floor just above your own."

"Is all there to make her comfortable? Is the fire lit?"

"Yes, sir."

"I shall move her at once, then. Is Arthur about?"

"No, sir. He left at dawn for London. Said he had urgent news for Lord Darby."

As Lucien scoured the sodden, frightful mess that had been Sarah's bedroom, he thought about Arthur's absence. Why had the servant left so quickly for the city? Was it to report the fire, or did the man suspect—or know—something else?

Sarah was right. To continue their affair would certainly put them both in jeopardy. He would not endanger her newly found freedom.

He hastily gathered a few things in his arms and headed back to his rooms, his resolve strengthened by the thought of the woman who rested there.

"I have found a few things not terribly damaged by the fire," Lucien said, laying a pile of garments on the bed. "The chifforobe seems to have protected some of your gowns from the flames, if not the smoke."

"Thank you, Lucien." Sarah picked through the heap, discovering a hat, two plain gray gardening gowns, and a green one that might be acceptable for dining.

"I took the liberty of taking some others to the laundress so that they might be ready for you soon. Until then, I am afraid these will have to do."

"I'm very grateful, Lucien. Were there any veils you could find?"

He was oddly quiet.

"Lucien? Did you find any veils?"

"Do you really need them, Sarah? You do not realize how lovely you are."

Sarah felt flushed. "I thought you understood. I cannot go without them. Did you even look for them?"

"I searched only your wardrobe. I did not want to disturb your private things. But I did find this in the laundress's quarters. I thought you might fashion it to your needs, if you insisted on hiding yourself again."

She took the length of cloth he proffered. It was a square of gauze the size of a kerchief. It would have to do, at least until she could find something more suitable.

"I need to change, I suppose, before I go tramping through the hallways."

"Of course. I will wait in the hall."

If circumstances had been different, she would have laughed at his sense of propriety; after all, they had seen much more of each other just a few hours earlier. "Turning your back will suffice."

He stared out of the window as she quickly shed her nightgown and donned one of the simple dresses he had brought her.

"Will you help me fasten it?"

"Of course."

Each whisper of his fingers against her skin fanned her desire for him. Button by button, his touch rose from the small of her back to the nape of her neck. She steeled herself against the sensation, trying not to recall the exquisite commotion those same fingers had wrought on her body just that morning.

She escaped his touch as soon as she was able, retreating to the fireplace.

"I'll never be able to repay you for what you have done, Lucien. You saved my life in more ways than one."

"It is I who am grateful to you. I care for you deeply, Sarah. I never believed I could care about another again. If anything had happened to you . . ."

Her voice softened. "I care for you, too."

Then he was beside her, holding her, framing her face in his hands. Sarah drew a sharp breath—waiting, wanting, unable to deny his kiss. It was sweetly savage, filled with desire and defiance.

She held nothing back. It was as if they did battle, each trying to conquer the other's fears, the other's torment, with a kiss. He coiled the hair at the base of her neck around his hand, drawing her head back to ravish her neck with his lips. She strained against him even as she willed herself to pull away.

If they didn't stop this madness, she knew where it would lead—into his arms, into his bed. It would lead exactly where they both hoped it would lead.

Exactly where it could not.

She broke free from his embrace and scuttled to the other side of the room. She braced herself against the wall, her entire body a shaking, trembling mass. "Please, Lucien. You know we cannot."

"I want you so badly," he said, his voice tight with emotion. But what emotion? Accusation? Pain? Regret?

She donned the hat and carefully pinned the square of gauze to the brim. The makeshift veil dropped over her face, cloaking her once again in a solitary world. On the verge of crying for a second time, she gathered her things up from the bed. "Where are my new quarters?"

As she left Lucien's room, she vowed she would shed not one more tear over this impossible situation.

Her vow lasted almost until she reached her new rooms.

In the hallway she fumbled with the key Lucien had given her, finding it an impossible feat to insert it in the keyhole when her eyes conveyed nothing but a rheumy blur.

"Come to your senses," she admonished herself, blinking hard to rid her eyes of the tears.

When she was able to open the door, however, her entrance did nothing to cheer her. The reminder that her own rooms, with all of her things, were now destroyed tipped the precarious scale on which her composure rested.

She raged against the circumstances that kept her hidden away at Elmstone, but then reasoned that if they had not, she never would have met Lucien at all.

She cursed James's protection, vowing to inform him of her feelings for Lucien, and then realized she could not. No matter how much James loved her, he believed he knew best when it came to her protection. If he wouldn't allow Sir Richard to court her, there was little chance for a landless artist.

She cried for the loss of a romance, but then rejoiced in the discovery of friendship. In the end, she knew this would sustain her. Having Lucien stand beside her as a friend was infinitely more desirable than his being driven away for being her lover.

When she could cry no more, she left her new apartment to sift through the rubble of her old one, hoping to find at least some pieces of her old life intact.

Chapter 23

He had but two hours before he was expected back at the town house in Berkeley Square.

James quickened his stride as he tried to formulate a reasonable story for the physician. He wanted simply to tell the truth, and he might do that very thing in the end.

He located the address given to him by a friend and, after taking great care to be sure he was not followed, slipped through a narrow door. The stairs in the dim hallway creaked beneath his weight, taunting him with the possibility of discovery. He climbed two stories before arriving at the physician's door.

A woman with a reassuring smile answered his knock. "Yes, sir?"

"I'm here to see Doctor Murfree."

"Are you the one who sent the note?"

"Yes."

She held the door open and waved James into the residence. With another furtive look over his shoulder, he followed her inside.

The room he entered was neat and well done up, not at all what he would have expected at such an address. Books lined a bank of shelves on one wall and lay scattered over tables in tidy disarray. The carpets were of fine quality and quite clean, if a bit worn. The same could be said of the settee, on which the woman who answered the door was now motioning him to sit.

"Thank you, no. I believe I will stand."

"As you wish. I shall go tell the doctor you are here."

James took a deep breath, still uncertain as to what story he would use. He practiced several variations in his head before the physician appeared.

James knew immediately upon seeing the man he would tell the truth.

Doctor Eston Murfree was the very picture of a learned, trustworthy gentleman. His head bore no wig, but rather a thick shock of gray hair which stood up at attention from his scalp. His dark brown eyes drooped slightly at the corners. Long of neck and lean of body, Doctor Murfree filled the doorway, a pipe held loosely in one hand and a book in the other.

"The missive you sent wasn't signed," he said.

"Forgive me, but I wished to remain anonymous until our meeting. I'm James Essington."

"Ah. Lord Darby," the doctor said as he bowed. "Mystery solved. You're the sort of man who would hardly wish to announce a visit to a poor physician's home in Stratford."

"The scandal sheets pay dearly for any bit of gossip naming a member of the peerage," James said. He knew that Julia read those very rags with some frequency.

"Not to worry. No one here will give you away."

The men settled into chairs, facing one another across a table strewn with papers and medical volumes. The doctor made a slight movement with his hand, and the woman hurried over to clear the clutter.

She bobbed her head and bustled from the room, arms overflowing with scholarly ephemera.

"Well, shall we get down to it, then? What have you, a touch of the pox? Syphilis?"

"Good heavens, no." That the physician might assume such a thing had never crossed James's mind. "No, I'm not here for myself, but rather a woman of my acquaintance. She suffers so. She . . ." His voice broke, and he took a moment to compose himself before going on. "She suffers from dropsy. While she was able to travel, I took her to Bath, where she was treated by several physicians. Nothing they prescribed helped her. I've heard you offer something different. Lord Talbot claims you cured his man."

Doctor Murfree chewed his unlit pipe. "I've studied the ravages of hydropsy with a very fine physician, William Withering. He's well known for his experiments with a certain herb."

"He practices in Birmingham, I believe?"

"Correct." Murfree drew on his unlit pipe a few times. His face wrinkled in frustration. "Several years ago, Withering had a patient who was cured of hydropsy by means of a gypsy remedy. He scoured the countryside for the gypsy, hoping to discover the secret of this powerful medicine. At first people believed Withering had gone mad. However, subsequent experiments have shown the remedy to be effective in many cases of hydropsy, and it has since been used for other purposes as well."

James leaned forward. "What is it?"

"First, I need to be sure of the symptoms. I must visit the patient."

"That will not be possible, I'm afraid. Our village is small, and a physician's presence would be cause for gossip. I cannot have anyone know of this."

Murfree studied him intently. For a moment, James feared he had ruined all hope of finding a cure for Leah's condition.

Finally the doctor said, "Very well. But we must be absolutely certain the ailment is hydropsy. The remedy has caused death in several patients, and should be used only as a last resort. Describe the symptoms, please."

James rubbed his eyes. It would be difficult to explain the changes the disease had wrought on Leah's delicate person. He could hardly stand to think of it, much less to describe the horrible metamorphosis. But he must, if he were to help her.

"Her size is nearly twice that of the woman I once knew," he began. "She looks heavy with child, though I know she is not. Her features, once fine, have been replaced by lumps that remind one of unbaked bread. And her legs . . . Dear Lord, her legs look like the trunks of small trees. She cannot lie flat, but must spend her days and nights sitting upright in bed."

"What has been done for her?"

James sighed. "Bleeding, of course. A soup made of garlic and horseradish. Juniper berry tea. Bark of elder."

"Has there been any success with these treatments at all?"

"Very little, I'm afraid."

Murfree's generous eyebrows furrowed into a line. He lit his pipe and smoked in silence, staring at the books lining the walls.

James leaned back in his chair, watching the doctor. Perhaps it had been a mistake to come here. Had he left Leah and risked scandal for nothing?

Without a word, Murfree stood and left the room. He returned a short time later without his pipe, holding a small sack in the palm of his hand. He withdrew a sheaf of parchment from a desk against the far wall and returned to the table, setting everything between them.

With great care, Murfree unbound the sack and poured the contents onto the parchment, then folded it into an envelope.

"Place this under her tongue three times daily," he said, handing James the packet. "Just a pinch at first, then more as the days progress and her body is able to bear it. This is all I have at the moment, but if you return in a few days, I will give you more."

"What is it?"

"The leaves of foxglove, dried and ground into powder."

James secreted the package in a pocket of his vest. "My sincere gratitude, Murfree. What is your fee?"

Murfree shrugged. "You may settle that with my wife. 'Tis she who holds the purse strings. But do keep me informed."

"I'll send word as soon as possible."

James settled his account and made his way back from Stratford, his mood lighter than it had been in months.

He would send for a courier immediately to take the packet of medicine to Whitford. If only he could take it himself, but now that his family had come with him, there would be no avoiding a short stay in town. He supposed he owed a holiday to all of them. A few days would be plenty. In the meantime, Arthur would handle things.

As he approached his town house in the heart of Berkeley Square, he thought that not even Julia's voracious socializing could dampen his spirits.

When he entered the foyer of his London home, the shrill, contrived laughter Julia affected whenever a guest was about scorched his ears. He attempted to sneak up the stairs before his presence was known, but just as he took the first step, his wife sailed out of the drawing room. He cursed under his breath. The woman possessed the hearing of a bat.

"My dear, there's someone here you *must* meet." Julia steered him to the parlor, pausing beside the doors to tug the bell pull.

Across the room, a woman dressed entirely in orange and equally as round as the fruit perched on the edge of a sofa. James half expected her to roll off the sofa and across the floor to greet him.

Julia addressed the orange. "Allow me to introduce my husband, the Earl of Darby."

The woman struggled to her feet. "Lord Darby!" She dipped at the knees, fluttering her fan before her face.

"Lord Darby," said Julia with some drama, "may I present Miss Mathilde Delacourte."

James issued a quick bow. "Miss Delacourte. Am I to assume you bear some relation to my sister's tutor, Lucien Delacourte?"

Miss Delacourte tittered. "But of course! We are cousins. I don't know him well, but I've learned quite a bit about him from Lady Darby."

"Indeed." James extracted his arm from Julia's grip.

What sort of trouble was she brewing?

Miss Delacourte wasn't the type of woman with whom his wife kept company. Even *he* could discern that her gown was hopelessly past the fashion.

"Come now, Mathilde," said Julia with one of her high-pitched laughs. "I simply shared what little I know of your mysterious cousin. My husband's sister Sarah knows him quite well, isn't that right, James?"

"I suppose."

"Where is your sister, Lord Darby? I've heard so much about her." Miss Delacourte's eager curiosity showed plainly on her face.

"She was unable to accompany us."

"What a shame. Everyone should come to London now and again, don't you think? Why, just the other day I was telling my sister-in-law, the Honorable Mary Weston, that I would have *expired* if I hadn't been able to make the journey myself. Mother was feeling a bit under the weather, you see, and I wasn't at all certain I would be able to make it. But here I am!"

"Yes, here you are," said James. "Now you must excuse me, as I've had a rather long day."

"Don't forget," said Julia, "we're due to sup with the Earl of Tewkesbury and his new bride tonight."

"Ooh, how positively enthralling. You must tell me all about them," Miss Delacourte gushed.

Julia winced ever so slightly.

It served her right.

James quit the parlor, leaving his wife to figure out how to extract the social-climbing fruit from their home before suppertime.

"I had hoped to do a bit of shopping on Thursday," Julia whined like a four-year-old.

"As I explained before, we must be on our way in three days' time. I did tell you this would be a short trip," James said.

"What's the hurry? We were supposed to attend the opera, and I haven't even had a chance to wear the splendid new ball gown from Godfrey's. I planned to show it off at London Assembly on Saturday."

"You can wear it when we return to Elmstone," he said.

Julia snorted. "When, pray tell, will I need a ball gown in Whitford? For afternoon tea?"

James had begun to feel frayed. "Wear it to tea, wear it to bed. I couldn't care less, Julia. But we are not staying in London for four more days just so you have a chance to wear some silly gown."

It was one o'clock in the afternoon. He, Julia, his mother, and Duncan were strolling through St. James's Park on their "morning" constitutional. James's disgust with London and the ton had quickly been renewed. He was anxious to return to Elmstone, not only to care for Leah but to again be amongst people who rose before noon and went to bed before dawn. With each sojourn to London the lifestyle James's peers embraced grew more loathsome to him.

Julia hurried ahead with Duncan, and the two soon became engrossed in conversation. As they spoke, Duncan withdrew a silver box from his pocket and displayed the contents to Julia. James had little time to wonder just what the box contained, for his mother gave his arm a tug.

"Were you able to see the physician?" she asked.

"I was."

"And?"

"And what?"

"James, you must stop keeping things from me. I love you, and I want to help you. If you're ill . . ."

James took his mother's hand. "All will be well, Mother. I promise."

"If only I could believe—Look! Over there. Isn't that Arthur riding toward us?"

James squinted in the direction his mother indicated. "By God, Mother, I believe you're correct."

James immediately recognized the mount galloping across the field. It was most certainly taken from the stables at Elmstone. The man riding upon it, however, slumped so low in the saddle James could hardly make him out until he rode closer.

Indeed, it was Arthur, limp with exhaustion. His face was drawn, and it appeared as if he hadn't changed his clothes since leaving Whitford.

James's heart pounded in his ears. Arthur was supposed to remain at Elmstone. If he'd left his post, it meant something terrible had happened.

Leah.

"Arthur, over here," James shouted.

Upon spotting his employer, the manservant leapt from the horse and hurried over. "My lord, the housekeeper told me you might be found here. We must speak in private immediately."

"Nonsense," said Merri. "Whatever you must say can be said in my company. Go on, Arthur."

The servant looked to James, discomfort obvious in his eyes.

"I insist," said Merri.

James gave Arthur a look of warning, hoping he would have enough sense not to mention Leah. "Go on, man. Come out with it."

Arthur cleared his throat. "Begging your pardon, Countess, but I didn't wish to upset you. However, if you urge me to speak candidly, I will do so." He turned to James. "Lord Darby, there has been a fire at the manor."

"A fire?" Merri swayed on her feet.

James led his mother to a bench. "Where?"

"In Lady Sarah's room."

"Sarah's room? Oh, dear." She wrung his hand painfully.

"Was she hurt?" James asked. His mother slumped against him, and he attempted to hold her upright. They'd begun to attract attention. Several fashionably attired ladies and gentlemen slowed as they passed the bench, attempting to catch a snippet of the conversation.

Arthur lowered his voice. "She suffered a brief loss of consciousness, but according to Delacourte, she has come around quite well."

"Delacourte? How is he involved in this?"

Arthur's face hardened. "I was forced to wake him, my lord, as no one had the key to Lady Sarah's room and we were unable to enter without brute force. I needed his assistance."

"Oh, dear," Merri said beneath her breath. She had managed to compose herself in the interest of dignity.

"Dammit. I should have insisted long ago that Sarah give a key to Miss Witherspoon."

"One could never have foretold such an incident, sir," Arthur said.

"What was the cause of the fire?"

"Who can say?" Arthur shifted uncomfortably on his feet. "In any case, Lord Darby, I believe you should return with some haste. Your sister may require your comfort."

"Of course."

James helped his mother from the bench. Julia and Duncan were nowhere in sight, but James guessed they would turn up at home for breakfast. Since Duncan had forsaken drink, he seldom missed a meal.

"Arthur, take a message to Lord Talbot at Grosvenor Square. Tell him I'll be unable to meet him this afternoon, but I appreciate his assistance in the Doctor Murfree matter. Then go to the stables and arrange for our carriages to be on the ready early tomorrow morning. It will take the rest of the day to prepare for the journey."

"You should ride ahead," said Merri.

He considered it for only a moment before memories of Sarah's accident invaded his thoughts. If anything were to happen to his mother or daughter, or even Julia, on the return trip, he would never forgive himself. "I'll ride with the carriages."

"Yes, my lord."

Arthur mounted his horse and rode slowly between the tight groups strolling on the lane. James would speak to him in private later. He wanted to tell him about the medicine he'd sent ahead for Leah. No doubt Arthur and the courier had missed each other by half a day, at least.

"Hurry along, Mother," James urged. "We have much to do."

Chapter 24

"*I want you to take the rest of the day for yourself,*" Sarah told Rebecca. "Perhaps a walk in the gardens will do you some good."

"Rebecca had just arrived at Elmstone, straight from the draper in Whitford, with two new gowns for Sarah. The maid's eyes were swollen from crying, having just bid her husband William goodbye for another two months.

"No, my lady. Work is just the thing to distract me from my thoughts." Rebecca withdrew a handkerchief from her bodice and gave her nose a lusty blow. "There. I'll think no more about it today. William will be home for Christmas, and until then I must do what I'm able. I'll keep him in my thoughts and in my heart."

"Very sensible of you."

"Not sensible. Necessary. It's hard to be sensible in matters of the heart."

Sarah thought of her forbidden attraction to Lucien. "I suppose it is."

She knew it was time to put her own misery behind her

and continue with life as she always had. Everyone lived with heartbreak, hers no worse than Rebecca's.

Lucien was still at Elmstone, still her friend. He could never be more, but he would never be less, either. That alone should have served to comfort her.

Unfortunately, it did not.

So she assumed an air of happiness she didn't feel, attempting to distract Rebecca from her gloom as the maid dressed her.

"Would you like to attend the Michaelmas celebration in Whitford?" she asked.

"Of course," said Rebecca. "But I've heard say that Lord Darby will never permit it."

"In the past he hasn't, but I believe he wanted only to protect my privacy. Any kind of celebration that would have put the Elmstone servants among the villagers would have opened the door to gossip. But now that I've been out, have been there, I hope I've quelled the rumors. Perhaps I can persuade my brother to change his mind."

"If you did, you'd win many hearts at Elmstone. Forgive my saying so, but it isn't the most pleasant place to work."

Sarah sighed. "James goes too far sometimes. He wasn't at all happy I ventured from the grounds. I imagine he wants to keep me here, where he believes no harm will come to me. I must talk with him when he returns."

"When will they return?"

"I'm not certain. But until then, please keep mum about Michaelmas."

"Of course." Rebecca finished buttoning Sarah's gown. "There you are, my lady. I don't know how Mr. Thomas and his wife managed to piece together two excellent garments in such a short time."

"I must remember to send them a token of my gratitude."

"Mr. Thomas has promised three more gowns next week, as well. He asked if you might wear one of them on your next visit to Whitford."

"Oh?"

"Will there be a visit soon, Lady Sarah?"

"We shall see."

"I'm sure Mr. Delacourte would accompany you."

Sarah's stomach fluttered at the mention of his name.

"Are you well enough to take supper downstairs to-night?" Rebecca asked.

"Yes. I suppose it is time to return to the dungeon."

"Will Mr. Delacourte join you?" Rebecca fussed with Sarah's sleeves and smoothed a puckered seam at her waist.

Sarah sighed. "I suppose so."

"Perhaps you could wear something special. The peach-colored silk, perhaps?"

"Becca, stop toying with my gown. May I ask why my wardrobe so interests you today?"

Rebecca looked surprised. "I'm sure I don't know what you mean."

"I think you do. Come out with it."

The maid wandered over to the dressing table and picked up a comb, running a fingernail over the teeth. "I swear I will never become accustomed to William's absences. Did I thank you for allowing me time to be with him?"

"Nine times."

"Well, I'll say it a tenth. Lady Sarah, we must steal every moment we can with the ones we love. Love is the only thing that matters."

Sarah watched her maid carefully. Did Rebecca suspect what had happened between her and Lucien? "It must be lovely to care for someone as deeply as you care for William," Sarah said.

"It is, my lady. It surely is."

"Well, thank you for your assistance, Becca."

"Will you need me this evening?" Rebecca gave her a pointed look.

Sarah smiled. "I'll ring if I do."

* * *

Though the day was cold and damp, Sarah donned a cape and went straight to the garden, avoiding the drawing room, the dining room, and anywhere else she thought Lucien might be. She needed time to think.

Rebecca's words echoed in her mind.

We must steal every moment we can with the ones we love. Love is the only thing that matters.

Of course, Rebecca was free to see William when she could, to love him with no restraint. That was the difference.

Sarah knelt beside a rosebush, raking fallen leaves and debris free of the base with her bare fingers.

Once again, her freedom was being stolen, this time not by her scars, but by propriety. She was not, like Rebecca, free to love whomever she wished without restraint. For Sarah, an indulgence in that sort of love would mean certain heartbreak.

For Lucien, however, it would mean so much more. He would lose his position and quite possibly his reputation. Could she, in good conscience, compromise his future to assuage her own desires?

But she wanted him. She could not deny it. The few hours they'd spent in each other's arms managed only to make her want him more. It was as if his touch had released her from an endless isolation, took her out of the walls of her small garden and into Eden itself.

She knew James would never understand, never approve of her love for Lucien. She also knew that the loss was inevitable. Their lessons would end. Lucien would leave.

The pile of refuse she'd gathered caught the wind and scattered over the lawn.

She could have Lucien now, while he was here. At least until James and the rest of her family returned. They could steal every moment together until there were no more moments to steal. She was willing to take the risk. But because it was Lucien who had the most to lose, the decision would have to be his.

He was in the drawing room with his back to the door, his silhouette framed in the gray of the sky through the window. His hands were clasped behind his back, his legs spread as if to hold him steady against some imaginary wind.

Had he been waiting for her?

She made a small noise and he turned. She felt a sudden rush of anticipation. She wanted to approach him but didn't dare, for fear she would fall to her knees and beg him to make love to her. Instead, she went to her stool before the easel.

"Will we resume our lessons today?"

"Is that what you wish?"

"Yes."

"Very well." He shed his jacket and moved beside her. "Will you wear the veils?"

How could she not? If she were to remove them, he would surely see her heart in her eyes. "I must."

He turned away. "Fine. Today, you will prepare the paints yourself."

She took up a mixing bowl and a tin of pigment. She shook the umber powder into the bowl and added a few drops of binder as she had seen Lucien do. He unrolled the pouch of brushes and chose one with stiff bristles for mixing the paint. When he handed it to her, his fingers grazed her palm, causing her heart to speed to a frantic beat.

She took a deep breath and held it, willing her heart to slow. With a shaking hand, she attempted to work the oil into the pigment.

"You must break up the lumps," he said. "Here. Let me show you." He covered her hand with his and stirred slowly.

His chest nearly touched her back, he stood so close. She could feel the heat of his body through her gown, and the warmth of his breath on the back of her neck.

"Lucien, I . . ."

"Yes?"

"I believe I understand, now."

He released her hand and stepped away. "What will you paint today?"

"I thought to try butterfly ginger. *Hedychium maximum*. I understand it's a favorite of the king."

"What colors will you need?"

"The leaves are dark green. The flowers are white with yellow centers."

Lucien busied himself at the table, opening tins of pigments, removing brushes from the pouch. She watched his fingers, so adept at their work. She remembered how easily those same fingers had loosened the ties of her night-gown . . .

Stop!

Lucien stilled. "You do not want the brushes today?"

Had she said that aloud?

"Never mind. I was speaking to myself. I believe I might be mixing this paint to the death."

He came to her side and looked into the bowl. "Not quite to the death, but perhaps to serious illness."

He took the palette from the table and hooked it over her thumb. "Take this. I will mix the rest of the colors for you. You can begin with what you have." He handed her a brush.

"Thank you. Lucien, will you . . ."

"What?"

"Nothing."

They worked in silence for a while. She experimented with different strokes on the canvas as Lucien gradually filled her palette with color. Each time he came near, the scent of cedar and spice teased her senses. Once she almost reached out to touch his hand. But she would make no overtures. He must be the one to revive their affair—if there was, in fact, to be an affair.

By the end of the lesson, she doubted it.

Two hours together had passed, but Lucien had made not so much as one suspect overture. He'd said not one word, made not one move that might be construed as anything more than friendly. Apparently he'd decided to respect her wishes and put their tryst out of his mind.

The Devil's teeth.

"If you would like to complete this work tomorrow, we can store the paint in sacks. When you wish to use it again, we will cut a hole in the sack and squeeze out the amount we require. It will save us from having to mix it all again."

He scooped the paint from the bowls and into several small bags, tying them tightly. Then he gathered up the brushes and washed them in turpentine.

"Will you scrape the palette?" he asked. He handed her a flat metal knife.

She took up the palette and began to remove the paint, watching Lucien as he worked.

With great care he cleaned each brush, inspecting the hairs and drying them well before returning them to their pouches. Then he lined up each implement on the table in the order by which they would be used during the next lesson. Sarah smiled. This thorough nature had proven most favorable in his lovemaking.

He hadn't overlooked an inch of her, kissing her fingertips, her elbows, the backs of her knees . . .

The metal scraper slipped from the palette, scoring the flesh of Sarah's hand.

"Oh, no!"

"What is it?" Lucien turned to her. "Oh, you are bleeding!"

He quickly wiped his hands on his breeches and grabbed a clean square of cloth from the table.

"It's not so bad," she said.

"Put the palette down," he commanded. He grasped her hand, palm upward, and wiped the blood from her cut.

"I'm fine, really."

"Let me see." He poked at her palm. A drop of blood escaped the cut, and he wiped it clean. Sarah trembled at the gentle pressure of his hand as it cradled hers. Lucien peered at her through the veils, his gaze seeking hers.

"Sarah, take off your veils."

She couldn't bring herself to do it, for she knew it would give her away.

"Show me your eyes," he said.

She shook her head.

Lucien released her hands and she buried them in her lap.

Slowly, he tugged at the bottom of her veils, freeing them from her bodice. The lace slid over her skin, making her shiver. Lucien's fingertips grazed the shallow valley of cleavage above her stomacher, causing her abdomen to draw tight.

The image of him grew sharp when he raised the veils over the brim of her hat. She drew a quick breath and released it, attempting to loosen the knot forming in her chest, but it grew even tighter when she looked into his face.

Everything she felt at that moment was mirrored in Lucien's eyes.

His fingers skimmed her cheeks, her chin, her neck. When he cupped her face in his hands and moved closer, a sigh escaped her lips.

"Lucien, I—"

"Shh." His lips brushed hers. She closed her eyes, wanting to feel each slight sensation without distraction. The kiss was light and warm, and opened her like the sun opens a rosebud.

Gentle pressure soon gave way to restrained urgency as Lucien buried his fingers in the hair at her temples. Her hat tumbled to the floor, releasing her hair from the loose knot in which it had been bound. It spilled over her shoulders, and Lucien wrapped it around his wrist, tipping her head back so that her neck was exposed to his kisses.

"Lucien, if James learns about us—"

"He will not," Lucien murmured against her neck.

"If he does, it will not be pleasant for you."

Lucien abandoned her neck to look into her eyes. "It will not be pleasant for you, either."

"I care nothing for that," she said. "What can he do to me? It's you who stands to suffer most."

His voice was thick with emotion. "I am suffering now. Can't you see how much I need you?"

His words broke the invisible barrier that held her in check. She reached up and wound her arms around his neck, pulling him to her. The kiss was deep. Urgent.

She reached out for him, resting the palms of her hands against the soft linen of his shirt, seeking the heat of his body beneath it. Lucien moved closer, sliding between her thighs. She could feel him harden through the thick wool of her skirts.

He reached down, sliding his hands over her ankles, her calves, her knees, beneath her underskirt and chemise, until he reached the span of naked flesh above her stockings. She moved forward on the stool and his fingers grazed the dampening curls between her legs. She cried out when his fingers gently entered her.

With his free hand he unfastened the hooks at her bodice, revealing the thin fabric of her chemise. He traced his tongue along the lacy edge. Her nipples grew taut with anticipation. In moments, the wet heat of his mouth covered them, one and then the other, until she could hardly stand the pleasure of it. His fingers and mouth continued to ravage her, taking her high atop a mountain of sensation where the air was so thin she could not breathe, dared not move.

And then she was falling. Lucien covered her mouth with his, muting her cry of release with a searing kiss as she tumbled back to earth.

She loved him. Dear God, she loved him. She would never let him go.

She fell limp into his arms and he gathered her against his chest, pulling her down from the stool to the thick carpet beneath them.

He stretched out beside her and she reached for him, stroking him through his breeches. Her trembling fingers worked to free him from the constraints. When her touch met bare skin, he groaned against her neck.

Without taking the time to shed his breeches, Lucien moved over her, pushing her skirts away until she was exposed to him. Unable to wait one more moment, she raised her hips to meet his, to take him inside of her. To surround him. To hold him.

Lucien cradled her head in the crook of one arm, kissing her eyes, her forehead, her chin. He moved into her like light into darkness, infusing every part of her until she couldn't tell where she ended and he began. His fingers twisted with hers as they met their climaxes together.

In the aftermath they lay with fingers and legs entwined, stretched out on the rough wool of the carpet. Sarah had nearly drifted off to sleep when she heard the clack of a latch. A cold draft of air tickled her bare legs. At once she realized their mistake.

They had forgotten to lock the drawing room doors.

Chapter 25 🍂

Sarah tensed in his arms.

"What's the matter?"

"Shh." She covered his mouth with her hand.

Then he heard them. Soft, shuffling footsteps near the doors of the drawing room.

"Lady Sarah?"

It was the maid, Elizabeth. Lucien recognized her voice from the night of the fire.

Fortunately, the alcove in which he and Sarah held their lessons was set off from the main area of the drawing room by a narrow wall that obscured them from Elizabeth's view.

Wrapping an arm around Sarah's waist, Lucien rolled with her until they landed behind a large armchair. He quickly righted Sarah's gown and buttoned his breeches.

"Lady Sarah?" Elizabeth's voice grew closer. From beneath the chair, Lucien could see the maid's shoes coming ever closer.

Just as she was about to enter the alcove, there came another voice from the door.

"There you are." It was a male voice, but Lucien could not place it.

Elizabeth giggled. "How did you find me?"

"I have my ways. Come over here, wench."

More female giggling. Lucien and Sarah watched beneath the chair as a dirty pair of boots met Elizabeth's functional lace-up shoes in the middle of the drawing room floor. After much heavy breathing and moaning, the pairs of shoes parted slightly.

"Did you bring it?" the man asked.

"The key, you mean?"

"The key, yes. Arthur asked me to make another today."

"But he's not even here. He's gone to London," said Elizabeth.

"I know that," the man said, his voice taking on a tinge of impatience. "He asked me before he left. He wants it done before he returns."

"Why didn't he just ask me himself?"

"I dunno. Maybe he's afraid of your big bosoms. You know how he shakes when he talks to you."

More giggling and breathing and moaning.

"A'right. Come with me an' I'll get it for you."

The shoes disappeared. Lucien and Sarah exhaled at the same time. He chuckled at their near miss, but Sarah had just the opposite reaction. She looked about to cry.

"Abominable. Absolutely shameful!" She stood in the corner like a child who had misbehaved.

"What?" Lucien guided Sarah to a chair, but she refused to sit.

"I am."

"Do you regret what we have done?"

She hung her head in silence.

"We have done nothing to be ashamed of."

She raised her eyes, wet with tears, to meet his. "I don't regret our lovemaking. But I'm ashamed of myself because I may well have imperiled your position here with my selfish desires. I wanted to be with you, and paid no heed to the danger of my actions."

Lucien laughed. "My dear Sarah, if what we did has imperiled me, then I hope to live in peril for the rest of my days. Lest you forget, I wanted you every bit as much as you wanted me."

She sniffled. "Elizabeth could easily have discovered us."

"But she did not."

"Nevertheless, it was foolish to take such a chance."

"I agree. From now on, we shall make love only where the maid will not discover us."

"Lucien!"

"Fine. We shall make love only where the maid, the cook, and the stable hands cannot find us. Does that suit?"

Sarah smiled. "What about Arthur?"

"We do not have to worry about him, remember?"

Sarah frowned. "Why do you suppose he went to London?"

"It doesn't matter."

She let out another breath. "Can you imagine if poor Elizabeth had discovered us? The shock may well have put her in Bedlam."

"Shock? She obviously is not the prudish type."

"No, the sight of my bare legs would hardly have shocked her, but one look at my face most certainly would have."

Lucien's amusement quickly faded.

He cupped Sarah's chin and looked into her eyes. "Your face is beautiful. Why do you still insist on hiding behind those veils?"

She turned away. "Please, no lies, Lucien. I'll accept anything but that from you. I know what I look like."

"Damn it, Sarah. I cannot abide such nonsense. It may have been Lavery's betrayal that sent you into hiding, but you remain there of your own free will."

Sarah retrieved her hat and veils from the floor where they had fallen. She secured the hat and lowered the veils. "And what of you? You hide behind your memories just as I hide behind my veils."

"I do not know what you mean."

"Why are you here, Lucien? Because you've run away." Sarah grabbed his hand and towed him across the drawing room, coming to a stop before his painting of the French garden. "You're wasting your talents here. You are no tutor, you are an artist. Why aren't you at Versailles, painting?"

He closed his eyes. "Stop."

"No. You take me to task for wearing my veils, but you're a hypocrite. You've not painted since you passed through our doors. You've forsaken your talents."

"No."

"Then why do you not paint?"

"Because I cannot!" His laugh was derisive, humorless. "You saw that for yourself. I cannot put a brush to canvas. It has not only been since I arrived here. I have not painted a stroke since . . ."

"Since Katrina and Tessa died?"

He opened his eyes. "I have lied to you, and to your family. I am little more than a charlatan. I would not blame you for despising me."

"Despise you? I could not."

"But you trusted me, and I betrayed you. Perhaps not in the same way Lavery did, but I betrayed you just the same."

"How? I wanted a tutor, and you have certainly been that. But more importantly, you have been a friend. The dearest friend I've ever had. Not only have you fulfilled your obligations as a teacher of art, you've given me back the courage I thought I had lost."

Lucien's throat felt raw. He swallowed. "But I have not painted in years."

Sarah took his hand and led him back to the alcove. She

placed her hat and veils on the table. "Until a few days ago, I hadn't left this wretched manor in years."

From the pouches of paint he had mixed earlier, she prepared a simple palette. She put him before the easel and took a brush in hand, dabbing it into the paint.

She held it out to him. "Try."

The look of hope in Sarah's eyes, the complete confidence in his abilities, reminded Lucien so much of Katrina he nearly turned away. But to have found another woman with such faith in him was a blessing. He could not refuse her.

He took the brush, balancing it in the crook of his thumb, testing the weight. It felt foreign in his hand.

With a ragged breath, he stretched his arm toward the easel. The instant before the brush touched the canvas, his hand retreated of its own will.

"I cannot."

"You will do this. Just as I walked through the gates of Elmstone, you will paint again. I promise you." Sarah curled her fingers over his. "Let me help you." She guided his hand, and the brush, to the canvas. A pain shot through his arm as the hairs of the brush skimmed the taut surface.

A stroke, blood red, was rendered.

It was but the width of hair, hardly visible, but they both had witnessed its creation. Sarah guided his hand to the palette, and he rolled the brush in the paint.

This time her touch on his hand was lighter as they moved toward the canvas. They repeated the sequence again and again. When the tension in Lucien's shoulders ebbed, when the last of his resistance melted away, Sarah released his hand completely. She stepped away.

His strokes grew bolder as he worked, until an image appeared on the canvas.

A rose.

It held none of the perfection of Sarah's summer blooms,

nor did it resemble his previous works, but its form was clearly rendered.

A knot formed in Lucien's chest as he studied the canvas. Thoughts of Katrina, of Tessa, of the whole of his life before Elmstone rushed into his mind on the speed of a hummingbird's wings.

Images blurred. Sights, sounds, smells assaulted him, pulling the knot in his chest tighter and tighter. When it seemed he would be pulled inside out, Sarah touched him.

The light stroke of her palm on his shoulder unbound him with the force of a hurricane. The knot broke and, with it, his control. Every moment of emotional release denied him when he was unable to paint came rushing to the surface.

Memories . . .

Katrina and Tessa laughing and playing in a field of fragrant wildflowers. Tessa's small hand in his. Katrina's body moving beneath him as they made love. Crowds of courtiers at Versailles. The fire. The stench of burning flesh. Katrina and Tessa, charred beyond recognition. Their freshly turned graves. The filthy hovels of Paris in which he had lived afterward. The cold mist on his face as he crossed the English Channel. The lonely journey from Weymouth to Whitford . . . The gardens. Sarah.

"Sarah."

Lucien's anguish reached into her, gripping her heart, even as his hands gripped her shoulders. Never before had Sarah witnessed a man's undoing. But she had never known a man possessed of such passion and emotion as he.

Why did he weep? Sarah could only imagine. She knew by her own experience that grief was a solitary thing. She only hoped her presence served to comfort him.

Lucien wrapped his arms around her, and she gathered him to her as she would a child, stroking his hair, his neck,

his shoulders. Then, as abruptly as it had begun, his weeping ceased.

His face was still buried against her, but his shoulders
had relaxed. She combed her fingers through his hair, and
he looked up at her.

"God sent me here," he whispered. "And you must be an
angel, for only an angel could cause such pain to leave."

"I'm no angel, Lucien, merely a woman. But perhaps
God did put us together so we could see, in each other, how
we've been wasting our lives."

"Then we must honor His wishes and waste no more.
Promise?"

"I promise."

"Our new lives begin now."

Sarah awoke to the sound of Lucien's snoring, and smiled.
It was a sound she never dreamed she would hear emanat-
ing from the opposite side of her bed.

She and Lucien had kept their promise to one another
by exploring the countryside, descending hand in hand to
Whitford to visit with old friends and new. Though they
didn't make their affair public, Sarah was sure there were
some in the village who suspected the true nature of their
relationship.

She doubted that news of it would travel farther than the
village limits. James didn't visit Whitford often, and those
she'd called upon would certainly understand the value of
discretion with him.

She languished on the bed, stretching her legs out until
her foot grazed Lucien's calf. He awoke in seconds, pulling
her on top of him and kissing her senseless.

"Good morrow, Lady Sarah." His voice was deep and
scratchy with the early hour.

"Good morrow, Mr. Delacourte. What shall we do today?"

He laughed. "Will you give me a chance to awaken, or must we sally forth in our nightclothes this instant?"

"I'm afraid we aren't wearing any nightclothes."

Lucien lifted the covers and peeked beneath them. "So I see. Well then, perhaps we should lie abed all day instead."

"Absolutely not. We have much to do. I promised Mrs. Endfirth we would visit."

Lucien nuzzled her neck and stroked her bare back with his fingertips, eliciting a sensual shiver.

"Well, perhaps Mrs. Endfirth can wait until after breakfast," she said.

"Breakfast, eh? If that is what you wish to call it . . ."

"Lucien!"

He smothered her admonishment with a kiss, and it was much later than noon before they finally started out for Mrs. Endfirth's tiny cottage on the outskirts of town.

As they walked, they discovered a small clearing in the woods, beautiful despite the lateness of the year. Tall brown grass, stark against the black-green of Scots pines and yew trees, whispered in the breeze.

"Sit with me awhile," Lucien said, plunking down in the middle of the tiny glen and pulling her into his lap.

"It's lovely here. I've never seen this place before."

"Will you paint it?"

"Will you?"

Lucien breathed deep. "We should paint it together. What are the trees?"

"Pine. Yew. Did you know it is possible for a yew tree to live for a thousand years? There is one in Scotland suspected of being more than nine hundred years old."

"Poor old man. I'm sure his hearing is long gone."

She laughed. "You make jokes about everything."

Lucien's face grew serious. He cupped her chin in his hand and kissed her lightly. "Not everything."

"No, not everything," she said softly.

His eyes searched hers. "I . . ."

"Yes?"

He cleared his throat. "I think we ought to be going. Mrs. Endfirth will surely wonder about us."

They departed the clearing in silence, Sarah wondering exactly what it was Lucien had wanted to say.

Chapter 26

It was still dark when they arrived home. It was madness to have traveled overnight, but James had insisted.

For the first time since her marriage, returning to Elmstone did not turn Julia's stomach. This day would mark a triumph, she was certain. This day she would, at long last, have Lucien Delacourte in her bed.

With the information she'd painstakingly culled from Mathilde Delacourte, she now would have him pinned to a wall, unable to refuse her. From experience she knew that she would only have to persuade him once. After that, he would come to her willingly.

"See to my things," she snapped to Agnes. "I want them in my rooms by daybreak."

Julia hurried up the steps and into the house, throwing her wrap on a chair in the hall. All was silent and dark. Instead of waiting for the servants, she lit a candle and mounted the stairs, anxious to set her plans in motion.

Upon entering her quarters, she lit several candles. The

room was bitter cold. She rang for Thora to set a fire, and waited impatiently for Agnes to arrive with her trunks. In the room beside hers, she heard the door open and close. The low murmur of voices beyond the connecting door drew her to press her ear against it. She could make out none of the conversation, but she could tell it was her husband speaking to Arthur. In a few moments, the voices faded and she heard the door open and close again.

Where could he be going at such an hour?

Julia's thoughts were interrupted by Agnes, who clumped noisily into the room with Thora in tow. Moments later, several exhausted servants arrived with her trunks and bags.

"Put them in the corner," she ordered. "Agnes, you may see to them later. I wish to remove my traveling garments immediately."

"Yes, my lady."

Never the most dexterous of maids, Agnes's bumbling nearly drove Julia to madness this day. She slapped the maid's hands away.

"Leave off. I shall manage myself. I'm quite tired, and wish only to crawl into bed and sleep until teatime. I don't want to be disturbed until I ring for you."

"Yes, my lady." Agnes shuffled from the room, leaving Julia to fumble with the fastenings of her gown.

Just as a thin, gray light seeped through her windows, Julia slipped from her rooms. Dressed only in a midnight blue silk wrapper newly purchased in London, she headed toward the stairs, praying she encountered no one along the way.

She arrived at Lucien's door with no disturbance. Glancing about, she tested the doorknob. It was locked, but no matter. From a gold chain around her neck, she withdrew a key pilfered from Miss Witherspoon's ring. Julia had carried it with her for weeks in anticipation of this very moment.

With a steady hand, she quietly turned the key in the lock before returning it to her neck. She would need it in the days to come.

Julia had forgone slippers for the silence bare feet would afford, and she tiptoed across the cold stone floors, nearly sighing with relief when her feet met the carpet that covered the floor beneath Lucien's bed.

He was on his side facing the windows, his back turned to the door. She took a moment to study his form beneath the covers, imagining what it would be like to lie with him, until the suspense drove her to his bedside.

As she rounded the end of the bed, she was greeted by a shocking sight. Lucien was wrapped, quite intimately, around another sleeping form. The woman's hair fanned wildly across the pillow, even as the rest of her was tucked neatly into the cup of Lucien's body.

Julia gasped. She would kill the harlot with her bare hands.

Who was it, a member of the staff? She couldn't recall any maid possessed of such dark tresses. Why, the woman's hair was almost the color of—

No. It simply could not be.

Sarah?

Julia squinted at the bed, but the thin light of the room didn't afford a clear view of the woman. She would have to get closer. Taking care not to breathe too loudly, she crept ever nearer to the bed.

She twisted her loose hair in a bunch and held it close to her chest as she bent over the sleeping form.

It *was* Sarah!

Though Julia hadn't seen her sister-in-law's face since before she was married, she recognized her instantly. Sarah had James's squared jaw line and Merri's decidedly unattractive cleft chin.

Only the slightest length of a silvery scar was visible on that chin. Julia was puzzled. The way Duncan had described the damage to Sarah's face just after the accident, Julia had pictured something akin to a toad caught in a spinning wheel. She could only assume the most wretched of the damage was hidden by the pillow on which Sarah's other cheek rested.

Well, well. The mangled toad had somehow found a man who pitied her enough to take her to bed.

Julia was disappointed with Lucien. He must have been truly desperate to do such a thing. Little did he know, she was about to rescue him.

She backed silently away from the bed and slipped out the door, locking it behind her.

Julia tapped her spoon on the table in the breakfast room, impatient to set things in motion. At first she'd been disappointed to learn that Lucien had bedded Sarah. After some thought, however, she realized it would only serve to make her liaison with him all the sweeter.

To take away something Sarah treasured would mean an added victory, considering all that Sarah had taken from her. Nights at the London Theatre. Balls. Dinner parties. Strolling at Vauxhall . . . the social events any other countess would consider mere convention. Were it not for James's vehement devotion to Sarah, Julia would live an enchanted existence. Instead, she'd been sentenced to this beleaguered outpost of humanity.

She heard voices in the hall and quickly returned her spoon to its proper place. She fluffed the curls at her temples and hoisted her bosom into place just in time for the couple's entrance.

Sarah clung to Lucien's arm like a barnacle, laughing madly as they passed through the doors. Her cackling ceased the moment she spied Julia.

Lucien was the first to speak. "Lady Darby. You've returned."

She graced him with a shining smile. "I have! And none too soon, by the look of things."

Sarah dropped Lucien's arm. "Julia. What a pleasant . . . What a surprise. How did you find London?"

"At the end of the road, of course."

They all chuckled a bit too heartily. Julia smiled. Could she enjoy anything more than watching Sarah squirm?

Sarah turned her attention to the table, taking her customary seat beside Merri's empty one. Lucien chose a chair in the middle, studying the trays of food with a meticulous eye.

"There are no figs today," Julia said brightly. "Mother is still abed, and after James learned that you suffered no serious injury in the fire, Sarah, he disappeared. So, I took the liberty of removing figs from the menu. I hope no one objects."

"Of course not," said Lucien.

Sarah said nothing. Julia noticed her plate was empty.

"Not hungry, Sarah?"

"No."

"Really? I imagined you would have quite an appetite, what with all that's gone on lately."

Sarah's head snapped around. "Gone on?"

Julia smiled. "I happened into the drawing room this morning, and I saw the paintings. So many! It appears you've been busy in our absence."

"The works aren't solely mine. Several of them belong to Lucien."

Julia turned to him in surprise. "You're painting, Mr. Delacourte? Why, with the way you've been so against it, one would almost have thought you'd given it up."

Lucien cleared his throat. "I find I am not so hungry as I thought. If you will excuse me—"

"Do stay," Julia said. "I have some news which may interest you, in particular."

Lucien sank back into his chair.

"I happened upon your dear cousin Mathilde while in London. We took to each other famously."

"I would not have imagined her welcomed in your circle, being only the daughter of a merchant."

"We're not so imperious as that, Lucien. And your cousin is quite resourceful. She's somehow managed to ingratiate herself into London society. We had the most enlightening conversation."

Lucien stood. "I trust you gave her my regards. But for as much as I would like to hear news of her, I am afraid Sarah and I have a lesson."

"Lucien, if you would like to discuss your cousin, our lesson can certainly wait," said Sarah.

Poor, stupid Sarah.

Lucien said, "We must not miss the morning sun. Your current composition requires it."

"Of course." Sarah followed Lucien from the dining room. She hadn't taken a bite of food.

Julia wondered exactly how long it would be before Lucien sought her out.

Just after noon, there came a knock at the door to Julia's chambers. She'd have stayed there all day, if necessary, to force Lucien to find her there.

She loosened the sash of her blue dressing gown—the same one she'd worn when she discovered Sarah in Lucien's room—before answering the door.

"Lucien. What a surprise."

He stood in the hall in his shirtsleeves, the cuffs rolled up to his elbows, his tie crumpled in his hand. Already he was half undressed.

She licked her lips. She could hardly wait to get to the other half.

"May I enter, Lady Darby?"

Julia pulled her dressing gown close. "Do you think it proper, Mr. Delacourte?"

"You are right, of course." He turned away.

Julia grabbed his sleeve. "I shall make an exception for you. No one is about, so I need not fear for my reputation as long as we're quiet."

She led him into the bedchamber, noticing he took great care not to look directly at the bed. "Why did you wish to see me?"

"I believe you already know the answer," he said. He came closer; so close she could smell the turpentine on his hands. She trembled with excitement as he reached for her. He stroked her bare neck with his fingertips, moving lower and lower, until she trembled at his touch. He plumbed the depths of her cleavage, and hooked the gold chain she wore.

He withdrew the key and dangled it before her eyes. "To my door, I assume. How did you get it?"

"How do you know it opens your door?"

"Because I saw you there this morning." He withdrew the chain from her neck before stepping away from her.

"You mean when you were in bed with my sister-in-law?"

"Yes. I said nothing to Sarah. I did not wish to alarm her. What were you doing there?"

She followed him to the other side of the room, trapping him in a corner. "I believe you already know the answer."

"Shall we pretend I do not? Make yourself clear."

She sighed. "Very well. I shall state my intentions, though I don't think you're half as thick as Sarah. I want you to make love to me. Beginning now."

"It is not possible."

"Not possible? Of course it's possible. James won't return for hours, if I know him at all. No doubt Sarah is holed up in her little rooms dreaming of you, if her whereabouts haven't already been discovered by Duncan. The dowager is as close to dead as she'll get before the actual blessed event. And the servants wouldn't dare disturb me unless I ring for them. So you see, we're free to do whatever we wish."

She wrapped her arms around Lucien's neck, pressing against him, reveling in the feel of his hard chest beneath hers. Until he pushed her away.

"You have forgotten one detail. *I* do not want *you*."

The heat of anger quickly replaced the flush of passion. "Of course you wish it."

"No, I do not."

Her hands balled into fists. "You do, and I'll tell you why. Because if you choose not to bend to my will, if you choose not to take me to my bed, you will pay handsomely for your actions."

Lucien moved toward the door. "What makes you so bitter that you would spoil everyone else's happiness?"

A spark of fury lit in her chest. "You should thank me. I'm saving you from certain ruin. If James finds out about you and Sarah, you will have nothing."

"No doubt my relationship with Sarah will anger your husband. But I hope to be able to convince him that my intentions are honorable. I hope to make him see reason."

Julia laughed, high and shrill. "Reason? That man is incapable of reason where his sister is concerned. Maybe you'd be able to convince him that you love her. And perhaps your avowal wouldn't solely cause him to reject your suit. But how will you explain your other deceits?"

Lucien stopped at the door.

"As I said at breakfast, your cousin Mathilde and I grew quite close. She confessed to me that your creditors in Paris have been in contact with her. They advised her you're no longer in service to the king, because you no longer paint. Therefore, you have no source of income to repay them."

A look of uncertainty crossed his face.

"Tell me, Lucien, how can one be the teacher of a craft he no longer practices?"

"But I *am* painting. You saw it for yourself, in the drawing room."

"That hardly matters. You accepted your position here under false pretenses, a fact that James won't ignore."

"I will speak with him immediately—"

"By all means, do. Tell him you arrived here a penniless artist unable to paint. Tell him you perpetuated a lie while seducing his beloved sister, who stands to inherit a good portion of his family's fortune. By all means, Lucien, tell him those things. For if you don't, I will. Unless, of course, you decide to come to bed with me."

The look in his eyes told her the answer even before it passed his lips.

"Never."

Chapter 27

Arthur's horse was tied in the clearing beside the little cottage when James arrived. The stack of firewood beside the door had dwindled considerably since he'd gone, proof that the cold had truly arrived.

Again he considered moving Leah to a more substantive house, but he wanted her close to him. Besides, to move her in this kind of weather might do more harm than good. The cottage was small, but it was warm and in good repair.

He let the door close softly behind him, in case she was sleeping. Arthur stood by the bed beside the nurse, his tall, lanky form bent in concentration.

It took just three strides for James to arrive at Arthur's side. "Have you administered another dose?"

"Just minutes ago."

James addressed the nurse. "Has it been effective?"

"'Tis hard to say, my lord. She sleeps so much I cannot tell if there's been a change in her."

"You see why I felt it necessary to fetch you from London," Arthur said.

"Yes. It was the proper thing to do. I wouldn't have gone at all, if not for the chance of meeting with Doctor Murfree. We must hope his knowledge as a physician matches his reputation."

The three stood shoulder to shoulder, watching the rise and fall of Leah's chest. She was propped up against three pillows, as she had been since the illness had taken hold.

"Her breathing seems easier," the nurse commented. The men agreed.

"Her color, too," said Arthur.

As they clucked over her like hens, Leah opened her eyes. James knelt at her side and took her hand, bringing it to his lips.

"My darling, my darling," he murmured against her fingers. "Speak to me."

"James?"

"I'm here. How do you feel?" He handed her a cup of water and she took a sip, wincing as she swallowed.

"Much better, now that you're here. Did London suit you?"

He laughed. "London never suits me. But I was able to meet with a doctor there. We're trying a new treatment."

Leah smiled sadly. "I fear there's little that will help me now, though my spirits are bolstered by your presence. Please, James, don't leave me again."

"It will be as you wish." He turned to Arthur and the nurse. "The both of you should go. Take some food and rest."

"But you haven't slept since leaving London," said Arthur.

"I wouldn't, anyway. Go on. I'll stay with her for a while."

The nurse disappeared into a tiny room at the back of the cottage.

"I'll return in a few hours to relieve you," said Arthur.

James nodded. His gaze didn't leave Leah's face. He

remembered her as she had been, fair-skinned and lovely, before the ravages of dropsy had taken their toll.

"How can you stand to look upon me now?" she asked, as if reading his thoughts.

"How can I not?"

A single tear escaped her. "I made your life miserable even before this wretched illness, and now—"

"Hush. My life would have been nothing without you."

She was quiet for a while, stroking his fingers, gazing into his eyes. "If not for me, you would have been with your sister that night. You would never have had to marry Julia."

"Leah, we've talked this subject to death. It was my decision to leave Sarah alone at the ball. It was a mistake, to be certain. But it was my mistake, not yours."

"But I wanted you to come to me."

"I wanted to be with you. Nothing could have prevented it. I wish I had been there to protect Sarah, to bring her home. But what's done is done, and I've paid for my error in spades. You shouldn't have to pay for it, too."

She smiled sadly. "No. I merely paid for the circumstance of my birth. If I'd been born a lady instead of a haberdasher's daughter, how different things would have been."

James rubbed the back of her hand on his cheek. "Let's speak of this no more. Are you thirsty? Shall I fetch more water?"

Leah shook her head. "Just stay with me."

"Always."

Lucien searched everywhere for Sarah. He had to find her before Lady Darby found her husband. Before Lord Darby found *him.*

Why had he not told Sarah of his debts? They would have meant nothing to her, he was certain. It was only his pride that had prevented him from revealing them. Now she would hear of them from someone else, unless he could find her first.

He headed for the orangery, hopeful he would find her there. It was the only place on the main floor of the house he had not yet checked, and she had once told him she liked to visit it on cold days. She said it warmed her soul to sit in the green when the world outside was so bleak.

When he arrived, there was, in fact, someone there. But it was not Sarah.

Arthur kneeled in a corner, rooting through the plants growing in a box beside the window. Lucien ducked behind a potted lemon tree, watching as the servant plucked some leaves and secreted them in a small leather pouch. He glanced about before exiting the orangery on the side opposite from where Lucien hid.

When Arthur had gone, Lucien strode to the box near the window. He bent down on one knee, surveying the plants growing there.

Foxglove. He recognized it from one of Sarah's drawings.

Why would the valet need the leaves of a foxglove plant?

And then he remembered what Sarah had said while she sketched the plant. If ingested in a sufficient amount, foxglove caused death.

Lucien raced from the orangery, the urgency of his mission suddenly doubled.

Julia paced the hallway, stopping before the mahogany cabinet clock for the hundredth time.

Damn James.

He had been gone for hours, as usual. Where could he be? As far as she knew, he had neither slept nor eaten since they returned from London. At least, not with her.

His absences no longer bothered her as they had in the beginning. She found she didn't enjoy his company enough to harp on him any further. Let him trot about the countryside. Let him mingle with farmhands and study crops and ruin his fine linen shirts with dirt. She cared not.

Except today.

This afternoon, she cared very much where her husband was. Or more specifically, when he would return. And she planned to wait here, in the hall, until he appeared. She wouldn't risk having Lucien speak to him first.

The mere thought of the artist set her blood to boil. That he would actually refuse her had never crossed her mind, at least not in any serious measure. His resistance had been alluring at first, and then challenging. It had all been a game to her. A very welcome game in which she always assumed she would be declared the winner.

Now, however, it was war.

Lucien would know his place in the world. Julia would make sure of it.

"Sarah!"

Duncan's voice echoed through the halls. Sarah silently cursed. She ignored his call.

"Oh, Sarah. There you are. I've been looking for you all morning." Duncan caught up with her at the rotunda.

"I'm sorry, Duncan, but I am in a terrible hurry," she lied.

"But I haven't seen you in almost a week. I need to speak with you." He hopped in front of her like an excited child, blocking her way to the stairs.

"Not now, Duncan."

"Just one moment. Please?"

She exhaled in frustration. "Very well. What is it that's so urgent?"

"It's just that I . . . well, I've missed you terribly. I

thought of nothing but you in London. I know that in the past I hurt you terribly, but—"

"We discussed that, Duncan. You're forgiven. Now may I please go?"

"Not before you guess what I have behind my back."

"Duncan!"

"Oh, all right. This isn't how I had pictured this moment, but . . ." He grabbed her hand, and slipped a ring onto her finger.

It was a silver band with two diamonds flanking a square-cut emerald. She stared stupidly at it.

"It's a ring," he said.

"I see that."

"A gift. For our betrothal. I want you to marry me, Sarah. Say yes."

"No." She pulled the ring off her finger and shoved it at him.

Duncan put his hands behind his back. "I won't take it back. Come, let's go find your brother and tell him the good news."

Sarah sighed. "What of your wife?"

He grinned. "It would seem I never had one. The marriage was declared unlawful. At long last, we can be together, my darling."

"Duncan, I said no. I will not marry you."

Before he could say another word, she skirted him and ran for the stairs.

"We'll talk about this later," he called after her.

Robert stood waiting for him on the drive before the main doors. James handed the reigns of his mount over and trudged up the steps. His boots had the weight of anvils. His head ached from lack of sleep and worry.

Though they had already administered half a dozen doses, the foxglove didn't seem as if it would cure Leah's dropsy. Her breathing was better, but the obvious, outward ravages had diminished little.

He hadn't wanted to leave her. Arthur's badgering had done nothing to convince him he needed sleep. It was only when he nearly pitched over into Leah's lap that she'd insisted he return home to take some food and rest.

James's already dark mood sank deeper when he entered the hall to find his wife glaring at him.

"James! Where have you been? I've been waiting hours for you to return."

"What is it, Julia?"

"I must speak with you immediately."

"Can't this wait a few hours? I've not eaten a bite all day."

"I'll ring for tea once we're settled." She grabbed his arm and dragged him to the drawing room, checking to be sure there was no one within before ushering him into the room. She closed the doors behind them.

James dropped into a chair, weary to his very bones, and Julia took the chair beside him.

"Tea?" he said.

She jumped from her seat and hurried to the bell pull, giving it several impatient tugs before returning to his side.

"Very well. What is it that's so urgent?" he said.

"It's about Mr. Delacourte. He must be sent away immediately."

James sighed wearily. "I know you don't approve of his attention to Anne, but I believe it does the child good to take an interest in something."

"It's not his attention to Anne which has me in a pique. It's his attention to Sarah."

"We've discussed this as well. Lucien is Sarah's tutor, and you shall not interfere with their lessons. If you care to learn to paint, I'll find someone else to teach you."

"No, no. It isn't the lessons! What he's done is quite shocking. He—"

The doors opened and a maid arrived with a tray. Much to the servant's surprise, and James's amusement, Julia snatched the tray from her hands.

"Thank you. I'll take care of this."

"Yes, my lady." The maid rushed for the door as if pursued by a ghost and ran straight into Delacourte.

"You're interrupting a private discussion, Mr. Delacourte," said Julia, intercepting him at the threshold. "Please leave us to speak in private."

"If I am not mistaken, this conversation pertains to me, does it not?"

James stood. "Indeed, it does. Julia, allow the man to enter. He should be here to defend himself against the charges you level."

For a moment James believed his wife might attempt to physically restrain the artist from entering the drawing room. She stepped aside, though, casting him a look of pure poison as he passed.

"I appreciate your sense of decency, Lord Darby. Whatever Lady Darby may have told you, you must hear me out."

"But she hasn't—"

"James," Julia interrupted. "By all means, allow Mr. Delacourte to speak on his own behalf."

James looked at his wife, confused by her sudden acquiescence. She nodded.

"Fine. What have you to say for yourself?"

"What Lady Darby witnessed this morning," Lucien began, "was no mere dalliance. Sarah and I have fallen in love. With your blessing, I plan to marry her."

"Marry her!" James felt the blood rush to his face. He put his fists on his hips to keep from using them in another capacity. "You had best tell me exactly *what* my wife witnessed."

"I assumed Lady Darby had already spoken to you about the situation," Lucien said, unable to disguise the note of surprise in his voice.

"Our conversation hadn't progressed so far. Now you may do me the favor of telling me yourself."

Lucien stood firm in the face of Lord Darby's menacing glare. Though he probably should have kicked himself for speaking out of turn, he was relieved to be the one to explain the situation to his employer. "I assumed your wife had revealed something of a personal nature, involving myself and Lady Sarah."

"Go on with it, man. What is it?"

Lucien struggled to find the words that would paint Sarah as blameless, while at the same time imparting the depth of his feelings toward her. He did not want Lord Darby to think that theirs was a frivolous affair.

"Perhaps we should sit."

A spark flared in Lord Darby's eyes. "I prefer to stand."

Lucien nodded. "I cannot begin without first conveying my respect for you and your family. I admire your devotion to Sarah, and I understand your need to protect her. But I assure you, there is no need to protect her from me."

Lady Darby made a small noise of disgust, but nary a muscle twitched in Lord Darby's face.

"Your wife discovered Sarah and me in a rather, ah, intimate setting."

"Intimate?"

Lucien cleared his throat. "My bed, to be exact."

Chapter 28

The force of Lord Darby's fist shattered Lucien's cheek.

Somehow he managed to remain standing. But the second blow knocked him to the floor. He rose, only to be knocked down again by the earl's hammering fists. Lord Darby hauled him to his feet by his jacket. Another strike to the chin drew a trickle of blood from the corner of Lucien's mouth. The temptation to strike back was great, but Lucien held himself at bay. The man had every right to defend his sister's honor.

"For God's sake, James! You'll kill him!" Lady Darby attempted to pull her husband away, but his fists kept flying. She ran to the other side of the room.

Not an inch of Lucien's body escaped the earl's wrath before the man's lust for blood was sated. Numb, Lucien staggered to his feet, expecting again to be beaten to the ground. Instead Lord Darby's blood-covered fists fell to his sides.

"Leave this house," he said, through labored breaths.

Lucien wiped the blood from his mouth with the back of his hand. "Forgive me, Lord Darby, but I cannot. I am deeply in love with your sister, and I believe she is in love with me."

The silence in the room was more threatening than Lord Darby's previous fit of rage. The two men stood as if suspended in wax, like Sarah's summer roses. Lucien steeled himself for another attack.

But Lord Darby sank into a chair and covered his face with his hands. "Go," he said quietly.

Lucien sensed he had been given a reprieve. He had no intention of leaving Elmstone, but he knew that should he ignore Lord Darby's magnanimous gesture, he would ruin any chance he had of convincing the lord of his honorable intentions. Nor had he made mention of the important matter that had caused him to seek the earl to begin with. Arthur's treachery.

It was a matter Lucien intended to address as soon as Lord Darby had cooled enough to listen to reason.

Lucien bowed as best he could and limped from the room, hoping against hope that he did not run into Sarah before he had a chance to wash the blood from his face and change his shirt.

It took a moment for Julia to gather herself. She'd never seen James hit a man. In fact, she'd never seen him show such emotion, ever. It made her wonder how things between them could have been, if he'd ever directed such passion toward her.

"I must say, I'm quite proud of you," she said. "I discovered so many unsavory things about him in London. Did you know he's no longer in favor with his king?"

James was silent.

"It's true," she continued. "Before he came here, he hadn't painted in years. He owes every merchant in Paris. The man is unconscionable."

"Unconscionable?" James issued a flat, mirthless laugh.

"Go and get me something to clean this blood from my hands."

"Me! Isn't that what the servants are for? I'll just ring—"

"Get out of my sight, Julia. Before I ask you what, exactly, you were doing in Lucien Delacourte's room."

Julia's face grew hot. "As you wish, *my lord.*"

She fumed all the way to the kitchen. How dare he accuse her? Where had *he* been at dawn? She'd never really felt anything for James, but the fact that he would question her fidelity when he was suspect, himself, angered her beyond reason. Without a doubt, the world was made for men in every single way.

She pushed open the heavy door to the kitchen, startled to see a tight knot of servants, heads bowed, huddled over something on the floor.

"What's going on in here?" she snapped. "Don't you all have better things to do?"

The servants turned to her, the same look of shock and confusion on each of their faces. The huddle parted, revealing the focus of their attentions. On the floor lay a motionless pile of fur.

"What is that?" Julia drew closer, and gasped. A dead cat lay there, its legs stretched out stiff as tree limbs. "What's the meaning of this?"

The servants were silent.

"Come, now. Someone tell me what this creature is doing here? Mrs. Hopstead?"

The cook broke away from the group, wringing her apron nervously in her hands. "The cat's dead, m'lady."

"I can see that. What is a dead cat doing in the kitchen?"

"It just died, m'lady." The cook's eyes filled with tears. "It took a taste of clotted cream and dropped over dead."

Julia frowned. "I don't understand. Clotted cream?"

The cook began to cry. "From Lady Sarah's tea tray."

The cook's words hit Julia like a rock. Her pulse quickened.

Just then another servant ran into the kitchen. "Just as you thought. It was open."

"What was open?" Julia asked, sharply.

The servant grew pale. "The cabinet in the pantry, lady. The one with all the poisons."

"Who has a key?" she asked.

"Jus' the housekeeper and myself," said Mrs. Hopstead. "Oh, and Arthur asked for one just recently. Said there were mice in Lord Darby's rooms."

"No one else?"

The servants shook their heads.

"What should we do, m'lady?" the cook sobbed.

"Tell no one. This is not to leave the kitchens, do you hear?"

The servants looked down at the cat, then back at her.

"Lord Darby must not know of this," Julia said. "He's not well right now. I will deal with this matter on my own."

The servants gawked at her in stunned silence.

She grabbed a basin and some linens and strode to the door. "If any one of you speaks of this, I'll make you wish you were that cat."

Julia flew from the drawing room just as Sarah approached.

"Sarah, there you are. Your brother would like a word with you. I just left him." Julia smirked, and Sarah once again wondered what trouble her sister-in-law was hatching.

"Close the door," James said quietly as she entered.

She spied the tea tray. "Shall I pour you some tea?"

"No."

"Would you care for a bite?"

"No."

James, refuse food? For the first time since she had entered the room, Sarah really looked at her brother. The hands resting upon his knees looked like skinned rabbits.

Beside him was a basin filled with pink-tinged water.

"What happened to your hands?"

His eyes were devoid of emotion. "I injured them defending your honor."

"My honor?" The meaning of his words sank into her consciousness like a dark, damp night. Somehow, he had learned of their tryst.

"Lucien!" She raced toward the door.

"As head of this family, I order you to stay," James said loudly.

"I will not."

"You will."

Her brother hadn't moved from his chair, but the tone in his voice restrained her the same as if he'd done so with his hands.

Very well, she would hear his accusations. She would bear out his ranting, and then she would tell him how much she loved Lucien. The brother she knew would never deny her happiness.

But when she came to his side, she quickly realized that James was no longer the brother she knew. In his place was a hard, stubborn man without compassion in his eyes.

"I've tried to be a good brother to you," he said, a note of bitterness hanging in his words. "I've tried to protect you and give you all that you need. I've been patient, I think, with your aversion to the world outside this home."

Sarah perched unsteadily on the edge of a chair. "Indeed, you've encouraged it."

"Yes, I have. I wanted to protect you. My protection, however, has come to naught. You've managed to place yourself in harm's way, despite my best efforts. I'm deeply disappointed in you."

"I assume you've learned what is between Lucien and me."

A cold smile crept over his lips. "Unless, of course, there have been others you've bedded in my house."

Sarah's throat squeezed shut. She fought against the tears welling in her eyes. "You have no call to question my virtue."

He pounded his fist on the chair, sending tiny splatters of blood across the carpet. "I most certainly do. You are Lady Sarah Essington, not some salacious chambermaid. You're not to leave the gates of this estate, do you understand? I'll not have you subjected to the gossip that is sure to arise from this disastrous affair."

"I no longer care about gossip. I'll live my life the way I see fit, James."

"You'll live a life befitting a lady of your stature while you live beneath my roof."

"Then I'll leave. You cannot stop me."

"If you leave here, you may not return."

Sarah was silent. She never before had cause to fear her brother.

"Where will you go, Sarah? You who have not ventured past the limits of Whitford since you were slightly more than a child? With no money and no friends, where will you go?"

"I've no need to leave Whitford. I'll get along very well there."

"Would you shame this family so? After all I've done for you . . ." James's look of anger melted into one of defeat.

Sarah sat on the arm of his chair. "You have been a good brother, James. The best I could ever hope for. But you cannot protect me forever."

"Then who will?"

Sarah took a deep breath. Dare she say it?

"Lucien."

James shook his head sadly. "Delacourte is the perfect example of the kind of man you need protection from. He's a black-hearted rogue."

Sarah rose. "You will not malign him to me. Lucien is a good man. A decent man."

"He's a fortune hunter."

"He's a well-respected artist with a fortune of his own."

"There! You make my point exactly. You know nothing about him."

Sarah paced before her brother. "I know a great deal about him."

James leaned forward in his chair. "Did you know he was unable to paint when he arrived here to give you painting lessons?"

"Yes. He told me."

"He told you when he arrived?"

Sarah hesitated. "No, he told me only recently. But he is painting again, as you can see." She pointed to the row of canvases propped against a wall.

"Very well. But did you know he is deeply in debt?"

"That cannot be true. He served the king of France. Why, just one of his paintings sells for more than my yearly allowance."

James leaned forward in his chair. "Ask yourself this. Why did he accept the position here?"

"Because he wanted to leave France. He wanted to get away from the place where his wife and daughter died."

James shook his head. "He needed the money. His creditors hunted him like dogs. Sarah, listen to reason. When Lucien was thrown out of the palace at Versailles, many of his paintings remained the king's property. Lucien drank and gambled. He acquired debts. He sold his remaining paintings, but it wasn't enough. He borrowed a small fortune."

Sarah searched her mind for some explanation for what James was telling her. "How could you know this?"

James sighed. "Julia found it out from Lucien's cousin Mathilde. It would seem Mathilde and her brother have been approached many times over by Lucien's creditors."

Sarah shook her head. "Lucien cares for me. Even if this is all true, it doesn't matter." Whatever Lucien's faults, she loved him. She would speak with him, and they would resolve this.

"You're right," James said quietly. "It doesn't matter. Mr. Delacourte will be leaving Elmstone tonight."

"You put him out?" She leaped to her feet and hurried toward the door, but again his words stopped her.

"Sarah, he made no argument. He wants to leave."

She stood in silence, her back to her brother.

James continued. "If you go to him now, I'll send for the magistrate. I'll make Delacourte pay for this deception in jail, or better still, on a hulk on the Thames. However, if you let him go, I will pay him double what's due for his services here and allow him to return to Paris. In addition, you'll promise not to leave the grounds of Elmstone for at least one month's time, until I can be certain there will be no damaging rumors."

Sarah crossed an arm over her stomach. Despite what James had told her about Lucien, she still believed in him. How could she possibly do as her brother asked?

But if she didn't, Lucien would suffer the consequences.

Without another glance at James, she fled the drawing room.

Chapter 29

Lucien peered into the mirror with one eye. The other was so swollen he could not hope to see out of it for at least a week. He moved his jaw, wincing at the pain. Chewing, too, would be out of the question for quite a while.

He dabbed his face with a linen, happy to see that most of the cuts populating his forehead and cheeks had ceased their bleeding.

Already, dark red, fist-shaped blotches had begun to appear on his shoulders and chest. They were too numerous to count, which Lucien had no desire to do anyway, so he just covered them with a clean shirt. He did not bother with a jacket. The weight of it would only add to his discomfort.

On his way out the door, he prayed for two things: that he would not see Sarah, and that Lord Darby's wrath had been sated.

Lucien discovered Lord Darby still seated in the same chair in the drawing room. The door was open, the room bathed in the deep brown shadows of late afternoon. Though it had been he who had taken the beating, it was

Lord Darby who looked defeated. His head hung low, almost touching his chest. Lucien wondered if the man had fallen asleep.

Lucien stopped before him, bracing for another onslaught. Lord Darby just stared up at him from the chair, as if unable to move.

"Why do you still plague us with your presence?"

"Forgive me, your lordship, but I cannot leave. As I explained earlier, my heart lies here, with Sarah."

Lord Darby looked past him, to the painting of the French garden Sarah so loved. "Sarah's heart, I'm afraid, doesn't lie with you."

The statement so took Lucien by surprise, it was a few moments before he could reply. "Begging your pardon, my lord, but you cannot know what is in your sister's heart."

"Indeed I do," said Lord Darby, still staring at the painting. "She left this room but a few minutes ago. I told her everything about your lies, your debts. I would be surprised if she ever wants to look upon you again."

The blood pounded in Lucien's ears. "It cannot be."

"Believe what you will, Delacourte. Perhaps she did have some sort of fondness for you. She asked me to pay your stipend before you left here. She also convinced me not to bring charges against you for your duplicitous claims. I promised those things, but not one thing more."

"I will not leave. I believe Sarah is in danger here."

"Danger?" Lord Darby's tone held a hint of amusement. "The only danger to my sister is you."

"No. It is Arthur."

Lord Darby's face turned stony. "Arthur?"

"I discovered him taking foxglove from Sarah's orangery this afternoon. And the night of the fire, he was lurking about the family's rooms. For all we know, he is the one who set Sarah's rooms afire—"

"Stop." Lord Darby's command seemed perilously calm. "Arthur is a loyal servant and a decent man. He would never, could never harm my sister, or any of us, for that matter."

"But the man could be dangerous."

"Leave, before my goodwill runs out."

Lucien left the earl, determined to seek Sarah out, his battered face be damned. But he got no farther than the bottom of the stairs before he met with Arthur. The servant blocked the stairs, holding Lucien's satchel in one hand and a leather purse in the other.

"Let me pass," said Lucien.

Contempt was plain on Arthur's face. "My orders are to escort you to the gates."

"I doubt you are able," Lucien said, pushing past. Out of the shadows appeared three large, well-muscled servants. Lucien recognized them as stable hands. The one who had helped put out the fire in Sarah's room grabbed Lucien by the collar and pulled him from the stairs.

"I will return, I promise you," Lucien told Arthur, his voice low. "And if any harm comes to Lady Sarah in the meantime, I will kill you. If I have to tear down these walls with my bare hands to get to you, I will kill you."

"Take him to the gate," Arthur spat, "and lock it behind him."

Lucien struggled, but won only more bruises for his trouble. Arthur opened the door and the three men dragged Lucien out of the house and onto the drive, his boots scraping on the gravel.

"Sarah! Sarah!" he yelled as they hauled him toward the gate. He prayed she would hear. He had to warn her. He had to protect her.

The three giants tossed him through the gate like a sack of feed. His satchel followed, skidding across the drive beside him. The purse came last. As it hit the stones, the contents spilled out, ringing like church bells on a Sunday.

Dozens of gold coins.

The last rays of sunlight turned them into little circles of fire on the drive.

The world had crumbled beneath Sarah's feet.

Lucien was gone without a word to her. She'd almost begun to believe her brother's warning. Had Lucien only wanted her for her fortune? It couldn't be! The way he looked at her, touched her. All they had shared. He must have felt something toward her.

She wandered about her temporary rooms, catching her reflection in the darkened window. Her scarred face stared back at her from the panes. Did he love her? How could he possibly?

She'd been such a fool, so willing to believe anyone with a kind word and sympathetic hand. The pain in her chest was nearly unbearable. So this is what it felt like to have her heart ripped out.

No, not her heart. Her soul.

Duncan had taken her heart, and somehow she'd managed to grow a new one. But Lucien—Lucien had taken her soul, and she knew she would never get it back. For as long as he lived, he would hold it.

She could never, would never, love another soul when her own belonged to Lucien Delacourte.

Chapter 30

"*Delacourte! You haven't the sense of a cow. Where's your coat, man?*"

Stagg's booming voice was exactly what Lucien wanted to hear.

"I assume my coat is in my room at Elmstone." Lucien eased onto a bench, rubbing his frozen hands together. Stagg sat, too, his meaty buttocks overflowing the bench on the opposite side of the table.

"Criminy, yer face looks like it stopped a scythe. What happened?"

"I had a bit of a disagreement with someone."

Stagg snorted. "*Disagreement* he says. Just so you know, you've got to move out of th' way when a fist is comin' at you."

"I'll try to remember that. Stagg, I need your help."

The farmer shook his head, digging into the pocket of his worn leather vest. "Lucky for you it was a good day at the market."

"That is not the kind of help I need."

"So you remembered your purse this time?"

"I have my purse, yes."

Lucien thought about the gold coins that littered the drive before the gate of Elmstone House. He could have used the money, Lord only knew, but he would not accept a farthing from Lord Darby.

"My purse is empty, but it is not your coin I need," said Lucien. "I must speak with you about Lady Sarah."

Stagg's eyebrows shot up.

Lucien raked his fingers through his hair, wondering where and how to begin.

Stagg signaled the barkeep and turned back to Lucien. "Go on, man."

"I am concerned for her safety. I need someone to look after her for a while."

"Why don't you look after her y'self? Living under the same roof would make it a damned sight easier for you than me."

"Unfortunately, I no longer reside at Elmstone."

Stagg plunked his elbows on the table and leaned in. "I guess you'd better tell me about it."

Lucien told Stagg what had transpired, feeling no need to omit the details of his own shortcomings. He excluded only the intimate nature of his and Sarah's relationship. He had the distinct feeling, however, the farmer had already guessed at that.

"You think this Arthur means Lady Sarah harm?" Stagg asked.

"I cannot imagine why, but he seems to be lurking in the shadows whenever there is trouble. If I could somehow get back in there to warn Lady Sarah, I would, but there are servants watching out for me at every entrance."

"Where will you go?"

"I must go to Paris. Not for long, but I must take care of something I should have done a long time ago. I will return to Whitford as soon as possible."

"How will you get there?"

"Same way I came, I suppose. Working my fare on a cargo ship. But I need someone to watch out for Sarah."

"There'll be no working in your current state. Why, you're no good to no one." Stagg drummed his thick fingers on the table for a moment. "Wait here."

Lucien watched Stagg through a haze of smoke. He spoke to the barkeep before disappearing into the back room. The farmer emerged with another man, who looked familiar.

"You remember Belk?" Stagg pushed the man down on the bench.

"Of course. Your cousin's daughter works at Elmstone, I believe."

"Me *wife's* cousin's daughter. 'Er name's Rebecca."

"Lady Sarah's maid?"

"'At's right," Belk said. "She done nothin' wrong, sir. Ne'er breathed a word to us about Elmstone."

"Of course not," Lucien reassured. "I need her help, though."

"What kind of help?"

"I need her to watch out for Lady Sarah, to report to Stagg if anything . . ." Lucien groped for a word that would not cause undue panic. "If anything *unusual* should happen."

Belk shook his head. "You know she can't. She been warned, like all of 'em, not to speak of Elmstone. Lord Darby would throw her out on her arse if she did."

"Will you ask her, at least? I know she is very fond of Lady Sarah."

"Aye. That she is. But—"

"I would not make this request if I did not believe Lady Sarah could meet with some danger."

"What danger?"

"I cannot say. I have no proof, just suspicion. Will you ask?"

"What would I tell 'er?"

Lucien thought for a moment. "Just tell her to keep her eyes and ears open. Do not mention my name. I am not certain what Lady Sarah thinks of me at the moment. Will you ask her to do it?"

Belk, who had been staring into his cup, raised his head. "For Lady Sarah, I'll ask it."

Relief warmed Lucien's limbs. "Thank you, Belk. You are a good man."

Belk nodded and drifted away from the table, allowing Stagg and Lucien to speak in private.

"What can I do?" Stagg asked. "Anything."

"Can you get me a few pieces of paper and a pencil?"

Stagg returned in a matter of minutes. Lucien scratched out a letter to Sarah and folded it into a small square. "Get this to Lady Sarah tomorrow."

"Should I give it to Belk for Rebecca?"

"No. This is extremely private. You must deliver it yourself."

"But how? I cannot get through the gates."

"I will draw a map of Elmstone for you. I want you to keep watch for Lady Sarah. Though it is cold, she often likes to walk in the gardens in the morning. If you must, wait until she comes to the village to give her the letter. She has promised Mrs. Endfirth a visit tomorrow."

Stagg took the note and tucked it into his pocket. "Consider it done."

"Thank you, Stagg. You are a true friend."

Lucien was shaking the farmer's giant hand when a barmaid approached. She placed a mug before Lucien. Instead of ale, it was filled to the brim with coins. She winked at him before taking her leave, her hips twitching saucily beneath her dirty skirts.

"What is this?" Lucien asked.

"Call it a cuppa cheer." Stagg's grin lit up his wide face like a crooked candelabrum.

Lucien stared at the mug in wonder.

"So you can get to Paris quicker. And get back here quicker, as well."

Lucien clasped Stagg's outstretched hand. "I will repay you. All of you. I promise."

"Nay," said Stagg, his face serious for once. "We wish to repay you, for bringing our Sarah back to us. Godspeed, Delacourte."

James peered out of the window at the trees bending in a howling wind. He wondered how far Delacourte could travel in such weather. He felt a twinge of guilt at the way he had handled the whole miserable affair. It was obvious Sarah cared for her tutor, and he for her. They should never have acted on their affections, to be sure, and Delacourte should have been honest from the beginning about his situation, but James knew firsthand how such things did not matter when the heart was involved.

He also knew firsthand how lamentable such a mismatched relationship could prove. He was experiencing it himself this very moment. James had loved Leah dearly for half his life, but their hope of being together was doomed from the start.

When he met her, he was the son of an earl and she the daughter of a haberdasher in Bath. His heart thought nothing of Leah's position in life before it cast itself at her feet. Unfortunately, his heart didn't have the authority to make decisions. That honor was held by James's father, and by the damned English peerage.

When James was forced to marry Julia, he stopped visiting Leah for a while. It was simply too painful. But eventually he found it impossible to stay away. She was the love of his life.

When she became ill, it seemed only natural to bring

her close so he could care for her. He suffered greatly for that decision. Every time he had to leave her in the cottage to return to a wife he did not love, all in the name of duty and propriety, he died a bit inside.

He wouldn't let Sarah fall victim to such a fate. She'd be better off loving no one than loving someone she couldn't have. In time, she would see the wisdom in this decision.

As he donned his jacket and a warm overcoat, preparing for another vigil at Leah's bedside, there came a knock at his door. He hurried to open it, expecting Arthur.

"Julia."

Her gaze took in his clothes.

"I'll not bother to ask where you are going on such a miserable night." She brushed past him and into the room.

"What do you want?" Any small twinge of guilt he might have felt was erased by his wife's sullen expression.

"I wish only to speak with you for a moment, and then you may take your leave."

James waited impatiently as Julia wandered about his room, touching this, peering at that.

"Well?"

"I'm very pleased you sent the artist on his way. Thank you," she said.

"I did it for Sarah, not for you."

"Of course. Sarah is always the recipient of your fond protection."

He pulled on his gloves. "Get on with it, Julia."

"Now that Delacourte is gone, I'd like you to consider something. Encourage Sarah to marry Duncan."

James laughed. "Do you think me mad?"

Julia smiled. "Not at all. I think you wish your sister happiness, which Duncan will bring her."

"As he did the last time?"

"Dredging up past indiscretions won't secure your sister's future."

"Indiscretions? Duncan humiliated Sarah. I would hardly call that an indiscretion."

Julia waved a hand impatiently. "Never mind all that. Duncan is quite in love with Sarah. Even you can see that. Or you could if you were ever here."

"In love with her?"

"Apparently. He tells me so every day. It's quite nauseating, really. But he wishes to marry her, and Sarah hardly has other options."

James was silent.

"Think about it, dear husband. Duncan's father is well respected. Duncan has had a, well . . . a rather dubious past, but he has changed. It would be an excellent match. Your father thought so, once upon a time."

"Sarah doesn't wish it."

Julia sighed. "Sarah isn't capable of making her own decisions, as you can plainly see. She fell under Delacourte's spell, after all. But she loved Duncan once, and I daresay she could again, given the proper encouragement."

"I'll give it some thought," James said, wishing only to end the conversation so he could get to Leah. He moved for the door, but Julia stepped in front of him, blocking his path.

"Watch them. You'll see the affection in Duncan's eyes. And you will see, too, that Sarah is not so opposed to this match as you may think."

"I said I'll consider it. Now, I must be going . . ."

He opened the door and stepped into the hall. Julia followed. She seemed small and fragile in the dark. Sad, almost.

"I want you to stay with me tonight," she said. "Tell me how I can make you stay. Tell me what I can do."

For a moment, he actually felt sorry for her. She hadn't always been so cold, so manipulative. In fact, when they first were married, he actually liked her. He supposed much of the change in her was his fault.

He touched her face, and she closed her eyes. Then the

thought of Leah, alone in the cottage, made him pull away.

"What can I do?" she asked again.

"Nothing."

"Where did Lucien go?"

Anne sat on Sarah's lap in the nursery as the two watched leaves swirl against the windowpanes.

"I don't know." Sarah hugged the girl closer to her. "He just left."

"Well, I don't believe it. Lucien would never leave without saying goodbye to me. He'll be back."

The confidence in Anne's words served only to heighten Sarah's own sense of doubt. She thought the same thing until she had gone to his room, only to find that everything he owned was gone.

"I'm sorry, my pet, but it's true. Lucien has gone. I'm sure he is thinking of you, though."

"Will he send me a letter?"

"Perhaps, if he's not too terribly busy."

Anne leaned her head back on Sarah's shoulder. "He'll write to me. He'll write to you, too, Aunt Sarah. I know it."

Sarah fought the tears. If they were to fall, they would soak her poor niece worse than a rainstorm. "Tomorrow, perhaps you and I will take a walk in the garden. What do you think?"

"Can we sit at the gazebo?"

"Of course."

"Lucien would love to sit at the gazebo with us. Maybe he'll return in the morning," she mumbled.

Sarah kissed the top of Anne's head. The child grew limp, and Sarah knew her niece had fallen asleep. Sarah held her for a long while, savoring the weight and warmth in her arms, the smell of her hair.

How she wished she had the hope of a child, she thought, as she stared out into the night.

* * *

"She seems much improved," Arthur whispered as James took the servant's place beside Leah's bed. "Her color has returned, and her face isn't quite so bloated."

James stroked Leah's hand as she lay sleeping. "How much of the foxglove have you given her?"

"Three doses today. We've almost finished the powder from Doctor Murfree, but the leaves I picked from Lady Sarah's orangery are nearly dry. I have only to prepare them to the doctor's instructions, and they'll be ready to use."

"Very good. Where is the nurse?"

"Sleeping, of course," Arthur whispered. "If it were not for her close-mouthed nature, I would think to use someone else. She's so callous."

James sighed. "It must be difficult to witness so much death and disease."

Arthur nodded. His shoulders drooped.

"Go on," James said quietly. "Go home for a rest. Let me stay with her a bit."

Arthur straightened and abruptly strode from the cabin.

James sat on the small chair beside the bed, gathering Leah's hand in his and bringing it to his lips. She did indeed look better. Though she still bore the ravages of the dropsy, her cheeks had grown pink and her breathing was less labored.

"Leah," he whispered. "Leah, can you hear me?"

Her eyes opened, and her lips formed a slow smile. "James."

He kissed her hand again. "How do you feel?"

"Better, I think." There was a slight wheeze in her voice. James poured a cup of water and brought it to her lips. She took only one sip before pushing it away.

"You look tired," she said. "Tell me, what has you so worried?"

"Nothing to concern you, love. We should concentrate on more pleasant matters."

"Such as?"

"Your improving health, for one."

Leah's smile was weak. "Yes, my improving health. James, you must promise me something."

"Of course, my love. Anything."

"When I go, will you take care of my brother?"

James's grasp on Leah's hand tightened. "Don't speak of such things."

"Please, James, promise me."

He brushed the hair from her eyes. "Of course I'll take care of your brother. Now shush. I want no more talk of dying. Shall we continue the book we began last night?"

As James read quietly, Leah drifted into a restless sleep. He closed the book and watched her breathe as he had so many times, and wondered what his life might have been like if he had thrown his wealth and his title to the wind and had married Leah instead.

Chapter 31

*Lucien followed a widow and her daughter down the gang-*plank of the boat, suppressing the urge to nudge them along. After two days bouncing in a coach and almost a full day on the rough waters of the English Channel, Lucien wanted only to be still.

He buttoned Stagg's huge coat, a last-minute gift from the farmer as Lucien left the Hog and Dove. The coins in the pocket of the coat slapped against his hip. Not for the first time, Lucien thanked the hand of fate for the generosity of the people of Whitford.

"Godspeed to you, Monsieur Delacourte," the widow said in French. Already the language seemed foreign to him.

"And to you, madame. Mademoiselle." He bowed quickly before slipping into the throngs of people milling about the waterfront, feeling a momentary twinge of guilt for not assuring the ladies' safety as far as their carriage. But he had not a moment to spare on this journey.

Though his throat was parched from the wind aboard the ship, his thirst would have to wait. Lucien headed straight for the Gallerie de Soleil. Straight for Valmetant.

The streets of Paris seemed at once strange and familiar. His last two years there he had existed in a fog; he had walked the streets mostly at night, to avoid his creditors as well as his memories. Now, his senses vibrated with the sounds, the sights, the smells. He tasted the air. It was sweet, none of the musky dampness of England. Before long, he stood at Valmetant's door.

His mentor's housekeeper answered at the first knock.

"Monsieur Delacourte!"

"Good evening, Monique. Is Valmetant about?"

"No, I am sorry. He is not." Monique hurried to close the door, but Lucien stopped it with his hand.

"Do you know where I might find him?"

Monique's nervous gaze flitted up and down the alley. "Perhaps Golvide's."

Lucien nodded. "If I do not find him before he returns, will you please tell him I was here?"

"Of course."

Monique closed the door, and Lucien heard the lock slide into place.

He could hardly blame her for being less than gracious. Lucien's relationship with Valmetant was well known throughout Paris. Undoubtedly there had been many unsavory callers searching for him there in his absence.

Lucien made the short walk to Golvide's with his chin buried in his collar. He entered the coffeehouse through a narrow door in the alley. Valmetant was seated at his usual table in the rear.

Lucien took a moment to observe his mentor before making his presence known. Valmetant had aged in the months Lucien had been gone. His hair, rarely hidden beneath a wig, was nearly white now, as was his beard. His shoulders had grown rounder, his stomach looser. His hands shook ever so slightly as he sipped from his cup.

The old man gave Lucien a blank stare.

"Henri." Lucien kissed the man on each cheek and sat down at the table.

Valmetant's eyes filled with recognition, then tears, as he returned Lucien's greeting. "I did not think I would ever see you again," his mentor said hoarsely.

"Did you receive my letter?"

"I did. So you took the position in England after all?"

"Yes. Thank you for suggesting it."

"It worked out well?"

Lucien was not quite certain how to answer Henri's question. "I will give you the details later. But if you do not mind, I would like to get back to your apartment as soon as possible. I am feeling a bit uneasy here."

"But of course." Valmetant threw a handful of coins on the table and the two men escaped into the alley. They arrived at Valmetant's door without incident.

Monique let them in with a pitying look for her master and a hostile one for Lucien. She settled them in the study and quickly disappeared.

"You must forgive Monique," said Valmetant. "There have been a few callers . . ."

"I am truly sorry," said Lucien as he paced before the fireplace. "I put many of my friends in danger, most especially you. I do not know how my life became such a shambles."

Valmetant shook his head. "You lost your mind when you lost Katrina and Tessa. You feel things deeply, Lucien. There is no shame in that."

"But there is shame in running from responsibility. You, and Monique, too, had to pay for it. So did many other people I cared for. I was wrong."

"Is that what brings you back? This apology?"

"In part."

"It is unnecessary." Valmetant poured two glasses of wine from a decanter on the sideboard. He handed one to Lucien with a trembling hand.

"I wanted to apologize, yes. But I also came to do something else."

Valmetant studied his face. "The painting?"

Lucien nodded. "There is nothing else for which I would risk returning to Paris."

"How will you carry it? Shall I remove it from the frame?"

Lucien stared into his glass. "No need. You see, I will be returning to England but I will not be taking the painting with me."

"You wish for me to sell it?"

"Yes."

The old man sighed—with relief, or pleasure, or pity, Lucien did not know.

"It is hung in the gallery, you know. I hope you do not mind, but it seemed a crime not to share it with the world. Many people asked to buy it." Valmetant paused. "Would you care to see it?"

The portrait was etched into Lucien's senses the way Katrina's touch was, the way Tessa's sweet voice was. He did not need to see it again. But could he let it go without one more look?

Lucien downed the rest of his wine. "Take me there."

The two men ascended the dark, creaking stairwell into the Gallerie de Soleil, Valmetant's place of business. The old man carried a single candle, which he used to light several more in sconces in the main room of the gallery. They passed a long wall of paintings with varying subjects— landscapes, horses, a scene from a Parisian market. Lucien's portrait hung alone on the back wall.

His heart stopped beating when he saw it. Every breath of air he took seemed laced with tiny daggers. Memory had not done it justice.

The painting was mounted, like a window to heaven, on a pure white wall. There were Katrina and Tessa, caught in a moment of sheer joy as they gazed into one another's eyes.

My God, why did he do this to himself? He could not sell it. He could not! It was all he had left of them.

Katrina's hair lay loose over her shoulders, curling against the delicate bow of her collarbone. Lucien reached out to stroke it with his fingertips. But it was not Katrina's hair after all. It was only an illusion. An illusion he created. Just as Tessa's silken cheek was an illusion.

His eyes stung. Their joy lived no more.

No, Lucien realized. *They do live. They live within me.*

Valmetant touched his shoulder. "Have you changed your mind?"

"I have not. Henri, will you sell the painting for me?"

"You are sure?"

"Yes."

Valmetant nodded. "Give me two days."

Though Valmetant asked Lucien to stay in his apartment, Lucien refused. He could not put his friend in further jeopardy. The simple fact that the painting would now be up for sale would have the jackals at his friend's door.

After spending the night huddled in a darkened doorway, Lucien started off, well before dawn, to Versailles. He would settle his debts quickly with money he borrowed from Valmetent against the sale of the painting.

And then he would have only one more piece of business to finish.

Chapter 32

"Where are you, little one?" Anne sang.

She walked alone through the red garden, a small, dull kitchen knife in her hand, looking for the plant her Aunt Sarah had sent her to fetch. She checked the drawing again, memorizing the triangular shape of the leaves she was seeking.

She wished her aunt would just have come with her. But it seemed as if the gardens had lost their magic for her. Aside from her work in the orangery, Aunt Sarah hadn't done any of her usual things. She hadn't gone to Whitford, hadn't walked in the gardens, hadn't painted, or even drawn. Anne knew it was because of Lucien. Though Aunt Sarah denied it, Anne knew his leaving made her sad.

Where had Lucien gone without so much as a goodbye? She thought they were friends.

Anne spotted the plant she was searching for and plopped onto her knees to take a cutting.

"Psst."

She started.

"Missy. Missy, over here."

Slowly, she turned. Peeking out from the hedge was the largest man Anne had ever seen. Big, but friendly looking all the same.

"Are you a giant?" she said.

The man muffled his laughter with a huge hand. "No, little lady. I be a friend of Lady Sarah. I need to see her right away."

"Go away," she said, trying to sound brave. "You shouldn't be here."

"Very true. But my business is urgent. Do you know what 'urgent' means?"

Anne put her hands on her hips. "Of course I do. It means 'importunate.'"

The giant scratched his head. "A'right. Will you fetch Lady Sarah, then?"

Anne stood and looked about. The garden was deserted. She supposed she should have told someone where she was going. She knew from the stories Miss Elsey told her that giants often made off with little girls. Especially little girls who failed to pay attention to their governess's lessons.

She gripped the tiny knife tightly in her hand. "What do you want with Lady Sarah?"

"I come to give 'er something." The giant doffed his hat and removed a folded piece of paper from inside it. He held it out to her.

Anne took a small step forward, then stopped.

"C'mon, child. 'Tis from Lady Sarah's tutor, Delacourte."

"Lucien! I knew he would write."

"Aye. He wished me to give it to her as soon as he left, but she ain't been out of the house in days."

With another quick look about, Anne hurried to the hedge and snatched the note from the giant's hand.

"Where is your coat, sir? Won't you freeze?" she asked, pulling her own cloak tightly around her.

"Nah. This hedge is warmer than my wife." He laughed.

Anne frowned. How could a hedge be warmer than a person? Then she thought of her mother. "I see," she said, and the giant laughed again.

"Will you deliver the note?"

"I will."

"Thank you, missy." The man tipped his hat and disappeared into the hedge as Anne hurried back to the house, the plant forgotten, the note tucked in the bib of her pinafore.

"The air in here is positively stifling," Merri complained. "Come back to the drawing room with me and have a game of cribbage."

"Perhaps later," Sarah said. She picked through one of the planting boxes in the orangery. "I wonder what's been getting into the foxglove."

"Do you intend to stay here all day?" Merri asked, not bothering to hide her annoyance.

"I have work to do, Mother. I'm sorry."

"No, I am sorry. I'm sorry Lucien left. But you cannot avoid the drawing room forever, my dear."

Sarah looked down at her hands. They were smudged with dirt. She wished they were smudged with paint, instead. But she honestly didn't know if she would ever paint again.

"Ah, here is Miss Witherspoon," she said. She hoped the relief she felt wasn't apparent. "Go on, Mother. Get out of the damp. I shall see you at supper."

Merri hobbled off with Miss Witherspoon, and Sarah breathed a sigh of relief. She plowed her hands into the soil of the planting box. It was damp and warm, and the musky scent of it filled her nostrils. She wondered if this was what she would smell for eternity when she was dead.

She shook off the thought. She didn't want to die, really.

She only felt dead. All the life Lucien had brought to her, all the color and warmth, was gone. And yet her heart did still beat, and her eyes did still see. She awoke every morning to the cold, and fell asleep every evening to the cold, and she hardly noticed it.

She had a sudden urge to defy her brother. To chase the wind to Whitford and visit her old friends. But she would not. For Lucien's freedom, she had given up her own.

She turned back to her plants, wondering again at the plight of the foxglove.

"Did you give her another dose?" James asked.

"Yes, it was the last. We'll have to use the foxglove from the orangery next." Arthur wrung his hands beside Leah's bed.

"She doesn't look good," said the nurse. "Perhaps you had better begin preparations—"

"Quiet! I'll not hear it. Not yet. There is still time . . ." said James.

The nurse backed away, returning to her seat in the corner. The two men stood over Leah like sentinels, watching her breathe.

"Stay with her for a while, Arthur. I shall return later and stay the night."

"But Lady Darby and the staff . . ."

"I do not answer to the staff. Nor to Lady Darby."

"Where do you think you are going?"

Anne skidded to a halt. "Good afternoon, Mother."

"It's long past afternoon. What are you doing out of the nursery? Miss Elsey is looking for you."

"I was taking a walk in the gardens."

"With your aunt?"

"No. I was alone."

Her mother eyed her with suspicion. "You took a walk in the gardens alone?"

"Yes." Anne tried not to look guilty. Her mother could always tell when she was lying. But she wasn't lying, really. She *did* take a walk by herself. The giant was already there when she arrived.

"Give me your cape."

"But I . . ."

"Come, now. Give me your cape. I'll put it away for you."

Anne reluctantly undid the ties. Her mother pulled the cape from her shoulders.

"What's this?" she asked.

The corner of Lucien's note peeked out from her pinafore.

"I . . . It's my morning's lesson. I studied it as I walked."

Her mother laughed. "Surely you don't expect me to believe such nonsense. Let me see it."

Anne considered defying her mother, but she knew from experience what would happen. She'd be banished to the nursery for weeks. She handed it over.

Her mother quickly unfolded the paper and read it. "Where did you get this?"

Anne began to cry. "From a man in the garden. He said he was looking for Aunt Sarah."

"You know, Mr. Delacourte hurt Aunt Sarah's feelings quite badly, and this note would make her very, very sad. Your father would be very upset with you, as well, if he knew about this. I think you should keep it quiet."

Her mother walked with her, holding her hand. Anne hadn't held her mother's hand in a long time. It was cold.

When they arrived at the nursery, her mother took Miss Elsey aside. Though she whispered to the governess, Anne could hear every word she said.

"Keep her upstairs until further notice. And do not, under any circumstance, allow Lady Sarah to visit."

* * *

Julia went directly from the nursery to her quarters, the folded square of paper she'd taken from Anne gripped tight in her fist. She closed her door and locked it, then opened the note again beside the fireplace. Damn Lucien Delacourte.

She read:

My Dearest Sarah,

You must know I would never leave you of my own accord. Your brother has sent me from Elm-stone on the grounds that I am unworthy of your love. He is right.

I am ashamed of my actions, not only at Elm-stone, but in Paris and Versailles. My only excuse is that my grief overwhelmed me. I have been so consumed with my past that I have given paltry thought to the future, until now.

I will return soon, I promise you. But you must do something for me. Please, beware of Arthur. I cannot say why, but I do not trust him. Keep away from him.

Know that I love you, Sarah. I will think of you every moment until I return. Give Anne a kiss for me, and pray for my soul.

Yours Always,
L.

Julia crumpled the letter into a tight ball and tossed it onto the flames.

"Would you like me to read to you?" said Duncan.

He followed Sarah around the orangery like a hungry chicken trailing a bucket of feed.

"No, thank you," she said.

"Shall I hold your basket?"

"No. Duncan, if you really want to be of help, you may go find Anne. She was supposed to bring some clippings to me from the garden."

Duncan's face went slack. "But I'll have to leave you if I'm to look for Anne."

"Yes, you will," she said impatiently.

"I don't want to leave you. Ever."

Sarah tapped her foot. Duncan's constant hovering frayed her nerves. She took a few deep breaths to calm herself.

"If you retrieve Anne, I'll meet you in the library later. I've just received a new box of books, and we can look through them together."

"Wonderful!" Duncan skirted the planting boxes and ducked beneath the lemon trees, headed toward the door. He nearly ran head-first into James.

"Darby! Pardon me."

"Where are you off to in such a hurry?" James asked.

"A small errand for Lady Sarah. Afterwards, she's agreed to let me read to her in the library. Must be going." Duncan scuttled from the room, unaware of James's bemused expression.

"So you've promised he can read to you?" James asked. His voice had an accusatory note.

The resentment she thought she had conquered flared anew within her. "Do you take issue with Duncan, as well?"

"Shouldn't I?"

"There is no reason to be concerned. Duncan and I have mended our fences. The past is behind us."

James raised his eyebrows. "Am I to understand that you have forgiven Lavery?"

"I have."

"Do you welcome his attentions?"

Sarah hesitated. She'd grown weary of her brother's coddling. She was a grown woman who could handle Duncan on her own. "Let us say that I'm not averse to his attentions," she said.

James looked at her as if she were some strange animal he'd never seen. For the first time, Sarah noticed how tired her brother looked.

"As you wish," he said, and left the orangery almost as quickly as Duncan had.

James made an appearance at supper that night, much to everyone's surprise.

Duncan was, as usual, expending all of his charm and wit on Sarah in an attempt to renew their courtship.

It would never happen, but James didn't have to know that, Sarah decided. At that moment, she wanted nothing more than to provoke her brother, to punish him for his conduct with Lucien.

So when James entered, she suddenly warmed to Duncan's attentions.

"You look lovely tonight, Sarah," Duncan said, as he had every night since he'd come back from London. This time she didn't ignore him as she usually did.

"I wore this gown especially for you. Green is still your favorite color, I trust?"

Duncan appeared stunned. "I . . . Why yes, it is."

"I remember a certain green waistcoat you used to wear," Sarah continued. "You looked quite handsome in it. You wore it to Lord Standing's ball."

"I did!" Duncan said, a look of sheer joy on his face. "I purchased it from a haberdasher in Bath. What was his name? You remember him, Darby. You used to visit that shop quite often, no?"

"No." James's expression was suddenly black. "If you all will excuse me, I must be going." Without another word, he stormed from the room like a fast-moving rain cloud.

Julia gave her cousin a scathing look.

"What?" said Duncan. "What did I say?" Then he turned to Sarah. "I cannot believe you remember the green waistcoat. What other fond memories have you?"

"Not now, Duncan," she said. There was no point in continuing the charade when James wasn't there to see it.

After supper, she stood outside the drawing room. She hadn't gone in there since Lucien had left. Her stomach rolled over when she touched the doorknobs. She took a deep breath, and pushed the doors open.

Her feet carried her directly to the alcove. The faint smell of linseed oil lingered. The table beside the easel was empty. For some reason, she assumed Lucien would have left his things. Maybe he had, and someone—the maid who almost caught them making love, perhaps—had taken them away.

Lined up on the floor beneath the windows were Lucien's and her paintings, intermingled with one another like ladies and gentlemen at a dance. She kneeled beside one of his works—a quick study of a horse in the field behind the stables. She remembered the day he had painted it. They'd gone for a long walk through the countryside. She'd left her hair loose, and Lucien entwined wildflowers in it as they crossed a meadow. He called her his walking garden.

Tears ran down her cheek, as useless as her memories. There was no point in this. No point at all. No matter how much she missed Lucien, he wasn't coming back.

She went in search of someone to remove the table and the paintings.

There were no names upon the two white crosses, nothing to indicate who lay beneath them.

When he had buried Katrina and Tessa, Lucien allowed no other mourners. They were his alone in death, as they were his alone in life, he had selfishly thought.

Only, they weren't his, really. They had belonged to each other. He had been no more than an occasional interloper in their lives.

"Mes chéres," he whispered. "My girls, please forgive me."

He laid a rose on each of their graves and left them at last. He had revealed their location to Katrina's closest friend, who promised to bring fresh flowers weekly. It was the least he could do for them.

He made his way back to Paris on the back of a donkey cart, his feet dangling almost to the ground. He watched the golden bricks of the palace recede into the background, and then he turned around.

Lucien reached the city at sunset. Reddish light bounced off the Seine, momentarily blinding him.

"It is good to be back in Paris, no?" the driver of the donkey cart asked.

Lucien just smiled.

He jumped off two streets from the Gallerie de Soleil and ran the rest of the way. He was out of breath when he arrived. Valmetant greeted him at the door, a look of satisfaction on his face.

"It is gone?"

Valmetant nodded. "Just today. I got a very good price for it." He handed Lucien a heavy purse.

Lucien extracted half the coins and gave them to Valemetant, along with a list of his creditors.

"Please see they get what I owe them," he said. "And keep the rest for yourself."

"When will you return to England?" Valmetant asked.

"Tomorrow."

"So soon? I had hoped you would stay for a few days . . ." His mentor's eyes welled with tears.

Lucien took him by the shoulders. "I appreciate all you have done for me, Henri, but I must go. I must get back to her."

Valmetant kissed him on each cheek. "Then tonight, we celebrate."

Chapter 33

Sarah met James in the library. He was dressed for riding.

"Are you leaving?" she asked.

"Soon."

"It is long past dark. Where are you going?"

He ignored her question, and asked one of his own. "What is your intent with Lavery?"

"I cannot see how that's any of your concern."

"It is, while you live beneath this roof."

Her temper flared. "You make me sorry each day for that circumstance."

His shoulders slumped. "Please don't say that. You know my only concern is your well-being."

"If so, you wouldn't have sent Lucien away."

Her brother sat on the arm of a winged-back chair. "As I told you before, he made no argument. I'm sorry, Sarah, but I don't think he had the same feelings for you as you did for him. For God's sake, look how he lied to you."

She began to cry silently beneath the veils. It had been almost three weeks with no word from Lucien. Perhaps it was time to accept the truth. He'd taken her for a fool.

"I want you to consider something," James said carefully. "Consider marrying Lavery."

"James!"

"You told me yourself that you've mended your friendship. You allowed him to read to you, and you flirted with him at supper. He obviously cares for you. I think you care for him, too."

Sarah sighed. "I only acted that way because I thought you disapproved. It was a childish thing to do, I admit. But I'm so very tired of you governing my life, James. I want to make my own decisions."

"Very well, I'll not push you. But I think you should consider Duncan. He seems to be a changed man. He might make a good husband. And you do want children, don't you?"

She was so confused, so hurt and furious, she didn't know what to say.

James slipped on his gloves. "I must be going, but I urge you to give it some thought. We shall talk about it more later."

As soon as he'd gone, Sarah let out a growl of frustration. She never, ever would have imagined her brother trying to push her into Duncan's arms. He must think her terribly desperate.

The horrible thing was, she actually thought about it. Could she take Duncan back? He *had* changed. And she *did* want children. She was relatively certain she would never meet another man who wanted to marry her, and without Lucien, the days stretched long and desolate ahead of her. Indeed, why not marry Duncan?

Lucien waited for someone to appear. He had rung the gate's bell what seemed like hours ago, and still no one answered. In all fairness, though, it was the middle of the night.

He rang again.

A few minutes later a servant Lucien did not recognize appeared, carrying a lantern. He wore a nasty frown, and a long coat over his nightclothes.

"What is it?"

"I've come to see Lord Darby. It is urgent."

The servant yawned. "Urgent? Who should I say is calling?"

"Lucien Delacourte."

The servant held the lantern close to Lucien's face and squinted at him. "Delacourte, eh? The staff have been wagering on your return. We've all been told to keep you from entering the grounds at any cost. We're to shoot you, if necessary."

The servant said this in a matter-of-fact tone, as if reciting the supper menu.

"Are you going to shoot me?" Lucien asked.

The servant scratched himself. "Do you see a pistol?"

"What is your name?"

"Daniel."

"Well, Daniel, what were the odds that I would, indeed, return?"

Daniel's smile was illuminated by the lamplight. "Fairly good."

Now Lucien smiled. "Tell Lord Darby I will be back in the morning."

True to his word, Lucien trudged up the hill to Elmstone just after ten o'clock. He would have gone earlier, but he spent the morning making arrangements with Mrs. Endfirth to stay in her carriage house, which had been renovated into a cottage of sorts. He also left messages for Stagg throughout the town. He wanted to speak with the farmer as soon as possible about Rebecca.

As he passed the little cottage on the hill, he peered

through the trees. Lord Darby's horse was tethered outside. He hurried along, hoping to reach Elmstone and see Sarah before the earl arrived home.

Unfortunately, it was Arthur who answered the bell.

Lucien gritted his teeth.

"Delacourte." The manservant said his name as if referring to a head of moldy cheese.

"I want to speak to Sarah."

Arthur smirked. "I'm so sorry. That will not be possible. Lord Darby has ordered that you shall never set foot behind this gate again. If you do, he'll fetch the magistrate himself."

Lucien put his hands on his hips. "Let me speak to Lord Darby. I will not hide from him."

"Lord Darby is not here at the moment. But heed my advice, Delacourte. Go away, and do not return."

Arthur trudged back up the walk as Lucien cursed him silently from the gate.

When he returned to Whitford, he found Stagg waiting for him at the carriage house.

"Good day, old friend," the farmer said, taking him into a viselike hug.

"It is good to see you. How have you been? How is Lady Sarah? Were you able to speak with her?"

"No, but I gave your letter to the little miss. Lady Sarah never showed in the garden."

Lucien frowned. "You gave the letter to Anne?"

"Yes. Lady Sarah hasn't come down for a visit since ye been gone," said Stagg. "Hasn't been in th' garden, either, so far as I know. I been watching for her."

"Have you spoken to Rebecca?"

"She's only been down once herself. Says it's too hard to get away."

"And?"

Stagg shook his head. "She says Lady Sarah refuses to say your name, or to let her say it either."

"I do not understand," Lucien said. He paced the tiny floor of the carriage house. "What of Arthur?"

Stagg scratched his head. "Rebecca says he hasn't been in spittin' distance to her ladyship. He's gone mostly all day, and when he ain't, he's with Lord Darby, or holed up in his room."

"When will you speak with her again?"

"Don't know. Soon, I think. 'Twill be her free day on Tuesday."

As it turned out, Lucien did not have to wait until Tuesday. Rebecca turned up at the Hog and Dove the following evening. She took one look at Stagg and Lucien, and burst into tears.

"What is it?" Lucien asked. His heart pounded against his chest like a mallet. "Is it Sarah?"

Rebecca sobbed. "Lady Darby dismissed me! Accused me of tellin' secrets to this oaf." She jabbed a finger toward Stagg. "Worse yet, she kept my pay."

"I am sorry, Rebecca," said Lucien. "This is my fault."

She sniffed, and took Lucien's mug of ale. As she finished it off, she hailed the barmaid. "Nothing to be done, now. Besides, it was time for me to go, anyway. William wants me in London."

They waited in silence for the barmaid. When she'd served them and gone, Lucien said, "How is Lady Sarah?"

Rebecca's eyes narrowed. "I wondered when you'd get round to her."

"Is she well?"

"Well as to be expected, with a broken heart. Why did you leave her, if you don't mind my asking?"

"I did not leave her. I told her I would return." He had a sinking feeling in his gut. "Didn't she receive my letter?"

"What letter? Lord Darby said you left without an argument. Made her think you were happy to go, really. I tried to tell her it weren't true, that you would never do it, but she wouldn't believe it. And when she didn't hear from you, she stopped speaking of you altogether."

Lucien rubbed his eyes. "She did not get the letter. Stagg, when did you give it to Anne?"

"A few days after you left. I gave it to her in the garden."

"My God. Sarah does not know about Arthur."

"What about that nasty codger?" Rebecca asked.

"I believe he's trying to harm Sarah."

Rebecca paled. "Good Lord. Then the rumors are true!"

"What rumors?" Lucien asked, close to panic.

"A cat died from eating poisoned cream. Some of the servants said it was meant for Lady Sarah, but I din't believe it. Who would want to harm her?"

Lucien leapt from his seat, scarcely hearing Rebecca's last words. He commandeered a horse from one of the patrons of the Hog and Dove and thundered up the lane. Both he and the horse were breathing hard by the time they reached the little cottage. As he hoped, Lord Darby's horse was tethered in the clearing.

Lucien dismounted and strode to the door. He did not bother to knock.

Chapter 34

&

"Lord Darby?"

The ravaged creature that stared back at Lucien was far from the man he had come to know during his tenure at Elmstone House.

Lord Darby crouched over a bed in the corner of the room. His eyes were pinpoints of black within circles of red. His once regal posture was as bent as a willow's limb.

"Had I the strength, I would pummel you again," he rasped.

Lucien moved closer. His first glimpse of the figure lying on the bed startled him. The lacy bedclothes and lack of facial hair were the only indicators of gender. "Who is she?"

Lord Darby looked down at the hand entwined in his. "The love of my life."

"I am sorry. Is it dropsy?"

Lord Darby nodded.

Lucien looked down at the woman on the bed. She slept

propped up, her breath rattling noisily in her chest. Her eyes were swollen shut. Lucien thought that a blessing, since she probably would not care to see how the disease had desecrated her body.

"I am sorry," Lucien said again. "But I need to speak with you regarding your sister."

Lord Darby stroked the woman's hand. "Leave me alone, Delacourte. Go now and I will not summon the authorities."

"I cannot leave. Not until I know that Sarah is safe."

Lord Darby looked up at him, surprised. "Why wouldn't she be safe?"

"Arthur, of course."

Lord Darby's look of surprise turned to one of amusement. The sound of his laughter was like a rusty hinge. "I've told you before, that is most absurd."

"Listen to me. He was at the stables the day the stallion nearly trampled Sarah. And he was lurking in the hallway near Sarah's room on the night of the fire. I saw him stealing foxglove from the orangery. Sarah told me it can cause death. It was probably he who poisoned the cream."

"What? What cream?" Confusion further contorted Lord Darby's face. "Listen to me well, Delacourte. Arthur would never try to harm Sarah."

"How do you explain his actions, then? And his apparent ill will toward me from the very beginning."

"Well, Arthur visits the stables quite frequently to alert them of my need for a horse. And I imagine he was in my quarters the night of the fire retrieving a purse of money I'd left to pay the nurse." Lord Darby gestured to the corner where, indeed, sat a nurse whom Lucien had not noticed before.

Lord Darby continued. "I know he took foxglove from the orangery. I asked him to do it, in order to make medicine for Leah. And I suppose the reason he's hated you since you've arrived is because he's generally an unfriendly sort."

Lucien mulled over Lord Darby's words. "There are too many coincidences. You must question him."

"I have no need. I trust him implicitly."

"You trust him with Sarah's life?"

"Yes."

"How can you?"

Lord Darby brought the woman's hand to his mouth and kissed it. "Because not only is Arthur my valid, he's Leah's brother as well."

Lord Darby's revelation shocked Lucien, but not as much as his next thought. "If Arthur did not try to poison Sarah, who did?"

Lord Darby's head snapped up. "Poison Sarah? I think you'd better tell me everything you know."

She had failed.

The reality of it gripped Julia like a malady. Lucien was long gone, and James no longer bothered to make a pretense of interest.

She stared into the mirror. Was she no longer beautiful? Had her abilities to seduce a man fled? What would become of her now?

A furtive knock at the door pulled her away from the mirror.

Robert.

"My lady," he said, breathlessly.

She pulled him into the room and kissed him, hard.

He gathered her up and ravished her lips with his. "I have wonderful news," he breathed.

She took his hand and led him to the bed. "Tell me after . . ."

"Wait. Look." Robert reached into his boot and withdrew a leather purse. He opened the strings and spilled the contents across Julia's bed. A small fortune in gold tumbled across the coverlet.

Julia scooped it up and let it fall through her fingers. "Where did you get this?"

"That stupid painter left it lying on the drive. The others didn't see it, so I got it all." He slowly unbuttoned the bodice of her gown, sliding it from her shoulders. He kissed her neck, her shoulders. "There was more, too. But I used it to find a place for us. A place where we can be together."

"But we're together here."

He pushed her down on the bed and ran his tongue into the crevice between her breasts. The coins were cold against her bare back.

"No, together forever. We can leave here. Isn't that what you wanted?" he said.

Julia almost laughed aloud. "Leave here with you? What would make you assume such a thing?"

Robert stopped fondling her. "You told me . . . You said if you could, you'd get away from them. From her, most especially. You said you wanted her dead, remember? I tried, but . . ."

Julia's blood ran cold. "You tried what?"

"I tried to get rid of her, but it weren't so easy. I really thought the tea would work."

She sat up. "You?" she whispered. "You poisoned the cream? How?"

"Got the key from a maid. Stupid, silly girl. She fancies me, I think."

"And the horse? And the fire?"

He smiled.

Julia leaped from the bed. With trembling hands she shoveled the coins back into the purse. She shoved the bag at Robert. When her fingers accidentally touched his chest, she gave an involuntary shiver.

"Hurry. Take this and go. If Lord Darby ever discovered your treachery, we both would hang."

"But you told me you hated her. I did it for you."

"My God, just go. *Now.*"

* * *

How had he let things get so out of his control? James won-
dered as he urged his mount up the path to the house. He
had failed once again to protect his sister, and this time
danger wasn't on a deserted country road. This time, it was
right under his nose, in his own home. In *her* home.

He intended to get to the bottom of this whole mess.

When he arrived at the house, he immediately sought
out Miss Witherspoon.

"Gather all the servants in the kitchen immediately," he
demanded. "And I don't want the family alerted to this
meeting. I won't have them worried until I know what's
going on myself."

He strode into the kitchen, his boots heavy on the gray
stone floor. The cook, her arms deep in the oven, nearly
burned herself when she saw his expression.

"M'lord? Can I be of service to you?"

"Take a seat at the table, Mrs. Hopstead. The others will
be about soon enough."

Within minutes, all manner of servants poured into the
warm, narrow room, their faces a mix of nervousness and
undisguised curiosity. A lord venturing into servants' terri-
tory was a rare thing, indeed.

"Is this all of them?" he asked Miss Witherspoon.

"All but your manservant, your lordship."

When they were seated, he leaned on the edge of the
long wooden table. "It has come to my attention that something unnatural occurred here recently. More specifically,
the untimely death of a cat. Can anyone here shed light
on this happenstance?"

The uncomfortable silence was broken only by the rustle of livery and the scraping of chairs.

"Come, now. Someone must know something."

One of the parlor maids looked down at her lap.

James barked at her. "You there. Have you anything to say?"

The maid's shoulders trembled.

"Out with it, girl."

She buried her face in her apron and sobbed. "I'm so sorry, m'lord. 'Tis all my fault. I gave him the key to the poisons cabinet. He said Arthur wanted him to kill some rats in the stables. I din't know he was out to do Lady Sarah harm!"

The servants broke into furious chatter.

"Quiet!" James shouted. In an instant, silence reigned.

"Now," he said, his voice tight, "to whom, exactly, did you give the key?"

The maid emitted great, loud sobs. "To R-r-r-obert."

"The groomsman?"

The maid nodded.

"Why didn't you come forward with this information sooner? Why wasn't I notified of this horror?"

The maid cried so hard she couldn't answer.

"Because Lady Darby forbade it," Mrs. Hopstead interjected.

"I see," said James.

Julia sat in a chair before the window. She didn't bother to turn when he entered.

His fury diminished when he noted the defeated slump of her shoulders. His wife was many things, but she wasn't a murderess.

"I wondered when you'd come," she said. "I knew the servants would never be able to keep their mouths shut."

"I think you'd better tell me what's going on, Julia."

Her shoulders straightened. "A certain young man, a servant, imagined he'd fallen in love with me," she said.

"Robert?"

Her head snapped around. "How . . .?"

He shook his head. "Continue."

"Somehow, he got it into his head that I would be happier with Sarah gone."

"Would you?"

"Of course. But not at the expense of her life."

James was silent.

"Do you believe me?" Her voice held a note of challenge.

He sighed. "Yes, I believe you."

She started to weep. He hadn't seen her do that since their wedding day. It occurred to James that Julia was just as miserable as he with their marriage. Still, she had caused danger to come to Sarah, however inadvertently, and she would have to suffer the consequences.

"Where is Robert?" James asked. "I'll kill him myself."

She wiped her tears on her sleeve. "I've no idea. Nor do I care."

He turned to go.

"James." Her voice quavered.

He looked over his shoulder at her.

"It's your fault, you know."

"I know."

James stepped out into the hallway to find Arthur waiting for him. His eyes were rimmed with red.

"You must come immediately, sir."

They met at the Hog and Dove, amidst much staring and whispering. Lord Darby hardly seemed to notice as he slid onto the bench across from Lucien.

"You do not look well," Lucien said. "You need some sleep."

"Leah died."

Lord Darby's patrician features crumbled into a look of such remorse, Lucien had to turn away. He hailed a barmaid and ordered two mugs of ale.

Lord Darby closed his eyes and pinched the bridge of his nose. "The end was terrible. She was in such pain."

"Her suffering is over now. Take comfort in that," said Lucien.

"It's a cold comfort, but it will have to serve." He cleared his throat. "Ah, well."

"May I ask why you summoned me here?"

"I wanted to thank you for warning me about the danger to Sarah. The culprit has been found out. Turns out he'd run off just this morning. He was apprehended in a barn not far from here and will pay dearly for his treachery."

"Thank God."

"Yes. Thank God, and thank you for protecting my sister. It would seem I failed her once again."

"You should not blame yourself. You had other worries."

Lord Darby shook his head. "None that should have distracted me from my duties as protector of my family."

Lucien was silent.

"How can I repay you?" Lord Darby said. "Name your price."

Lucien's heart stopped. "I want nothing save your permission to court your sister."

Lord Darby stared pensively into his mug. "What exactly is it that you expect to happen?"

"I believe you know the answer to that. I love Sarah. I want to marry her."

"Again, I will say what I said in the drawing room that day not so long ago. You do my sister a disservice by pursuing her. She deserves better."

"Sarah deserves a man who loves her without condition, as I do."

"What sort of future have you? You're a penniless artist and she's a woman of noble blood."

"I am no longer penniless. I have sold the last of my works I completed in Versailles and have returned if not with the fortune of a king, at least with a full purse. I intend to continue to paint, as well. Your sister has been a great inspiration to me, and I believe I am doing some of my finest work now."

"And what of your debts?"

"I have paid them all."

Lord Darby drank, observing Lucien over the top of his mug. His fingers drummed on the tabletop.

"I cannot allow it," he said finally. "You see, I know firsthand what heartbreak arises when two people who love each other should not. I lived it, with Leah." His voice broke as he spoke her name.

Lucien allowed Lord Darby a moment to collect himself before stating his case again.

"With all due respect, your lordship, our situations are nothing alike. If you and Leah ever wished that you could have been together, could have been married, then you know what Sarah and I feel."

Lord Darby looked more than a bit uncomfortable, but Lucien knew he may never have this opportunity again. He pressed on.

"You and Leah could not act on such wishes, and for that I am truly sorry. But do not punish Sarah for it. You know Sarah cares nothing about society's expectations. How could her life possibly be worse for marrying me?"

Lord Darby was silent.

"She is my soul."

"She is my blood, and I am bound to protect her." The nobleman finished his mug of ale and headed for the door.

"I will not give up," Lucien called after him.

The earl hesitated only a moment before pushing open the door and disappearing into the cold night.

"Have you given any more thought to marrying Lavery?"

Sarah should have been ready for James's question, but

she wasn't. She had tried to think about it—about what it would be like to be Duncan's wife—but she found it didn't come as easily as it had when she was young.

If she didn't want children so badly, the thought would never have crossed her mind. But Duncan was quite attentive, and truly seemed to desire their union.

She had, if not encouraged him, at least not turned him away for the past two days. She found his company to be like porridge—lukewarm and comforting in its familiarity.

"I don't know," she said. "I shall have to think about it some more."

"I'm afraid there isn't time to think about it," James said as he removed his riding gloves. "If there is to be a wedding, I must know immediately."

"But why? What is the hurry?"

Her brother wandered over to the window. "I'm anxious to see you married, Sarah. I wish to know you're happy before I leave."

He sounded so sad. So ominous.

"Leave for where?"

"I plan on making an extended visit to Blakely Hall. I don't know when I'll return."

"Your holding in the north? But when? Why?"

James scratched the stubble on his jaw. "I'll leave soon. I need a change . . . some time away from Elmstone. Besides, if you marry Lavery, you'll need a place of your own. He's confessed to me that his estate may not suit you. So you may have Elmstone. It's more yours than mine, anyway."

Sarah was stunned. She'd never considered having to leave her gardens if she married. And she'd never considered living apart from James.

"Where would you live?" she asked.

"I don't know. I haven't given it much thought. So, what will you do? Will you marry Lavery?"

Sarah's heart raced. She imagined nights spent reading

by the fire with her husband. She imagined never being lonely again. She heard the laughter of children in the gardens.

The only problem was, it wasn't Duncan by the fire, and they weren't Duncan's children laughing in the gardens. God help her, she was still in love with Lucien, despite his betrayal.

"I cannot, James," she said. "I cannot marry Duncan."

Her brother was quiet for a long while, staring out of the window. Then he said, "Shall I ask him to leave?"

"No. I'll do it."

Chapter 35

Sarah examined the paintings propped against the wall of the drawing room. The four represented the best of her works. One of them would be framed for the king and sent, along with the finished volume she had compiled, to the Royal Botanical Society.

The thought of it held no thrill. Right now she wanted nothing but to choose a painting and retire to her recently restored rooms to wallow in dejection.

It hadn't been an easy morning. The scene with Duncan had been, if not ugly, at least unattractive. When Sarah had asked him to leave, he became morose. He poured a glass of brandy and drank it almost defiantly.

"I don't understand you at all, Sarah," Duncan said. "We could be so happy together. Why won't you marry me?"

"I'm sorry, Duncan, but it's for the best."

"The best for whom? Me? I think not." He poured another brandy and downed it in two gulps. "I shouldn't think it was best for you, either. You haven't any other offers, my dear."

"No, I haven't. And yet, I still choose not to accept yours. I do not love you anymore, Duncan. It is as simple as that."

He shook his head, as if unable to comprehend it all.

"Take care of yourself," she said, sadly. She knew it was the last she would ever see of her one-time love. His bags were, by now, packed and waiting at the door.

Duncan's leaving made everything so real. She would never marry now. She would never read before the fire with anyone other than her mother. And she would never hear the laughter of her children in her gardens.

She chose one of the paintings. "What do you think?" she asked Merri, who sat beneath a lap blanket near the window. "Is it suitable for a king?"

"Lovely, my dear," said Merri. She seemed almost distracted. "What a gloomy day."

"Indeed."

The door to the drawing room opened and closed, but she paid it no heed. Until she heard his voice.

"Sarah."

Lucien!

She felt as if she'd been at once doused with cold water and buried in hot coals. The pain was exquisite.

The painting slid from her hands and landed with a dull thud on the carpets.

"My dear boy, how good to see you again!" said Merri.

Lucien strode to her mother's side and kissed her cheeks loudly. "You look well, Dowager," he said.

"As do you," said her mother. "Sarah, what have you to say? Lucien has returned!"

"I see." She regarded him coolly, although her heart pounded fiercely. "How did you get in? I understand the servants were given orders to shoot you."

He laughed. The timbre of his voice shook her to the core. "I bribed the new stable hand."

"Bribed him? Do you mean to imply you're no longer the pauper who arrived here in June?"

At least he had the decency to look ashamed. He crossed the floor and stood before her. "I have missed you, Sarah. Terribly."

"Really? So much so, you didn't see fit to write?"

"But I did! A friend of mine gave a note to Anne, but for some reason she never gave it to you."

Sarah stiffened. "Anne would never keep something like that from me. Especially when she knew how I— When she knew how worried I was about you. Turns out I had more to worry about than I thought."

She picked up the painting. "If you will excuse me . . ."

Lucien looked stricken. "Sarah, wait. You're angry. Is it my lack of fortune? If so, I assure you, I—"

She laughed. It sounded harsh, even to her. "You think me so shallow, my *friend,* that I would care only for a man with a fortune? I'm angry, but not at your lack of coin. It's your lack of honesty and trust that makes me angry."

"I was wrong, so wrong to keep things from you. In my note I tried to explain."

"There was no note, Lucien. If there were, Anne would have given it to me. I think you should leave now."

"Sarah!" Merri interrupted. "You are acting in a most wretched manner."

"Bring Anne here. Ask her for yourself," he said.

Lucien's voice held a note of desperation she couldn't deny. She wanted him to be telling her the truth for once. She desperately wanted it.

She crossed to the bell pull, giving wide berth to Lucien's body. Still, as she passed him, she smelled the faint scent of linseed oil, now an intoxicating aphrodisiac to her.

A maid appeared in moments.

"Fetch my niece, please. Tell Miss Elsey I will require but a moment of her time."

For what seemed an eternity they stood there facing one another in the room in which they fell in love, and fell apart.

Finally Anne arrived, but she was not alone. It was Julia, not Miss Elsey, who held her hand.

"So, it really is true. You've returned." Julia's look to Lucien was malevolence distilled. "Haven't you caused enough damage?"

"Silence, Julia," Merri threatened. "We need to ask the girl a question."

"Be quick about it. She has lessons to learn."

Lucien approached Anne slowly and knelt before her. He smiled, and she smiled in return.

"Anne, did you receive a note from a friend of mine to give to your Aunt Sarah? He told me he gave it to you in the garden one day."

Anne opened her mouth. "I did—"

All of a sudden her smile faltered. She looked up at Julia.

"I did not."

"Are you quite certain?" Lucien said. "Perhaps you misplaced it, or forgot to give it to her. Your aunt will not be angry, and neither will I."

Anne's eyes filled with tears. "No. I received no note."

"There. Are you satisfied?" Julia directed the question to Sarah.

"Quite."

"Then we shall take our leave."

Anne looked back over her shoulder at Lucien as Julia dragged her from the drawing room.

"She is lying," Lucien said quietly.

Before he had time to rise, a small army of servants arrived at the door.

"Mr. Delacourte, Lady Darby ordered us to remove you from the premises," one of them said. They all seemed reluctant to follow those orders.

"Sarah?"

She turned her back to him. She could not bear to see him leave her again, even if he could sink so low as to use her niece in his lies.

"I have an announcement."

James tapped his knife on a glass, though the action was hardly warranted. The women of Elmstone House were as quiet this supper as they always were.

Sarah, her mother, and Julia stopped eating and looked toward the head of the table. James stood there with his hair in his eyes and two days' worth of stubble on his chin. Sarah wondered when he had acquired such a wild look about him.

"Out with it, will you?" said Merri. "I'm hungry."

James raked the hair from his eyes with his fingers. "I've made a decision. We shall leave for Blakely Hall in one month's time."

"James, it will be winter. No one travels to the north in winter," said Julia, her tone dismissive.

"As much as it pains me," said Merri, "I must agree with your wife. It would make for a wretched holiday."

James smiled. "This won't be a holiday. We're going to live there. Or at least, Julia is."

"What do you mean, *live* there?" said Julia.

"We're going to take your things to Blakely Hall, and you will remain there with them."

"Permanently?" Julia squeaked.

"Permanently," said James. "Haven't you begged me to get you away from Whitford?"

"But *Blakely Hall?* For God's sake, James, it's practically *Scotland.* It's *overrun* by Catholics."

"Then perhaps you should convert."

Julia looked ready to swoon.

"Oh, James, you must stay," said Sarah. "Since I'm not marrying Duncan, there's no reason for you to go."

"I told you, Elmstone is yours," he said.

"I knew it! I knew this had something to do with her."
Julia rose up from her seat like a mummy from the grave,
pointing a bony finger in Sarah's direction.

"Sit down, Julia," said James. "I've made this decision
for a number of reasons. Not the least of which is your
questionable moral fiber."

Julia's face turned red. "How dare you accuse me, after
the way you've behaved of late? I don't know where you
have been off to in the middle of the night, but it's going to
end, or you'll be sorry."

"You're right," said James. "It is going to end." He turned
to Sarah. "I had hoped you would allow Anne to stay here
with you. Take care of her."

Sarah was stunned. "Of course. You know I adore her.
But James . . ."

He shook his head. "She deserves a peaceful life, out of
the clutches of a hopeless father and the viper she calls
Mother."

Merri's jaw hung open. For once she was at a loss for a
comment.

"You're free to join us at Blakely if you wish, Mother."

Merri regained the use of her voice. "I cannot leave
Sarah here alone."

"She'll hardly be alone. We'll take Arthur with us, and
Julia's lady's maid, but the rest of the servants will stay on
here."

"Servants are hardly family," Merri said.

James drummed his fingers on the table. "True. But
there is one other person . . ."

Her brother turned to her. "Sarah, I must apologize for
the way I've acted. I've stolen your freedom from you just
as the accident has. I wanted to protect you, but I did you
harm, instead."

James waved toward the door. Arthur entered, carrying
something beneath a sheet. James took it from the servant.

"This arrived for you this morning, Sarah."

He pulled the sheet away to expose a painting. The women gasped.

"Is it you, Sarah?" her mother said in a whisper.

My God, was it?

The woman staring back at them was captivating, her expression one of serene contentment.

"It can't be Sarah," said Julia. "The woman is beautiful."

Only the faintest hint of a scar was visible on the milky planes of her face. It looked almost like a tiny wrinkle in the canvas. Sarah approached the painting breathlessly. What had Lucien once told her?

The greatest works are those for which the artist has a great love, an intimate understanding of the subject's soul.

James said, "I understand your feelings toward Delacourte. I may not wholeheartedly approve, but I do understand. If you still love him, I won't deny you your happiness."

Sarah's throat constricted. "Thank you. Your words mean everything to me. But Lucien lied so many times, how can I possibly trust him?"

Julia stared down at the tablecloth.

"Tell her," said James. "Tell her what Anne told me."

Julia sighed. "He didn't lie as much as you think. He did, indeed, give Anne a note. I found it and burned it."

"He never wanted to go, Sarah," James said. "I forced him to leave."

Merri grinned. "I knew it."

Sarah felt light-headed. The image of the beautiful woman in the painting swam before her eyes. Could it be true? Did he really care for her?

"He's residing in Mrs. Endfirth's carriage house," James said.

Her entire body went numb.

"Go on," said James. "Go to him."

* * *

Sarah flew down the hill toward Whitford, mindless of the cold stinging her cheeks through her veils. What would she say? She'd behaved abominably, accusing Lucien of betrayal, refusing to trust his word. Would he still care for her? Would he forgive her?

She raced up the lane to Mrs. Endfirth's carriage house, her boots slipping on the stones.

As if he sensed her presence, the door to the carriage house swung open and Lucien was there, in the shadows. Sarah wanted to see his face, to lure him into the light.

But she could not move.

"The portrait," she said. "It's lovely."

He remained in the doorway, bathed in shadow.

"Lucien, I was so wrong. I should have trusted you, as you trusted me. I know that now."

Silence.

What could she say to him now? How could she make him understand? There was but one way.

She took a breath and clenched her fists.

"I love you, Lucien."

Chapter 36

He met her in four long strides, sweeping her into his arms and kissing her hard through the veils. "I love you, too, Sarah. So much you cannot know."

He picked her up and carried her over the threshold of the carriage house and into paradise. Stacked against all four walls were paintings. Paintings of her gardens. Paintings of the serene woman in the portrait. Her.

She sat in the middle of the floor. "When . . .?"

"Anywhere. Everywhere. Right here in Mrs. Endfirth's carriage house. I'm always painting. Always thinking of you. I cannot seem to stop. You have been my inspiration."

He pointed to an easel in the corner. On it was another portrait of her, holding a rose. It was her rose—the one she had yet to name.

For the first time, she noticed that Lucien's hands and shirt were covered with paint. She'd interrupted his work.

She removed her hat and veils and kissed him properly. "Perhaps you can take a bit of time to be inspired further?"

He let out a deep sigh and buried his face in her neck. "You smell like summer," he said. "Sweet and warm."

A small cot stood against the wall. Lucien pulled it to the center of the room and surrounded it with the paintings. He unbuttoned her cape and laid it over the cot.

"I want to make love to you in your gardens," he said, "but I fear I cannot wait until spring. Will this do?"

Sarah looked at the beauty that surrounded her. Her flowers, his paintings. A part of her, a part of him. Together they created this beauty.

"This will do very well." She sank onto the cot and pulled him down with her, kissing him deeply.

He wrapped them both in the folds of her cape and undressed her slowly, kissing each limb as he exposed it, taking the tips of her fingers, one by one, into his mouth.

She watched his hands caress her body, the streaks of paint on them moving over her skin as if it were a canvas. Lucien was creating her. Or rather, he was recreating her—changing her into a woman who never before existed.

"You are so beautiful," Lucien whispered as he entered her. And she believed him.

She counted his breaths and measured them with her own as he moved inside her. She wrapped her legs around his hips, her arms around his neck, bringing him as close as their bodies would allow. And this time, when she sailed from the earth on a cloud, Lucien came with her.

Much later, as they lay quietly in the garden they had created together, Sarah kissed the tip of Lucien's nose. "I've thought of a name for my rose," she said. "That is, if you approve."

"What is it?"

"The Pink Tessa."

Emotion clouded his eyes. He kissed her gently on the forehead and settled a lock of hair behind her ear. "Thank you."

"We're not meant to forget our past, are we?" she said. "It's made us who we are, after all."

"No, we should not forget it," he said. "But we should not let it steal our future, either."

She lay her head on Lucien's chest, listening to his heartbeat, and knew that he would be her future.

They walked hand in hand through the town, and up the hill toward Elmstone.

"I intend to ask your brother for your hand," Lucien said as they approached the house.

"You'd best hurry," she said, smiling. "James is leaving. He's taking Julia to his estate near the Scottish border. He wants me to have Elmstone, but I don't want to stay here if this isn't where you want to be. If you would rather return to Paris, I will go with you."

Lucien stopped at the crest of the hill. The house sprawled before them like a stone giant. "Behind those walls are your gardens. Could you really leave them behind?"

"For you, I could."

"I would never ask you to do such a thing. I will stay with you, but you must do something for me in return."

"Anything, my love."

"Remove your veils. Forever."

Her heart quickened. Could she face the world again without walls? Could she stop the past from stealing her future?

With trembling fingers, she removed her hat and ripped the veils from their pins. The wind made them flutter in her hands. She opened her fingers and they flew away, dancing across the countryside as if they had always longed to be free.

BERKLEY SENSATION
COMING IN OCTOBER 2004

Tempting Danger
by Eileen Wilks

Enter a bold new world where the magical and the mundane co-exist in an uneasy alliance—and a cop must balance her own life to stop a brutal killer.

0-425-19878-2

Hardly a Husband
by Rebecca Hagan Lee

Jarrod, sixth marquess of Shepherston, is asked by a childhood friend for help in the art of seduction. Jarrod is wary of a marriage trap—but love has a way of softening the hardest fall.

0-425-19879-0

Master of the Night
by Angela Knight

A tale of supernatural seduction from the author of *Jane's Warlord.* American agent Erin Grayson has been assigned to seduce Reece Champion. But she's been set up. Reece is not only an agent—he's also a vampire.

0-425-19880-4

The Kitchen Witch
by Annette Blair

When a single dad and TV exec hires Mellody as his babysitter, he knows she's rumored to be a witch—but when she magically lands her own cooking show, the sparks really begin to fly.

0-425-19804-9

NICOLE BYRD

Widow in Scarlet
0-425-19209-1

When Lucy Contrain discovers that
aristocrat Nicholas Ramsey believes her
dead husband stole a legendary jewel, she
insists on joining his search.
Little does she know they will be drawn
into deadly danger—and into a passion
that neither can resist.

Also Available:
Beauty in Black
0-425-19683-6

BERKLEY SENSATION
COMING IN SEPTEMBER 2004

Beloved Impostor
by Patricia Potter
Rory Maclean has been away at sea, but now he returns to end a feud between his own family and the Campbells—and risks everything by letting the enemy into his heart.

0-425-19801-4

A Hint of Seduction
by Amelia Grey
Everyone thinks Catherine is in London to find a husband. The truth is she's looking for the father she never knew. But when she meets a handsome stranger, it could be love—or he could be her half-brother.

0-425-19802-2

Snap Shot
by Meg Chittenden
Diana Gordon thinks she is safe from her past. But a killer is watching her every move.

0-425-19803-0

Available wherever books are sold or at
www.penguin.com

Barely a Bride

by
Rebecca Hagan Lee

The noblemen of the Free Fellows League have vowed to "avoid the inevitable leg-shackling to a female for as long as possible." But when Viscount Abernathy is called off to war, he must obey his father's wishes that he marry—and fast.

Two years later, Abernathy returns from battle scarred and weary, hoping to love the wife he hardly knows. Now he must try to win his wife's heart by wooing the bride he left behind.

"REBECCA HAGAN LEE TAPS INTO
EVERY WOMAN'S FANTASY." —CHRISTINA DODD

"REBECCA HAGAN LEE WARMS MY HEART AND
TOUCHES MY SOUL WITH HER DELIGHTFUL AND
BEAUTIFULLY WRITTEN ROMANCES."
—TERESA MEDIEROS

0-425-19124-9

B186